A September Day and Shadow Thriller

HIDE AND SEEK

Book Two

AMY SHOJAI

Copyright

Second Print Edition, February 2017
Furry Muse Publishing
Print ISBN 978-1-944423-19-3
eBook ISBN 978-1-944423-20-9
Hardcover ISBN 978-1-948366-36-6

First Published by Cool Gus Publishing
First Printing, January 2014
COPYRIGHT © Amy Shojai, 2014

FURRY MUSE
PUBLISHING
P.O. Box 1904
Sherman TX 75091
(903)814-4319
amy@shojai.com

September & Shadow Pet-centric Thrillers
By Amy Shojai

LOST AND FOUND

HIDE AND SEEK

SHOW AND TELL

FIGHT OR FLIGHT
Introducing Lia, Tee, and Karma

HIT AND RUN

WIN OR LOSE

Prologue

Tommy Dietz grabbed the car door handle with one bloody fist, and braced his other hand against the roof, worried the carcasses in the back would buck out of the truck's bed. Despite the precaution, his head thumped the muddy window. He glared at the driver who drove the truck like he rode a bronco, but BeeBo Benson's full moon face sported the same toothless grin he'd worn for the past two weeks. Even BeeBo's double chins smiled, including the rolls at the nape of his freckled neck.

The ferret thin guy in the middle snarled each time his Katy Railroad belt buckle chinked against the stick shift he straddled. Gray hair straggled from under his hat and brushed his shoulders. He had to slouch or he risked punching his head through the rust-eaten roof. Randy Felch's snaky eyes gave Dietz the shivers even more than the freezing temperatures spitting through windows that refused to seal.

Three across the cramped seat would be a lark for high school buddies out on the town, but the men were decades beyond graduation. Dietz was in charge so Felch could either ride the hump or share the open truck bed with two carcasses, and the new Production Assistant.

Dietz stifled a laugh. Not so high-and-mighty now, was he? The man must really want the job. Vince Grady had turned green when he was told to climb into the back of the truck. Just wait till he got a load of the dump. Dietz remembered his first visit three years ago when he'd been out scouting locations. He wondered how the spit-and-polish Grady would react.

He'd hired locals for the rest of the crew. They needed the work, and didn't blink at the SAG ultra-low pay scale, the shitty weather, or the stink. In this business, you took anything available when pickings were slim. Then the show got picked up and union fees grabbed him by the short hairs. Amateur talent screwing around and missing call times cost even more money, so he needed a Production Assistant—PA in the lingo—with more polish and bigger balls to keep the wheels greased. A go-to guy able to think on his feet, get the job done. No matter what.

If Grady wanted the PA job, he'd have to be willing to get his hands dirty, and stand up to BeeBo and his ilk. Riding in the open truck bed was illegal as hell, though here in North Texas even the cops turned a blind eye unless it was kids. This was an audition, and Grady knew it.

He had to give Grady props—he'd not blinked, but clenched his jaw and climbed right in when they collected him at his hotel. He'd been less enthusiastic after following the hunters most of the morning, tramping to hell and gone through rough country until his eyes threatened to freeze shut. Something drove the man, something more than a PA credit for piss-poor pay and worse conditions. Hell, something drove them all to work in this unforgiving business. Dietz didn't care about anyone else's demons as long as they let him feed his own.

Dietz craned to peer out the back to be sure the man hadn't been tossed out the tailgate. Grady gave Dietz a thumbs-up. *Probably wants to point a different finger,* Dietz thought. Grady wore the official *Hog Hell* blue work gloves and ski mask—dark blue background and DayGlo red star on the face—or he'd be picking his frostbit nose off the floor.

Prime time in the back woods. Dietz's quick smile faded. Nothing about this trip was prime, not even the butchered Bambi in the back. Deer season ran November through early January, and it was always open season on hogs, so they were legal for any follow up film footage. The two deer hadn't looked good even before BeeBo dropped them, but that's what viewers wanted. Crocodile wrestlers, duck dynasties, and gold rush grabbers with crusty appeal and redder necks.

Nobody wanted actors anymore. Casting directors looked for "real people." So he'd caught a clue, jumped off the thespian hamster wheel, moved to New York and reinvented himself as Tommy Dietz, Producer. He'd found his calling with a development company relatively quickly.

A movie star face didn't hurt. Everyone these days had a little nip-and-tuck; it was part of the biz. He'd been selling his version of reality for years anyway, and always came out on top. He hit it out of the park on his third project. *Hog Hell* kicked off the next step with a Texas-size leap. He'd show them all, those who'd laughed at his dreams, calling him a loser. And he'd make them sorry.

The shabby pickup lurched down and back up again, and its engine growled and complained. Dietz was surprised the seat hadn't fallen through the floor. The overgrown road the hunters called a pig path consisted of frozen ruts formed from previous tire treads. They damn well better not get stuck out here.

"Don't worry, she'll make it." BeeBo talked around the stub of his unlit cigar. "This ol' warhorse made the trip so often, she could drive herself. Ain't that right, Felch?" BeeBo reached to downshift and Felch winced as the other man's ham-size fist grabbed and jerked the stick between his knees.

Dietz sighed. Out the window, skeletal trees clawed the pregnant sky. Weird flocks of blackbirds moved in undulating clouds, exploding from one naked tree after another to clothe the next with feathered leaves. Spooky.

Thank God the icy weather stayed dry. Heartland, Texas had dug out of a record-breaking snowfall, and the locals hadn't quite recovered. It put a kink in *Hog Hell* filming and they'd barely met the deadlines. Delay turned his balance book bloody with red ink.

Back home in Chicago they'd been hit with the same blizzard and so had NYC. But big cities knew how to manage winter weather. Apparently North Texas rolled up the sidewalks with even the hint of flurries. He wondered if BeeBo and Felch knew what to do in the snow, and didn't want to find out. The thought of hunkering down overnight in the truck with these men turned his stomach.

Dietz adjusted his own ski mask. He'd folded it up off his face so the blue cap hugged his head while the red star painted a bull's-eye on his forehead. He wore the official coat, too; dark blue and a bright hunter-safe star on the front and back, with the *Hog Hell* logo. The Gore-Tex fabric crackled with newness, and his blistered feet whimpered inside wet, dirt-caked boots. No way would he wear his new $300 Cabela's, purchased for photo ops at the upcoming watch party. He had a gun, too. In Texas nobody cared if you carried. They expected it.

BeeBo's preferred weapon, an ancient short barreled shotgun loaded with deer slugs, contrasted sharply with Felch's double gun he'd had custom made last season. Felch shot 44 Magnums, and the cut down double barrel rifle boasted enough firepower to take out an elephant, or a charging feral boar hog. They sleeved the guns in canvas cases stowed in the back of the truck, but the hunters cared far less about their own attire.

BeeBo and Felch would wear official *Hog Hell* gear at the watch party in five weeks, but not before. Dietz didn't want them stinking up the outfits. Today they wore wash-faded coveralls, heavy work coats, earflap hats, clunky boots with thorn-tangled laces, and frayed gloves with fingertips cut out. A bit of peeling DayGlo tape formed an "X" on the back and front of each coat after Dietz insisted on the nod to safety, even though he knew the two hunters paid little mind to official start and end dates during hunting season.

That was the point of the original reality program *Cutting Corners* that focused on people forced to skirt the rules to make ends meet. The unlikely stars of a single episode, though, turned Felch and BeeBo into overnight sensations and birthed the new show after *Cutting Corners* tanked. The two hunters were experts at skirting rules. Dietz was no slouch, either.

In the truck bed, Grady swayed back and forth. He'd pushed up the ski mask enough to expose his mouth. White breath puffed out in a jerky tempo, and Dietz wondered if the man would pass out. If Grady took a header off the truck bed, the liability would kill the show. "Find a spot to stop, BeeBo. I think our new team member has had enough."

Felch grunted. "No place to stop till we get there. Unless you want us to get stuck." He grinned, but the expression never reached his eyes. "You don't want us lugging that shit back to your hotel. The stink ain't something you want close by."

BeeBo guffawed. "Got that right. With all the hunters unloading, it's what y'all might call a 'renewable resource.'" He twisted the wheel and the truck bucked, jittering the decades old pine-shaped deodorizer suspended from the rear view mirror. "The critters take care of the stink pretty quick, though." His hairless wide-eyed face was a ringer for the Gerber baby. "It's around that next bend. You might even catch a whiff of Jiff by now."

Dietz wrinkled his nose. The pungent aroma wasn't assuaged by the air freshener that had probably come with the vehicle. He shielded his head from another thump, and squinted ahead through the crusty windshield. Wiper blades had torn loose on the passenger's side and smeared the detritus rather than clearing the view. It didn't bother BeeBo.

The trio remained silent during the final bump-and-grind through the trees. They pulled halfway into the clearing, and Dietz waited impatiently until BeeBo cranked the steering wheel, turned, and backed beneath a massive tree with pendulous clusters decorating the branches. Grady ducked, or he would have been scraped off by low limbs.

Several similar trees bordered the clearing, and another smaller truck squatted at the far end of the area. An elderly man stood in the truck bed and flailed tree branches with a long pole, while the woman dodged and weaved beneath to gather the resulting shower in a bucket.

"What's that?" Grady wasted no time jumping off the truck bed. He gagged when the wind shifted.

"Nuts." Felch unfolded himself from the cramped middle seat. "Pecan trees. They're gleaning the nuts."

Dietz's stomach clenched. He pulled the ski mask over his lips and breathed through his mouth, imagining he could taste the odor that closed his throat. Neither Felch nor BeeBo seemed to notice the stench.

Grady wiped his watery eyes. The breeze paused and he gulped a less contaminated breath. "Pecans? To eat?"

The truck squeaked, rocked and grew two inches when BeeBo stepped out. "Back in town they'll pay $8 to $10 per pound, once shelled. I got my daddy's old commercial sheller—held together with baling twine and spit, but works okay. I only charge fifty-cents a pound to shell." He shrugged. "Every little bit helps. It's too early for most of the big-name commercial farms, but for the gleaners, if ya wait too long the squirrels get 'em off the trees, or the pigs root 'em off the ground. Pigs eat lots of the same stuff the deer and turkeys eat, acorns and suchlike. But they get ground-nesting bird eggs, too. Pigs'll root up and eat damn near anything." He jerked his chins at Felch. "Gimme a hand." He lumbered toward the back of the truck and waited by the taillights.

Felch vaulted in the bed of the vehicle, and adjusted his gloves. He pointed. "Smorgasbord, y'all. Hey Slick, you might want to get video of this. Bet your big-city cronies never seen the like." His yellow teeth gleamed. He bent low, and grunted as he pushed and tugged the black plastic bag to the tailgate, hopped down and joined BeeBo. Together they slung the truck's cargo into the pit.

Yipping and growls erupted from below. Dietz stayed back, he'd seen it before. This stuff he wouldn't put on the air. This'd be too much even for the hardcore viewers without the added value of aroma.

Grady covered his mouth and nose in the crook of his elbow. He edged closer to the deep trough, a natural ditch-like runoff that sat dry three-quarters of the year. Piles of gnawed and scattered bones mixed with carcasses in various stages of decomposition. A family of coyotes tried to claim BeeBo's tossed deer remains, but was bluffed away by a feral boar.

Grady ripped off his ski mask, puked, wiped his mouth, and grabbed his camera with a shaking hand. He spit on the frozen ground and jutted his chin at Dietz. "So?"

Dietz smiled. "You got the gig."

***

The damn ski mask dragged against his hair so much, the normally clear adhesive had turned chalky. Victor had removed the wig after dissolving the glue with a citrus-scented spray, a much more pleasant olfactory experience than the afternoon's visit to the dump. A shower rinsed away any lingering miasma, but he gladly put up with the stink, the rednecks, and the sneers. The payoff would be worth it.

Until then, he couldn't afford for anyone in Heartland to recognize him. His tool kit of fake teeth, makeup and assorted hairpieces kept him under the radar. For the price, nearly fifty bucks for a four-ounce bottle of adhesive, it damn well better hold the new wig in place for the promised six weeks. He rubbed his hands over his pale, bald head and grinned. Even without the wig, she'd be hard pressed to recognize him.

Muscles had replaced the beer gut, Lasik surgery fixed his eyes, a chin implant and caps brightened his smile. He'd done it all, one step at a time, over the eight years it took to track her down. He'd even changed his name and transformed himself into a man she couldn't refuse.

He'd done it for her. Everything for her.

He dialed his phone. "I want to order flowers. Forget-Me-Nots, in a white box with a yellow ribbon. Got that? And deliver them December eighteenth. It's our anniversary." He listened. "Use red ink. The message is 'payback.' Got that? No signature, she'll know it's me." He picked up a news clipping that listed the address, and admired the picture. She was lovely as ever. "Two-oh-five Rabbit Run Road, Heartland, Texas. Deliver to September Day. The name is just like the month." He chuckled softly. "Yes, it will be a lovely holiday surprise." He could hardly wait.

Chapter 1

Five Weeks Later

"I'm dreaming of a brown Christmas, just like the ones I used to know . . ." September stopped singing when her voice cracked. There was a reason she played cello.

She settled the instrument between her knees and caressed the silk-smooth wood. The pungent scent of the Christmas tree, a cedar cut from the back of the property, made her smile. After the recent freak Thanksgiving blizzard, a holiday without snow would be a gift. Boring would be nice, too.

The phone in the nearby kitchen rang, and she let the machine answer. "You've reached Pets Peeves Behavior Consulting. We're closed for the holidays. If this is a medical issue, please call your veterinarian. For new behavior clients, please complete the questionnaire on the PetsPeeves.com website or leave a brief message after the tone."

She'd stopped leaving her name. People thought *September Day* was a joke, and lately, she agreed. Her maiden name made it worse. Growing up with the name *September January*—no middle name needed—created its own kind of kid hell. But at least her parents gave up the birth-month names by the time her brother Mark came along.

The caller began to speak, quiet and determined, with an underpinning of anger. "This is Clare O'Dell again. You're the only one that can help Tracy. Please call me back!" She left the number, and disconnected.

September wrinkled her nose. Too many pet owners expected miracles. Was Tracy a cat? A dog? What was the problem, was it new or long-term, had a veterinarian been consulted... The questionnaire saved so much time if only people would use it. She hated to ignore the calls, but most of them never followed through with the required information anyway. She made a note to include a referral name for all those frantic pet parents, though.

The cool surface of the cello would warm as she played. The Reynaud's syndrome meant her fingers needed help staying warm even though the furnace kept frigid outside temperatures at bay. She wore light blue sweat pants, a matching top, and insulated socks but no shoes in deference to the new carpet she hoped to keep fresh. September tugged on funky hot pink knit gloves—they'd been cheap, so she'd bought half a dozen. Each fingertip poked through the cut-off portions and resembled pink paws with claws poking through. She leaned forward, and long hair matching the rich chestnut of the aged wood spilled over the instrument until she tied a ponytail over her right shoulder to keep from tangling the strings.

The familiar routine unclenched her shoulders. She breathed deeply, thumbing each string, cocking her head to judge the tone, and made small adjustments with the tuners before picking up the bow. As she drew the horsehair across the strings, the cello's rich voice warmed the room, baritone to tenor vibrations resonating in September's body until she became part of the music.

"Ah Melody, I've missed you." She breathed the words, eyes half closed, and welcomed the slight discomfort when her tender fingertips smarted after a finger-slide shift to thumb position. They'd soon regain the string-fed calluses necessary for optimal performance. Nobody else would notice or care, but Melody deserved her best.

"Ack-ack-ack-ack-ack..." Macy prowled into the room from the adjacent kitchen, ducked under the Christmas tree and stared through cedar greenery like a jungle creature, his chocolate ears twitching with kitty criticism.

"Yeah, sure, everyone's a critic." September paused, arms embracing the cello, and grinned at the Maine Coon. "I'm not a big fan of your singing, either, big guy. But I've only got a week to get ready for the performance, so lion-cough all you want."

She reached for the *Son-Of-A-Peach* oversize coffee mug on the piano bench beside her and sipped the hot beverage. The cat eyed one of the ornaments, nosing it before patting it with a white paw to make it dance. It was one of the unbreakables she'd placed on the lower branches, but September didn't want the cat practicing potentially dangerous behaviors. "Macy, come."

Macy's ears swiveled forward. He left the ornament and trotted to her, and sat when she signaled him with the closed fist as he'd been taught. She rubbed the base of his tail with the back of her bow, and he responded with an elevator-butt pose. Macy mewed and stroked the length of his chocolate-furred body against September's leg and then pawed her bow arm with sugar-dipped toes.

His claws snagged her sleeve, and she had to set down the mug before she could unhook him. "You need a claw trim." She leaned down, and they did kitty Eskimo kisses, rubbing noses as she stared into the cat's green eyes that looked so much like her own. Sometimes she thought Macy could read her thoughts, too. Didn't all pet lovers feel that way? "Here, why don't you go scratch your log? Macy, go scratch."

She picked up one of the many pen lights stashed around the house for the cat's entertainment, and flicked it on. He'd follow a light beam anywhere, and it wouldn't hurt his eyes like a laser might. It worked better at a longer distance than the retractable treat sticks she used for clicker training.

Macy followed the light beam with interest, raced across the room, and pounced on the length of cedar log that lay against the wall. "Kill it, Macy, kill it! Good boy." He shredded the papery bark, making a mess she'd need to vacuum later, but it was worth it. "I know you'll make me pay a treat for each claw clip. Why don't you go find Mickey?"

He stopped and his tail drew a semaphore of disappointment in the air. She shouldn't have said the "treat" word when none were within reach. But after a quick grooming lick to smooth fur and hurt feelings, Macy dropped to the floor and dashed back into the kitchen. September smiled when she heard his claws at the cupboard door where he stashed his favorite toy. Too late she remembered what the *skreeee* of the opening cupboard signaled.

Overhead, a loud THUMP shook the ceiling, the sound of a seventy-pound dog's vault from bed-to-floor. Shadow's scrabbling claws clattered the length of the upstairs hallway, and his paws thundered down the back stairs into the kitchen proper. He slid on the slate floor, thumping sideways into the island at the center of the room and then levitated in a rear-paw dance to reach the cat teasing from the counter.

"Shadow, settle! Leave the cat alone. "

The black German Shepherd remained focused on Macy's stuffed toy mouse. The cat hissed at the pup, grabbed Mickey by its one remaining ear— the other ear a victim of the dog's gnawing—and dragged it out of reach when Shadow braced massive front paws on the counter.

The pup barked, frustration and excitement coloring the sound.

"Guys, enough!" September stood but she couldn't risk leaving the cello unprotected with the dog so aroused.

Macy dropped his toy in the kitchen sink, the risk of a hated dunking less onerous than dog drool. But September knew that wouldn't stop the pup.

At ten months old and still growing, Shadow easily accessed the sink. He'd grabbed a thawing pork chop from the sink two days ago. Never mind previous training as an autism service dog, Shadow had entered doggy adolescence and embraced canine delinquency with all four paws. The teasing cat made things worse.

Shadow snagged the Mickey toy and raced away with Macy in hot pursuit. The black dog loped toward September and barely skidded to a stop, nearly taking her out at the knees. She lifted the cello and turned away, sheltering the fragile instrument with her body as the dog shook and "killed" the toy.

Macy stalked forward and crouched in the kitchen doorway, back paws treading like a racecar revving its engine. He launched himself at the dog, a silent flash of coffee fur that dashed beneath the dog's tummy before rearing up on his hind legs to box Shadow's face—but with sheathed claws. Shadow growled around the Mickey toy and wagged, big tail nearly clearing the piano bench.

The dog dropped the toy and open-mouth grappled the cat as Macy hugged his neck. Macy, still silent, retaliated with bunny-kicks from pistoning rear paws, escaped and launched himself into the middle of the Christmas tree.

"That's enough!" September's roar stopped the dog in his tracks, but it was too late for the tree. After teetering to and fro, it crashed to the floor, Macy leapt clear and sprinted from the music/office area to the front of the house, perhaps fearing the tree would give chase. Shadow gathered himself to follow.

"Wait. Down." Her whip-crack voice brooked no nonsense.

Shadow dropped to the ground. He gazed longingly toward the doorway and fidgeted when Macy returned to view and washed himself with a studied nonchalance.

"Don't even think about it." Her disapproval dragged the dog's attention away from the teasing cat. He squinted sideways at September with ears pressed flat and tail thumping. He scooted two feet on his belly—without getting up from the "down"—and grabbed the Mickey. The expression mimicked a doggy apology, and may well have worked on a less savvy human.

"You blew it." She carefully set Melody down, turning the bridge of the cello toward the wall. "Yes, I know Macy teased you. And you fell for it, again. Outside. You can go outside and cool your jets."

She grabbed up the toy on the way to the kitchen, pointing ahead so Shadow would move to the back door. Bright light spilled through the stained glass windows, courtesy of her brother Mark. She shoved the cat's tattered plush toy back inside the cabinet and set her coffee mug on the stained glass tabletop.

Although Macy could easily stay out of dog reach via the granite counters and his favorite refrigerator perch, teasing the dog had become his game of choice. The cat knew getting the dog in trouble banished Shadow to a scary uncharted outdoor land Macy rarely wanted to visit.

Spending time outside wasn't punishment to Shadow. It was more a break for both of them. He helped September deal with the PTSD, but she knew service dogs became emotionally drained and suffered burnout if not provided with their own downtime to recharge. It was good for her to practice being alone, too. Shadow could burn some energy sniffing out varmints. She'd probably have to hose him off, his paws anyway, before he'd be fit to return inside.

Mark's partner, Aaron Stonebridge, had begun the garden redesign after she threatened to finish pruning with a blow torch. The dug up portion of the rose garden proved irresistible to Shadow's digging. The feral hogs had had field day, too, and had torn out one corner of the fence.

September sighed. Shadow and Macy were bored. Wasn't that rich? She solved other folks' pet behavior problems, but neglected her own.

On cue, the wall phone rang again. There'd been a rash of pet runaways recently, and she'd been called to track missing dogs, cats, and in one case, a guinea pig. Shadow had loved that one after he figured out it was legal to follow the weird smell. The behavior advice requests still came through, but she'd had an equal number of crank calls and even a few death threats so now she screened everything.

September recognized the number before picking up the receiver. "Hey Combs, today's the big day?"

She'd met Officer Jeffery Combs during a day-long nightmare after his mother's murder a week before Thanksgiving. Instead of blaming her, as was his right, he'd become a friend.

"Yep, soon as I drop off the kids. They're not happy, and I don't blame them. We'd planned on another few days together. But I can't blow off my first day back."

Combs was one of her few friends in Heartland. She ignored hints he'd like to be more than that. Her world these days had no room for further complications.

September grabbed her coffee mug, a gift from Combs, and took a swallow. "At least they reinstated you as a detective. That's what you wanted, right? Vindication."

He laughed. "More likely punishment. Still waiting to find out about my new partner." He hesitated. "We still on for tonight?"

Her forehead wrinkled. She'd put him off twice before, and couldn't reasonably get out of it this time. "Sure, you can tell me all about your new partner—we can celebrate or bitch and moan, your choice. Anita dropped off some of her famous lasagna, and I've got wine. Bring beer if you want that." She hung up the phone. She'd have to change clothes. Sweats were fine for dumping around the house, but she should make an effort to be presentable now and then. Not date-clothes—it wasn't a date. But jeans and a nice sweater would be an improvement.

It was time she got back to a normal routine. That's why she'd agreed to bring Melody out of retirement and play the cello for Mom's church Christmas cantata. She sipped her coffee, not sure what constituted "normal" for her anymore.

September struggled for nearly thirty seconds and finally managed to unlock the reinforced steel door to take Shadow out. She shrugged on her coat, but didn't bother with gloves since she still wore the cello mitts. After hooking the leash on his collar, she slipped stocking feet into garden shoes, closed the door behind them and automatically dodged one of the low-hanging wind chimes suspended outside the door. Shadow tugged toward the car, anticipating a ride.

"Nope, this way. To the roses." He corrected himself and hung a quick left to the garden entry, his tail a happy flag.

She hugged herself in the forty-degree wind. Felt like thirty or less. The dog leaped and bounced at the gate two or three times before he managed a wriggly sit, a doggy request for the gate to be opened. "Wait." She unhooked his leash, gratified when he didn't move. At least he remembered some training.

The rusty gate squealed and Shadow's nose twitched with anticipation. She gave him the release word before he lost his composure. September crossed her arms, smiling despite herself as he raced into the three-acre garden to explore. She noted the time and shivered. A twenty-minute romp would have to suffice in this weather.

She hurried back to the kitchen. Wind had pushed the door ajar a few inches—the door was a bitch to latch—and once back inside, she hip-bumped it closed. She didn't bother with the kitchen door's cranky lock since Shadow would need to come in shortly. She congratulated herself that the unlocked door didn't bother her. Well, not much anyway.

September left the muddy shoes in the laundry room, and shed her coat and dropped it over her office chair before she returned to her cello. "Ah Melody, sorry for the interruption." She took her place once more on the piano bench, embraced Melody and tried to recapture the feeling of reverie.

But before she could draw the bow across the strings, the doorbell chimed. Her shoulders hunched. Aaron wasn't due for another twenty minutes, and he wouldn't ring the bell. Carefully she set the cello aside, replaced the bow on the bench, and hurried to the front door to peer through the stained glass sidelight.

For a while after the recent trouble she'd had uninvited visitors, especially after she stopped answering the phone. Her family knew to call first. Strangers had seen pictures of Shadow in the paper and remained cautious of the imposing black shepherd. The ragged gunshot notch in one ear made him appear ferocious.

Nobody waited on the front stoop. The front circle drive remained deserted. Maybe a kid on a dare rang the bell to her notorious 'house of blood.' That's how the local papers reported the tragedy. With Christmas next week, kids on school holiday had another week of boredom to fill.

She caught the motion of a fluttering sticker glued to the stained glass and felt cranky the ground delivery guys couldn't be bothered to wait. They pitched the package, rang the bell, and ran like she was an ax murderer or something.

September unlocked the three deadbolts, and swung open the door. A cloud of jackdaws, black tails as long as their bodies, descended onto surrounding trees like an invasion of ants, bending limbs to breaking, their raucous cries polluting the air.

But she saw only the package sitting on the top step. The long, narrow white box boasted a yellow ribbon and bow.

Her heart hammered. She whimpered and couldn't catch her breath. When the world tilted, September grabbed for the doorframe but fell to her knees and scooted away from the poisonous package. The yellow ribbon could mean only one thing.

He'd found her.

Chapter 2

Dietz watched impatiently as BeeBo unzipped his new official *Hog Hell* hunter's coat, doffed his blue and red cap, and took a good sixty seconds to squeeze into the provided chair. His massive thighs spilled over both sides.

The tiny office barely accommodated a single person, desk and computer set up, let alone two more grown men. BeeBo's girth should count as at least two and maybe even three. Thankfully, Grady's athletic but slight build easily perched on one side of the desk with such grace one would think it had been designed for such a purpose. That left the third vacant chair available.

He'd gotten lucky when Grady answered his plea on a national email list that served as a kind of Craig's List for the industry. Grady handled all the scut work Dietz hated, and was a problem solver of the highest order, especially the niggling details necessary to make a reality show seem real but run smoothly. The locals couldn't handle or understand some of the tech issues that challenged original programming. Once they got this next season rolling, worries would be behind them all. Grady understood that.

"Where's Sunny? And Felch?" He wasn't too worried about Sunny Babcock. The token girl on the team was little more than eye candy, and never stepped out of line. It made for great TV when she shot the lever-action Winchester deer rifle, never mind that she rarely scored with the cut-down barrel. But the last empty chair in the room looked ominous. Felch's loose cannon behavior helped make the show a hit but kept Dietz on pins and needles wondering whether he'd continue to produce. "This isn't an optional meeting."

Grady sipped his double skinny cafe latte. He was never without coffee, and between that and the energy drinks, the man fairly bounced off the wall. Now he grinned, teeth dazzling in their perfection, and pulled out his ever-present phone and dialed. His teeth were his best feature. That and his wavy blond hair, a style that was too young for him. Somehow he pulled it off along with the yuppie cargo pants and sweater. He disconnected the phone. "Sunny texted, running late. Nothing from Felch. He's not answering." He rolled a silver pen in his hand, a nervous habit he might have inherited from giving up smoking.

"I thought you got him a phone."

"Yep. But Felch hates it, leaves it off most of the time." He shrugged in a *'what can you do'* expression. "Promised to be here. Should be here any time."

"Better be." Dietz groused, and rubbed a hand over his stubbled chin. They all played at this like a second rate drama club when it was his life, by God. He needed a shave, hadn't slept well in days, and wanted to get this meeting behind them. He had to impress upon them the importance of the next two days. How they behaved, and what they said, would make or break the show and they couldn't go freelancing and shoot off their mouths. That's what got them into this mess.

Felch needed the dressing down more than BeeBo. The huge man was a cross between Frankenstein's monster and Jonathan Winters but despite a scary appearance, he only wanted to please. Felch, an Ichabod Crane clone, needed someone to ride herd on his free spirit. Of all the reality stars, Felch needed the money the most but hated the limelight the worst, and routinely dodged anything that didn't involve wind-in-his-face he-man activity.

Dietz didn't have time to play nursemaid. Grady handled the talent, got them where they needed to be, so Dietz could manage the money matters. He checked his knockoff Rolex. In six months, the watch would be real. With diamonds.

"That reporter came to see me last week. He talked to Felch, too. He's all riled up about us." BeeBo stared at Dietz, a kicked puppy expression that begged for a comforting word. He shrugged out of the coat, letting the DayGlo fabric slide off and fall over the back of the chair.

Dietz sighed, an exaggerated sound that ruffled the wavy fringe of hair that spilled over his brow. Leave it to BeeBo to point out the elephant in the room. "Let me worry about that. I told you, Grady sets up all interviews. I've got media appearances lined up to promo the big pig roast launch party for the new season." He leaned forward over the tiny desk. "BeeBo, we need to coordinate our messaging. Let me put it this way: It's like fishing—you got to use the right bait."

BeeBo nodded, eyes glued on Dietz, but still acted puzzled.

Patiently, Dietz explained. "If you throw all your bait out in the lake at one time and the fish gobble it up, they won't be hungry when you drop in your empty line."

"Why would I dump my bait…oh wait, I get it." BeeBo smiled, the gap of two missing front teeth a perfect fit for his stubby unlit cigar.

Central Casting couldn't have picked better. "We want the news people hungry, ready to swallow every word we feed them. If you grant interviews to everyone, we won't have any fresh bait to feed the big fish. And some of them are sharks so we have to be extra careful." Words would be carefully practiced, no room for error. "I don't want you or Felch or any of the production crew or talent—" His scowl included Grady, who crinkled sparkling green eyes at him. "Nobody talks to anyone without my say so. Got it?"

BeeBo agreed. "If you say so, Mr. Dietz."

Grady fingered his phone again. "Got a text. Felch is on the way; Sunny found him. Go ahead, I'll fill them in later." Grady pocketed his phone, slid off the desk and appropriated the empty chair.

Dietz breathed again. One less thing to worry about. He could count on Grady to get it done, no nonsense, no excuses. That was a pro. "Good. Give them this." He handed over several copies of the preprinted calendar with media and shoot dates noted. "Distribute to the rest of the staff. Have them clear their calendars and be on call for the next two days, until we get the big-ass launch behind us."

Grady's claim to fame included a number of indie films during the height of the martial arts craze, and a few guest star roles in TV cop shows as the victim or bad guy du jour. But like Dietz, when Grady reached the purgatory age—too old for romantic leads, too young for character roles—work dried up despite the obvious cosmetic work he'd had done. Facelift on a budget was never a good thing, and Dietz wondered how bad his face had to be to warrant such a gamble. Grady had to switch to behind the scenes work anyway. Turned out, he was good at it.

"What if he's right?" BeeBo turned his cap around and around in his meaty fingers. He tried to shift his pose in the chair, and it rode his butt until he gave up.

"Who? Right about what?" Dietz handed BeeBo his own copy of the calendar and sample questions and prepared answers.

"My dawg acts like he said. That reporter has a cat that's sick. What if it is our fault?" BeeBo folded the paper until it fit easily into the breast pocket of his shirt. "Hunting hogs is different. They tear up property, hurt folk's livelihood. And we don't waste 'em, just butcher what we bag and pass it on to folks that needs the food. But I never hurt no dawg or cat in my life, not on purpose anyhow." His lower lip stuck out, cherry red and wet, trembling a bit.

"Aw man, don't let reporters rattle you." Grady leaned forward and rested his forearms on muscular thighs. "The press always want an angle to get Joe Blow excited." He turned to Dietz, kicking his argument into high gear. "Besides, it could be good for us. Get the warm-and-fuzzy crowd shouting about their poor pets. No such thing as bad publicity, right?"

Grady's smile made male investors open their wallets, and women open their legs and thank him for the opportunity. Dietz wished he had that charisma. Money worked as well, though. Once *Hog Hell* became the cash cow he expected, no woman would refuse him.

Better put the brakes on Grady's publicity notion. That would make the rumors worse when they needed to be erased. "You're killing me. The only publicity I want pre-launch is *good* publicity. Got it?" Dietz's slapped the desk for emphasis, and BeeBo jumped at the whip-crack sound.

Grady's toothy smile pinched white at the corners. "You're the boss."

"Got that right." Turning to BeeBo, Dietz softened his tone to a placating purr. "Nobody's hurting pets. Hell, you've been feeding your dogs the same ol' same ol' for how many years?"

"Thirty." BeeBo whispered.

"How many? Speak up, put some of that *Hog Hell* holler into it, brother." He played the part of cheerleader and hard-ass coach in turn, whichever was needed.

"Thirty years I been feeding my dawgs the same food. And they done good!" BeeBo raised his voice, the baritone rich and thundering in the small office. He stood up, scraped the grabby chair off his butt and slapped the desk with his own beefy palm. "By damn, they done fine!"

"That's what I'm talking about." Dietz beamed, his brow smoothing. "You don't talk to anyone, especially the media—I mean reporters or TV or radio people—unless I'm there and say it's okay. Grady will help you practice answering questions so you won't get stumped."

"Want me to take a meeting with that reporter? Get him to bury the story?" Grady straightened in the chair. "I can discourage him from bothering the talent. Maybe give him some new stories to chase, until after the launch."

Dietz rubbed his face and waved BeeBo back into the chair. The big man's looming height and girth made the room even more claustrophobic. "We want publicity, so you'll have to finesse it. I don't want any negatives about the show to surface in the next five days. Media appearances today, tomorrow night the launch party, and over the weekend build positive buzz. I want positive impressions about 'local boys make good and help the economy.' You know, a feel good Christmas story."

"Hogs for the holidays." BeeBo's gap-toothed expression was a sharp contrast to Grady's high-dollar caps.

Grady barked a laugh. "Not bad." He stood. "I'll take care of it, Boss. Better follow up on Felch. And I'll get the talent together with the staff later today for some media training fine tuning."

"Lots riding on this." Dietz stood as the two men headed for the door. "Hang back a minute, Grady. BeeBo, he'll catch up, so go wait in your truck." They watched him lumber out of the room. He moved quickly for a big man, he moved quickly, and probably could take down a hog without the help of one of his several dogs. He turned to Grady. "One down, two to go. Make sure Sunny gets to the TV studio on time for the satellite media tour. The rest of us need to be at the radio station a half hour early." He scowled. "You've got to get Felch squared away."

"It's covered, no worries."

"Sure, you say that, but he's not here, is he?"

"Not my fault. The reporter got to him before I could, and hustled him into his car. You said no scenes, no bad publicity, and there were too many people around."

Dietz groaned. He needed a drink, never mind the morning hour. "We can control BeeBo—just tell him what he wants to hear. Sunny's a mercenary bimbo, and a paycheck will keep her in line. Felch takes convincing."

"He's a dumb ass."

"Hardly! Sure, he's unsophisticated, but he's not stupid. Behind that ugly face is a thinker. And a conniver. Find out what he wants and give it to him."

Grady shrugged. "Whatever. I can handle him." He sipped his coffee. Rolled the pen.

"You haven't so far. I need a cutthroat attitude, someone willing to get his hands dirty to get the job done. Are you hearing me?" He tried to calm his breath and failed. "Felch had me fooled. Makes me wonder if he's even from around here. If he's not a native Texan, that could blow up and derail this whole deal."

Grady didn't need to know Felch came out of nowhere and contacted him with the idea for the *Cutting Corners* show. You can't copyright ideas, after all. And it was Dietz's connections and expertise that turned the "idea" into *Hog Hell*, Dietz who got the barbecue sponsorships, Dietz the spin-off *High On The Hog* cooking show. And this season's show launch would announce the Piggy Panache gourmet gifts franchise during the watch party at the local Hog Heaven BBQ Restaurant, right in time for the Christmas rush. "We need Felch to stay in the show one more season, and make an appearance at the launch. The other guys get the job done, but Felch and BeeBo have star power."

Grady blew a raspberry. "'Star power?' Hell, they don't know what camera to play. You want an on camera backwoods goof? Just say the word." Grady pooched out his gut, let one eye cross and jutted out his chin, assuming a shambling gait and lisp. "Dem hawgs be the devil, sho' 'nuff."

Dietz sucked in a breath, shocked to momentary silence. The mimicry was uncanny. If not for the expensive hair style and clothing the man could be a smaller version of Felch. He shook himself. "They're the golden goofs.

They're why viewers tune in, and viewers keep sponsors happy, and sponsors keep producers funneling in the big bucks."

Grady straightened and turned sulky. "I could do it."

"Sorry, we went in another direction." The words were familiar to every rejected actor, including himself. Even the love of his life had gone in another direction. Literally. She'd be sorry, soon enough.

Dietz brushed off the memories. That was then, this was now, and as a director and producer he had a responsibility to the show and everyone involved, and couldn't let personal feelings get in the way. Not yet, anyway.

"Didn't hire you to be the talent; I hired you to manage the talent. If you can't handle the job, there's a dozen like you lined up to take your place."

"So what else is new?" Grady's jaw tightened.

"It's your paycheck, too, you know. Hell, I'll double your salary for the next week for the extra aggravation. Deal?"

The younger man twirled the pen, considering, and then grinned.

"All righty, you get your designer butt in gear. Go catch up to BeeBo, and do what you need to do to keep a rein on the talent before him and Felch tank everything."

Chapter 3

Shadow cocked his head at the sound of the distant doorbell, raised his tail and woofed with concern. Doorbells meant visitors. Visitors might be friends with treats. But a visitor could be a scary stranger. It was a good-dog's job to know the difference.

He listened, but nothing else tickled his nerves. He yawned and then shook himself in a canine shrug until his shoulders relaxed. Some visitors didn't matter. His tail began to wave as he returned to sniffing the frozen mud, happy to stay outdoors and explore.

At first he didn't want to leave the house. His tummy hurt if he couldn't see September, and she didn't like the outside. He'd only take-a-break to potty if she clipped on his leash and stayed by his side. That way he kept her safe from scary strangers. He barked with loud ferocious warnings at anything that moved or made noise or smelled different, anything that made September startle—just in case. She'd make the CLICK-sound with her mouth, and say, "Good-dog, Shadow," and stroke his cheeks.

September's CLICK-sound meant he'd done something right, and often meant treats, too. He'd already learned lots of things, like how to walk on the leash without pulling ahead or lagging behind. He knew how to "sit" and "down" and knew what "wait" meant, though he didn't like that word even when he got a treat. Shadow liked treats, but he liked making September happy even more.

Playing games made her laugh. Shadow's tail waved harder at the thought of Frisbee-fetch. If September said, "Where's your ball?" he'd race to bring it. Other times she asked him to find objects he'd learned in the *show-me* game, like *book* and *paper* and *gun*.

Lately September partnered the *show-me* game with *hide-and-seek*. She let him examine a scented sock and it was a good-dog's job to track down the same scent hidden somewhere in the house. He'd learned how to play the game by following trails of smelly treats dribbled along the floor. Sometimes the puzzle-smell was treats like cheese, or some stranger's socks, and one time a strange dog's toy. He wondered if he'd get to meet the dog. Wouldn't that be fine! Or maybe even a cat. Macy wouldn't let him but Shadow wanted a really good sniff of cat-butt.

The best part about *inside* was September's bed at the top of the narrow stairs. She always asked him to jump up and share the sleep spot with her; especially late at night after she cried out in her sleep and her eyes rained water and her fear-stink made him start awake. When that happened, he nose-poked her and then dodged her fists until she knew him again. He'd figured that out on his own. Shadow was smart that way.

His bruised paws healed, but torn nails took longer. He trod carefully, and flinched when one of the thorny branches whipped close to his nose. The wind puffed through bone-dry overgrowth, shaking the prickly branches against each other in a rattled staccato.

Lately, the world outside teased more than Macy's sly looks. Shadow spent hours staring through windows. He longed to run and play, snap leaves out of the air, and roll to scratch his back against smell-rich ground. Once he knew everything about *inside,* it became harder and harder to be a good-dog the way September expected.

September didn't like it when he sneaked treats from the cat's sandbox. She'd made it clear that good-dogs steer clear of all-things-cat. Shadow hated to disappoint September, so he practiced paw-stealth to sneak close and snack on the yummy bits. But treats and sleeping on the bed, and sucking on Bear-toy, even sneaking quick tastes of cat-stuff weren't enough entertainment for a good-dog.

The icy vegetation crunched beneath his paws. Tough clumps of tall grass brushed his belly and parted for him when he ducked and weaved between scraggly thickets that crowded each side of the narrow path. Wind stroked Shadow's fur, and he slicked back his ears and squinted into gusts that carried scent-glimpses of distant treasures. Naked shrubs shivered in the wind, and limbs bristling with thorns claw-combed his fur if he misjudged the opening.

The pathway wound down a gentle slope hidden by bristling overgrowth and surrounded by a battered metal fence. When Shadow push through the final bushy barrier, he huffed and tasted the air with anticipation. He bounded toward the farthest fence pole.

Shadow sniffed the base before balancing on three legs and letting fly with a poorly aimed stream of urine. Lately, he wasn't sure why, it felt right to lift one leg. He sniffed his work, appreciating the steam that rose into the frigid air, and then moved further along the edge of the cleared fence line, and paused to sniff and pee, sniff and pee until he had no more pee to spend.

The center of this bottom half of the garden served as a morgue to brittle bodies of dead rose bushes stacked higher than the fence. Brown grassy areas bled across the lot where something had ripped into the thick sod leaving roots bared to the frosty air. Shadow padded to inspect the irregular furrows. His hackles raised at the rank odor that spoke of odd creatures—too many to count—that trampled through muddy soil before the clotted surface froze. He pawed the icy dirt for a fresher sniff, and stifled a yelp. He dropped his head to lick his tender toes.

Car tires screeched at the front of the house, a loud BANG echoed, and September screamed.

Shadow whirled. He drove back through the pathway toward the sound. Thorny branches tore at a good-dog's fur like an angry cat, but Shadow bulldozed on. He had to reach September. He could tell the difference between play-scream and scared-scream, and September was scared. She needed him.

Shadow reached the gate. He slammed into it, but it didn't move. The latch rattled when he pawed the metal and tried to push his long muzzle through the bars. The cross pieces, too narrow for him to squeeze past, stopped him dead. He turned his face sideways to try again, yelping with frustration.

He listened. Nothing. September hadn't called out to let a good-dog know everything was fine. So Shadow leaped up, placing his paws on the top of the gate, rear legs searching for purchase to climb over, but his paws slipped down and made no headway. Dropping to the ground, he backed away from the gate as far as he could, but the tangled shrubbery blocked a solid running start.

He couldn't go through. He couldn't vault the gate. Shadow dropped his nose to the dirt, checking for a way under. Yelps turned to barks and finally howls as he pawed the frozen ground. He had to reach September.

Chapter 4

Theodore "Teddy" Williams sat in the car for a long time, listening to the cooling engine tick long after it had been shut off. One of the women inside the two-and-a-half story brick monstrosity flicked the curtain to peer out, and then quickly ducked out of sight. He took off his wire-rimmed glasses, and rubbed his weary eyes. Unruly eyebrows bristled beneath his fingers.

Molly always trimmed his eyebrows. She could no longer be trusted with scissors, let alone something sharp near his eyes. Giving away Molly's garden stuff seemed wrong. It signaled giving up, meant he'd finally accepted she wouldn't get better.

He hunched his shoulders, gripping the steering wheel with gloved hands until creaky arthritic joints popped. After a long, shuddery breath, Teddy opened the car door and pried himself out of the driver's seat, popping the trunk. He limped to the front steps, slowly climbed them and fixed a cordial smile on his face. It wouldn't fool anybody, but he needed to make the effort.

The door swung open, and he faced half a dozen women ranging in age from thirty to seventy. Cassie held the door wide and motioned him inside, and his smile slipped. Teddy cleared his throat. "Thanks, but I can't stay. Molly's expecting me."

No, she wasn't. Molly likely wouldn't know if he visited or not, but he couldn't stay away. He visited every afternoon. On good days when the nursing home scheduled an outing, they used to meet at the local mall for coffee and a walk. Today they'd called to tell him to meet at the mall, and he couldn't wait to get there. Good days didn't happen so much anymore.

"We talked and Molly wanted me to bring her stuff over for the club to use. It's in the trunk of the car. Help yourself."

She should be here. Molly loved her Master Gardener club meetings, and delighted in sharing tips and bringing in expert speakers. After these special meetings, his wife came home filled with as much excitement as a teeny-bopper sighting Frankie Valli or whoever the young kids liked these days, and gushed about pruning timeliness, mulch components, grafting and the latest in weed pre-emergent technology.

"Thanks for coming, Teddy. We all miss Molly so much." Cassie folded her arms. "She was a driving force in the club. How generous to share her materials." The other women murmured agreement, but their sympathetic expressions stiffened his spine. "Maybe with Molly's secret ingredients, the rest of the club will carry on her legacy of winning blooms." Cassie's warm tone contrasted with her flinty expression. Despite her groomed yard and manicured flowerbeds courtesy of a hired army of lawn care specialists, Molly beat the pants off Cassie time after time.

"Molly never shared her garden secrets with me. Probably had something to do with her singing to the plants." A couple of the ladies smiled at his comments. "Me, I can't carry a tune in a tin bucket, but Molly and Patricia challenged the birds with their singing." He glanced around the room. "Where's Patricia?"

Cassie shrugged.

An older birdlike woman—he thought her name was Ethel, he couldn't keep all of Molly's friends straight—came forward and gave him a hug. "Patricia hasn't been here for the past several meetings, either. She and Molly were very close. Well, we all were. We miss her."

He swallowed past the lump in his throat. "Thanks. You meant a lot to Molly, too. She loved these meetings."

Molly wanted to share the supplies and pass on the savings to her friends, because not everyone in the club lived in mansions like this one. Cassie married up after her divorce, but acted like she'd been born lady of the manor. Others in the club pinched pennies and shared resources to create showcase gardens for boasting rights more than any income. The quiet rivalry between the iris club and the rosarians culminated at the spring garden tour each year. With only a dozen slots available, the gardeners angled for every advantage, and in the fall and winter months prepped the soil for winning blooms.

"We just started the meeting. Would you care to stay? I've got coffee brewing, and one of the ladies brought cookies." Cassie's crossed arms tightened, and she made no move away from the door. The other women, with the exception of Ethel, wouldn't meet his eyes.

He was a reminder of their mortality. They'd already pruned Molly out of the little clique before the disease infiltrated the rest of the group. Teddy spun on his heels, pushing Cassie aside. "Sorry," he mumbled. But he wasn't. "Come get what you want. Maybe some of Molly's magic will rub off on you."

She'd always been magical to him, a creature out of a fairy tale that somehow agreed to marry him, a mere mortal more adept at talking to computers than people.

He rushed back out the door, and had to consciously slow himself to keep from pitching headfirst down the brick front steps. The gaggle of biddies inside jostled each other, four finding coats to then clamber out the door after him. He stood at the trunk waiting for the women—they did remind him of geese, muttering and honking under their breath to each other—to line up and each grab a sack before trundling it into their own cars to stow.

Molly talked him into buying the truckload of fertilizer three years ago from the local man making the rounds. Mostly, she'd wanted to help out the hard-luck fellow. With the economy tanking, folks turned to all kinds of homegrown moneymaking schemes. But with the Molly magic, the contents of a dozen or so burlap bags labeled with neon yellow tape made a huge difference in the blossom production.

Their house had been on the tour four times in the past seven years Molly had been a member. Her roses rivaled any they'd seen in Tyler, Texas, arguably the rose capital of America. She kept her garden small due to the limitations of their postage stamp backyard, and used vertical space to advantage. Cherokee Rose took over the north side of the yard, spanning more than twelve feet in height and width, while Fortune's Double Yellow and Seven Sisters rambled up each side of an arched trellis that framed the back patio. Miniature roses lined the paving stone pathways painting carnival colors everywhere. But when she became ill a year ago, the garden took a back seat.

Teddy smiled when one by one, four of the women filed past the car to return to the house. Cassie and Ethel stayed at the door. "There's still a few bags left. Some gardening tools, too." He wanted all of it gone. It reeked of normal, happy times that would be no more. The reminder hurt too much.

"I don't want to mess my clothes." Cassie hugged herself, not budging from the doorway. "Leave a bag there on the drive. I'll have one of the kids tote it to the garage when they get home."

He adjusted his glasses. It would serve her right for him to accidentally-on-purpose break open the bag and dump it all over her sidewalk. But when Ethel hurried down to join him at the car, he stifled the impulse and offered a weak smile.

"Don't mind Cassie. She's all tied up in knots trying to be someone she's not." Ethel spoke softly, for his ears only, and patted him on the shoulder.

"Molly always knew exactly who she was, and what she needed. That was—and is—you. She adored you—still does, I'm sure."

He grabbed up Cassie's bag of fertilizer and carefully set it on the ground so he wouldn't have to look at Ethel. "There's two more bags." His voice cracked and he cleared his throat. "I could carry them to your car."

"Just leave the rest here for Cassie, if you don't mind. I'll pass on the fertilizer, but would love to have one of Molly's gardening tools. Not to use. But as a memory, you know?" She patted him again. "As an honor to her. What happened to Molly could happen to any of us. That's got them scared. But she'd be pleased what you're doing here. Never doubt that, okay? Let your heart lead you and it'll never fail."

He smiled, blinking hard, and covered her hand with his gloved one and squeezed. "Is that what you do? Let your heart lead?"

She nodded. "Been with my cowboy for going on forty-five years, through the fat and thin times. The heart never lies, not if you listen close enough." Ethel leaned closer. "Even when it seems mighty silent, you can hear the echo."

"Thank you." He indicated the open trunk, filled with a variety of gardening implements. "Help yourself." He muscled the last two bags out of the car and dropped them beside the others.

At first, he and Molly laughed about the memory lapses. After all, neither of them were spring chickens, and he had nearly a decade on her. When she left her eyeglasses in the microwave they chuckled about "see-food" for a week. Then she called the pastor by the wrong name, and the embarrassment stopped the laughter dead. Shortly thereafter, he found notes she'd made to herself to keep track of the must-do items of daily living. The list included "take a shower" and "turn off stove." That scared him.

He'd begged her to see a doctor. Molly refused. She'd always been pig headed—it took him nearly three years to convince her to marry him. But after she drove across town to a dentist appointment and had a meltdown when she couldn't find her way home, he scheduled the appointment despite her protestations.

They'd held hands in the waiting room, anchoring each other against the desperate tide that threatened to sweep them away. The diagnosis drowned their hopes, and they'd been treading water ever since, knowing the time would come when they could no longer stay afloat in the flood.

Ethel picked out an old pruning shear, the yellow handle grip stained with sweat and scarred from use. "I remember seeing Molly use this." She hugged it to the breast of her coat. "I'll treasure this, and take good care of it. Betcha it's full of Molly magic, more than that old dusty fertilizer."

He saw Cassie in the doorway, waving a hand at the stacked bags. "You got that right." He slammed the trunk of the car. "Everything had to be yellow, or have sparkles. I'm proud you'll have it. Molly will be glad." If she could remember, that is.

It developed so quickly. Even the doctors whispered puzzled conversations in the face of Molly's swift decline. Teddy kept her at home as long as he could, but his age prevented him from providing the care she needed and deserved. Finally he'd found her a nursing facility, and continued to see her every day.

Some days she was bright as a penny, the Molly he'd always known. Those days they packed every moment with fun and laughter, memories of good times. The medications supposed to slow down the disease progression gave them hope for the future, a future they measured in days and hours, no longer months or years.

After cracking computer code for decades and figuring out circuitry and neural networking puzzles, Molly's brain disease thumbed its nose at him. Alzheimer's played fast and loose with logic, a moving target that stymied the doctors and wrung emotions dry.

He climbed back into the driver's seat, and watched until the ladies disappeared back into the house. Ethel pushed aside the blinds and waved the yellow-handled pruner, and he waved back. Teddy started the car, but before he could push it into gear, his cell phone rang.

The number wasn't familiar. Teddy still consulted with a few companies, and figured it might be an unlisted number from a client. "This is Theodore Williams, how may I help you?"

"Mr. Williams? This is Alison? Over at SunnyDale Nursing Home?" She spoke in constant questions, a young person's habit that drove him nuts.

"Yes, Alison, I'll be at the mall in another twenty minutes. Is the group already in the food court? I've got my car today since it's good weather, and can park around back." He shoved the car into gear and pulled out of the drive.

"Well, there's a change of plans. That's why I called." She hesitated, and then hurried on. "How soon could you get here? I mean, to the facility?"

"What's wrong?" His heart quickened.

"Nothing is wrong. It'll be fine, I'm sure? I mean, don't worry at all, not at all. But, could you come here instead? Soon as you can?"

He disconnected the call without a word and gunned the engine.

Chapter 5

September's heart thumped and she held onto the door as blood drained from her face. She backed away, unable to breathe, slamming the door to fumble the locks closed with palsied fingers. She didn't have to open the beribboned package; she knew what it contained.

She won a place on a prestigious concert tour but Mom didn't want her to go. September should instead give music lessons to children of the town's elite, volunteer in the right organizations, meet the right sorts of people, marry a fellow with the right social standing and the ultimate goal for Rose January—produce grandbabies. After weeks of arguments and cajoling and promises, Mom agreed on one condition: that a family friend watch out for September while she was far from home. And thus, the nightmare began . . .

The squeal of tires and metallic crash startled a scream from September. She should phone…who? Who could she call? Not even Chris had known the whole story, but he loved her and married her anyway, tried to protect her, and got himself killed along with their dog Dakota. April knew, but her sister would never help, even if she could. Hard to help from a hospital bed and pending arraignment. Combs knew some and probably guessed even more. She couldn't bear to share her shame with him.

The package waited on the front steps, identical to the cheery deliveries she'd learned to dread. That's why she and Chris had left Chicago, yet he'd followed them to South Bend. She braced herself and moved closer to peer through the front door, quickened breath fogging the stained glass.

The circle drive boasted a screen of newly planted live oaks on each side of a recently installed metal gate that fronted Rabbit Run Road. A car engine revved, wheels spinning, but the accordioned hood wedged between two gnarly cedar elms on one side of the open gate. Like a coward, he must have dropped the package and run and crunched his car. Good!

She'd changed after the recent Thanksgiving debacle. She wasn't the trusting innocent any longer. Afraid of him? Hell, yes! But more than that, she hated him for wrecking her life, or trying to. If he came after her this time, he'd get the surprise of his life.

"Uncle" Vic looked like six miles of bad road, his cheeks pocked with acne scars, crooked teeth, and a lanky string bean physique with massive belly more Peewee Herman than the leading man he wanted to be. He was a stray mutt so ugly and needy, folks bent over backwards to be extra nice to him and make up for the short straw he'd drawn in life. He chaperoned outings, vetted parties, and steered September away from missteps. Mom and Dad considered Uncle Vic the ideal shepherd. They'd been wrong.

She heard Shadow barking, his yelps and cries testament to the shepherd's protective nature, and her spine stiffened. She wasn't alone. She wasn't sixteen. This was her house, dammit!

September picked up the office phone and without taking her eyes off the distant gate, dialed Jeff's number from memory. She didn't have to give him details. But the phone went to voicemail. She fumbled with what to say, and instead hung up without leaving a message.

Her gun was in the car. Just the thought of the gun ratcheted up her nerves, and made bile burn the back of her throat. She hated guns, but Victor made owning one a necessity. September retrieved her coat, shrugged it on, and unlocked the deadbolts again, her fingers still clumsy with fear.

She shuddered, but grabbed the baseball bat left within reach by the door. It felt like an old friend, and her pulse steadied. She stuffed sock-clad feet into tug-on rain boots left at the entry. Her grip on the bat whitened her knuckles, but she took a deep breath, and strode out the door.

To reach the gun, she'd lose sight of the front gate, and risk Victor doubling back and trapping her in the garage. September hefted the bat, liking its weight. Shadow's barks grew more insistent, bolstering her courage. But she had to do this herself. Victor had killed Dakota, a trained protection dog, just to hurt her. She wouldn't risk Shadow by bringing him along.

September grabbed up a pair of binoculars she kept near the door, and trained them on the distant car. Red spiky hair. Victor was bald. Huh. He'd sent a delivery boy to do his dirty work. She'd confront him, find out more about Victor. This had to end. No more risking those she loved. No more excuses. And no more hiding. She clomped toward the crumpled vehicle, jaw tight and breathing fire.

Her face grew hot the closer she got to the Gremlin. It sat nose down in the slight depression between the trees. The engine made a hissing sound as it revved, trying to back out of the ditch, and she dodged clotted dirt kicked up by spinning wheels.

The driver's door butted against a tree trunk, blocking his exit. He'd need to clamber out through the passenger's side. She positioned herself to meet him, and held the bat ready. September ducked to see inside. He faced away from her, red hair moussed into spikes, and wearing a yellow windbreaker. She rapped on the window with the bat, resisting the urge to hammer the glass, and he spun around, a panicked expression on his face.

She stepped back, deflated. "What are you doing here?" September checked all around, but saw no other car or anyone else nearby. They were alone.

Sylvester Sanger gave a sheepish buck-toothed grimace. "You wouldn't phone me back. So figured I'd make a house call." His face was burned, probably from the airbag deployment.

"I don't talk to sleazy tabloid reporters about my personal life." Her shoulders remained hunched. She searched both sides of the road for signs of her stalker. "Was anyone else out here?" September forced herself to loosen her grip on the bat. Her hands had begun to hurt, and she flexed them, suddenly conscious of the goofy pink gloves.

"Some delivery van nearly T-boned me racing out your drive as I pulled up. That's how I ended up in the trees. I should have put the seatbelt around the kitty carrier." He jerked his head to indicate the back seat, where a pet carrier canted on its side, the door sprung open.

"Really? You brought a cat bribe?" She scanned up and down the road, nerves thrumming. She should get back to the house. The front door was unlocked. She turned to go.

"Wait. No, wait a minute. At least hear me out, now I pried you outta that fortress of a house." His voice rose in a whine, and he struggled to wiggle across the seats to get out of the car. "You made the national news last month. Sure, I wanted a piece of the action. The whole country wants to know what makes September-the-hero tick, her secrets, the tragic story of lost love."

She stiffened. The brisk wind whipped hair into her mouth, and she pushed it out of her eyes. He'd pestered her for an exclusive, wanting to raise his own credibility, and she'd dodged him for weeks. She eyed the battered car and flourished the bat. "Don't tempt me, Sly. Your car's already totaled and I need to work off some steam."

Sly levered open the passenger door, tumbled out, stood, and dusted himself off. "Never mind that. Your secret life, whatever it is, got trumped. Me and Fish are working on something bigger. Ginormous! It'll put us on the map and make us heroes. And it's right up your furry alley." He lisped with excitement, again gesturing to the pet carrier.

He fear began to abate, replaced by anger. "I can't believe anyone bought your line of crappiocca." Humphrey Fish, a local radio host, helped save her bacon during the recent blizzard, but he couldn't care less about her personal life. He only cared about the next story and getting out of Heartland to reach the big time. He still called her a couple times a week to push a return to the Pet Peeves radio show spot, but she'd had enough media attention to last a lifetime. What pet story would be big enough to tempt Fish to work with a sleaze bucket like Sly?

"You wouldn't answer the phone, or return my calls. So I came to you, but I'm not empty-handed. I brought you a gift." He jerked a thumb toward the back seat, pleased at his ingenuity. "I figured you'd come running to see who left it. I didn't count on ramming the tree before—"

"Wait. That package was your idea?"

"Package? That's what you call it?" His brow furrowed, and then cleared as he shrugged. "Well, yeah. Totally my idea."

"Son-of-a-bitch!" She swung the bat, and relished the satisfying "thunk" when it dented the hood of his old car.

He flinched and dodged. "What are you doing?" His voice sirened two octaves when she walloped the car a second time, even though the bat's whoosh never came close. "Stop with the bat, lady. If you don't want it, say so! Sheesh, I thought you were an animal lover."

The words stopped her third swing in mid-air. Animal lover? She had no compunction about putting the fear of God into Sly, but no pet deserved being scared spitless even if the owner was a clueless piece of toilet fish.

She lowered the bat and craned her neck to see into the car. On the back seat, the carrier jittered slightly as something inside shifted weight but remained reluctant to leave the security of the open carrier. It wasn't just a prop to enlist her attention.

She'd gone from fear to anger and now disgust at Sly's attempt to manipulate her. Even so, her shoulders unclenched with relief. Better the clueless reporter than the alternative. She hated to let him off the hook, but threw the bat to the ground so hard it made her arm ache. "Did you think a fancy-wrapped gift and cute puppy—"

"Cat. He's a cat." He opened the rear door, and struggled to maneuver the plastic container out. "He's my kitty security force, keeps interlopers out of my private office. That's why I named him Pinkerton. That, and his bright pink nose."

September put up both hands in a warding off gesture and backed away. "I don't need another pet. You don't show up with a cat like a box of chocolates. What were you thinking?" She tried to calm her hurried breathing, still fuming. What were the odds Sly would use the same wrapping as Victor? "You're trespassing. Clear out of here, and don't come back." She whirled, clutching her coat close against the chill. Her pink fingerless gloves and dumpy rain boots lent a ludicrous air to her retreat.

"But Pinkerton is sick. Don't you want to see him?"

September stumbled, but forced herself to keep walking. She couldn't rescue the world. And she wouldn't expose Macy to a strange, sick feline. "Take him to a vet. And get the hell off my property before I file charges for stalking." It wouldn't be the first time.

Chapter 6

Nikki scrubbed her tearful face with mittened hands, and stepped into the three-wheeler's path with hands overhead to flag down her brother. Twice he and his friends had raced by as they ran the track. She risked getting run over, but it was better than being ignored in the icy wind.

Hank applied the brakes. His fair skin flushed from wind-burn and embarrassment, but Nikki didn't care. "I'll tell. It's not fair." She had to shout over the engine noise.

"Quit following us." He forced a nonchalant expression when Zeke and his no-neck older cousin zoomed past on their own spanking new four-wheeler, and then Hank turned to scowl at her. "Mom told you to stay home. I can't babysit while me and the guys run the course."

"It's my turn. You always let me ride. I'm as good as those guys, you said so." She hated the whiny way she sounded, but couldn't help it. Hank was only three years older, but he treated her like a baby when she was nearly ten. He'd been riding since forever, while she'd stood out in the cold until her nose turned snotty. "Mom said to share."

"No, Mom said you should go shopping with her." He revved the engine like he wanted to spin out and leave her in the dust. Except the ground was froze solid.

"I already got my Christmas shopping done. Mom told you to watch out for me, and instead you ditched me soon as she pulled out of the drive. Maybe I should take back your present." She stuck out her tongue. He wasn't going to let her ride. Not with his friends around to see.

Nikki's friends had left town with their families for the holiday, except for her bestie Gina, whose mom just had a new baby. Gina was all, "Oooh, the baby this and the baby that," until Nikki wanted to puke. It was bald and prune-faced, and smelled like pee. Nothing cute about it, as far as Nikki could see. Not like the kitties over at the barn. Nothing was cuter than kitties.

Mom wouldn't let them have pets, especially cats, because she got sneeze attacks. Nikki didn't care about being with the popular kids at the barn. She wanted to spend time with the cats. So as long as Hank let her tag along to visit the kitties, she'd keep his secret.

Usually Hank was pretty decent, for a boy. He didn't mind when she tagged along, and she took seriously being sworn to secrecy about the barn hangout. That's where the older kids, boys mostly, hung out and smoked dope and bragged about all kinds of things that would make parents' eyebrows curl. Mom would have a cow if she knew Hank hung out at the barn, and she'd totally stroke out if Nikki did, too.

"I gotta catch up with the guys." Hank adjusted his blue and white Dallas Cowboy's gimme cap, the one he got for his birthday four months ago. "Sorry. I'll make it up to you later. Promise." His eyes shifted away and he ducked his head. "It's Zeke's rules, ya know. His trail, his four-wheelers..."

"Zeke's a stupid-head." She bit her lip to stop the tremble.

Hank smiled. "True. But he lets us ride, and got us both into the barn. He says his cousin visiting from Austin gets dibs over my kid sister." He shrugged. It made perfect boy-sense, she guessed. "You gotta wait until he goes home. Then it'll be back to normal, okay?"

"Promise?" She wouldn't cry, she wouldn't.

"Swear on my Cowboy's cap. Dustin—that's the cousin—he's heading out day after Christmas." Hank touched his hand to the cap, and saluted the way Daddy taught him. Daddy had bought it for him before he left.

She smiled. He looked like Daddy, too; they both did, with white-blond hair and freckles. Looking at Hank made her miss Daddy even more.

Hank revved the engine again. "Now go back home before Mom finds out you're here. She'd ground both of us." He pulled away in an impressive cloud of dust. She guessed it wasn't that frozen after all.

Ever since Daddy got deployed—a fancy word for "gone away to serve America"—Mom got this pinched expression on her face. She didn't laugh so much anymore, and mostly said "no" to anything new. Mom said she had a lot on her mind, keeping everything going till Daddy got home. She didn't want any bad surprises, and said Hank and Nikki had to suck it up and pull together like good soldiers right along with Mom. They all had their fingers crossed (toes too, and eyes if it'd help) that Daddy could come home for a holiday visit. That would be the bestest Christmas present of all.

She and Hank tried not to be any trouble. But the barn was too good to resist. You only got invited by the cool kids, how could anyone turn that down? If Mom found out about the barn hangout, that would be a *very-bad-thing*. Even though Hank and his friends didn't smoke or anything, Mom said an omission was bad as a lie. Nikki wasn't exactly sure what that meant, but she didn't want to find out.

Nikki watched Hank go. She scrubbed her salty cheeks where the tears had dried and itched in the cold air, and waited until he turned the corner over the hill out of sight. Since he wouldn't let her hitch a ride, she'd hike to the barn by herself. It wasn't *that* far. Up the hill and down the path to the left. She knew better than to ask Hank to look after the kitties. He wouldn't stop the trail ride for such a thing, and even if he did, she didn't want the boys to know how much she liked the cats. Hank was okay, but some of the older boys acted mean sometimes.

With school out until the Monday after New Year's, most of the big kids had better things to do than sneak out to the barn. She should have the place to herself. Hank, Zeke and his cousin wouldn't stop riding until the sun started to set. She checked her pink sparkly cell phone, the one Mom said only to use for emergencies, and saw she had at least an hour before dark-fall. There was plenty of time to travel there and back home without anyone being the wiser.

Twenty minutes later Nikki arrived at the old barn. The walk took longer than she'd figured, and chilled her to the bone. Before going in, she did what the big kids did, and walked all the way around the structure to be sure nobody else was there. The weathered wood had long since lost its original color, and the gray planks blended with the bare bois d'arc trees. Its witch-claw limbs grabbed at the shaky walls, and drooped clear to the ground as though to gather up the horse-apples shed around its gnarly feet.

Nikki shivered, from the cold, not the spooky trees. After all, she was nearly ten years old, and stupid trees were nothing to be scared about. She didn't see anybody else around, but listened carefully at the door anyway for whispers or boy laughter before shoving aside the loose wall plank enough to bend low and squeeze through.

She straightened, and turned her head this way and that. Nikki hadn't noticed so many shadows before when she'd been here with Hank. "Just shadows, nothing scary." Her voice didn't even shake. See? Nothing to get stupid about.

A soft mew replied.

"Mama Kitty? It's me, Nikki. I brought you treats." It wasn't proper cat food, but she'd discovered the cats liked baloney and cheese during her first visit when she'd dropped part of a sandwich.

The fluffy gray cat eeled out from one of the empty stalls and padded toward her. "How are you? Where's your family?" When they'd first met last spring, she'd had half a dozen babies, but over the weeks and months, some had disappeared.

Nikki brushed off a wooden box and sat, crooning to Mama Kitty when the cat cheek-rubbed her ankles. "Kitty-kitty-kitty?" She called again, hoping the three remaining young ones would come out of hiding when she pulled out the plastic baggy of food. Unlike their mother, the kittens remained shy and she'd not managed to pet a single one, although they would sneak close enough to grab a treat or two she tossed in the dirt pathway down the center of the building. "Guess you need a new name, huh? I mean, if your babies are all grown up, I can't call you 'Mama Kitty' forever. So what's your name?"

The gray cat hopped into her lap and nosed the plastic bag, trilling and mewing with excitement. "Always hoping for treats, aren't you?" The cat's bony hips stood out prominently beneath the fur. Nikki shredded the cold cuts into strips, and hand-fed her two before the first kitten appeared. Two more kitten-shaped shadows hung back in the doorway to the stall.

Nikki tossed a cube of cheese near the first youngster, and he pounced on it, crouching over the treat to lick and finally pick it up and chew, head turned sideways to more efficiently munch. She offered another strip of baloney to the gray cat on her lap, and thrilled at the sound of cat purrs.

Like always when she visited the cats, she fantasized about taking them home. "I keep hoping you could come live with me. Would you like that? Hey, I'll call you 'Hope' for luck. Maybe that'll make it happen."

Hope purred and head bumped Nikki's hand, as if approving the new name. Nikki had researched on the internet and found out some cats didn't cause allergies. There was one called a Siberian that people said was a safe kind for sneezy people like Mom, and the gray cat had long hair like a Siberian.

She tossed another piece of cheese to the kitten, and made trill sounds with her tongue. The blond again pounced on the food. "You like that, don't you?" She smiled when the two other furry figures finally dashed out of the shadows toward the food.

The blond kitten screamed, and raced away. Only then did Nikki realize the other two creatures weren't kittens, but raccoons.

Hope dug her claws into Nikki's pant leg and arms, and puffed up to enormous proportions. Screaming, Nikki scrambled to stand up, dumping the terrified gray cat off her lap.

The raccoons hissed and fought over the cheese, gulped it down and then stared up at Nikki. They took wobbly steps toward her. They acted sick, bad sick. Maybe they had rabies.

Nikki backed away, one slow step at a time, fearful the sick raccoons might attack her. She should never have come alone. She was just a stupid nine-year-old kid, and made a baby mistake. Hank would know what to do. She wanted to find the loose board and make her escape, but was afraid to turn her back on the threatening animals.

She still clutched the baloney and cheese baggy, and flung the plastic toward the sick raccoons. The creatures fell on the treats, making awful noises, and the gray cat pressed against her leg, wailing. Without further thought Nikki scooped up the bony feline, turned, and dashed to the loose board and backed out of the barn butt first.

Panting, she straightened and whirled to run back home. She nearly ran into the man, and stopped dead, juggling the yowling, struggling cat.

"What y'all doing with my cat?" The giant scarecrow-man leaned forward, long scraggly hair flying, and shrugged off a heavy sack slung over one shoulder so it slammed to the ground. He scowled, revealing broken, stained teeth. In the other hand, he held a gun.

Chapter 7

September broke into a run back to the house when Shadow yelped. "Baby-dog, I'm coming, everything's okay." He sounded frustrated but without the warning snarls she'd learned to recognize and heed. He fed into her emotional state and mirrored it back, and she felt equally attuned to the pup. She no longer questioned it. They were family.

He paw-punched the garden gate and his woofs punctuated the metal jangle. At least his torn claws had healed, but she winced at the memory of the bloody damage. September trotted around to the garden.

Shadow flattened his ears when he saw her. He yawned and voiced a squeaky trill and wagged with clear relief.

She took a big breath herself, mentally shedding the stress from the argument with Sly. "I'm fine, baby-dog, did you worry about me? Sorry for all the noise." She unlatched the gate and knelt for a moment to thwart his impulse to jump up, squinting her eyes shut and laughing as he nosed and washed her face in a proper exuberant doggy greeting. "Okay, already, I love you too. Ready to go inside? Gotta call somebody about Sly's car." He stood tree trunk solid when September braced against his broad shoulders to lever herself upright.

Shadow raced her to the back door, sat, and waited for her. "Good-dog,

Shadow." He wriggled and grinned, watching with expectation for her next words. "Shadow, open." She coupled the command with a wavelike hand signal, and the young shepherd lunged onto his rear legs and punched the door with his chest and paws.

The door rebounded from the dog's weight. September bit her lip to keep from smiling, instead tipping her head with one raised eyebrow until Shadow backed out of the open doorway and planted his tail. "Good-dog! Inside." She gave the final command in the chain, and watched him sprint across the kitchen's slate floor, nails a tap-shoe clatter on his way to slurp mouthfuls from the oversize water bowl.

She hip-bumped the door closed, kicked off her boots and walked past the stained glass table to retrieve her cell phone from the dark counter. September noted the missed call. Humphrey Fish. She made a face, and deleted without listening. If he'd partnered with Sly on some hair-brained scheme she had even less inclination to return the call.

Her website traffic exploded after the national news turned her into an overnight superhero, and the real pet problems got lost in the tidal wave of curiosity seekers. Good for Fish, his dream came true, but she didn't need the aggravation or the money. Well, maybe the money. At some point, the lottery winnings would run out, even with her careful investments and management. Meanwhile, the news coverage painted her with a huge bull's eye. Anyone could easily find her now. It was only a matter of time before she'd have to deal with Victor, for real.

Shadow whined and pressed close as if he could read her mind. He wiped his wet muzzle on her sweats and she absently stroked his head as she dialed the insurance company and explained the situation. Sly would pay for the damage.

The big dog stiffened, muscles rock hard against her thigh. A low growl bubbled in his throat.

"What?" She disconnected but hung on to the phone as she followed the trotting shepherd from the kitchen through the music/office to the front door. His hackles raised, he stared at the door, head tilting to one side. The growls erupted into alarm barks, and he danced around the door with his tail flagged high, begging for it to be opened.

She thumbed one of the deadbolts home before peeking through the adjacent window. A huge cobalt pickup pulled into the drive, and September's shoulders relaxed. Aaron was early.

He swung down from the driver's seat with the practiced grace of a cowboy's dismount. She knew Aaron still rode as often as he could despite her brother's worried disapproval. She pasted on a smile, opened the door, and used one sock-covered foot to boot Sly's gift box inside. She'd toss it later.

Aaron loped toward her, one hand waving behind him toward the highway. He yelled something unintelligible.

"What?" She shivered. Despite the clear sunny day, the wind cut like glass.

"Nearly hit it." Sun-bleached eyebrows shaded his gray eyes, and the corners of his mouth turned down, accentuating his dimples. Women still hit on Aaron, and it drove Mark crazy, but Aaron laughed it off.

"Oh, that car off the road? I called for help." She gestured with the cell phone. "He missed the curve."

He didn't act mollified. Aaron never lost his composure. He balanced Mark's emotional highs and lows the way her husband had steadied her. When she'd lost Chris she'd run home to Heartland to hide. She bit her lip, and stared at the box she'd kicked into the corner. She hadn't run far enough. Reminders, even fake ones, reached out to bite when least expected.

She and Mark shared dark hair and a tall slim build, and had also inherited Dad's tender heart. In the past few months, she'd managed to toughen up. Aaron knew she'd kick his butt if he hurt Mark, and it didn't bother him because, well, Aaron was that genuine and nice, despite her own initial suspicion of anything good. She hoped Aaron would never lose his fresh-faced optimism.

Now something beyond bad driving had him riled. "Come on inside, you'll freeze your nibblets."

He finally laughed. "Yeah, I hate when that happens." Aaron pulled the door shut behind him before he noticed Shadow's raised hackles. His scowl returned. "Are you okay? Where's Macy?"

Aaron was a cat guy and Macy knew it. "He's around somewhere. Had to separate them for a while, so he's probably sulking somewhere with his Mickey toy."

White eyebrows climbed higher, but Aaron had the good manners not to say anything. "You don't let Macy outside, do you?"

"Perish the thought." She gave a theatrical shiver. "He'd take on a coyote if he got the chance, but Macy's no match for them. Shadow's run off a few, and I worry they'd gang up on him, big as he is."

"I nearly hit an animal up by the gate. Maybe it was a big skunk, but it's the wrong time of day. I only caught a glimpse. Yeah, I know Macy isn't black but it was in the shadows and moved more like a cat." He craned to see up the sweeping front staircase, and then turned to scan the living area. "Are you sure Macy's inside?"

September glanced around, uneasy. Unlike many cats that dove under the bed with anything new, Macy loved visitors. And the big cat especially loved Aaron, almost to an embarrassing degree. "Macy? Kitty, where are you?"

When he didn't appear, Shadow kept by her side, the frown on his furry brow mirroring her own concern. She checked the cat's favorite perch atop the refrigerator. Empty. She opened the cabinet and pulled out Mickey, but the cat wasn't there. She crossed to the kitchen stairwell to call. "Macy, come! I have treats." She waited, head cocked to listen. Shadow woofed under his breath at the "treat" word and licked his lips.

Macy wouldn't snub both Aaron's visit and the promise of treats. Granted, even a trained cat wasn't above blowing off requests now and then. She peeked back over her shoulder, where Aaron leaned against the kitchen island with an odd, vacant expression on his face. "You're sure you saw him, that he got out?"

Aaron raised his eyebrows as if surprised to see her there. "Who got out?"

Shadow whined, and barked more sharply. He poked his nose at September's hand for the mentioned treat.

The dog's bark sharpened Aaron's focus and he straightened and blinked hard. "That's…Shadow, right?" He shook his head. "Not firing on all cylinders lately, haven't been sleeping too well. Better keep the dog inside, he'll get in my way. I brought the fertilizer mix for the first section of the garden."

"You said a cat dodged across the road on your way in. I can't find Macy."

"Oh, yeah." He rubbed his eyes. "He's not in the house after all? I'm sure it was a cat."

"Maybe he snuck out when I let Shadow into the garden. Macy loves spending time in the garden, but at least it's fenced and more or less cat-proofed. He's only been out there on leash, though, with Shadow to keep tabs on his furry butt." At his name, the dog barked once more.

"Want me to go out the front? You do the garden. We'll cover more ground that way." Aaron held up his own phone. "I'll call you if I catch a glimpse."

She waited until Aaron left before pulling on heavy tracking boots from the laundry room, and grabbing Shadow's harness and leash from the wall hook. He cued on the tools and could barely contain himself from bouncing up and down, muttering doggy comments under his breath. The newly trained *hide-and-seek* game had become one of his favorites, almost as adored as Frisbee fetch or Bear-tug-o-war. "Calm down, baby-dog. Sit."

He sat. His tail polished the kitchen floor, ears slicked back against his head as she put on his harness and attached the leash. Shadow's muscles trembled with the effort to contain himself. The dog finally exploded in joyous bounds aimed at her face when the last clasp snicked into place. "Shadow, settle." He leaned against her, sighed heavily and slurped her hand. "I love you too, baby-dog." She whispered so that only he could hear, and then stood and squared her shoulders. "But you're not the only fur-kid in my life. Shadow, want to play *seek*?"

His head cocked to one side, ears came forward with interest and his happy panting paused. She'd begun teaching him the *hide-and-seek* game so he'd be able to track missing pets, a skill that would have saved her much heartache a month ago. He'd been successful a few times, but now Macy counted on her, on both of them.

Most cats that got out of the house stayed close to home but remained hidden, and wouldn't even answer a beloved owner's call. A tracking dog, one trained to trail pets, was the answer.

After she grabbed Mickey, she led Shadow to the kitchen door, manhandled it open, and stepped outside. If Macy got out, it would have been from this door. September took a deep breath, and waited a moment until the dog's full attention focused on her. She held the stuffed toy for him to sniff, just as they'd practiced, so that he'd know the scent to track. "Where's Macy? Macy's hiding. Shadow, *seek Macy!*"

Shadow's eyes lit up, he woofed understanding and his nose dropped to the ground.

Chapter 8

The young woman fidgeted with the collar of her pink-koala-print smock, and glanced over her shoulder toward the closed door of the administrator's office. She whispered. "Mr. Williams? Mrs. Bradshaw doesn't know I called you?"

Again with the question. "We've known each other for almost a year now, Alison. When will you start calling me Teddy?" He adjusted his wire-rimmed spectacles, set the iPad on the counter and unbuttoned his lightweight jacket. "It's okay you decided not to go to the mall. Probably easier to spend time with her here; she prefers the familiar these days. Maybe take Molly for a walk with Trixie, and then take a trip down memory lane." He forced a smile and gestured at the album.

"You know the policy? We got to be respectful. Always Mister or Miz?"

"Good golly, she hates being called Miz Molly." He waited for Alison to giggle at the old, tired banter. Molly would have hee-hawed with delight.

But Alison busied herself with a pencil and pad, averting her eyes. "Could you take a seat for a minute?"

He'd worried for nothing. Allison would have said something, or the administrator Mrs. Bradshaw would have met him if there were a problem. He shrugged, grabbed the photo-filled tablet from the counter and shuffled over to one of the uncomfortable orange Naugahyde chairs, and lowered himself slowly with a grunt. His old bones didn't take kindly to the up-and-downs of sitting these days, and it irked him that the usually perky Alison was so prickly. Besides, the assisted living facility depressed him. He'd never imagined life would come to this.

Theodore Williams, maverick computer nerd, loved the predictability of technology. He'd been an early adopter of all things cutting edge when pocket protectors weren't cool, enjoyed the challenge of cyber-anything, and delighted in the ability to upgrade, re-boot, and download the latest advances. Hard drive failed? Replace it with a newer model. Software infected? Re-write the virus code to ricochet and destroy the sorry-assed wannabe player. Never mind Teddy officially "retired" from his teaching job ten years earlier; he still got called for freelance jobs from time to time, often from white-glove entities that needed discretion. His reputation as Mr. Fixit hadn't dimmed, although his hair had turned to snow and his knees made popcorn sounds.

But he couldn't re-boot Molly. Alzheimer's had stolen her away.

They met a lifetime ago. The girl with the giddy-making smile and ballerina grace made him crazy-happy for more than forty years, she the sequin shine to his stark practicality. Teddy liked to think he'd balanced her impetuous impulses as much as Molly had taught him how to laugh, laugh at life, laugh at failure, laugh at success, but always laugh together. Their happy expression had two F's, the "laff" a code for a personal shared hilarity nobody else understood.

Alzheimer's stole the laffs.

It happened so fast. Within six months, Molly disappeared, locked in a void of vacant stares, crying jags and fist-flung waking nightmares he couldn't breach. Most days he spent researching the digital world for the latest options, until his eyeballs bled from strain and he wanted to take a baseball bat to the computer. He hoped the iPad pictures from their happiest moments might spark a smile.

The front door squeaked open, and Teddy looked up. "Lewis? What're you doing here?" He struggled to his feet, and held out his hand to the much younger man.

"Same as you, I suppose. Visiting." Lewis's big hand swallowed Teddy's when they shook. He tugged off his gimme cap to reveal a well-worn groove in his brow. "Patricia finally got the point . . ." His throat worked and he turned away.

"I didn't know. God, I'm sorry." The news was a blow, although he hardly knew the man. As the local high school football coach, they frequented different circles, and Lewis's much younger wife worked in social services. But Patricia and Molly called themselves "professional volunteers" and spent hours together in various club meetings. "Patricia can't be more than forty year's old." His voice quavered with the shock.

"She's thirty-seven." Lewis throttled the cap in callused hands, but the words were void of emotion, as though he'd already used up futile anger and must conserve any remaining energy for grief. "They tell me it's a particularly aggressive form of the condition." Dark bags under Lewis's eyes aged him a decade beyond his mid-forty age.

Alison returned to the front desk. "The administrator wants a word, Mr. Williams. Through that door." She pointed, and then turned a full-wattage smile on Lewis. "Miz Patty is ready and for waiting your visit? Follow me?"

Lewis stuffed the hat into his pocket and followed Alison down the left hallway. Molly's room was at the end of that same corridor. The patients—or "guests" as Alison characterized them—needing more advanced care stayed on that side of the facility.

Teddy reclaimed his iPad from the chair before he hurried to the administrator's office, the first door on the right-hand hallway. He'd visited the office only twice before: six months ago when he realized Molly needed more than he could give, and a week later when together they'd introduced her to the facility. Neither visit had been pleasant.

"Mr. Williams, come in, have a seat." Mrs. Bradshaw met him at the door. Stiff decorum that served as her professional mask—and emotional protection, he guessed—had fled. Her hands fluttered, birdlike, smoothing the front of a dark tailored blouse and matching slacks. No koala print for her.

"I'll stand, thanks. What's this about? I want to see Molly." He gestured with the iPad. "I brought her favorite photo album. Is she having a bad day?"

"Actually, she's had a very good day." Mrs. Bradshaw moved around the tidy desk and perched on the edge of the overstuffed rolling chair. She scooted it back and forth, back and forth until Teddy wanted to nail her feet to the floor.

"A good day. Terrific. So what's the problem? You want me to authorize adjustment to the medication?" She'd been taking Damenia until the blowup in the news over the off-label use of the drug caused the company to pull it from the market. Maybe the new drug had better results? His heart jumped and he cautioned himself against false hope.

She pursed her lips. "We're doing everything we can, and I'm sure she's fine. You know how she loves Trixie."

His heart thumped louder. "I'm not liking your tone, Mrs. Bradshaw. What does Trixie have to do with this?" The resident Golden Retriever had been the deciding factor between this facility and others, and Molly acted much calmer when in the dog's presence. He put his hands on the desk, and leaned toward her. "Where is my Molly?"

She shrank back. "Like I said, I'm sure everything will work out fine. But you see, at the moment, we don't know exactly where Molly is."

He straightened. The iPad dropped to the floor with a loud crack.

Mrs. Bradshaw stood, the rolling chair rebounding from her narrow butt. "Truly, Mr. Williams, it should be fine. I've already called in a Silver Alert, and the police should find her quickly. Besides, the day's pretty mild, and she talked about walking the dog. Before we could get an aide lined up, she and Trixie were gone."

Chapter 9

Shadow snuffled, drawing the cool air deep, tasting the flavor of the paving stones. His own signature odor and that of September remained fresh, where they'd recently trod this path from the back garden. Cat smell drifted from the door, and he cast first right and then left in a semicircle, seeking the odor that identified Macy like a name-tag.

In his before-life, when he lived with his-boy at that other house, he'd learned what to do only because September visited and taught him what a good-dog should know. She taught him what special words and hand signals meant, like "sit" and "heel" and "come" and called him "good-dog" more than anyone else. Shadow liked to learn, liked hearing the "click" noise September used to tell him he'd done something right. He worked and worked, so hard it made his head hurt, to show September he could be a good-dog so she wouldn't ever leave him behind again.

She'd left him behind in his before-life, and he didn't like that, not at all. He still worried sometimes that he'd be left behind. He'd finally found his family. It was a good-dog's job to stay with his family—even cats could be family—teach them how to laugh and play fun games that kept dogs and their people from feeling bad.

Nobody taught him that. Shadow figured it out all by himself. He was smart that way.

The *hide-and-seek* game made September laugh and call him 'good-dog' a lot. He wagged at the thought, and huffed another breath. It wasn't as exciting as Frisbee-chase, but finding Macy always prompted the cat to make interesting noises.

When he'd first come to live with them, Macy scared Shadow with paw-thumps as he raced by, until he figured out that was cat language for wanting to play. Macy-talk confused him, but he learned quickly. He figured dog-talk confused cats, too.

He liked to steal Macy's mouse toy, a guarantee Macy would play with him. That game he invented all by himself. Macy slept with the toy and the aroma of cat fur and spit smelled almost as good as the real thing. So far, Macy only allowed long distance sniffs. Shadow was certain if he played the game right, he'd get to sniff Macy up close and personal, push his nose deep into the cat-fur-body, and not have to make do with second hand sniffs. Wouldn't that be fine!

September missed out on lots of smells and sounds that made the world such an interesting place. Shadow figured that the *hide-and-seek* game was a way for her to understand. It made him happy he could teach her, like she taught him. Family helped each other like that.

Shadow found nothing on the sidewalk, so he began pulling steadily toward the front of the house, towing September behind. The tug of the long line at his shoulders provided a direct physical connection with September he relished. Tension vibrated the line, more than when they'd played *hide-and-seek* in the house. It puzzled him that he couldn't immediately target Macy-smell but maybe the game had changed? September did that; made simple tasks harder to test him. He liked surprising her with success. His tail swept back and forth at the happy thought.

At the front of the house, September asked him to sniff bushes along the windows on both sides of the entry steps, even though he found no Macy-smell. He did find interesting bunny stuff, and a place where two raccoons had slept for a time, but no evidence of the cat.

For the first time, Shadow worried he might fail the test. He trusted that September knew lots of things, more things than a good-dog could discover, so it must be his fault he couldn't find Macy-smell. He didn't want to let her down.

From there he ranged back and forth on the hard circle pathway where cars arrived and left. Shadow liked cars. He got to ride in the back of September's car and stick his nose out to taste rushing wind when she made it go fast. He'd rather stick his whole head out, but the narrow opening wouldn't allow more than the tip of his nose. The pavement spoke of bird droppings, people shoes and coyote urine. Shadow's hackles bristled a bit, wanting to track the interloper. But he resisted the urge to pee over the mark, and concentrated on the job.

The garden-man's truck sat to one side, and it smelled of chemicals and mice poop and green growing things. But no cat. He spent several moments huffing and testing spore surrounding the vehicle anyway. He paid particular attention to the doors, and even jumped into the back of the truck to see if Macy had found a hidey-hole inside. Macy did that a lot, finding and curling up to sleep in tiny places a good-dog wouldn't fit. He snuffled up potting soil and dust that coated stacked bags, and sneezed twice before he hopped back out onto the ground.

September pointed underneath, and he sniffed a second time but found no Macy-smell, only the trail of the garden-man's boots. He whined and stared at September's face. Had Macy stopped smelling like Macy? How could that happen, for a cat to become invisible to smart-dog noses? Maybe this was a game he couldn't win.

Deep lines in September's forehead spoke of worry. Tension in her hand fed down the line and made his shoulders clench. Shadow's tummy hurt at the thought he might fail the test. He had to find Macy. Then the cat would hiss and paw-pat his face, September would laugh and stroke his brow and call him 'good-dog.'

"Shadow, *seek* Macy." She held out the cat's toy again for him to sniff. He licked it, too, in case that made a difference, but Macy-smell must still be the same. September's voice sounded fearful. He understood this wasn't the usual game, and sniffed Mickey again to please her. Nose-to-ground hadn't worked, though, so instead he lifted his face into the breeze.

His mouth opened and he panted quietly, sorting the threads of scent that tangled the breeze. Some were neon bright and shouted for attention while others barely nudged the itchy smell-center deep inside his muzzle.

He turned his head around, huffing out and discarding those that held no bearing, and—there! He came to attention, nose poised with purpose, and inhaled deeply, holding and tasting and teasing out the one thread that came oh-so-close to what he sought.

Cat. He'd found cat smell. He turned to September, and she'd already read his intent, and her half smile mirrored his anticipation at winning the game. That was the puzzle! She wanted him to find this other cat, and Macy-smell was the clue.

He pulled hard, letting his nose lead him to the origin of the cat scent, tugging September in his wake until she had to trot to keep up.

"Good-boy, Shadow! That's it!"

Her happy tone spurred his paws faster until they were both running down the long car path to the front gate. He slowed momentarily when he reached the strange car half in the ditch and crushed against the gate. Two of the doors swung open, and he took a moment to compare the scent he'd found on the breeze to the one strongest in the back seat of the car.

"Shadow? What're you doing, boy? *Seek* Macy, your kitty. Macy. Please, let it be Macy you're tracking!"

He didn't let her worried tone slow him down. Scent firmly in his brain,

Shadow obeyed the command to find the lost cat. Nose barely skimming the ground, he located the freshest paw-treads.

Sick, the cat smelled scared and sick, not like Macy at all. Maybe that's why September wanted it found. He pulled hard to follow the trail, towing her so fast behind she stumbled and he had to slow down so she could keep up. The cat had run from the car across the road into the bushes of the nearby field. Shadow dug in his paws, leaping ahead with excitement that the goal was so close.

Chapter 10

Despite the pink gloves, September's hands hurt with the effort to hang on to the tracking line as Shadow eagerly led them to the source of the scent. Her hope took a hit when he stopped to investigate Sly's car. She didn't see the man anywhere, or his cat. She debated aborting the hunt. But Macy could have made it this far, perhaps even investigated Sly's abandoned car on his way to explore the great outdoors. That could be Macy's scent near the car.

No, she couldn't stop now. She couldn't take the chance. It wasn't the dog's fault if she'd given mixed signals. Besides, it was Shadow's job to track, and it was her job to believe the dog. She needed to reward him if he found any cat.

The field across the road from her renovated Victorian house offered a maze of Johnson grass hummocks, and cedar trees sprouted everywhere, an unwanted green plague ranchers fought to eradicate. She nearly turned her ankle in a pig wallow, thankfully dry, where a sounder—feral pig herd—must have recently camped and uprooted turf seeking food. Between the hogs and the armadillos, the field offered ample opportunity for injury.

Shadow tugged her steadily toward the center of the field where a gigantic bois d'arc tree held court. Spiny branches scratched the sky. As kids, she and Mark had called them "witch trees." Like most cats, Macy wanted to claim the highest perch possible. It made sense Macy had headed for the tallest tree around.

Parts of the old tree split, exposing the gnarly orange wood inside. Shadow slowed, sniffed and pawed the trunk and stared up into the tree branches. He jumped up, placing front paws against the rough bark, and whined before dropping off. He lay down and stared at her with a happy grin, his signal of a find.

"Good-dog, Shadow. Good boy." She offered the praise and stroked his throat and he wriggled with delight. She stared into the dark, bare branches overhead, trying to see Macy through the twisty jigsaw. "Macy? Macy-cat, come." She waited. Nothing happened. She'd expected at least a meow response. "Macy? I've got treats." A shadow on one of the branches shifted, revealing the silhouette of a large fluffy cat. "Thank God!" She dropped the tracking line, and searched for a way to climb into the boughs. Cats often acted like it was too undignified to come down once they managed to climb aloft.

"Shadow, wait." She found a scraggly branch so heavy it drooped nearly to the ground, and pulled herself up onto the broad wood. Careful with hand placement to avoid the spikes, September tight-roped toward the trunk of the tree until she was able to use smaller ladder-like limbs. "Macy, I'm here. Hang on, kitty." She realized Shadow had wandered some distance from the base of the tree, probably enamored of some critter scent now that he'd nailed the *hide-and-seek* game.

She climbed twenty feet into the tree on the opposite side of the cat's perch. September inched around the girth of the trunk, finally at eye level with the furry miscreant. The cat hissed—not Macy, but a strange longhaired tabby cat with a bright pink nose and crusty eyes—and leaped from the tree to the ground. Crap. This must be the cat Aaron had nearly hit, probably Sly's sick cat, Pinkerton.

September grappled to maintain her balance, and bear-hugged the trunk. Below, Shadow's head jerked to follow the cat's flight, and without a backward glance, he leaped after the cat in a joyous chase.

"Dammit, Shadow, no!" She struggled to dismount the tree, her descent less graceful than the climb up, and jumped the last five feet in her hurry to stop the dog. Not only was Macy gone, now Shadow had disappeared.

"Shadow, come." He knew the command, but wasn't particularly reliable. She should have tied the line, she knew better.

He yelped—a sound of frustration, not pain or fear—and September dodged through the cedars and burr oak stands, eager to catch up. Vining brambles festooned cedar elms like overdone Christmas garland, smothering and bending saplings double. She ducked beneath swags of the prickles, and tore through green drifts that clawed her pants and scored her ankles. Shadow's tracking line must have snagged. That was good and bad; good that she'd be able to catch him, but bad if she hadn't been around. A caught line could trap the pup and make him easy pickings for coyotes. "Shadow, where are you, boy?"

He barked an answer, then twice more, and barks morphed to yodels of distress.

"What the hell?" September redoubled her effort, leaving torn fabric and skin behind, and broke through into a grassy opening.

Shadow barked and cried, leaped forward and back. His tail thrashed with conflicted emotions, his hackles erect. She bent to gather the long line of the lead that trailed in the grass at her feet. Three strides closer and she saw her wooden baseball bat creasing the tall grass. Puzzled, she retrieved the bat, and then dropped it with revulsion at the sight of the dark stains and clotted matter covering the business end of the wood.

The big tabby and white cat hissed from its perch. Shadow had cornered the feline against a downed barbed wire fence, the deadfall offering shelter but no easy escape. "Shadow, come." The dog turned his head, and backed up to press his shoulder against her thigh. She could feel him trembling.

The strange cat hissed again, and shifted to face them. Its enormous paws worked rhythmically, treading in the universal feline kneading behavior against the soft yellow fabric upon which it rested, perhaps in an effort to self-calm.

"Pinkerton? Hush, kitty, I'm here to help." She cautiously drew near, her boots crunching on dry vegetation, not wanting to spook Sly's cat. Finding Macy would have to wait until she caught this stray cat. She couldn't let her dislike of the reporter keep her from saving a needy animal.

September nearly tripped on a hummock of Johnson grass, and caught her balance on Shadow's broad back. He whined, and licked where her fingertips poked out of the gloves. The breeze died for a moment, and a smell smacked her in the face, the stink so thick she gagged. She stopped, heart hammering. She'd know that smell anywhere. Blood.

The cat's bright pink nose tested the air, but its eyes never stopped scanning, scanning, head turning first left and then right with a vague unfocussed expression as though blind and unable to see. A low keening sound, more growl than purr, made her scalp itch and mouth go dry. She gagged when Pinkerton's furry toes squished, and red liquid pooled beneath its paws steaming in the cold air and soaking into the yellow cloth. September prayed the cat was crouched on a still-warm deer carcass. Cats were heat-seekers, and sometimes a hunter's aim failed to drop prey in its tracks, and it ran for miles before collapsing.

But deer don't wear yellow. Or have spiky red hair.

Pinkerton cheek-rubbed and head-butted the figure until a gloved hand fell sideways in the brittle thatch. He stared into the bloody mess where a buck-toothed smile had been, and yowled a feline lament for Sylvester "Sly" Sanger.

Chapter 11

Shadow followed closely beside September, nearly tripping her on their rush back home. She'd taken off her jacket and wrapped the sick cat inside, even though it wasn't Macy. The cat smelled scary-bad, not only sick, but coppery rich with the dead man's blood.

He'd smelled that awful odor before. It made him want to squat-and-pee like a puppy. Instead, he growled to boost his courage, and his confidence increased when September touched his neck and smoothed the bristling fur.

"Aaron? Aaron, call 911." September barged through the kitchen door, waiting for Shadow to enter before bumping the door closed with one hip.

But the garden-man wasn't in the house. Shadow knew the big man worked among the dead plants inside the fenced back yard. When he didn't answer, September hurried into the nearby laundry, set the cat on the floor and shut the door before she picked up and held the small talk-box to her ear. She played with his tracking line as she talked.

Shadow drank deeply of the house smells, snuffling the slate floor with deep inhalations quickly huffed out as so much background noise. Acrid detergent. Spilled coffee trace. Lingering bacon—he licked his lips—but that scent, faded with time, had no merit in the current *hide-and-seek* game. No, he needed Macy-smell. His person—she who made all things right—had asked him to *seek* Macy. He'd found the sick cat, but read September's disappointment. He wouldn't pass the test until he found Macy.

He unraveled skeins of scent painted across the floor and floating at nose-level throughout the house. Macy smell filled the house. Only the freshest mattered. Shadow found the brightest trace, nose glued to the invisible trail, and pressed forward. The tracking line unraveled behind him, but stopped short and pulled against his harness when September's grasp anchored him in place. He stared back at her from the kitchen doorway, and whined.

"Shadow? What are you—" She dropped the line to finish talking.

He barked once, twice, impatient for her to grab the line so he could show her. She had to follow, he'd found Macy just as she'd asked. He barked once more.

"Give me a minute." She said something else into the talk-box and then pocketed the object. "Shadow, we've kind of got an emergency here. If you found Macy in the house, everything is fine and we'll play another time." But she picked up the line and let him tug her after him, despite the scary tension he heard in her voice.

Claws clicked across the cold hard floor of the kitchen, paws padded past plush carpet with the funny inside-tree, and onward to the smooth wood near the front door. He both heard and felt September hold her breath—everything traveled down the leash-line—and then she breathed again when his nose lead them away from the exit.

There! The freshest scent yet, at the bottom of the entry stairs. He huffed loudly, and scrambled up the staircase, slowing a bit when September dragged on the line. Good-dogs with four feet moved much faster than their two-footed people.

Shadow paused at the landing, wagging with low, loose wags as September caught up, and then he turned the corner and surged on up the remaining steps. He pulled and pulled—it was okay to pull with this harness but not the collar leash—and led them past September's room. He could tell she wanted to go into the sleep place, but the Macy-smell wasn't as fresh there as the paw-treads in the hallway.

Close now, and closer still. He even heard quiet cat breath, quick and jerky like Macy had run a race, and followed his ears down to the last door at the end of the hall. He nosed it open, walked to the cold shiny potty seat next to the cabinet, and lay down. That's what September taught him to do when the game ended. He woofed softly in case she didn't understand.

"Macy! Kitty, what are you doing in the sink?" September dropped the leash, and hurried past Shadow to reach the cat.

The cat roused enough to offer a half-hearted mew. But he didn't get up, and leap away to invite another tag-and-chase game as Shadow expected. Macy panted, eyes half shut, like he was sick. Macy's head fell forward, chin thumping the sink basin when he passed out.

September made a choking sound in her throat, and carefully gathered

Macy into her arms. Shadow followed after, dragging the long line as she bounded down the stairs with his cat friend.

Chapter 12

The first dozen notes to the theme song of *Hog Hell* identified the caller before Dietz heard Grady's voice. "So? Did you find Felch? What's his excuse this time?" Heavy breathing but no words sounded. "Grady? You there, brother? Did you butt-dial again?" He started to disconnect, when the man finally spoke.

"Yeah, I'm here. Boss, we're screwed. Oh God, we are so screwed!" Grady's tone squeaked and broke like a voice-changing adolescent, the stampede of words muddled in the rush. "It's Felch, the crazy son-of-a-bitch. Christ, don't know what to do, couldn't stop him."

"Slow down, I can't understand you. Get a grip." Dietz sat and pulled the chair closer to the desk. He'd been prepping for the radio spot, but that could wait. "What'd he do? How much will it cost me this time?" Lord, couldn't the man stay out of trouble longer than a few hours? Three days, they needed three days of calm.

Grady's anguished voice broke again. "Remember I told you how he got in the car with that reporter? Felch called, said there's been an accident. Wanted me to pick him up." Heavy breathing again.

Dietz groaned. "So pick him up, take care of any insurance or cop reports, and send me the bill. And then don't let Felch out of your sight. I don't have time for this; that's your job."

"You don't understand. Took a while to find the place. They slammed into the front gate at this old Victorian monstrosity. Felch tells me he beat up that reporter, maybe killed him."

Breathing stopped for a lifetime. Then Dietz licked his lips, and whispered. "What did you say?"

"Felch went off on that reporter. I'm trying to tell you! He says the guy had this story ready, drove here to talk to some woman about it, and planned to release it before the show launch. Felch had to shut him up, protect the show. We all have a lot to lose if that story gets out."

"But he made it up! There's nothing to the story, Felch has to know that." Dietz stood up so fast, the rolling chair hit and dented the back wall. Even a fabricated story would ruin everything, though. "Felch beat him up? He can't be dead." He sat on the desk and put his head in his hand. "This isn't happening, I don't believe it."

"Believe it, all right." Grady's voice grew steadier. "I got Felch calmed down, got him in the truck, and he says the reporter spilled everything to this animal expert. What do you want me to do?" He paused, and then added, "Want me to talk to her? Warn her off? Hell, the reporter probably has notes stashed somewhere, too." His voice had gone squeaky-high with excitement. "We call the cops on this, and the show's toast. You know that, right?"

"Let me think, let me think." Dietz ran his hand through his hair until static electricity crackled. "Wait. Animal behavior expert? September Day?" He straightened. She could spoil everything. "Does she know about Felch and the reporter?"

"No. Maybe. Hell, I don't know." Grady rushed on. "Nobody's going to stumble across the body. Took all my powers of persuasion to get Felch in the truck and get the hell out of Dodge."

"Where's Felch now?"

"Haven't a clue. I dropped him at his place, but for all I know, he's circling around ready to jump me." He breathed heavily. "I'm sitting here in my car, with the doors locked, wishing I had a gun instead of this phone. If we're lucky, Felch is halfway to Mexico by now." Grady paused, and Dietz could almost hear the wheels turning. "You want me to call the police? Why don't you call the paper, give them the scoop about Felch getting fired from the show. That would distance us from him. I mean, before the body shows up. And it *will* show up."

The timing couldn't be worse. "The press will want to know why he got fired. When the reporter's found this will come out anyway, or even sooner if that woman talks to anybody." Think, think! Dietz stood up from the desk, and paced. Damage control, he needed time to manage and massage the story, discredit the reporter, and delay any negatives until after tomorrow night's launch. Longer, if possible. "First, get hold of the reporter's pack of lies, and burn them." He ground his teeth, silently cursing the whole situation.

"Where are you?"

"Rabbit Run Road, half a mile from the behaviorist's house. Sunny's getting her hair and face done for the TV gig so I got to take her place talking BeeBo down about his sick dog. You know he's a baby about his mutts." His grim tone spoke volumes. "I know the job can get down and dirty, but I never signed on for this. We gotta call the cops."

"We will, of course we'll call the police. But if the man's dead, waiting a day or three—until Monday, after the launch party—that isn't going to hurt him any worse, right?" He waited a long moment, and then prompted again. "Right, Grady? Tell me you understand."

"If somebody finds out before we report it, we're screwed even worse. I'm not going to prison for your stupid show."

Dietz groaned. "I have more to lose than any of you. My name's on the show. I cast *Looney Tunes* Felch. We need some wiggle room. If the news doesn't come out until after the launch party, and until after the holiday premium orders roll in, it won't matter. We can handle BeeBo. We can manage Sunny. And we can re-cast Felch."

"So you want me to keep a lid on it until. . .when?"

"Hell, until forever! What do you think?" He wanted to punch the wall. Success within his grasp, finally after years of failure, and now this. "Fix it. Find Felch, put a sock in it, make sure he talks to no one." He thought for a moment, and then added, "Especially keep him away from that September Day woman. You know, it'd be terrific if she left town for a while."

"Sure. I understand." Grady hesitated, as if weighing his next words with care. "Say the word, and I can arrange for her to take that trip. I can make the reporter's body disappear. But I need some guarantee this won't come back on me. I'm taking all the risks."

Dietz sank back into the chair. "What are you saying?" But he knew.

"I want to bury this problem as much as you, but a little more incentive would go a long way toward making the risk worthwhile. Don't you think that's fair?"

Blackmail? "I already doubled your pay this week. But that was to keep Felch and BeeBo in line. Haven't handled that too well, have you?" Dietz's face flushed with heat, and he was glad Grady couldn't see him.

"Do you want to argue the point? What's it worth to have this problem go away?"

Dietz took in the stack of bills on the desk in front of him, and the notes for the upcoming media events. He didn't have time to argue. And Grady knew it. "All right. Triple your weekly salary."

"I want a cut, too."

"You want *what?*" Dietz leaned his head in his hand. Damn Felch! The man better stay in Mexico or he'd beat the shit out of him, too.

"Triple salary. Named as a full producer on the show. And a fifty percent—"

"You're bat-shit crazy!"

"—or I could call the cops and let them handle it."

Dietz blew out his breath. Grady waited. He didn't need to say anything else.

It occurred to Dietz that he had no way of knowing how much the other man might be making up. Maybe he'd better have a private conversation with Felch before he slapped the snot out of him. Meanwhile, he had no choice. Promise whatever it took, for now anyway.

"What'll it be? Boss? I mean, *partner?*" Grady's words gloated.

"I don't want a sniff of my name or the show connected. And I don't want to know how you do it." Dietz slapped his palm against the desk and stood up. "Just make it go away, Grady."

"Done."

Chapter 13

Jeff Combs pulled the car to a stop in front of the brick colonial, and checked in the rear view mirror. Twelve-year-old Melinda sat with her arms crossed, red curls a jumble as she turned away to stare through the passenger window. Her lower lip pooched out, and high color on pudgy cheeks offered silent testament to the angry set of her shoulders. She looked so much like his wife, Cassie—ex-wife, he corrected himself—with a temper to match.

His eyes met William's serious expression, and the nine-year-old shrugged and leaned to pat his sister on the arm. Melinda jerked away from her younger brother's comfort, and her lip trembled with the effort not to cry.

The divorce had blindsided them all, but hit Melinda particularly hard. While William was a glass-half-full kind of kid and forgave pretty much anything, Melinda held each disappointment tight to her heart, taking it personally when life proved unfair. In that, she took after him, (Lord help her) and these days nothing seemed fair.

The custody arrangement gave him the kids for the two weeks leading up to Christmas. That would have worked out great except his leave of absence was cut short when Detective Kimberlane Doty took a new job in Chicago. His former partner's defection left a hole the department wanted to fill fast. Ironic that Doty not only got him busted from Detective down to beat cop, but her departure gave him back his ranking sooner than he could have hoped. He couldn't say no, the opportunity wouldn't come again anytime soon.

He unbuckled his seatbelt and strained to turn around, and tapped Melinda on her knee. "I'm sorry. I'm disappointed, too. But I'll make it up to you."

"I'll believe it when I see it." She wouldn't meet his eyes.

Hell, the sulky tone even sounded like Cassie.

"It's okay, Dad. Like you said, we'll make it up with an outrageous New Year's celebration." William addressed the words to Jeff, but pointed them at his sister. Always the peacekeeper. Like his grandma, God rest her soul.

Jeff blinked hard at that thought. This would be the first Christmas without Mom, and the first year after the divorce. Melinda had a right to be a cranky-pants, and he'd like to join her. But sadly, he had to be the adult. He sighed and opened the car door. "C'mon, troupes, I gotta get to work. Your mom's expecting us." In fact, he'd seen the curtains twitch and appreciated Cassie giving him time for private goodbyes before beckoning from the door.

The kids unlatched their seatbelts, grappled backpacks from the floor (a pink kitty-theme for Melinda, and the latest super-hero-du-jour for William), and tumbled out of the car. Melinda slammed her door extra hard and stomped toward the house, but William ran to Jeff's open window for their traditional "man-hug" and knuckle-bump. "Go get some bad guys, Daddy."

"You got it, champ." Jeff called hopefully after Melinda's back. "Hugs?"

She paused, hand on the doorknob, and glanced back. The scowl slipped, and she dropped the backpack and took a half step down the steps, tremulous smile fighting to blossom. Then Cassie opened the door. And the moment passed.

Melinda grabbed the backpack and shoved past her mother through the door, quickly followed by William. Jeff held out his hands, palms up, and shrugged, but Cassie said nothing. The door swung closed, blocking off the view of the sumptuous hardwood entry and formal appointments her new husband could provide.

"Happy holidays to you, too." He rolled up the window, threw the car into gear and left tire treads on the brick drive that Cassie's husband, Rick-the-Prick would pay someone to scrub clean. He scowled. Petty? Sure, but he had to take his pleasures where he could.

Forty minutes later, Jeff shook hands with his new partner, Detective Winston Gonzales, and his shoulders relaxed. He could have been partnered with anyone, even one of the cronies who still blamed him for the department's black eye that had led to his demotion a year ago. Maybe his luck had changed.

Gonzales smiled past his carefully trimmed black mustache, handshake firm, tidy suit and tie matching the studied assessment as he met Jeff's eyes. He sported a big dog attitude despite his small stature, and Jeff recognized his ability to face down most opposition with a steady stare, like a Chihuahua besting a Doberman on its home turf.

"Deja vu. You look a whole lot better than the last time I saw you." Gonzales led the way to desk space on the far wall. "You still on that diet of caffeine and cookies?"

"Don't knock it till you tried it. Sleep is highly over-rated. Trying to measure up to Doty's standards." Combs pulled out the rolling chair in front of the bare desk where the blond Amazon used to work. "How ironic is that? Both of us partnered with her until she takes credit for the bust, and moves on to greener pastures. So to speak."

Gonzales snorted, and shed his suit coat, hanging it carefully on the back of his chair. "From where I sit, you measure up just fine. Doty is what she is. Let her take the credit. Got you back in the saddle, didn't it?" He planted his narrow butt on his own chair and trundled back and forth, his version of a hamster burning energy on a wheel.

They'd briefly worked together last month to investigate Jeff's mother's murder. When Doty froze him out, Gonzales at least met him halfway despite the rumors around the department. The younger man treated Doty with the respect reserved for a more experienced partner, but everyone in the department knew she maneuvered for high profile cases to help her climb the career ladder.

Gonzales cared as much or more about justice for the victims as he did clearing a case. That reason alone was enough for Combs to like the younger man. He envied Gonzales's ability to capitalize on the good and ignore the bad of the job—a glass-half-full kind of guy.

There it was again, he needed to be more like his son William and new partner Gonzales. Maybe that would balance out his own innate pessimism and suspicious nature. But it took a lot to balance getting kicked in the balls by your peers, wife leaving you, and kids' disappointment.

"Here's the current cases." Gonzales shoved the stack of files on his own desk closer to the edge and watched Combs cage the first one from the top of the pile.

Before he could give more than a cursory read, a shadow fell over the desk. Combs stood quickly and held out his hand. "Thanks for the opportunity, Captain." He had to raise his face to meet the towering man's flint-gray eyes.

"We needed to fill the hole. I trust you won't step in a big ol' pile of stink this time?" Captain Felix Gregory crunched the offered hand, dropped it and addressed both detectives. He nodded at the pile of cases. "That can wait. We've got a body."

Chapter 14

September stroked Macy's tawny fur, cradling the big cat in her arms and rocking him gently. They sat huddled together in their favorite overstuffed chair in the living room. It faced the floor to ceiling window view of the circle drive. Normally the cat preferred to snooze on the back of the chair above September's head, giving him an added elevation for scolding the dog. He rarely agreed to lap sit, except on extra cold or cloudy days. The fact that he didn't protest her arms spoke volumes. Macy was sick.

She'd thrown away the bloodstained pink gloves and hurriedly changed into stone washed jeans and a green sweater that matched her eyes, and now wore boot-cut zipper boots. She'd wanted to race to the emergency vet with Macy and the dead man's cat. But with the police on the way to address the murder, the cats had to take second place no matter how much she wished otherwise.

Pinkerton remained sequestered in the distant laundry room, meowing now and then in protest at the incarceration. September had belatedly scrubbed her hands and changed out of her shirt, but worried she'd exposed Macy to whatever had made the tabby cat sick. Feline illnesses easily transferred from cat to cat, and any virus or bacteria contamination of her hands could also infect.

Shadow lounged beside the chair, his stuffed bear braced between front paws, and mouth around the toy's soft, misshapen head. He sucked the fuzzy pacifier with eyes half closed, body leaned against one of her legs. The contact that usually calmed September's nerves did nothing to ease her tension.

"Please, don't let my cat die." She whispered the words, more of a hope than a prayer, not convinced God listened to her after all the awful things she'd done. But Macy was innocent. God had taken Chris and Dakota, but had spared Shadow. Maybe she'd been punished enough.

A car pulled into the drive, and September recognized Jeff Combs when he got out. When Detective Gonzales followed Combs, a dizzying sense of deja vu rocked her, and she squeezed Macy in reaction. He mewed in protest, and kicked with his rear legs, showing a bit more energy than he had in the previous twenty minutes. September soothed him with a soft murmur before placing him inside the fabric pet carrier she'd set next to the chair.

Shadow beat her to the front door. He still wore his harness, although she'd removed the tracking line and stuffed it in her coat pocket. When the doorbell bonged, he woofed twice, checked in with September, and sat quickly, anticipating the closed-fisted signal that always followed a doorbell chime. "Good-dog. Away. Go to bed." She waved one hand, and pointed across the room and he reluctantly trotted over to settle on an overstuffed dog pillow near the fireplace.

She unlocked the deadbolts, unlatched the chain and pulled open the door. Managing a weak smile, September motioned the two men inside. As soon as Combs entered, Shadow wiggled his body with ears pressed flat, and woofed a greeting. But he didn't break, and kept his butt planted.

"Hey Shadow, good to see you, too." Combs kept his eyes on September, though, raised eyebrows requesting answers. Gonzales already had a notepad and pencil out of his pocket.

"Thanks for coming so quickly." She motioned to the pet carrier. "Macy's sick. So could we speed up the statement? I can answer any follow up once I get him to the vet." Her voice caught. "I don't mean to be unfeeling, but the man is beyond help."

"If needed we can do follow up at dinner tonight." Combs entered and crossed to the wagging Shadow to pat the dog's neck before turning back to September.

September caught Gonzales' surprised expression. Great, now the whole police department would think she and Combs were an item. But he only smoothed his dapper mustache, and didn't move from the doorway. "Where's the body?"

"Across the road." She pointed out the open door, past the gate. "There's a bois d'arc tree about a third of the way in the field, and his body is a few yards to the left of it. West of the tree, I mean, near an old fence."

As if through a prearranged signal, Gonzales tucked his notepad back into his pocket and hurried down the front steps toward the crime scene.

September slowly closed the front door after him. She latched each lock before taking a deep breath and turning to face Combs.

He'd settled on the arm of the sofa, and motioned her to take a seat. Combs pulled out a digital recorder, and took up the questions. "Start from the beginning."

"This morning I heard a crash." She pointed out the front window. "I ran out to see what happened—"

"By yourself?" Combs stared pointedly at Shadow. He knew she took self-protection seriously.

"Shadow was in the garden. And I'm getting better about that." Her words sounded defensive, even to her own ears.

Shadow thumped his tail against the floor at the sound of his name, and she dropped a hand to touch his back. Should she tell Combs about the bat? Maybe she shouldn't have thrown away the pink gloves. Then it was too late to mention, as he prompted her to go on.

"You spoke to the car's owner? You know this person?"

"Sylvester Sanger." The name left a sour taste.

"Sly?" Combs grinned. "He's a piece of work. What'd he want?"

"He's been calling and hounding me ever since…well, you know. Wouldn't leave me alone, wanted to write a big tabloid piece, and didn't respect my privacy." Her cheeks heated at the memory. "He was a worm, but nobody deserves to die like that."

Combs paused, pencil in the air. "Killed in the car crash? That his Gremlin by the gate? Nobody inside when we drove up."

September stood from the sofa, and Shadow followed her pacing with his eyes, whining in response to her agitation. "Sly was fine, a little bruised up but out of the car and talking and walking when I saw him. Had his cat in the car with him and said he wanted my help researching some lame story. I was so mad he'd messed up my new gate, I didn't listen. I blew him off." She turned away sheepishly. "When I got back to the house, Aaron said he saw Macy outside."

"Your brother's partner, right?" Combs craned to look toward the kitchen. "He still here?"

"He wanted to wait in the garden. I can get him." She started toward the kitchen but Combs called her back.

"That's okay, we'll get his statement later. He didn't talk to Sly or see him?"

"I don't think so." September rubbed her face, and settled back in the overstuffed chair. She let her hand press the mesh top of Macy's carrier, anxious to grab him up and go. "When I couldn't find Macy, I had Shadow search for a trail outside the house. We found Sly." She shuddered.

"Did you touch the body?"

She ducked her head. "Didn't have to. I could see he was gone." Now would be the time to mention the baseball bat, but at that moment, Pinkerton yowled from the laundry room. She gestured that direction with a grimace. "The cat made contact, though. It was crouched on top of his body like a furry guard." She shivered. "I couldn't leave it out there. I called the police, and then Shadow found Macy." She finished in a rush. "He's sick. So's the other cat. That's all." She waited. "Can I please take them to the vet?"

Combs shook his head. "You need to sit tight. Sorry about that, but you know the drill." He stood.

Yes, she knew the drill all too well.

"Do whatever you need to do while I talk with Aaron. Gonzales will secure the body. We need you to stay out of the way. Stay in the house until I give you an all clear." He started toward the kitchen.

At least she could get the animals ready for the trip to the clinic. September picked up Macy's carrier and hurried after Combs to the kitchen, setting the carrier on the stained glass table before turning to the laundry room where Pinkerton continued to wail. She waited until Combs disappeared out the door, and resisted the urge to lock it behind him. He was a cop, after all. Another cop was across the road.

The sick feline's tortured cry sounded again when September carefully entered the laundry room, prepared to block any escape attempt. But the tabby cat continued to yowl, tail held high—for the first time she could see it was a boy—and the kitty's head pointed into the far corner of the room. He pawed the wall, crying with a frustrated vacant stare as if convinced a doorway should open for him. Shadow stuck his nose into the doorway, but politely kept his distance from the strange cat.

"Kitty? Pinkerton? I'm over here." When the cat didn't acknowledge her presence, she stamped the floor and slammed the door in case the cat was deaf. The tabby boy flinched from the sound, but continued to dig at the wall.

September wondered what sort of illness the cat had caught. *Please don't let it be contagious to Macy.* The cat had no collar or tags but the white blaze on the cat's muzzle and chin spotlighted the bright pink nose Sly had described. The vet clinic would be able to scan for a microchip—sadly, not all cats had them—and hopefully confirm if he belonged to Sly or not.

She found a clean pillowcase, held it open, and slid the bag over the top of the cat. The dazed creature walked right into the opening. September gently lifted the big cat, which began to purr and finally settled in the cradling material.

After she washed her hands one more time, September picked up the bagged cat, and deposited it on one of the cast iron chairs next to the glass kitchen table. She sat in another one. Her leg bounced up and down. She stood and paced, Shadow following her and whining. She opened the door and stuck her head out—technically, she hadn't left the house—and saw Combs in the bare spots through the fence. He stood dwarfed by Aaron. She couldn't hear what they were saying, but the tone of the bigger man's voice sounded confused and strident.

September hated that she'd somehow managed to get family once again involved with her troubles. She'd make it up to him later.

She saw Combs pull out his phone. He listened a moment before whirling to look toward her. September quickly ducked back into the house, gently pulling the door closed, not sure why she felt guilty. She'd done nothing wrong. Thirty seconds later, Combs pushed open the door with one foot and stood in the opening, phone in one hand and recorder in the other, and said nothing for a long moment.

"What? Did Aaron know something?" She licked her lips. "Can I go now? Take the cats to the vet?"

He dropped the recorder in one pocket, and gestured with the phone. "Gonzales called. There's only one big-ass bois d'arc in the field. You said west of the tree, right?"

"Right."

"Are you sure he was dead? If you didn't check for a pulse, didn't touch the body, you can't be sure."

"He had no face!"

Combs dropped his phone into his pocket. He wouldn't look at her, and instead waved a hand at the pet carriers. "Go on, you're in such a hurry, get out of here. Any other questions, we can cover tonight."

"Wait, tell me what happened."

He finally met her eyes with his own. Cop eyes. Hard. Questioning. "Gonzales can't find anything. There's no body."

Chapter 15

Tommy Dietz paced in the waiting area of the WZPP (aka "ZAP105") radio station, and checked his watch for the third time. BeeBo had yet to arrive, but the interview would go on with or without the big man. He had to make nice with the locals, especially with the kickoff to the new season imminent.

The brunette—wait, did she have blue hair?—stood behind the glass partition. She leaned forward and spoke with a nasal twang. "We're ten minutes away from air. Where's your guys?" The smell of a peppermint-scented candle clogged the room. She finger-combed her metallic blue nails through the matching streaks in her wavy hair.

"On the way; don't worry. And I can fill in until they get here." The radio show could barely be heard in the waiting room but grew louder when he walked to the counter and leaned toward the receptionist. Dietz eyeballed the nameplate on the desk. "After all, Anita, I'm the host with the most, and the brains behind *Hog Hell*."

"Yeah, that's great." She waved one hand in the hair to speed the drying time of the nail enamel. "But Fish wants the stars. He wants the on-camera characters the listeners recognize, not the producer or director or whatever. No offense, but nobody cares about you. They want to hear all that down-home redneck talk."

Dietz hid his irritation with a bright smile, the practiced expression calculated to melt female hearts. "You like the redneck attitude, do you?" He turned up the wattage, knew that his blue eyes proved irresistible to women of a certain age. His bad boy good looks and expression promising a dangerous good time had booked him countless TV commercials back in the day.

Anita cocked her head and stared at him for a long moment. "Nice try, honey, but I've been schmoozed by the best. Better save your A-game for Fish if your talent is a no-show." She returned her attention to painting the nails on her other hand, holding up the middle finger in a mocking gesture. "I'll give you another two minutes, and then y'all need to get your cute boy buns back to the studio."

His anger seethed and he turned away and took several calming breaths. That's what he got for working with amateurs.

He'd turned BeeBo, Felch, Sunny and the others into stars, but the fickle tastes of the public could reduce them to has-beens twice as fast. Never mind the network ordered another six shows—they could and would cancel in a heartbeat if sponsor money dried up, and the whiff of scandal puckered wallets faster than anything. He couldn't let that happen.

In a way, Felch did the show a favor by getting rid of that rumor-mongering reporter. As long as Grady kept everything under wraps, the show had nowhere to go but up. Sponsors would beg for a dozen more episodes, book two or more years out. When that happened, he'd sell the property outright and be set for life.

"Hey there, Mr. Dietz, you ready? I'll let Fish know you're going solo." She arched one thinly plucked brow and pointed toward the security door, releasing the door-lock buzzer with the jab of one blue nail. "Down the hall, glass studio booth, wait for him to wave you in. He's live right now." She smiled with sympathy. "He'll want to cut the interview short. Probably would've given the lovely Sunny a whole hour." Her expression soured a moment before she added, "But I'll buzz your guys in right away if they show."

Dietz ignored the heat that warmed his neck. He grabbed the door handle and hurried through before she changed her mind. BeeBo would pay for this.

The radio show that had been muted in the waiting area overwhelmed the hallway at full volume. The host's voice boomed in a basso profundo so low that Dietz could feel sympathetic vibration in the studio windows.

"I have a tasty treat for you today, boys and girls. We'll be talking to the stars of the hit reality show, locally filmed *Hog Hell*. So hang tight. I'm Humphrey Fish, and we'll have a scrumptious knee-slapping interview after this brief message from our sponsor."

Dietz paused, surprised by the host's appearance when a bowling ball-shaped man waved for him to enter the studio. Fish hopped off the tall stool, and held out his hand to shake.

"I'm Fish. You must be Tommy Dietz." His bald head barely reached Dietz's shoulder. Fish jutted his red goatee toward the door. "Where's BeeBo? And what's-his-name, the other guy?" He made a point of craning his neck right and left, pretending Anita hadn't alerted him to the situation.

After shaking his hand, Dietz took the chair Fish indicated. "I told Anita they're on the way. Thanks for having us on the show. We wanted to give you the scoop and first crack to share the exciting news." He knew Fish craved the limelight as much as his TV colleagues. After last month's notoriety with the Blizzard Murders, the glorified DJ considered himself a journalistic star in his own right, and a bit of flattery couldn't hurt. Fish's show, now syndicated and aired both live and via the internet, reached a wider audience than the local TV affiliates, and his audience shared similar tastes with the viewers that had put *Hog Hell* on the map. "Nobody else could do the story justice."

"My listeners expect the best. Let's not disappoint them." Fish motioned to the engineer, and reclaimed his tall perch. He pulled the football shaped fuzzy mic closer to his mouth and signaled Dietz to do the same with his. "We're live again in fifteen. I'll intro, pitch to you for a quick comment, and we'll go from there."

Dietz tugged at his collar. No matter how many media appearances he'd done over the years, nerves never went away. He noticed Fish sipped something murky from a puce colored mug, and wished he'd thought to stop for a decaf chai. He'd been trying to cut down on the caffeine and finally found a local cafe that did justice to his favorite blend.

"We're back, gentle listeners, and as promised, help me welcome Tommy Dietz, the producer, show host and creative genius behind *Hog Hell*, a reality show that's made stars out of local hunters BeeBo Benson, Randy Felch, the lovely Sunny Babcock and a host of other characters. Welcome to the show, Mr. Dietz."

"Call me Tommy. Thanks for the opportunity." He licked his lips, took a breath, and settled into the prepared pitch. "*Hog Hell* has won a huge following thanks to fans like your listeners. The show began as an experiment in edu-tainment that celebrates the unique culture of the hog hunting community."

Fish widened his eyes. "I didn't know hogs had culture. But that show really brings home the bacon."

"Ha, right. Good one." Dietz faked a laugh, and pushed on. "Feral hogs damage property and cause enormous financial hardship to the tune of $52 million a year, and that's in Texas alone. Nationwide, conservative estimates of annual cost damages due to feral hogs reaches $1.5 billion—yep, that's with a B. Hog hunts help manage the problem, and combine a dog sport—everybody loves dogs—with a worthy charity that benefits the community. The pigs harvested during the show go to local food banks. That barbecue is not only tasty, it's a win-win for everyone."

"The pigs might disagree." Fish slurped his coffee. "Listeners, what do you think?" He nodded over at the engineer. "Caller, you're on the air. Do you have a question?"

A female voice spoke with soft determination. "This is Gracie. I listen to your show all the time, Humphrey, it's such a delight. But I watched that Hog H-e-double-toothpick show one time after my son turned it on. Disgraceful!"

Dietz started to reply, but Fish held up a hand to stop him. "What didn't you like?"

"Everything! The guns, the violence, the vicious dogs biting those poor little piggies. Those Pit Bulls are killers, you know. Now my son wants one."

"Thanks for your call." Fish pointed at Dietz to speak.

"We take great care to manage the hunt in a humane manner." This wasn't the interview he'd envisioned. "The pigs are not dispatched on-camera. Feral hogs in this situation are much more dangerous to the people and the dogs than the other way around." He'd bet a year's salary the caller wasn't local. Probably some bleeding heart wanted the piggies adopted out in some hog sanctuary.

"Caller, you're up. What do you have to say?"

"Thanks for taking my call, Mr. Fish. I've got real problems with these so-called sportsmen playing target practice with the pigs. That won't solve the problem."

"Is that right?" Fish again held up a hand, cutting short Dietz's comments. "You have a better solution? And what's your name, sir?"

"Fred Jones, I'm the County Ag Agent. Now, I agree the rooting behaviors cause no end of habitat destruction, but shooting a stray pig now and then won't control them. Only way to control 'em is to round up and trap the whole sounder."

"Sounder?" Fish cocked his head.

"Sounder, that's a herd of wild swine. One sow can have two or three litters a year, or about thirty piglets, and even with fifty percent attrition, that's fifteen more pigs for every sow. Feral pigs are so smart, if you only trap one at a time, you educate the other pigs to be more wary and avoid the traps. The best way to control them is to trap the entire sounder at once."

Dietz sniffed. Viewers wouldn't tune in to watch a corn-sprinkled pig lot and wait for the piggies to stroll into the trap. But he'd play along. "Mr. Jones, we've had this conversation before. We're on the same side. And I applaud the job you're doing with the traps, and we'll keep on going after our pigs one by one."

"Sounds reasonable enough. Next caller, what do you have to say?" Fish twirled his finger in the air, and the engineer cued up the next guest.

"This is BeeBo Benson, y'all. Don't you be talkin' down my dawgs."

Dietz started. "You're supposed to be here, doing this interview."

"Sorry, Tommy. My best dawg got sick, so Grady drove me over to the vet." His voice caught on the last few words. "I don't think he's going to make it. But I can't have Mr. Fish's listeners thinking bad about my dawgs. That's a shitty thing to say about a man's dawgs, especially when they're sick and all." He paused and blew his nose. "Mr. Fish, I am right sorry that I missed out meeting you. I got to go now, but maybe I can make it up to y'all sometime?"

Fish shrugged a "what can you do?" gesture. "BeeBo, thank you for calling in. I'm sure all the listeners out there will send some positive vibes out to your dog." He turned pointedly to Dietz. "What do you know about this rash of sick critters everywhere? Now even your star hounds are affected. Some of my listeners complain about diseased raccoons and coyotes out and about, maybe infecting their pets. Since you and BeeBo are out amid the varmints, so to speak, is it contagious to pets? Did BeeBo's dog catch a critter cootie? Rabies, maybe?" His tiny eyes shined with excitement.

Dietz counted silently to five. It was that damn reporter's fault, raising suspicion for no good reason. "You'd have to ask a veterinarian about BeeBo's dog. There have been reports of raccoon distemper in the south part of the county, but that doesn't affect our show in any way." Had the reporter talked to Fish, too? This was his chance to put a lid on potential bad publicity before it went viral.

Fish was on a streak. "Here in North Texas, guns, dogs and barbecue go together like prom night and shotgun weddings. I kid. Well, maybe not. There's been some talk that the actors, I mean stars of the show, are scripted."

"Wait a minute, I—"

"We're still waiting for your other stars to show up. At least one had the courtesy to call in. BeeBo Benson, the lovable three hundred-pounder with the eagle-eye aim, rock hard gut and soft spot for his hog dogs. Randy Felch, thin as a copperhead with a temper to match. And the lovely Sunny Babcock, hotter than a coal stove even when covered in muck. Are you telling me they're not from Central Casting?" He glared. "Now, if BeeBo's dog is sick, my sympathies. Listeners know I'm a big fan of pets—you could say that "putting on the dog" put me on the media map. So I hope your stars will deign to show up and prove my suspicious nature wrong."

Dietz returned the stony expression. "If they were professional actors, they'd be here. These are real people with real feelings and allowances must be made. That's the tradeoff for getting the unexpected, exciting show our fans love. Believe me, BeeBo, Felch and Sunny are as real as they get." He lightened his tone. Wouldn't pay to piss off Fish before he'd gotten the news announced. "Two years ago to celebrate the wrap of the first season, we held a pig roast and barbecue locally to thank everyone for their help."

"I remember that. It was over at the Hog Heaven BBQ Restaurant." A beat. "I wasn't invited."

Aha. That explained some of the man's attitude. "My bad. Let me make it up to you, Humphrey."

"Don't be a tease. What do you have in mind?" Fish raised his eyebrows.

Dietz smiled. "The first show of our new season airs Friday, tomorrow night—right in time for Christmas. We're shipping out a special Piggy Panache Premium Package, official holiday gifts to Super Fans with sausage, jerky, bacon and more samples. You can't buy these. Viewers must watch the first show to find out the Piggy Password to order."

"A piggy password?" Fish nearly fell off his stool, guffawing. "Let me guess. Pig-in-a-blanket? Pig-in-a-poke? Porky Pig. Pig Newton?"

"Not even close, Humphrey. Guess you'll have to watch the show." Dietz's shoulders relaxed a bit. The little man had bought into the promotion. "Tomorrow night we have a watch party barbecue celebration once again at the Hog Heaven restaurant with an invitation-only audience. I've got spots for 200 guests—199, actually, because Humphrey Fish will be the first guest in the door." He noted Fish's pleased expression and continued in a rush. "The guests will also be on-camera in a future episode of the show as extras— so get ready for your close-up!"

"Now Tommy, that sounds like my kind of party. Can't wait to pig out at the big event! But what about those other 199 tickets? Do I sense a whole hog give-away in the offing?" Fish put his hand to his ear, pantomiming a phone.

Dietz grinned. "You read my mind. What do you say we give spots away to your listeners?"

The phone lines lit up.

Chapter 16

September rocked back on her heels in surprise, and had to consciously close her mouth. It wasn't possible they couldn't find Sly's body. She should have led them to the place. Hell, she would have missed it if the cat hadn't led Shadow to the crime scene.

Before she could say a word, Combs pushed past her and hurried out of the kitchen to the front of the house. She heard the door swing open and shut, probably on his way to rejoin Gonzales. Her lips tightened. Fine. She'd reported the crime. The police didn't want or need her help to do their job. She had her own job to do taking care of the cats.

"Shadow, wanna go for a car ride?" September looped his leash over the back of her neck, gathered up Macy's carrier with one hand and Sly's cat-bag in the other, and nearly ran out the door to the car. The big pup bounced and twirled in response, following so close behind her she nearly tripped. "Stay with me, baby-dog."

Shadow jumped into the back seat without prompting. After belting Macy's carrier in the front seat and setting the pillowcase on the floor, September deactivated the passenger side airbag just in case. Even a minor fender bender deployed the airbag and would crush a small pet, but she couldn't have the cats in the back with Shadow.

Her car swung out of the renovated carriage house garage. She carefully threaded the needle past Aaron's big truck to the front gate, avoiding the sight of Sly's battered car, which was now a crime scene. Combs didn't look up from collecting evidence, and Gonzales joined him by the car as she drove past.

Once on the road, she fished out her cell phone from a pocket and dialed the veterinary hospital. "This is September Day, and I'm bringing two sick cats in for exams. Yes, I'd call it an emergency. I'm on my way, should be there in ten or fifteen minutes." She briefly outlined the two cats' symptoms before disconnecting.

She set the phone on the dash and pressed the accelerator, ignoring the speed limit to make the twenty-minute drive in record time. The tires slipped on wet pavement, and September leaned into the turn. She glanced in the mirror when Shadow lost his balance. He yelped when he bumped against the door.

"Sorry."

He put his ears down and thumped his tail. Shadow stuck his nose through the pet barrier and poked her arm, and she smoothed his muzzle.

While her left hand steadied the steering wheel, she braced Macy's cat carrier nested on the passenger seat with her right hand. The cat's green eyes peered out of the mesh webbing, and he head-bumped the material and mewed, trying to reach her fingers. Sly's cat in the pillowcase on the floor said nothing.

Macy's breathing problems seemed to have resolved and now he seemed normal. But she didn't want to take chances, and Pinkerton needed a look, too. Besides, it had been too long between checkups. Macy loved meeting new people and enjoyed vet visits where strangers complimented him and offered pets and treats.

She couldn't bring herself to visit the vet clinic back in South Bend. She knew it was wrong to blame them but couldn't help it when they couldn't save Dakota. At the thought of his name, her heart skipped a beat. She still missed him. Always would.

"Macy-cat, feeling better?" She steadied the carrier as they again rounded a curve. When he meowed, Shadow nosed her once more. Although the pair had only lived together a short time, they'd already become fast friends.

Macy had always been healthy, and at four, he was the picture of a strapping adult boy cat. Maybe he'd eaten something toxic. Her own mouth tasted bitter at the thought. She knew all the holiday plants to avoid—holly, Jerusalem cherry, mistletoe—and decorated with an eye toward pet safety. She didn't even have the fake plants in the house.

She'd been rocked by Combs's revelation. It made no sense for the body to disappear. She hadn't fumbled for a pulse, it hadn't seemed necessary with the state of his concaved face, but if Sly had managed to stagger off, Gonzales would have found him.

Combs didn't mention the baseball bat, either. That thought chilled her. There had been plenty of time between her finding Sly's body and Gonzales's arrival for someone to move it.

Someone who stumbled upon the crime scene would raise the alarm and call the police, would get help, not hide the victim. Instead, they didn't want Sly found maybe because they killed him. And that someone had the murder weapon that could incriminate her.

"Shadow, tell me I'm paranoid." He woofed happily, and she smiled despite herself. The pup always knew how to lift her spirits. "We're a team now, right? We'll protect each other."

She felt lucky to have survived Uncle Vic with nothing worse than PTSD, although *nothing worse* seemed like an oxymoron. She shivered.

He'd listened to her teenage angst. He'd cheered her musical successes, and kept would-be romantic wolves at bay, deeming none good enough for his "princess." After being overshadowed for years by her sister—April was the pretty one—September felt flattered and vindicated by Uncle Vic's attention and fierce protectiveness. Her folks thought the world of him. And so she trusted him completely. Until her eighteenth birthday dinner, when everything changed.

"He can't hurt you." She said the words aloud, the mantra one she'd recited for more than eight years. But the package, another crappy joke from Sly, brought everything back. He couldn't hurt her. But he had. Because of Victor, she'd never feel safe again; never open herself to such hurt. Never trust again, not fully.

She kept the horrific memories buried and had no intention to share what sort of damaged goods she truly was. Chris had known, and ended up dead. "Safest to stick with cats and dogs. Right gang? You don't care about the past." And pets never lied about love.

She pulled into the parking lot of All Creatures Veterinary Hospital. Shadow's breeder had been married to the clinic's owner, Doc Eugene, an internal medicine specialist. Heartland didn't have a pet emergency center, and instead several smaller clinics rotated after-hours emergency availability. They'd treated Shadow's gunshot wound last month, along with his paw injuries, and she'd been relieved not to see Doc Eugene. For sure, he didn't want to see her.

September put the car in park and cracked both rear windows two inches before turning off the engine. The warmth of the heater followed her briefly as she stepped into the cold. Her breath puffed in white clouds when she hurried around to the passenger side to heft the twenty-pound Maine Coon's carrier out of the car. The cat in the pillowcase weighed less than half that amount. She slammed the door, and briefly touched a gloved hand to Shadow's nose sticking out the window.

"Wait here, baby-dog, I'll be out soon." Shadow's worried whine fogged the window, but he quickly settled to await her return.

The door squeaked open on a tile-floor waiting room lined with padded benches on three walls. Large windows on the front side gave September a clear view of her Volvo and the black doggy nose stuck halfway out one rear window. Clenching the pet caddy in one hand and the bagged cat in the other, she lugged them to the front counter—deserted—and waited a moment before setting both gently onto the floor.

"Anybody here?" She leaned over the chest-high counter, craning to see into the back room where muffled voices droned.

A hidden door squealed opened. "September, that you? Be right there." The youthful voice belonged to Timothy Beamish, the office manager and vet tech September had called on the way to the office. "Meet me in the cat room, exam three." The door clunked shut.

Macy's meow turned into a drawn out yowl as his carrier swung in September's grasp and accidentally bumped into a wall. "Sorry, buddy." She balanced Macy in one hand with Pinkerton in the pillowcase in the other, and hurried down the hall to the last small room on the left and elbowed open the door.

Three people stood in the room around a stainless steel table upon which a brown and white Pit Bull reclined. An enormous man, at least 250 pounds, turned a tear-streaked face toward her. The white-coated veterinarian's nostrils flared in aggravation, and September sucked in her breath and backed out of the doorway. "Sorry."

A short stocky man wearing a smock covered in pink and blue puppies and kittens saw her and smiled, and September glimpsed his name-tag. Timothy didn't move from his cradling grasp of the recumbent dog. "Cat room is across the hall. We'll be with you shortly."

"I'm so sorry." Heat flooded her face. She pulled the door closed and hurried to an identical room that smelled faintly of alcohol and cat pee. She shut the door and leaned against it. So much for dodging an encounter with Doc Eugene.

She busied herself getting Macy out of the carrier and onto the metal table for the exam, but left the tuxedo cat in the bag on one of the chairs. She settled into the other chair. The voices in the room across the hall carried, and it made her uncomfortable intruding on the big man's grief but she couldn't block out the sound. Obviously something serious afflicted his dog.

"He got all his shots. I give 'em myself, except that rabies one that y'all have to give." His voice trembled. "He's my best hog dawg, a real natural on the hunt. But he's been off the past couple weeks, you know? Not himself."

"Mr. Benson, we'll have to run tests. What kind of changes have you noticed?" Doc Eugene was all business.

"Wandering, can't get settled. Acts deaf, or at least he don't pay attention too good. Used to beat me to the truck. Now he trots on over, but don't know what to do once he gets there." BeeBo's voice had steadied. "Can you fix him? He's only four-years-old, but acting like an old fogey with half a brain."

"Like the others." There was a pause before a defensive note crept into Timothy's voice. "Well, it is. The other doctors said so, too."

September paid closer attention. Macy jumped into her lap and began kneading rhythmically against her thigh, acting fine. Maybe she'd over-reacted, but she couldn't take a chance. Macy had been with her through the bad times. She'd been alone, adrift, and he provided a furry anchor. September smoothed his dark neck and shoulders and scratched his white chin and chest. She wondered if the other pets Timothy had mentioned also suffered fainting spells.

"How's his appetite? What do you feed him?" Doc Eugene continued his no nonsense tone, intent on collecting an accurate history.

"Raw, it's healthier." Defensiveness crept into Benson's voice as well. "I fed that way thirty years, before it was a fad. My dawgs do good on it. This ain't the food, Doc."

"That's fine, Mr. Benson, we want all the facts so we can figure this out. I'd like to admit him. We need to run some tests, take blood samples, run a urinalysis, and go from there."

A long silence followed before the big man managed a choked answer. "Do what ya gotta do, Doc." His voice hiccupped, steadied and went on. "I'll pay whatever's needed. Just fix my dawg."

September heard the door across the hall open and close and pictured the big man returning to the front lobby area. She felt for him.

The door in the opposite side of the room opened and Timothy stuck his head inside. "We'll be with you shortly, we're getting that dog squared away. We're a bit shorthanded today. Only me and Doc Eugene scheduled, but lots of weird emergencies." He bit his lip. "I didn't say that. Doc wouldn't want me talking like that."

"Weird stuff?" September struggled to keep Macy on her lap when the big cat wanted to race over and greet Timothy. "Weird how?"

A canine whine turned into a drawn out howl. "Tim, I need your help." The veterinarian's soothing baritone murmured and the dog's distress calmed. Timothy handed her a form on a clip-board with a pen. "Fill out the basics about the cats, and we'll be back in a flash." He ducked out the door without answering September's question.

After another fifteen minute wait, the door opened again, this time admitting Doc Eugene. His long, narrow face masked emotion, and he wouldn't meet September's eyes. She'd feared his reaction. She'd seen him last at his wife Pam's funeral, where she'd been turned away.

"This is Macy." The cat wriggled out of September's grasp and leaped onto the exam table to meet Doc Eugene with a trill of welcome. The big man's eyes softened when the Maine Coon met his offered hands with head butts and cheek rubs.

September stood, and took a deep breath before speaking. "I gave Timothy the history over the phone, and completed this form. But I brought another cat—in the pillowcase. He needs an exam, too. I think it's Pinkerton, a cat that belongs to Sylvester Sanger."

"Tim?" He waited until the technician came in, and handed the bagged cat over. "See if we have a chart for owner Sylvester Sanger. If not, make a Good Sam chart, and get the basics." The door closed and he turned back to Macy. "Tell me again." He still didn't meet her eyes, but stayed focused on the patient, deftly examining the cat from nose to tail.

"Macy's four. He had his last exam a little over a year ago in South Bend, Indiana, a wellness exam with updates on his vaccinations. He got a three-year rabies at that time so isn't due for at least another year."

"You said it was an emergency when you called." He finally looked at her. She could tell it took great effort for him to keep his voice neutral, but his manner could have frozen fire. He had reason to dislike her. Pam would still be alive if not for her.

"I thought it was an emergency." September kept her eyes on the cat, anywhere but at the vet. Macy purred and trilled, delighted by all the attention. "He acts fine now, but he passed out at home."

His hands tightened on Macy, and he pulled the stethoscope from its necklaced position to listen to the cat's heart. "Has he ever fainted before?"

"No. He's always been active; he eats well. Chases the dog, teases Shadow, they're still testing boundaries. But they played this morning racing around and around, and he had no problem. This is the first time I've noticed anything." She paused. "I overheard what Timothy said. Is there something going around? Sly—I mean, Sylvester—mentioned that his cat had been acting odd."

He held up one hand to silence her, and continued to listen to Macy's heart. A half smile transformed his face for a split second. "He won't stop purring. But there's a distinct murmur." He flipped the stethoscope back around his neck. "Did the previous exams detect any abnormal cardiac sounds?"

"Nobody mentioned it, no." September's stomach clenched. Maine Coon cats could be prone to heart defects.

"I want to get a cardiac ultrasound." Doc Eugene scribbled a note on the chart, all business once again. "I don't like guessing, would rather get all the facts before we speculate. There's also a DNA test for Maine Coons that can tell us if he has the gene mutation responsible for HCM—hypertrophic cardiomyopathy, a heart ailment. That okay with you?" He continued to scribble, taking her silence for agreement.

She buried her face in Macy's mahogany coat, and her hair spilled over him, the color a perfect match. She struggled to maintain composure. *Just breathe.* "You want me to leave him here? Can't I wait while you run the test?" The three of them, as a unit, felt right. Leaving Macy behind took away one leg of their virtual three-legged stool.

He shook his head. "He's so friendly he probably won't need to be sedated. But I've got a kennel full of cases ahead of him, also the other cat you brought in. We need to mail the sample for the DNA test, and won't get results for at least a week." He opened the door and beckoned Tim before coming back to September. "We'll call you when we're finished. If it's what I suspect, we can get Macy on some medication to help relieve the symptoms and slow progression of problems."

Leaving Macy felt like a mistake, but September had no good reason to argue. Even if Doc Eugene didn't like her, she couldn't question his professionalism and dedication to furry clients.

When Timothy came into the room, Doc Eugene took September's completed form and strode out as though he couldn't wait to get away. The tech smiled and scratched Macy's chin before gathering the cat into his arms. "I'll meet you at the front desk as soon as I get kitty-kins squared away. Oh, I found Sylvester Sanger in the database. His tabby Pinkerton is the same age as your boy." Macy's big head bobbed over Timothy's shoulder and he blinked and meowed before disappearing into the rear clinic area.

September's throat tightened. *He'll be fine.* She collected Macy's pet carrier and returned to the front desk, heart as hollow as the empty container. She forced a smile when Timothy bustled back into the reception area, brandishing the paperwork for Macy's tests.

"What a sweet cat. Lots of them get stressed and hard to handle. Pinkerton won't stop yowling." He wrinkled his nose. "Cats don't like all the strange smells and critters."

"Macy's always been a people cat. He'd run up to an ax murderer and ask for a pet." She dug in her handbag for her wallet. "Thought I'd lost him out the door this morning. Scared me to death."

"You should microchip him." Timothy read the chart. "Wait, he already is."

She smiled. "So's Shadow."

He crossed to a shelf behind the counter and returned with a brochure. "What about these? Got in some trial packages, they attach to the collar. Kind of big for most cats but Macy's huge. You can get one for Shadow, too."

"Tracking system for pets? Couldn't hurt."

"They're sort of pricy." He sounded apologetic. "I can get it set up for you, though, no charge."

"Thanks." September handed over a credit card, barely glancing at the total. The amount didn't matter. Only getting Macy the right help mattered. Besides, between Chris's life insurance and the lottery winnings, she'd not have to worry about such things ever again.

A car engine roared and September started. She checked out the front window as a large truck revved outside.

"That's Mr. Benson." Timothy shook his head and frowned. "He's one of the stars of that local reality show, where he hunts with his dogs. He's pretty torn up. Sad situation." Timothy sighed. "I think he's got someone driving him, thank doG, or else he'd probably skid right off the road, the state he's in."

September strained to see around the truck until she saw Shadow poke his nose out her car window. Her shoulders relaxed. At least he was healthy. "What's the deal with Mr. Benson's dog?" She pushed her hair back behind her ears. "I couldn't help overhearing. Is it something that Shadow could catch? Or Macy?" Maybe she should get out the bleach and disinfect everything when she got home.

Timothy shrugged. "Something's going around, we don't know exactly what. There's been increased reports of sick raccoons, too. Maybe other wildlife."

"Rabies? Should I get Shadow another booster?" He'd cornered a raccoon in the garden a couple of weeks ago but he'd not had any contact before she called him off.

"Not rabies. The wildlife guys think it's a mutated dog distemper because there's more neuro signs than anything else. Raccoons can get dog distemper, but it's not contagious to cats. The feline distemper is a different disease—the panleukopenia virus usually causes vomiting and diarrhea and can make raccoons sick, too, but it doesn't cause the neuro signs like the dog disease. This illness has neurological signs like dog distemper but affects cats, especially the feral colonies, so maybe it's a variant. So sad." Timothy leaned pointy elbows on the counter and lowered his voice, enjoying a fresh audience and freedom to share juicy gossip. "The hospital's full of cats and a few dogs with similar weird signs like Mr. Benson's dog. Doc Eugene won't confirm or deny, and he's sent off a bunch of labs and been talking with some of the other internists." He whispered. "Don't say anything; he hates me to speculate."

September thought of how Pinkerton had acted in the laundry room, lost in one corner and unable to find his way out. "They catch it from raccoons?"

"Haven't a clue." Timothy handed back the credit card. "It'll be late this afternoon before the doc can run the echo. But don't you worry; we'll take good care of Mr. Macy. Oh, and honey? Don't let the Doc get you down. He knows it wasn't your fault. He's still hurting."

September flinched, but forced an unsteady smile that quickly crumbled.

"Oh dear, I shouldn't have said anything. Honey, it's okay." Timothy hurried from around the counter, ignoring the fact they'd only just met, and enveloped September in a bear hug. "You don't have to hide your feelings, it's safe here." He stood back and grabbed up a box of tissues. "We should buy stock in Kleenex."

She choked a laugh, grabbing one and smashing it against her eyes. "It's the worry over Macy." That, and Sly's ill-timed yellow-ribboned delivery. And disappearance. She scrubbed her face with the wet tissue as if that would also erase the helplessness she couldn't quash. "He's such a good kitty. Got me through some pretty desperate times, you know?"

"Don't they all." Timothy patted her on the shoulder, grabbed up the cat carrier to set it on the counter. "Want me to keep this here for Macy?" She agreed, and he escorted her out the door to the car. He gave her another quick squeeze and hurried back to the clinic, hugging himself against the chill.

BeeBo sat on the passenger side of the huge truck next to September's car. His shoulders shook, and September turned away to give him the privacy she'd want. The truck's engine revved, shuddered into gear and peeled out of the parking lot.

Shadow stuck his snout out the cracked window and whined. Her heartbeat a trip-hammer, unable to catch her breath, she clutched at the car door. *Get inside, get arms around Shadow, hands against his warm fur.* She needed contact to counter the chill in her veins. She should have brought him inside with her. She knew better, but had been overcome with worry over Macy, the strange cat's symptoms, and Sly's disappearance.

The pulse in her temple pounded, pounded, vision narrowed to a pinprick tunnel, and invisible bands crushed her chest. Numb fingers and toes betrayed her intent, and September stumbled, fumbled, failed to get IN— *must get INSIDE!*—the car's safety. A scream built in her lungs that she couldn't release past the constriction of her throat—*can't breathe! can't see!*— blinded by tears, sweat drenching her body despite the freezing air. Suffocating, dying, falling forever, no escape from the abyss that claimed her body, her soul…

A lifetime later her heartbeat slowed and breathing eased, and she found herself in the car's back seat with no memory of how she got there. The dog's weight pressed into her. "Sixty, fifty-nine, fifty-eight…" She counted backwards, out loud, a trick she'd used before she'd had Shadow. In those days, Macy's solid weight in her lap anchored reality so she could find her way back from the darkness. Now it was Shadow who licked her face, and she smiled and pushed him off her lap. "Good-dog, what a good-dog. Thank you, Shadow, I'm okay now."

Opening the door, September slid out of the car. "Wait." Shadow cocked his head but didn't attempt to leave the car, and sat when she latched his door and climbed into the driver's seat. "I'm ready to go home, how about you?"

Shadow woofed. Before she could start the car, her phone rang. She noted the display before quickly answering. "Hi Teddy, what's up?"

"I need you to bring Shadow." He sounded as breathless as she'd been moments before. "I'm at Sunnydale Nursing Home. Molly's gone, her and the dog are both gone."

Chapter 17

Teddy limped as fast as he could from the overly warm building when September pulled into Sunnydale's parking lot. He waited impatiently for the car to stop. Despite the clear blue skies, the December weather made the inside of his nose freeze, and he buttoned the front of his wool coat with stiff fingers.

Shadow's black muzzle poked out a rear window. Teddy hurried to the car when it jerked to a halt, and scratched the dog's chin. "Who's a good boy? Gonna help me find Molly, aren't you, fella?" The dog licked his hands and thumped his tail.

Blinking back grateful tears, Teddy smiled when September clambered out of the car. "You got here quicker than I thought. Thank you."

"Don't thank me yet." September straightened and flexed her back. "We were at the vet, a few blocks over when I got your call. Macy's sick." She pulled a scrunchy out of one pocket, gathered her long hair and bound it up with a practiced motion, all while taking in the cramped parking lot and shiny modern facility. "How long has Molly been missing?"

"They won't say. Covering their asses." He didn't hide his disgust and worry. Her own expression was pinched. "Sorry about Macy." He knew her animals were the world to September, but right now all his concern was focused on finding Molly.

"They're running tests this afternoon. So, what do you know? Have the police been called?"

He held his palms up with a helpless gesture. "The administrator called in a Silver Alert, but the police haven't shown up yet. I called them again right after I talked to you. They said all the units were out on other calls." He couldn't help the indignation.

"Maybe a police team will be available shortly." She wondered how many men had been deployed to her house to search for Sly.

"What's more important than finding a sixty-two-year-old Alzheimer's victim? She's not dressed right, she'll freeze in this weather." He shivered elaborately as if to illustrate the danger. "A couple of the staff said they canvassed the immediate neighborhood, and I'd go, too, if it wasn't for this bum knee." Between the arthritis and a needed hip replacement he'd put off, Teddy had enough trouble getting on and off of the HARTLine bus. He didn't like to drive at night anymore, didn't trust his eyes. "The police don't have a tracking dog unit, either. Said they used to contract that out, but the person shut down the service."

She flinched. "That was Pam and her dogs."

"Oh. Right." He avoided her eyes. "I guess her husband doesn't work the dogs now that she's gone."

"Doc Eugene doesn't have time to run the dogs and the vet hospital." She stroked Shadow's face. "Remember, Shadow isn't trained to track people. I drilled him on tracking lost pets. Lately there's been a lot of those and he's getting very good at it. But since he's the only dog available, I'm willing to give it a shot if you are."

"Molly's with Trixie." He couldn't help the hopeful note. "That's the resident therapy dog. Molly loves dogs, and the feeling's mutual. She used to spend hours and hours in the garden with our old dog, Rocky, and Trixie could be his twin. Dark red Golden Retrievers, not the pale yellow that's so popular now. Trixie spends as much time in Molly's room as she can. I think it helps remind Molly of the good times, you know?"

Shadow whined and pushed his face further out the car window when he saw September retrieve the long tracking line from the front seat. "Baby-dog, settle. You want to play *hide-and-seek*? Three times in one day, how fun is that?" September jollied the dog, getting him keyed up for the challenge, but Teddy could sense her worry even if the hunched shoulders hadn't revealed her stress.

"I appreciate this." He stuck his hands in the pockets of his long coat. "Wish I could tag along but I'd slow you down."

She let the black shepherd out of the back seat. "Shadow, sit. Wait." The dog obediently plopped his tail onto the cold pavement. He had a hard time containing his excitement, but allowed her to clip the long line to the D-ring centered between his shoulders on his harness.

Shadow seemed bigger than the last time he'd seen the dog over Thanksgiving. That had been one of Molly's good days, and they'd enjoyed the family dinner atmosphere. He hadn't tried to explain to his wife why the giddy, celebratory dinner meant more than the usual turkey-day holiday. Teddy noticed Shadow's gunshot ear had finally healed, although the ragged end lacked fur. It gave the dog a more grim appearance. "He's not a puppy anymore."

September paused. "I see him every day, so it's hard for me to tell the difference. He still has some filling out to do. He won't be a year old until Valentine's Day." She smiled at Shadow. "This is a game to him, though, we want to keep it fun so he always wants to work. What exit did Molly use? Also, I need something to cue in to Trixie's scent. A dog brush, or a toy that smells like the therapy dog." She led the way to the front door of the nursing facility. "Otherwise he won't know what to track, and might generalize to who knows what. We've been tracking cats today, including Macy."

The black shepherd's ears flicked at the name, and he nudged her thigh with his nose. She dropped her hand to stroke his brow. "That's right, you played hide-and-seek with Macy, didn't you? But this is a new game."

Teddy hurried to catch September's arm before she opened the lobby door. "Let me find the administrator and give her a head's up first. She's a piece of work." He pulled hard on the door. "I don't want her screwing our chances to find Molly by citing some weird rule book." He limped inside, and September and the dog entered right behind him. "Wait here." He whispered. "They're strict about animals." He arched one eyebrow. "I know he's your service dog, too, but Molly doesn't have time for arguing the case."

September spoke softly to Shadow, and he sat and panted happily.

At the front desk, Alison smiled at Teddy, and then half stood when she noticed Shadow. "You can't bring that in here."

Shadow's black nose twitched, he sneezed, and his tail swept the spotless floor.

The smells Teddy now took for granted would be odd to most folks. Institutional smell; a mix of disinfectant, urine and maybe desperation, if emotion could have a smell. He gritted his teeth and crossed to the administrator's office without acknowledging Alison.

Teddy knocked briskly, cracked opened the door and stuck his head inside without waiting. "Mrs. Bradshaw, a tracking dog is here to find my wife." She started to say something, and he spoke over her words. "I'm not asking permission, this is an FYI as a courtesy. I'm taking them down to Molly's room."

"That's fine, Mr. Williams. Of course we'll help any way we can. Tell the police dog team they have the run of the place, whatever is needed." She didn't get up, and acted relieved that Molly's recovery was out of her hands.

Alison stood behind the counter, attention moving back and forth between Shadow and Teddy when he shut the administrator's door. "It looks ferocious...does it bite?"

"Only bad guys." September's humor attempt fell flat. She crossed closer to the counter, Shadow in tow, and the girl shrank back. September made a fist gesture, and Shadow sat, cocking his head up at Alison. "Can you tell us where Mrs. Williams—Molly—left the building? She's with a dog, right?"

Alison smiled at Shadow despite herself. "Probably through the side entrance, 'cuz I never saw them pass through here. Trixie is our therapy dog, she's certified through Delta Society." She dropped her voice to a whisper. "She belongs to Mrs. Bradshaw. I think she's as worried about Trixie as Mrs. Williams." She pursed her lips and made kissy noises, and Shadow cocked his head and thumped his tail. "Is he going to track Mrs. Williams?"

"Actually he's going to track Trixie. So we'll have to keep our paws crossed the dog stays with Molly."

"Oh, Trixie adores her! She spends a lot of time with your wife, Mr. Williams. That is, when she's not raiding residents' rooms. She's a sneaky thief, but it's not out of meanness. She only borrows stuff. I think she does it so they'll tell her how pretty she is when we make her give stuff back." Alison sipped from a large cup, and then giggled when Shadow licked his lips.

"We need something that smells like Trixie." Teddy wanted to get Shadow on the trail. Too much time had already passed. "Does she have a toy or maybe a dog bed where she spends time?"

Without answering, Alison ducked down behind the counter, scrounged for a moment, and came up with an oversize blue ball on a rope. "She sleeps with this, carries it with her, and even eats with it. I'm surprised it's not with Trixie now." She offered it to September.

She took it gingerly, holding it carefully by one end of the rope in her gloved hands. "Perfect." She turned to Teddy. "Take me to Molly's room. We'll get a sense of the start point, and go from there."

He felt better once they began moving. "She's in the room at the end of the hall." He led the way and stopped at the designated door. Inside, a small bed with a garden themed spread dominated the room. A small table contained a picture frame of one of the last family portraits they'd had made before. . . Well, when Molly was still Molly.

Teddy furnished the room with things that mattered to Molly, or used to matter, anyway. Pictures from her garden. One of her posed with a tail-wagging Rocky—God, how she'd loved that dog, and he'd loved her back. A crocheted pillow cover that had spent years on their shared four-poster and now kept her company in her lonely twin bed. A tattered robe—her favorite that she wouldn't give up. The small vanity in the corner contained an assortment of toiletries, scented hand lotions and perfumes, a hair brush. A small blown glass bowl of jellybeans held court. He had a glass paperweight in the same colors on his desk at home. They'd purchased them as a pair on a trip to Scotland years ago, and Teddy wondered if she sometimes held the bowl and thought of him as he thought of her when holding the glass globe.

They'd had to remove the mirror when Molly's reflection, a stranger looking at her, caused her first panic attack.

Sighing, Teddy made room for September and Shadow to enter. "This is it." He waved a hand at the towel on the floor. "I think the dog spends time lying on that, too. Now what?"

September brought Shadow into the room. She showed him Trixie's ball-on-a-rope toy. "What's that, Shadow? Time for *hide-and-seek*?"

She watched him sniff the ball, but he didn't attempt to take it as he might have when he was younger. Shadow was all business, inhaling with purpose. She showed him the towel on the floor, and he moved over to it and explored with snuffles and snorts. She showed Teddy her crossed fingers and he answered with his own. This had to work!

She waited until the dog signaled readiness with an expectant expression. "Shadow, *seek*!"

He dropped his head, returning to the towel, and then moved quickly toward the door. September had gathered the long line, taking up the slack with one hand, and kept him on a short leash as he guided her through the doorway.

Teddy followed, stumbling in his effort to keep up. He saw Shadow cast first one way and then the other on the immediate outside of Molly's doorway, and held his breath. Suspecting that September might accidentally cue the dog in one direction over the other, he was surprised when Shadow hesitated and then drove forward—the wrong way.

"Wait, September, the door is—"

She glared at him, finger to her lips, as the dog towed her past the rear door that Alison had indicated. Instead, Shadow padded quickly, sure of his nose, toward a rear area with a crash bar on double doors. "Seek, good-dog Shadow, seek!" She repeated and encouraged him, and he wagged without lifting his head when she pushed through the barrier.

The kitchen. Shadow had led them into the kitchen. The staff were nowhere to be seen, since mealtime was still hours away. Teddy's anger grew. Trixie wasn't allowed in the kitchen. There was no way Molly and the therapy dog had passed this way. But before he could speak, the dog towed September faster straight through the wide corridor, paying not the slightest attention to anything but the invisible trail on the floor.

A second pair of double doors on the far wall stopped Shadow, but he leaped up, pawing the crash bars and whining with excitement until September banged them open. She rushed behind the dog, playing out the long line but keeping it taut, and jogged to keep from frustrating his eagerness. Teddy struggled to keep up.

The doors opened on a hidden courtyard off the kitchen. A tiny garden, currently barren due to the time of year, shivered behind one concrete wall. Sacks of bone meal fertilizer created a second wall, forming a small alcove that sheltered from the wind.

Shadow abruptly stopped at the entrance to this cave-like opening, made eye contact with September, and planted himself in a down. He woofed, his tail banging happily.

"Good-dog, Shadow! What a good boy!" She knelt beside the black shepherd, rubbing his throat and letting him lick her face.

"Good-dog, Trixie, good girl, what a pretty girl." Trixie raised her shaggy head and wagged back. She deftly caught the rope-ball toy when September tossed it to her, but didn't stray from the woman's side.

Teddy pushed past September, relief palpable. "Molly! Are you okay? I was so worried." Finally he could breathe.

Behind the Golden Retriever, Molly had a child's orange plastic bucket and toy shovel, something that might be used at the beach, and had broken open one of the bags of fertilizer. "We must get rid of it. Rid of it all. It's bad, makes you crazy." Her ghostly face glowed dusty white with the bone meal, tears tracing wet tracks down her cheeks. "Isn't that right, Rocky...I mean, Trixie?" The dog licked the powder from her face and sneezed.

Chapter 18

Back in the Sunnydale parking lot, September waited as Shadow sniffed the front tire for the ideal spot to take-a-break. He'd done a great job finding Teddy's wife. Rather, finding Trixie.

"Good boy, Shadow. Ready to go?" She stroked his neck as he paused beside her before leaping into the back seat. "Pull in your tail. Good boy." She slammed the door, and he immediately turned around to stick his muzzle out the three inches of open window. He didn't care but Shadow risked eye damage if he stuck his whole head out.

She knew Teddy worried about Molly. How awful to have someone you love no longer recognize you. What if it happened to Shadow? Very old dogs did develop cognitive disorder, but she wouldn't have to worry about that with Shadow for years and years.

She started the car, shoved it into drive, and slowly pulled out of the parking lot. By the time they'd left, Molly had started talking nonsense to Trixie while calling her Rocky. The dog didn't care, though, and Trixie refused to leave Molly's side. Heartbreaking. She wondered if Molly knew, or was beyond recognizing what was happening to her mind. September hoped it was the latter. Bad enough that Teddy knew.

Thank goodness Molly stayed with Trixie. Shadow loved tracking other animals, and it had been a big day for the pup.

She hadn't known what to tell Doc Eugene about the reporter's cat. She probably should let someone know about Pinkerton. September rolled to a stop sign, pulled out her phone, and dialed. The reporter's number was stored in her phone even though she'd never returned his call. She left a message for whoever might get it through his service, and disconnected. It'd be hours before they could return to the vet clinic to get Macy. "What should we do now, baby-dog?" She smiled at the happy doggy expression reflected in the mirror. Nobody was around to see her talk to him, but she wouldn't have cared if they were. Shadow listened with more attentiveness and intelligent expression than most people she knew.

She still felt responsible for Sly's cat, and was curious about his investigation, especially if it might affect Macy's wellbeing. She could talk to Timothy about the reporter's suspicions. He acted more open to speculation than Doc Eugene, but she'd have to wait until it was time to retrieve Macy.

"Wait. Sly said he talked to Fish. He's got to know more." She dialed the radio station by memory, prepared to dodge the DJ's pressure to return to the radio show.

"WZPP, you've reached ZAP105 FM Radio, home of THE Humphrey Fish, bringing you easy-listening 24/7 with your favorite Fish Stories. How may I direct your call?"

"Hey Anita, it's September. Oh, and Shadow's with me."

"You want to talk to Fish? He's on-air for another twenty minutes or so." The brassy voice was pure West Texas, and turned honeyed when she asked, "How's the big guy? When you going to bring Shadow to visit again?"

September took one hand off the steering wheel long enough to make a "speak" signal, and Shadow woofed and wagged. "There, he said 'howdy.'"

The other woman laughed. "Seriously, you know Fish hates returning calls. So how about you stop by? I want to show you my new hair-style. Oh, and bring the baby-dog. I need a puppy fix. Tell Shadow I've got treats."

The dog tipped his head to one side as if he'd heard the magic word. He probably had. September laughed at his selective hearing. "Okay, I'm already halfway there. Shadow's ready for some treats and love." She teased. "Didja get tired of being a redhead?"

"I need to mix it up."

"So what color this time? Blond? Silver?

"Brunette with blue streaks. Thinking about getting my nose pierced, too. Maybe some tats."

September grinned. Nothing Anita did got Fish's attention, but that didn't stop her trying. "I'm sure it's stunning." She hesitated. "We had to help Teddy with his wife at the nursing home."

Anita tsk-tsked. "How's she doing? I feel so bad for them. For him especially."

"Not good. I think our Thanksgiving was the last good day she's had."

She hesitated, and pressed harder on the gas to beat the light. "Sylvester Sanger came to my house this morning."

"That weasel? He's been here confabbing with Fish off and on the past few weeks, too. What does he want?"

"You don't know?" September's tires crunched as she turned into the gravel lot, pulled up to the brick building, and parked. "He had his sick cat with him. Said he and Fish needed my help on some story, so I guess it's about pets." She felt guilty now for whaling on Sly's car with the baseball bat. "I thought he wanted an interview about, you know, Steven and the other kids. He'd left several messages I ignored, and frankly, it pissed me off to have him show up and run into my gate."

Anita hee-hawed. "He ran into your new gate?" Anita laughed again, and then with an effort, stifled the guffaws. "Not funny, I know but—Jeez, what a piece of work." She hurried to add, "I've got other calls. Phone when you get here and I'll buzz you in."

September pulled off her seatbelt. "We're here. Give me sixty seconds to get Shadow out of the car."

When she exited, Shadow whined and paw-danced on the seat and clawed at the door. "Settle, Shadow." The insides of the doors carried scars from his impatience, but at least she'd remembered to set the child-proof lock on the windows. He'd been known to hit the button and scroll open the window.

Opening the door, September caught up his leash before he hopped out, but when Shadow tugged the line on the way to the radio station entrance, she didn't argue. She chose her battles, and actually preferred having him take point. She suspected, though, that he was focused on the prospect of treats, but trusted he'd alert to anything untoward in the vicinity.

Besides, she was so much better. Today she'd been out almost all day, with only one knuckle-biter episode. Having the big pup nearby did more for her than the dozens of locks and security system she'd installed at the house. Still, her heart always galloped anytime she left the relative safety of a building or her car.

They entered the empty lobby and her pulse slowed to a more reasonable rhythm. Shadow wasn't a "certified" service dog, and she had no documentation. There wasn't any official certifying body for service dogs. Those that had graduated from a program sometimes carried documentation, but self-trainers like her wouldn't have any proof. Nor did the law require it. Oh, she had his harness with the "service dog in training" badge from his short-lived partnership with her nephew. September didn't feel right using that since Steven would never need Shadow's services again.

The law said you weren't required to reveal your specific disability, but business owners could ask if the dog was a service animal or used for a disability. To avoid the whole issue she told them she was a service dog trainer. They didn't need to know it was for her.

She released the leash. "*Check it out*, Shadow." His head came up. He scanned the small waiting room—chairs, table, out of date magazines, glass wall and counter below, closed inner door, speakers mounted on the walls— and then he sniffed the perimeter of the room. September smiled. Her confidence rose in the security of the empty room, but every opportunity to train helped ensure Shadow's behavior would become automatic.

September crossed the empty reception area to the glassed-in counter next to the locked inner door. Shadow returned to her side, and at her signal, performed a "paws up" at the counter. He nose-smeared the glass, tail wagging, and September figured he recognized Anita's scent and anticipated the treat to come. "She'll be here soon. Meanwhile, want to play *show-me?*"

The pup pushed off, backed away and sat, cocking his head with expectation. He enjoyed these training games as much as she did. September examined the sparse room. Not much to choose from, but she finally crossed to the small table and picked up the vase of fake flowers in one hand. Quickly she pulled out the artificial blooms, holding them in the other. "This is *glass.*" She held out the vase. "This is *flower.* Shadow, show-me *glass.*"

He bounced forward, nose-punching the vase so hard that it nearly fell from her hand.

"Good-dog! You're so smart." She paused, and said, "Show-me *flower.*" He obligingly poked the blooms.

"You like?" Anita had returned, and peered at them through the reception window. She stopped, indicated her billowing dark bluesy curls, and twirled.

"Stunning."

Anita took a seat at the desk. "Fish's show winds up in another ten minutes." At her voice, Shadow bounded to the window, tail swinging, and woofed softly. She laughed, and leaned forward toward the small opening in the glass. "How's my boy? I got treats for my buddy." She crooned, her copper-bright voice softening. "What were you doing now?"

"Playing the show-me game."

Anita's eyes widened. "Teddy told me about it. He said Shadow's a canine Einstein or something." She waited, expectation painting her face. "Is that how you taught him to take away Steven's gun?"

Chapter 19

Nikki sat in the back seat of the car, arms crossed and still shivering over the encounter with the weird guy at the barn. She hadn't told Hank. Not yet, anyway. Not till she could tell him in private.

Hank sat beside her, but leaned forward with his head between the two front seats to talk with Zeke, while Zeke's cousin Dustin drove. They'd gotten permission from Zeke's folks to run into town for BBQ from Zeke's favorite restaurant. Several of the popular kids would be there, and Zeke acted all puffed up to introduce his older cousin to the gang. Big whoop.

Once again, Nikki was a tag-along, and not by choice. Mom wasn't home yet from shopping, so she had no choice and neither did Hank. But she didn't want to say anything in front of the others. They wouldn't believe her. Even worse, they'd make fun of her, maybe even tell Mom. Then Hank would get in trouble, too, and be mad at her. That'd be even worse than not getting to see the kitties anymore. No, she'd better wait to tell Hank in private.

When the stranger showed up, she'd nearly peed her pants when she saw his gun. It had two barrels but was way shorter than Daddy's rifle. She rubbed the deep scratches on her arms, hidden by her jacket, where the gray cat had gouged her. She hated leaving Hope-Kitty behind, and worried the sick raccoons might attack her. But when she saw the gun, she'd not thought, just ran. And the loud "boom-boom" that followed after made her think the scary stranger might have shot at her!

Hank had to believe her. He couldn't go back to the barn, not with the crazy man there. She didn't want him to get shot. Or tore up by attacking rabid raccoons.

"It's up the block, turn right at the light, and it's on the left." Zeke twisted halfway around in his seat to talk to Hank. "Did you hear about the watch party? I think maybe we can score tickets. Xavier's going to check it out, he's working today."

Zeke's older brother Xavier worked holiday hours at Hog Heaven. He got them discounts on hot wings and fries, and free drink refills, but only on Tuesday nights. Today was Thursday so they'd have to pay full freight. That's what Daddy called it, paying full freight.

"What's a watch party?" Nikki rubbed her throbbing arms. Once they got to the restaurant, she could go to the ladies' room and wash off the scratches. The cat didn't mean to hurt her, but she didn't want the sores to get infected. The barn wasn't all that clean. She thought again about the sick raccoons.

"Watch party for the first episode of the new season for *Hog Hell.* Doncha know nothing?" Zeke rolled his eyes, and turned back to the front. "Dustin, turn there. No, don't park under the trees or we'll get nailed with bird poop all over and have to wash the car."

Nikki blinked hard. Zeke was a stupid head, why'd he have to be so mean?

"It's this reality show, Nikki, a hunting show where they shoot wild pigs." Hank explained with quiet kindness. "Mom won't let us watch, says it's too violent."

"Ka-pow! They shoot the sons-of-bitches, and then barbecue their ass." Zeke licked his lips and made smacking noises. "Hank, ol' buddy, you're missing a great show. I got some of 'em TiVo'd, so you can watch at my house if you want."

"Barbecued oinker, huh?" Dustin grinned.

Nikki thought he had a hot smile. That's what Gina said about the boys when she wasn't talking about the new baby.

"Those feral hogs destroy lots of property. They eat anything." Dustin preened in the car mirror and smoothed his hair, and then winked at Nikki when he caught her staring. "Might even want to chomp on a cutie like you, Nikki."

She blushed and turned away. Dustin was cute, with his curly brown hair down to his collar. And he was seventeen, nearly twice as old as she.

Zeke smacked his lips again. "They'll be serving special eats at the watch party. The stars will be here. That Sunny Babcock is smokin'." They got out of the parked car, and he pretended to aim and fire an invisible gun. "Maybe they'll bring their guns. Nailed your butt, Porky-Pig!"

"I'm hungry. Let's go." Hank yanked open the car door and scooted out, impatiently waiting for Nikki to join him. He whispered as they followed the other two toward the entrance. "Never mind Zeke. He's trying to be a big man around Dustin."

She caught at his sleeve. "Gotta talk to you." Maybe he'd hang back a minute and she could tell him about the guy at the barn. The car door slammed, and a cloud of blackbirds rose from a nearby tree, swarming like bees until, as one, they roosted domino close, turning power lines into a creepy clotted string.

"Sure. Inside, where it's warm." He caught the door before it slammed shut, and hurried into the place.

She didn't like the birds. About a million beady birdy eyes stared at her like in a scary movie she wasn't supposed to watch but did anyway.

Nikki wasn't fast enough getting through the door, and it caught her sore arm. She hissed with pain, and her eyes watered, but she wiped them before anyone could see and call her a crybaby. Once inside, she found the boys had already claimed one of the tin-covered picnic-style tables at the back of the space.

Zeke grabbed the head of the table as well as the bucket of peanuts. He popped the nuts into his mouth, tossing shells on the sawdust floor. Nikki made a face. He chewed with his mouth open. What a pig. She giggled and covered her face. Daddy would have liked that; he said puns all the time.

Hank took a place next to Zeke, while Dustin grabbed a menu. When Hank waved at her to come over, she shook her head and pointed to the ladies' room.

There were only two stalls, both occupied. That was okay. She no longer needed to pee. Nikki shrugged off her jacket and tied the sleeves around her narrow waist, and then gingerly shoved the sleeves of her favorite purple unicorn sweatshirt halfway up her arms. She winced at the deep angry gouges, still seeping red. At least the inside of her purple top wouldn't show the blood. Mom would want to know what happened, and that'd be the pits.

She ran the water in the sink, and shivered when it wouldn't get hot. Nikki soaked one of the brown paper towels—they always smelled funny, but beggars couldn't be choosers. That's what Mom always said. She applied greasy pink soap and gently washed each forearm. It stung, and she gritted her teeth. "Means I'm killing germs," she whispered. That's what Daddy always said.

After drying off with another wad of the brown paper, Nikki carefully pulled down the sleeves. Mom would demand an explanation so she better keep her arms covered up until the sores healed. At least the cold weather meant she could wear long sleeves without getting weird looks. They still stung, but at least the wounds were clean.

One of the ladies came out of the stall, and Nikki hurried out of the bathroom before the woman could say anything or ask about her arms. Grownups were always so nosy. When she grew up, she'd give her kids some privacy. And a cat, if they wanted. Maybe even two cats.

She rounded the corner, clumping in her muddy shoes, and stopped when she saw the table now crowded with kids. The populars. All older than Nikki except for the cop's kid Willie Combs. She knew Hank had a crush on Willie's sister Melinda, even though he'd never admit it. But why else would he get the stutters and turn red around her?

Nikki slowly approached, keeping her head down so they wouldn't notice her. Having all their eyes on her would be worse than the gazillion birds outside. Maybe she could blend in and hang back behind Hank? But Willie's face lit up when he saw her, and she groaned.

"Hey, Nikki, you going to go to the watch party, too?" He bounced around like a kitten chasing a moth.

Melinda saw Nikki, and her mouth made a funny fake pout. "You had to bring your kid sister, I had to bring Willie. At least now they can keep each other entertained, right?" She batted her eyes at Dustin.

To Nikki, the gesture looked so fake she could have puked.

"Why don't you two kids find yourself a kiddie table?" Melinda made shooing gestures with her hands.

"Sure thing. C'mon, Nikki. It'll be our private place." Willie skipped to the next booth. He didn't act bothered at all.

When Nikki turned to Hank for help, he shrugged, handed her a cup with soda, and turned away. The back of his neck turned red when Melinda accidentally-on-purpose bumped into his arm.

Give me a freaking break. Nikki huffed and dragged her feet but it was easier to give in and join Willie than argue and create a scene. Besides, they could still hear the conversation from their so-called kiddie table.

"Are you?" Willie had his own drink. He'd taken the plastic lid off, and tried to stab his straw through one of the hollow ice cubes. "Gonna come to the watch party? Lindy says there'll be autographs from the stars, and a red carpet entrance, with a limo and everything. We'll get to see the first show before anybody else. It's a sneaky preview, with surprises and stuff. Mom's bringing us. She got tickets and my step-dad has to work, so we get to go. So, you coming?"

"Sneak preview." She automatically corrected him. "To watch somebody shoot a pig?" She shuddered. "Pigs are cute. My grandma used to have a pet pig named Pinky, and he wasn't stinky or dirty or anything. I don't even like bacon anymore."

"They're not shooting the pigs in the restaurant. It's a TV show." He dropped his voice. "I think it's special effects, you know, with green screen. I watched this behind-the-scenes special how they made that movie *Life Of Pi.*"

"C'mon, how do you think they get ham sammiches and pork chops? From the pork chop tree?" Willie was so immature, she thought, brushing off the cat hair stuck to her unicorn sweatshirt.

"Here's your food." Melinda carried a basket of fries and messy buffalo wings over to Willie.

"Tell Nikki about the watch party, Lindy. It's gonna be killer, right?" He grabbed one of the tiny sauce-covered drumsticks, dipped it in ranch dressing, and chomped down.

Red sauce dribbled from the corners of his mouth. Like blood. A boy-vampire. Nikki shivered at the thought. Hank said vampires were made up stories but she wasn't convinced.

"I don't know if they can let just *anyone* come." Melinda arched her brows and cocked her head, taking in Nikki's stained jeans and the frayed sleeves of her jacket. "The show is so gruesome. The stars are so bad-ass."

"So, I'm not invited?" Dustin sauntered over, hands stuck in the pockets of his leather jacket, peering out from under the curly shelf of his hair. "I'm not *anyone*. Am I?" He smiled at Melinda, and when she turned away, briefly flustered, Dustin winked at Nikki.

Nikki covered her mouth to keep from laughing.

Melinda grabbed up one of her brother's fries, dipped it in sauce and bit off a taste. "I bet my mom could get you a ticket. You've got to come! It's going to be THE BEST!" Her voice rose, and the rest of the other table turned to listen.

Now the "kiddie table" had become the place to be. Nikki liked being part of the crowd. Her arms didn't sting so much, either. Being included worked better than aspirin. She sipped her drink, happy Hank had decided to drag her along after all. Dustin didn't treat her like a baby, he saw through Melinda, too. Nikki smiled to herself.

Melinda rattled on, delighted to be the focus of attention. "You know they harvest the hogs and give away the food to needy people. That's why my mom is such a fan; she works at the Hot Meals soup kitchen. Volunteers, I mean. She doesn't work anymore since we moved in with my step-dad." Her words faltered a moment.

Nikki started to say something when Willie punched her softly. She shut her mouth, surprised when he shook his head. So she didn't say anything.

Hank didn't notice. "Could your mom score me a ticket?" He gazed back and forth between Dustin and Melinda, his face stricken. "I've never seen the show, but Zeke said he'd let me watch his TiVo."

"My fave is that tall guy, Mr. Felch." Melinda ignored Hank, and he shrank a bit, even as she turned her face up to Dustin. "BeeBo is sort of gross, he's a ginormous Michelin Man." Her laugh tinkled. "Mr. Felch, though, he's a creeper." She shivered delicately, for the benefit of Dustin.

"Sounds spooky. Feral hogs are dangerous, too, so anyone goes after a tusker must have some brass balls." Dustin showed his teeth again.

Zeke barked a laugh. "Texas size!" He made a rude gesture at his crotch, and Hank slugged his arm. "Hey! What's the deal? Oh." Zeke shrugged when Hank jerked his head toward Nikki. "That's what she gets for tagging."

With one pinprick word, Nikki's bubble of belonging burst. She bit her lip. Why'd Hank have to punch him? She wasn't a baby; she'd heard Daddy use worse words when he didn't think she could hear. She had to do something, show she deserved to be here. "You got pictures? Of the show stars?" Nikki jutted out her chin at Melinda, acting like a big shot around Dustin and making Hank get all weird. "How scary can they be? Bet it's fake TV like you said, Willie."

"Yeah, show us some pictures." Dustin smiled at Nikki, and she liked him even more. "I never saw the show, either. But if the pictures are as good as you say, maybe I do want to come to this little watch party soiree."

He said the word with a foreign accent and everything. Nikki hugged herself with delight.

"Sure, I can show you pics." Melinda dug in her tiny purse and pulled out a phone case with her initials in glittery sparkles. She fiddled with the buttons to engage the browser, typed in a search, and quickly had the TV show website on the screen. "There. See? I told you. Creepy as all get out. Doncha love it?" She held out the phone to Dustin and he took a quick look and then, despite Melinda's irked expression, handed the phone to Nikki.

"That's BeeBo with one of his dogs. He's got lots of dogs. Hounds that track them and Pit Bulls that hold them. The nice kind, though, his Pit Bulls aren't mean at all. He's always talking about how he wants his dogs to represent the good side of the breed." Melinda pointed, before changing the picture to the next frame. "And that's Mr. Felch, with his favorite piece. Can you imagine? He says he named the gun 'Trudy' after his lost love because she always shot off her mouth." She giggled.

Nikki leaned close to the picture, and then jerked backward. Her lips trembled. "That's him. That's the scarecrow man. He…he shot his gun at me."

"What? Where?" Hank pushed Melinda aside to hurry to Nikki. "What are you talking about?"

"At the barn." She whispered. Now everyone would know. "While you were riding the four-wheelers. I had to visit Hope, that's what I named the momma kitty, and there were sick raccoons and this scary man came with a big sack and carrying a gun. Maybe there was a body in the bag!" She'd just thought of that. Could it be true? He didn't have blood on his face, but he was white like a vampire. "I know it was Mr. Felch. I swear, Hank, it was him."

"She's lying. Can't you see she's lying?" Melinda, no longer the center of attention, had been pushed to the outskirts of the circle. "Give me back my phone. Why would a big movie star bother with you? You're making it up to get attention." She pocketed the phone and crossed her arms.

"I'm not lying. He was there, and he scared me. He was at the barn."

Dustin grabbed her arms to make her sit down, and she flinched and cried out. He backed off like she had cooties. "What'd I do? I only touched her. Sorry!"

Hank gently pushed her onto the bench. "Are you hurt?"

"My arms." She shoved up her sleeves. Now Mom would never let her see the cats again.

Dustin's face drained of color while Hank's turned rosy. Melinda's mouth dropped open. Willie said, "Ouchie," and patted her on the shoulder.

"Get in the car." Dustin pulled out his wallet and tossed a couple of bills on the table.

"What? Why?" Melinda found her voice. She reached out a hand toward Nikki's gouged arms, and stopped before she touched them. Brow wrinkled, she asked, "Does it hurt? We need to wash that."

"Already washed." Tears coursed down her face, hot and sticky. "Hank, you can't tell Mom. She'll never let me see Hope again." Her voice hiccupped.

"Get in the car. Now!" Dustin grabbed Zeke's coat sleeve and tugged, and pushed at Hank's shoulder. "Melinda, get your brother. Nikki, come on." He put one gentle arm around her shoulders.

Heaven. It was almost worth getting scratched by Hope. Almost. "Where are we going?" Her voice sounded so small, like a baby, she thought. But Dustin didn't act like it mattered.

"To the barn." Dustin hugged her. "We're going to kick some pig-sticker ass."

Chapter 20

September frowned at Anita. The news stories made Shadow out to be super-dog.

"So he grabbed Steven's gun? Shadow knows how to disarm bad guys?" Anita covered her mouth with her hand. "Sorry, I don't mean to imply Steven is a bad guy. How could a little kid like that…"

"It's okay, I know what you mean." She tucked stray hair behind her ear. "It's complicated. Shadow knows what the word means. He sort of nose-poked the gun at the right time."

At the word *gun*, Shadow cocked his head and his ears flicked backwards. The word probably had unpleasant connotations if he associated it with his shot ear. "The *show-me* game helps teach Shadow vocabulary. By holding two different objects, one in each hand, and naming them, he learns what each is called." Shadow knew nearly a hundred name-words by now. She scanned the room, and then turned back to the patiently waiting dog. "Shadow, show-me *paper*."

His mouth clicked shut and he danced across the room to the small coffee table, and nosed the stack of magazines.

"Good-dog!" September turned away to speak over her shoulder to Anita. "He prefers to learn new words, but we need to practice the known words to keep him sharp."

"He needs new ones?" Anita shuffled around her desk. She held up a coffee mug, and raised her eyebrows.

"Cup, he knows that one. But okay. What else you got?" September reached through the opening when she pushed it through.

Anita moved a few items around the desk, and then opened the drawer. "How about this? Got it on a trip to England years ago."

"Nice." September took the shiny silver letter opener, shaped like a hand wielding a sword. She turned to Shadow, the coffee mug in one hand and letter opener in the other, and he backed away and sat down, anticipating what would follow. "Shadow, this is *cup*. This is . . ." She hesitated, fingering the cool metal. She held it carefully, not wanting Shadow to hurt himself. "This is *knife*. Show-me *knife*."

He leaped forward, and nosed the hand with the letter opener.

"Good-dog!" She handed the objects back through the window. "I want him to generalize objects. No matter the size or shape, they're always cups. Not mugs, or glasses, just cup." She shrugged. "Could get fancy and add colors, the ones dogs see anyway—blue cup, yellow ball, green Frisbee—but at this point I don't want to confuse him."

Shadow woofed. He stared hard, probably willing her to produce the Frisbee. "Sorry, baby-dog, that wasn't nice of me, I shouldn't tease the dog." She scratched the top of his head and he tipped it sideways and pressed into the satisfying scratch.

Anita took the items, her blue highlights waving. "So now he'll identify any letter opener as a knife?" She dropped it back into the drawer.

"You got it. He already knows *knife*. I don't want to confuse him using terms like dagger or machete or butter knife."

He wasn't suited for Schutzund work—the type of training typical of police and protection dogs—and September wasn't interested in training an attack dog. During his temperament tests at seven weeks old, Shadow's breeder chose him as the best suited of his litter to be a service dog. He needed to have a confident but biddable, loyal and focused personality to partner with an autistic child like Steven, and bite-work had never been in his future. Dogs trained to help those suffering from PTSD often were expected by their human partners to offer warnings of perceived or imagined threats. But protection training wasn't necessary. The bond between human and dog partners grew so strong that feeling protective of each other happened as a byproduct of their love.

Even protection trained canines like Dakota weren't super-dogs. She wanted Shadow to know enough to alert her and protect them both, but not so much that he'd rush in and get himself killed.

It had taken every bit of courage to open her heart to another dog after Dakota died with Chris. Caring so much, loving so deeply opened the heart to future hurt. So much safer for her to keep others at a distance. Safer for them, too.

The phone rang, and Anita adjusted her headset on her blue-striped locks before her accent disappeared and she morphed into her husky-voiced alter-ego. She beckoned September closer and pointed at the door, pressing a hidden button to unlatch it. "Go on in. Maybe if he sees you, Fish will get the hint." She punched the phone line. "WZPP, you've reached ZAP105 FM Radio, home of THE Humphrey Fish, bringing you easy-listening 24/7 with the best Fish Stories. How may I direct your call?"

September held the door for Shadow. She hadn't bothered to switch to the short six-foot leash, and had to stoop to reel in the long tracking line before it got caught. Anita winked as they walked by, and tossed a treat that Shadow snapped out of the air and gulped in one graceful motion. September laughed when Anita lobbed a second treat at the end of the hall. "You're spoiling my dog." But she dropped the line, said, "Okay!" and he bounded after the prize.

Anita hung up the phone. "Spoiling them, that's what dogs are for."

"That's my line." Laughing, September hurried after the pup to the glass-walled studio of the radio station.

The red "on air" light over the outside of the door was off. A dorky headphone-wearing young man straddled a tall bar stool while he fiddled with the controls on the U-shaped bank of controls that surrounded him. Fish stood behind the engineer's shoulder, making notes on a computer tablet. He saw her and visibly tried to stand taller and suck in his pear-shaped abdomen. It didn't help.

She opened the door but didn't want to go inside. Fish had a history of ambush-interviews, telling visitors mics were off when in reality they were hot and broadcasting. When Fish saw Shadow, his hopeful expression shuttered to a scowl. "We'll wait till you're done." September let the door swing closed.

Fish tucked the tablet under his arm and strutted to the door. "It's about time. Are you allergic to returning phone calls?" The petulance turned his bass voice into a cartoon.

"I told you, I'm done with radio."

He wilted, and then brushed by her, swerving to avoid contact with Shadow's inquisitive nose. "You mean you're done with me? Then we've got nothing to talk about."

"Humphrey, don't be that way. I appreciated you giving me the Pet Peeves spot. But I don't need it anymore."

He whirled. "Did you ever think maybe *I* needed it?" Two bright spots of color sat high on his cheeks, and he blinked hard. "Might as well bury me now. My life is over."

Was he crying? Humphrey Fish, king of his little fiefdom, overnight sensation, needed her? Before she could ask, he turned away and entered one of the small offices at the end of the hall. She followed, catching up Shadow's leash to prevent the pup from returning to Anita-the-treat-dispenser.

The short man walked around his desk, keeping his back to September when she followed and shut the door. He stared out the small window.

"Why in the world do you need me?" Shadow dropped his nose to the carpet and began vacuuming crumbs. She wrinkled her nose. The place smelled of stale French fries and something sour. Fish was a pig. "You're the radio king, flying high after saving the day. Like the ad says; *all the best Fish Stories*. Right?

"Don't be catty." He turned around, eyes hard. "What'd I do to get kicked to the curb? We had something good, September, good chemistry. You owe me—"

"What? I *owe* you?" Shadow whined and pawed her leg, reacting to her tone. "This place is like a chemistry experiment gone bad. I don't owe you anything." She turned to go. "I *thought* we were friends."

"So did I. When you asked me to help, I was there. But you can't even return my call, and then show up here to rub my face in it."

That stopped her. She hadn't realized how he must feel. "I'm sorry but I can't come back. Holy crap, it was only a stupid five-minute weekly slot." The weirdoes already phoned her with relentless glee, determined to get a rise out of her. "We did have chemistry. You're right. I'm sorry. I should have called and explained."

What made for great local radio banter risked her sanity once it went viral. The national publicity killed her privacy, and opened the door to the past finding her again. She shivered.

"Radio's dead. My career, anyway." His choked words stopped her.

"And Pet Peeves would save your career?" She couldn't help the sarcasm. He had to be joking, playing the victim in the hope for a pity favor.

"Hell, radio's been on oxygen for the past couple of years. Now the owners issued the station a DNR. Unless there's a miracle healing." Fish waved his hands in the air like a televangelist, but quickly dropped the campy imitation. He set the tablet on the desk. "You became a star last month. The station got lots of attention."

"Attempted murder on live radio will do that for you."

Fish winced at her dry tone, but didn't take offense. The little man's usual buoyant personality kept him higher than helium, but he'd deflated into a sad balloon cartoon. "The station owner got some offers. He's going to sell."

She sat down so she wouldn't add insult to injury making him crane to meet her eyes. "But that's good, right?"

"You'd think so." After a moment he sat down, too. "The new owners want to take it to a younger audience. And they're cutting staff. They'd keep *you* as long as your star power lasts, and I figured maybe as a favor you could say we're a package deal." He wiggled his eyebrows and they squirmed like dark caterpillars. "Barring that, I need another killer story, something that knocks their stinkin' socks off. Otherwise I'm gone as of the first of the year."

Her mouth dropped open. "But that's only a couple of weeks. What'll you do?" He'd been the voice of ZAPP for twenty years.

"Make a deal with the devil. Actually, he's not the devil. Maybe one of the devil's minions." He pretended to shudder. "Can't believe I'm so desperate I'd even consider working with the likes of him." He leaned forward over the desk. "Sylvester Sanger brought me a killer story. His editors won't touch it."

"That's hard to believe." Must be a doozy if his sleazy tabloid got cold feet. "That's why I'm here. He came to see me this morning." She scowled. "Did you put him up to that?"

"Yeah. I told him to talk to you, sure. You're the go-to pet person. I figured once you heard his theory, you could tell me if it's a load of fertilizer, or there's something to it." He fell back in the chair after seeing her expression. "You thought it was bogus, huh? Well, that settles it. I'll start packing."

Shadow whined again, and September stroked his brow and immediately her pulse slowed. "I didn't give Sly the chance to say anything. Thought he was someone else, so I went all Babe Ruth on his car." She pantomimed swinging a bat, and when Fish winced, she became defensive. "He deserved it. Ran his car right into my new front gate." It sounded lame when she said it aloud, and she felt ashamed since the man was dead. "Anyway, he mentioned his sick cat had something to do with a story he researched with you. I left Pinkerton at the vet."

"Pinkerton. Good name for an investigator's cat. Not a great writer, but he sure can ferret out the dirt." The old fluorescent lighting flickered, and he pursed his lips. "Damn place is ready to crumble, and the new owners sit on their thumbs." He cleared his throat. "So, why'd he leave Pinkerton with you?"

She paused. Fish wouldn't help unless she met him halfway, and he was already more than a little pissed at her. Better go all in. "Pinkerton slipped out of Sly's car after the accident, and Shadow tracked him."

"Oh, that's right. You're doing that pet tracking deal now. Hope it pays better than radio." He slurped coffee, making a nasty sound. "Sylvester ask you to track Pinkerton? Did he pay you yet? Careful he doesn't stiff you. His job's as precarious as mine."

September took a breath. "He's missing."

"Missing?" He laughed. "That's one way to dodge paying."

"Look, I found his body, okay?"

Fish's mouth dropped open. She could see the wheels begin to turn.

"I didn't realize the car crash was that bad…"

"It wasn't. Someone murdered him." Before he could interrupt further, she rushed on. "Fish, he was dead. I think he was dead." She rubbed her face. "I know he was dead, had to be, with that head injury." She held up a hand to stay his questions. "I called the police, they came to investigate and couldn't find the body." He didn't need to know about the missing baseball bat. She couldn't very well tell Fish about it when Combs remained in the dark.

"Somebody killed him, let a witness see, and then hid the body? That makes no sense."

She shrugged. "Tell me about it. If Shadow hadn't tracked the cat, there'd just be an abandoned car at my gate. Nobody would look for him, at least not right away."

Fish's eyes sparkled with excitement. "He made lots of enemies over the smear journalism he wrote. Nothing to kill him over, though. Unless the new story struck a nerve. Someone wanted to shut him up before he published."

"Exactly." She leaned forward, ticking off items on her fingers. "His cat is sick. Sly's dead. His body disappeared at my house. You sent him to me for help with a sick pet story." She didn't list Macy exposed, sick and at the vet, but couldn't help feeling there must be a connection. "Whoever came after Sly probably thinks I'm involved, too. You made me a target by sending Sly."

He held his hands in a prayerful pose, teasing. "So you need to help me. Work with me. Come on, September, what do you say? We make a good team. You said so yourself."

She'd had enough of high profile publicity and yearned for peaceful anonymity. "No more radio." Before he argued, she added, "But like you said, I owe you. I'll help get you the scoop, if there is one. So tell me what you know. What were you and Sly working on?"

He jumped to his feet, the bounce back in his attitude, and fairly rubbing his hands together with glee. "It's not only pets, September. Not by a long shot."

Chapter 21

Dietz shoved the truck into gear. The tires squealed like a pig and it handled like a rhino in heat. No way to sneak around town in this bad boy, so he had to hope nobody would be home at the behaviorist's house. He hoped Grady had already gotten rid of the reporter's body.

The extended cab truck made Dietz feel like a king on a mountaintop staring down on ant-like traffic. The truck could handle equipment needed for shoots in the field, or serve as a rolling office with his laptop, files and other equipment in the back seat.

But it was a truck. A blood-red truck with a snarling blue feral hog plastered on the door, and flaming *'Hog Hell'* emblazoned the length of each side. The vehicle took up nearly two spaces so he had to park on the street at his apartment. It guzzled so much gas he suspected a hole in the tank. A date would need a ladder to get in.

He'd dreamed of riding in a limo to his triumphant launch where he'd sip champagne or throw back some high-dollar beverage at an exclusive venue. Instead, he'd vroom up to a glorified take-out joint wearing a *Hog Hell* getup complete with ski cap and shit-kicker boots.

He'd choked down disappointment when his acting career cratered. For a time, he'd tried his hand at mentoring other artists, and got kicked in the teeth for his efforts. Writing and directing indie productions kept him busy but frustrated. Like others in his shoes, when unable to pay for top-of-the-line, he'd settled for in-kind trades with other wannabe film pros, yet despite his comatose bank account, Dietz continued to fantasize about awards, invites to the best parties, appearances on Letterman, a home on the beach, and above all, to rub the naysayers' noses in his success. Payback would be sweet.

After years of failures, *Hog Hell* could take him all the way. He'd smile and be gracious at the pig jokes, and proudly wear the stink of "reality show" in exchange for a fat bank account. Money was freedom.

And then the reporter threatened to take it all away. If Felch hadn't killed him, Dietz would have been tempted to arrange a little hunting accident. Now the sweet taste of almost-success soured so much, the thought of the watch party gave him hives.

He couldn't allow September Day to interfere. He'd watched her from a distance, just in case. Always good to keep your friends close and your enemies locked up. Time to put the fear of God into September Day. Make sure she shut the hell up or better yet, left town for good. She'd run before, more than once. After the new season launched, he'd have offers to sell his interest in the show, and get away clean to start new projects.

He drove fifteen minutes before he found the small road sign, and turned right on Rabbit Run Road. The road snaked through brown countryside where only a few scattered houses with ramshackle outbuildings dotted the landscape. At the rise of a small hill, the road pulled a dog-leg turn and sloped downward. Dietz saw the tall gate at the bottom of the curving road. He'd been told that the reporter had run his car into a metal gate. That must be it.

He slowed the truck, hoping to avoid other traffic. His God-awful pig-mobile stuck out bright as a blister. Best to park on the road and walk in, so she didn't discover any connection to the show.

He found a spot a few hundred yards from the entry, pulled off on the shoulder, and stopped. Dietz swung down from the truck cab, gently latched the door, and jogged toward the waiting sedan. He winced. The car's dimpled hood and door panels must have lost a fight with a hailstorm. Golf ball size hail wasn't unusual here in Tornado Alley but these were fresh dings. Maybe Felch had warmed up on the car before going after the reporter.

Dietz adjusted his blue gloves before cranking open the passenger door to the car. The floor to the sedan, littered with candy wrappers and empty fast food containers, smelled rancid and he found no notes on the back seat, under the front seats or in the glove box. His luck, the guy kept everything digital, and that would complicate things.

September wouldn't recognize him, so he could claim to be Sanger's boss. He could do this; he was still a damn good actor. He'd be pissed Sanger wasted her time on a story with no merit. That way he could pump her for what she'd been told, and debunk it at the same time. Yes, that could work.

Dietz jogged down the bricked drive, and circled around to the front, seeing the results of lots of cash. So that's how she'd spent the lottery winnings.

A pair of trucks sat in front of the house, one old and well-worn with a tree logo on the driver's door advertising garden services. The other could have been held together with baling wire and spit, and he wondered how it passed inspection with the exhaust pipe trailing and a rear headlight gone. Before Dietz could make his way past the two trucks, someone approached from the side of the house. Tall and gaunt, shaggy gray hair. Shambling gait. Unwieldy sack balanced on each narrow shoulder. A stained paisley bandanna covering his nose and mouth turned him into a cartoon bandit.

Felch.

Dietz froze in the middle of the drive, and resisted the urge to duck behind something, anything. The tall man had his head down, though, and hadn't yet noticed. Instead he carefully placed his big feet to keep from losing control of either or both of the sacks. He reached the falling apart truck, slouched forward, and shed first one and then the other bag into the truck bed with a muffled thump. White dust poofed in a cloud and immediately settled. It turned the truck's rust to ocher.

Felch straightened, saw Dietz, and stiffened. He held his hands out. "Stay back."

"What're you doing, Felch? Everything okay?" Dietz didn't make a move. He kept his voice calm. Had he already spoken to September? If she knew he and Felch were together, the show was toast. And his future gone.

"Nothing's okay. It's all gone t shit." Felch kept the truck between them. "You clear out of here. I'm trying to clean up, that's all. What ya call it, damage control."

"Where's Grady? He called me, said he's taking care of things. Didn't Grady tell you to go home and chill?"

"Can't remember." Felch's forehead creased and his sunken eyes searched the sky for the missing memory. "It's getting worse, don't you see?" He pulled down the kerchief around his neck and it became his trademark Western accent for the TV show—but it fell flat. "Don't know why I bother with this. Too late, figured it out too late. And now it's too late for that poor sonofabitch back there, too." He flapped one hand toward the house.

"Who?" Dietz took a step toward the man.

"Didn't believe him. But I saw coyotes go loco. Raccoons, too. My cats and deer and hogs and BeeBo's dogs caught it. With critters it's humane to put 'em down, right? And I caught it bad." He rested his head in his hands, and then pounded his temples. "Can't think! Got to do something, got to fix this, got to remember before I disappear." His voice turned to gravel and tears spilled unnoticed as he forced the words past sandpaper lips. "I had me a lady friend once. Love of my life, till she disappeared. If I disappear, too, maybe we'll find each other again."

Dietz's mouth tasted like he'd chewed cotton. "Uh, right. Whatever you say." They were screwed, they were absolutely screwed and ruined and going to jail if he couldn't get this nut-job the hell out of sight. He took another step toward the man. Where the hell was Grady, anyway?

"No! Stay away!" Felch pounded his head again. "If I can remember how to get her back, I know she'll keep me from disappearing. Ain't that right, Grady?"

Dietz started when Grady appeared, dragging another sack along the drive. "Whatever you say, Felch. You're the boss, the star of this drama." He nodded pointedly at Dietz and held a finger to his lips. "This is the last one, need some help here." He whispered to Dietz, "We're fine. Nobody's here, and I got all the reporter's notes from his car before I grabbed the body. But we have to work fast." He raised his voice to add, "Move that out of the way first, will you?"

Dietz grabbed one end of the baseball bat and tossed it to the other side of the truck. He bent to catch one end of the sack, Felch supported the sagging middle, and the three of them lifted and slung it into the battered truck. In the bed of the truck Dietz saw stacks of gunnysacks with white powder spilling out, cardboard boxes of fabric-wrapped objects, a rolled up rug, and even some sort of guitar case. "Moving day?" He grinned.

"It's your plan. Scare her off. Take a few things special to her, items she'd never leave behind. Just having someone poke around her house should make her run." Grady's tight sweater showed off an impressive six-pack before he zipped up his coat.

Dietz brushed white powder off his hands and sneezed. "What you got in that thing? Must weigh a couple hundred pounds."

"Get in the truck, Felch." Grady waited until the fellow had clambered into the passenger side and managed to shut the door, and then turned to Dietz. "Got back here too late."

Dietz felt a chill. "Too late for what?"

Grady shook his head. "Felch had a breakdown. You saw it. All I could do was clean up once I got here. Or did you want me to call the cops after all?"

"No, you said you'd handle it." He paced away from Grady, and back again. He should never have come. Now he'd been at the scene, maybe left incriminating evidence. "What's in that bag?"

"You don't want to know. I'll take care of it. Nobody will be the wiser."

"Christ! I want out of this." Dietz jammed his hands into his pockets to keep from punching something. "I'm making calls soon as I get back to the office. And I'm taking the first offer and selling this god-forsaken show. Take a loss if need be. But getting out from under." He whirled and started back through the gate.

Felch's ramshackle truck started with a grumbling roar, circled around the gardener's truck and drew abreast Dietz as he stomped back up Rabbit Run

Road toward his monstrosity of a truck. Grady cranked down the driver's side window. "You won't sell the show."

"The hell I won't." Dietz kept walking.

"You forget. I'm part owner now."

Dietz stopped, and the truck stopped with him. Felch faced the passenger side window, head turned away with his forehead pressed against the glass.

Grady smiled, a bright sickly expression without humor. "Mr. Felch and I will dispose of our *problems*." He jerked his head to indicate what now rested in the bed of the truck. "I will see you back at the office, where you will have drawn up a legal agreement making me full partner in everything to do with *Hog Hell*." He held up a hand to stem any protests. "That show is my way out of limbo. Yours, too. Trust me."

"Do I have a choice?"

"See you back at the office. *Partner.*" Grady gunned the engine, and was gone.

Chapter 22

Shadow fidgeted in the back seat of the car. It had been an eventful day and he yawned loud and long.

In the front seat, September made the car go, turning the wheel this way and that, while peering at him in the mirror now and then. Each time their eyes met, he beat his tail on the soft throw that covered the car seat. He couldn't help it. Looking at her made his chest thump faster. Maybe his tail was connected to that thump-place in his chest?

She'd told him "good-dog" many times when he found the dog and lady. The Teddy-man did, too, and patted his head but only for a minute before he took the lady inside. Shadow wanted to play with the other dog—they called her Trixie—but he could tell Trixie wanted to stay with Teddy's lady. He understood. That other dog fretted about Teddy's lady the way Shadow worried about September.

He worried about September sometimes, too. Earlier when they'd been in the car together, she'd grabbed and squeezed him hard, but not to wrestle-fight the way dogs do. Instead she shook and trembled, raining tears and spilling acrid fear-stink that made him wrinkle his nose. He stayed still and quiet, licking her face to show he meant no harm until her breathing quieted and she pretended to be all right.

But it was pretend. A good-dog knew the difference.

"Tired? Ready to go home?" She met his eyes in the mirror again and smiled.

He thwacked his tail. The tension in her voice had faded and her shoulders relaxed. He turned and lifted his nose to the window where wind blew through the crack. Most of the fear-stink washed away in the cold air but some clung to his fur where she'd grabbed him. He shook his head, flapping his ears hard, and breathed deeply to clean the stink from his nostrils. Shadow liked sticking his nose out the window, liked to drink sips of the many smell-flavors they drove through as they sped along the car path.

Cars stayed on these paths and never veered off. Well, mostly. Sometimes cars got confused. He sniffed hard again as September slowed and turned the wheel to the driveway. She stopped and stared for a moment at the stranger's car squashed against the gate.

Turning from the window, he pushed his nose through the grill barrier, as much as would reach, to get a closer sniff of where Macy had rested on the front passenger seat. He was confused by much of the cat's behavior, but September cared about Macy, maybe as much as she cared about Shadow. Even if Macy paw-swatted a good-dog's nose for trying to get a sniff, Shadow didn't like having his cat gone. He wondered why September had left Macy at the clinic. Why didn't Shadow get to go inside? The people inside always gave him treats.

He wondered if Macy got treats, too. He'd like a treat now. Maybe he'd get a treat when they went back into the house. Shadow licked his lips.

"I can't get my gate fixed until the police tow Sly's car." She made the car go again, and they drove into the big building where the car slept when they didn't use it. Shadow woofed. He didn't know what she said, but it seemed polite to talk back when she spoke to him. She talked to him a lot, and he only understood some of it. People knew lots more than dogs. September was always right. Well, almost always.

He waited impatiently for her to climbed out and open his door. For a moment he thought she might leave him to wait in the car again, and he yelped and pawed the door. The window smoothly scrolled down, and he happily stuck his head and chest out of the opening.

"Crap! Shadow, wait." She hurried to open his door before he managed to climb out on his own. He'd done that before, and didn't understand why she objected.

"You're too darn smart. Forgot to engage the child-lock on the windows." Her voice scolded but she couldn't hide her smile so Shadow knew she wasn't mad. He hopped out, and offered a butt-high invitation to play. "Go on, big guy. I'll meet you at the door."

He bounded away, taking advantage of the opportunity to sniff the area. The garage smelled of small furry creatures tucked away in shadowed nests. Nothing new there. Shadow dashed through the double barn doors, and despite her permission to forge ahead, he waited for September. She got nervous if they were apart, and that made Shadow feel funny, too. So instead, he pretended to sniff the pavement until she made the big doors slide closed.

The usual sounds and smells filled his world. Fresh cut and burned cedar—the gardener had cleared the scrubby trees behind the house. A coyote. Sick raccoon. Shadow wrinkled his nose and wanted to investigate but wouldn't leave September.

Metal creaked and squealed from the swivel atop the car house, screaming like an angry Macy. And something else. He lifted his nose from the spore and paused, waited until the wind shifted. The several sets of toys hung all around the house echoed in bongs, chimes and cricket-chirp pitches, some glittery like shattered ice falling to the ground. In the *show-me* game, September named them 'wind chimes.'

"Shadow, let's go." September stood beside him, tapping her foot and swept a gloved hand toward the front door.

There! Floating on the wind, now strong and then gone, but definitely there. A familiar scent, from the back garden, Aaron the gardener again. But different. He growled, his notched ear twitching with sense memory, and his hackles rose. He pressed against September's legs, putting himself between her and the smell.

Blood. Lots and lots of blood.

Chapter 23

September took a step backwards. Shadow's rumbled growl shook his fur. He never growled, except when playing tug with Bear-toy. His tail carved a scimitar in the air above his back, jerking back and forth while his head lowered, pointing toward the back of the house.

"Is anyone there? Aaron?" His truck was still here. September kept one hand on Shadow's neck, and could feel his slight trembling.

A loud screech made her jump, and she ducked and then half laughed when she looked up and saw the rusty weather vane swinging in the wind. The dozen or so wind chimes that hung every six feet around the house played a clanging concert.

She'd hung the chimes for several reasons. The sound helped identify her home with a distinct sound for both Shadow and Macy, to help them find their way home, just in case either got out. The low hangers also doubled as early warnings of intruders if someone ran into them in the dark. And finally, she liked the sound.

Combs questioning what she'd seen irked her no end. It scared her, too. The police should have found some evidence of the attack—tracks, blood, something—even if the body was gone. At least they'd treated Sly's car like evidence and designated the field a crime scene, so they hadn't totally discounted her story. Someone had been very careful if they'd found nothing. She took a breath and had to consciously relax her jaw, and flexed her neck to shake off residual nerves.

Shadow must be feeding into her emotions. They tuned into each other in the same way she'd known Macy was in trouble, and sometimes September thought they could almost read each other's mind. She'd been so much better the past weeks, but today, nothing had gone right. Two steps forward, and three back. Crap, she hated PTSD. Sometimes she hated her life.

Stop. Suck it up, sweetheart. Nobody said life was supposed to be easy, and she had Shadow and Macy counting on her to hold things together.

"I'm okay, baby-dog." If she said it enough, she'd start to believe it, and that could make it so. "For I wish it to be so. Let's go in." She nudged him with her knee, and pushed past on her way to the house.

At the door, she gave the command. "Shadow, *check it out.*" It had become a habit, to send Shadow into the house ahead of her after they'd been gone. Usually he used the exercise to flush Macy from nap time. He'd never found anyone in the house. But no matter how much better she got, September couldn't bring herself to go in until Shadow "woofed" the all clear.

By the time she'd keyed open the last deadbolt, Shadow was tap dancing with impatience. September swung open the door and he didn't wait for her to repeat the command. He burst into the entry, nails scrabbling for purchase on the slick wood, and leaped without hesitation into the living room. Growls and barks exploded, echoing in the high ceilinged space.

September froze. This was a first. She didn't move, scanning the rooms from her vantage in the open door, poised to backpedal and race to her car. She dug in her coat pocket for her phone. Combs was on speed dial.

Shadow quieted only long enough to thoroughly nose the area immediately to her right, beside the entry. Then he whirled, raced back across the hardwood into the office-music room and again put on the brakes as he kept his nose to the floor. Nobody here, or he would have already flushed them out, but she yelled anyway.

"I'm calling the police." She yelled, proud her voice didn't shake. "Better clear out before my dog nails you." Shadow wouldn't bite without a good cause, but the intruder wouldn't know that.

She heard no reply. Heard nothing but Shadow's snorts and low growls, and then the dog returned to her, huffing and whining. He pushed his head beneath her hand for a pet, his signal for 'all clear.' Although his hackles stayed raised, his loose tail wags and forward-pointing ears showed no immediate threat. She clutched the phone and took a careful step to follow him into the room and recoiled. Someone had been here.

Melody—her cello—was gone.

"Oh, no." She wanted to weep. Other items had disappeared. A sob hiccuped in her throat with the aching absence of the small Persian carpet, one she'd chosen during her exile in Chicago. She'd painted the jewel blue ceiling to match, and now the room appeared top-heavy without the balance of reds, blues and greens covering the floor.

Another empty spot shouted the absence of the stained glass desk lamp Mark had made as a going away present when she first left home at sixteen. The wall above also looked bare—the Eichenberg wood engraving, "The Peaceable Kingdom" was gone, a gift from her father to celebrate Macy's adoption.

A stupid burglar. A robbery. Fear bled away, replaced with anger. He'd chosen only those things with special meaning for her, and left behind the desktop computer, CD player and other impersonal items. She wouldn't cry, she wouldn't. That gave the jerk power over her.

Shadow hurried to nose her, and shoved his head beneath her hand to force a pet. She smoothed his ears. "The perfect end to a crappiocca day. Anything else?" His hackles had smoothed, telling her the house held no strangers, only their scents.

He woofed, and bounded into the adjoining kitchen and she slowly followed, noting the kitchen door stood ajar. "Dammit." Combs knew better, so did Aaron. They'd blame themselves and probably offer to pay for everything, even though neither could afford it. Besides, nothing could replace such personal items any more than a new kitten would make up for Macy. *Don't even think that.* She jerked the door the rest of the way open, ducked to dodge one of the wind chimes, and hurried to follow Shadow when he raced to the garden gate. It also stood open.

Aaron had been back and forth from his truck to the garden all frickin' day. She strode through the garden gate with mounting anger, ready to chew him out and her brother be damned. Noticing the white powder on the walkway that needed to be swept up, she added that to her list of complaints. He knew how she felt about security.

September fought through the overgrown roses, following Shadow as closely as she could. He'd traded growls for whines, and kept his ears flat, clearly concerned. He could duck beneath the worst of it, while her legs and ankles caught thorns the jeans couldn't thwart. She stumbled to keep from tripping.

She floundered into a small clearing at the back of the garden, breathing heavily. "Aaron?" No answer. And no big man wielding tools. Hard to hide someone his size.

"C'mon, baby-dog. Let's go inside, and call the police. Again." She turned and fought for several steps back through the vegetation before noticing Shadow lurking in one corner of the cleared space. "Shadow, let's go." He ignored her, nose to the ground, and finally lifted his head and howled.

"What the..." She hurried to his side. "Shadow, what's going on?"

He pawed her leg, whimpering. His paw left a blood smear on her light colored jeans.

The wind died for a moment, and September smelled it, too. Coppery.

Cloying. Oh God, she'd know that smell anywhere. With a trembling hand, she reached down to touch the still damp earth, warmer than the weather should allow, and stared at her crimsoned fingers.

She recoiled, falling backwards on her butt in the soiled earth. From her new perspective, furrows in the gore-soaked soil marked the path the big man must have been dragged. Shadow leaped around her, whimpering and barking until she managed to scramble upright. She raced back to the house, ignoring torn shins and thighs, scanning for shadowy figures and prepared to fight them off should they leap from the scraggly shrubs.

The house, she had to get back into the house, lock the doors. And call Combs, who cares what he thinks. She tried to speed dial her phone but dropped it into thorny undergrowth. Sobbing with frustration, she left it behind.

Shadow beat her into the house and whirled, tail wagging a frenetic tempo and barked with excitement as she slammed the kitchen door and struggled to shoot the lock. September whirled, ready to race to the front door and secure her stronghold. That first, before calling the police.

The sight of the beribboned package, now open on the center of the kitchen's stained glass table, stopped her dead. A card lay inside the box of carefully arranged clusters of tiny blue flowers. Forget-Me-Not blossoms.

September whimpered. Her knees turned to rubber. "Please God, no."

She didn't need to read the card, didn't care what it said, she knew Sly had lied. The package wasn't from the reporter. It was from her past. The simple message, on a cheesy anniversary card, spelled out the *why* in blood-red block letters:

Payback.

Chapter 24

Combs cursed under his breath. Late again. September expected him a half hour ago. He'd tried to call, but her phone kept going to voicemail. That bothered him. She never went anywhere without her cell phone. Last month, that had saved her life.

No matter how much he planned, Combs always ran out of time. Not on the job, that was different, and partly why his private life came last. He knew she'd been screening calls on the business line to avoid the sickos badgering her over her fifteen minutes of fame from last month. But she wouldn't answer her cell, either.

It had taken him a long time to get her to agree to this "not-a-date" as she insisted on calling it. The earlier visit with Gonzales might have been too much deja vu for her. She saw threats in the shadows. Not good, not good at all. He liked her too much, wanted more for her, than hiding from the world.

He didn't think she'd told anyone the whole story about her stalker, certainly not him, and not even her family. Last month during the Blizzard Murders he'd found out more about her past than she'd want him to know, and out of respect he'd not pressed her for details. But Combs understood why September kept relationships at a distance. Besides, the circumstances when they'd met were hardly conducive to dating. He hoped someday September would trust him enough to share her burden. That's what friends were for.

Combs was ready to move on from his divorce. The internal affairs investigation that derailed his career had been the final straw, but to be honest, his marriage with Cassie hadn't been healthy for a long time. He'd been so angry and defensive at the injustice of it all that he'd had no interest in dating again. How ironic that the horror that introduced him to September also ultimately caused the Department to reinstate him.

He switched on the turn signal for Rabbit Run Road, and waited for a huge flame-red truck to pass. He hoped September's failure to answer the phone meant she was pissed he'd questioned her story about Sly's body. Combs saluted the truck driver, and made his turn.

The gate stood sentry at the bottom of the twisty road. Sly's car still squatted like a crushed bug against the gate, ready to be towed as soon as the department got the chance. They'd found nothing in the car to suggest any reason for his disappearance, and canvassing local hospitals had produced nothing. The crime scene in the field had been processed, and a few blood samples collected, but it would take time to know if the evidence would help.

Once he got out of his car, Combs grabbed the carton of cold beer, skirted the gardener's truck and headed for the front door. His steps slowed when he realized no downstairs lights brightened the interior of the house. And the front door stood ajar.

He fell back two steps, dropped the beer and drew his gun. Combs dug the cell phone out of his pocket to call for backup. He hesitated, and instead dialed September's number again.

Combs heard the phone inside the house ring, ring, ring, ring, before the machine clicked on. He disconnected, and once more approached the front door, slowly climbed the steps and pushed the door open with his foot, screening himself as best he could by standing next to the door but away from the leaded glass sidelights.

"September? You there?" His cop voice switched on with sharp authority. "This is the police. Show yourself."

No answer.

He quickly entered low, stopped on the wooden entry and swept the room from side to side with his gun at the ready. Down two steps and to the right, the living room area with adjoining dining room stood empty. The table's place settings for two was a nose-thumb jab at the evening that apparently wouldn't happen.

To the left, September's music/office space was different, something was off—and then he saw it. The carpet was bare, a bright throw rug missing from the room.

"September? Where are you?" He took the steps to the left at a near run. Items were missing. He couldn't pinpoint the changes. But not a burglary.

The expensive computer equipment hadn't been touched. Something else. Like she'd packed away items or rearranged the furniture.

"What the hell?" He holstered his gun and scratched his head. He noticed the bunch of blue flowers on the stained glass kitchen table, probably for a centerpiece for their dinner. Maybe she considered it was more of a date than she'd wanted to admit. The dinner table settings said she'd planned to be here, so her absence must be unexpected.

That's right, she'd been in a rush to take Macy to the vet. The pets won over dinner with him, paws down. "Some date." More disappointment than anger made him wince. It'd been years since he'd been stood up. "Guess I'd better get used to it." Thank God he'd not called Gonzales for backup after all. The man would never let him hear the end of it.

Combs headed back to the front door to collect his beer and stopped short at the sight of the gardener's truck. Aaron seemed scattered earlier during his questioning, but that happened when people talked to the police. Nothing like a cold one to get a guy to talk. He took two, and popped the top on one can as he walked, wishing he understood women better.

His face smacked into the seashell wind chimes hung at head level directly outside the door. "Bastard!" Combs made a point to dodge the others, and rubbed one eye that got nailed.

A fine white powder dribbled a path along the paved walkway from the front drive to the back garden entrance. Before Combs pushed open the metal garden gate, he stooped closer and touched some of the powder to his glove. It coated the fabric, almost like talcum. He stood, noting the trail led beyond the gate into the garden proper. A new trail had been torn through the weedy overgrowth. He could see why September wanted to get a handle on the mess. It was a far cry from the rose arboretum the place used to boast.

The old house was a landmark as a showplace until it fell into disrepair. They'd called it a haunted house when they were kids. He remembered lobbing stones to crash windows, ashamed to have broken into the place with other high schoolers to smoke and drink beer out of sight of their parents. September hadn't been part of that crowd, though.

For the past dozen years, the place stood vacant until September came back home, bought it and began renovations. Complete with triple locks that even the gardener should know to keep latched.

The hairs stood on the back of his neck. He couldn't see any movement. "Hey, is anyone there? Aaron Stonebridge, this is the police!" He pushed through the fresh path, holding the beer away from wicked thorns that grappled his pant legs to trip him up.

When he broke through into a cleared spot at the back of the fenced enclosure, he saw nothing and no one. The ground had been plowed and then raked. A towering stack of dried cuttings piled against the fence spilled to the other side where dead roses and other vegetation had been dug out by the roots. Dozens of blackbirds played hopscotch inside the prickly bundle, tree lice colonizing the dead and probably debating the merits of nest building within thorny protection.

"Hello?" He called once more, turning 360-degrees to capture any human motion. He idly wondered if any of the old roses were worth saving, or if all would be discarded and new ones planted. Somehow, the thought made him sad. The old house's garden was a reminder of his childhood.

As he trudged back through the weeds he pulled out his cell to try September one last time. When her phone rang, he heard an odd echoing ring-tone nearby. After three rings it stopped, going to voicemail, and Combs canceled the call and immediately re-dialed, this time standing still and cocking his head.

There! He dropped the beer and hurried back the way he'd come. Combs had to dial a third time and listen before he was able to pinpoint the source of the ring-tone. He knelt in the mud, reached through the undergrowth and pulled out September's ringing cell phone.

Chapter 25

September drove aimlessly. For the first time in memory she'd run out of the house without latching or locking the door. Hadn't even bothered to pack.

She'd been careless, let down her guard. He'd been in her house. He could have killed Shadow, done with her what he wanted. Security be damned, he could reach her anytime, anywhere. She was at his mercy.

What could she do? Nothing. Nothing at all. She couldn't even call for help. The loss of her cell phone plunged her back into the helpless void she'd left behind eight years ago. The flowers, the message, all brought into focus the hell she'd escaped and hoped never to see again.

Victor Grant. Or whatever the chameleon called himself today. He sucked you in, became what you wanted and only then shed his mask to play snake to your mouse. September shuddered. Her wrists and ankles throbbed with the memory of the restraints—that, and what came after.

Publicly, Victor lamented her "nervous breakdown" while gloating how grateful her parents were for his care and protection, his superb mentoring of her career. Weeks locked away schooled her in what he expected. She learned not to fight. She learned to please him. And she learned to despise herself, loathed herself even more than the monster. September believed him, knew it must be her destiny, that she owed him everything. She never doubted he'd hurt her family. That she had no choice.

Shadow's whimper brought September back to the present. She reached through the pet gate to stroke his face, but this time not even Shadow's touch helped.

Victor had found her. He wanted her to worry, wonder what he'd do, guess whom he'd hurt next. She choked on a sob. She couldn't ask the police for help without Combs finding out. He'd try to help and end up a target, like Chris. Everyone she touched, anyone who got close to her, was in the line of fire. Nobody in her family would expect danger from dear old "Uncle Vic." After all this time, nobody would believe her if she raised the alarm. By staying silent for eight years, she'd given Victor even more power.

She should never have come home. It would have been better to disappear without a trace. For a moment, her eyes pricked, and she pushed away the feelings. She'd been right to keep Combs at arm's length.

She had to get Macy. Her breath quickened. Victor knew she had a cat, probably knew about Shadow. Victor knew the best way to hurt her. The pets would be his first targets, just as he'd focused on Dakota.

If she could, she'd hide them away but Victor would find a way. The crippling thought of separation from Shadow or Macy made her throat ache. No! They were her family; they'd stay together, no matter what. She'd already lost too much because of Victor. She wouldn't give them up, too.

God, her head hurt! Glancing in the mirror for vehicles, she worried that Victor might be on her tail. Two copies of Fish's file, a copy of Sly's research, sat on the passenger seat. She'd made an extra copy to share with Combs and hadn't told Fish. He'd hate the police 'scooping' his story, but saving lives—including his—trumped any job.

Victor changed everything. He'd expect her to run.

To run meant Victor won.

Stay, and she risked everything.

September pounded a fist on the steering wheel. "Shadow, I'm not letting him win. Not this time."

She'd stay. Victor's sudden appearance the same morning Sly disappeared couldn't be a coincidence, there had to be a connection. Blowing the whistle on a potential epidemic could save lives. She owed it to the animals, to the pet owners, and the people who might also be affected. Besides, September had little she truly cherished, other than her pets, but she always kept her word. Somehow she'd help Fish investigate and find the proof to break his story. More than that, she owed it to Teddy and his wife Molly.

She slowed and stopped at the light, knee jittering with eagerness to move. The roadway remained clear. To reach the clinic and pick up Macy, she should turn right. If they called her to get him, she wouldn't know. "What should we do, baby-dog?" Shadow woofed, and his tail thumped the back seat. September adjusted the mirror to see him more clearly. He still wore the tracking harness from finding Molly.

"Teddy! Of course." The light changed, and September swung left and headed toward the man's house. He might not be home yet from the nursing home. She'd been saddened by Molly's condition, but because of it, Teddy was the perfect person to connect with Fish's investigation, and find the connection to Victor, too. Teddy could be a bulldog when he devoted his mind to a cause, and his computer-hacking skills should cut down any time needed to dig out juicy pieces that mattered.

The fifteen minutes it took for September to reach Teddy's comfortably shabby ranch house felt like hours. The crick in her neck from straining to watch all directions at once made her back ache, and she flexed and arched her spine until it popped. She pulled into his narrow drive. The closed garage door and light in the front living room indicated he was home.

September checked both ways, but none of the other houses in the neighborhood showed activity. Quickly she gathered one copy of Fish's file, and raced Shadow to Teddy's front door. She rang the bell, and danced from foot to foot, craning to see over her shoulder until the old man opened the door.

"September, what're you doing—" Teddy's mouth made an "O" of surprise when she pushed past him into the house. "Don't let me get in the way," he said, offering a sweeping bow to punctuate the sarcasm. "Hey, big fella. How's the super-pup?" He shut the door and offered his hand to the dog to sniff, followed with a chin scratch that Shadow clearly enjoyed.

"Sorry for coming without notice. I lost my phone, happened to be in the neighborhood..." She hesitated at his puzzled expression.

"My house is not in your neighborhood. And I saw you today, so I can't think this is a social call. By the way, thanks again for helping with Molly."

"How is she?" September followed him into the living room, fell into the squishy sofa cushions and scooted to make room for Shadow when he climbed up beside her. She crossed her legs, and when Teddy stared at her jigging boot she uncrossed them. She leaned forward with elbows on her knees. That also gave her a view of the front window. It was all she could do to keep from jumping up to close the curtains from prying eyes. A cloud of blackbirds fluttered onto the front lawn to graze for whatever buggy morsels they preferred.

"Molly is sometimes here and other times not. Today was a "not" day." He settled in the big La-Z-Boy that had clearly seen better days. "Very agitated. Kept saying somebody poisoned her. Frantic to keep *Rocky*—the dog we used to have—from being poisoned, too." He took off his wire-rimmed glasses and rubbed his eyes. "She confuses Trixie with our old dog. But at least we found Molly before she got too cold, got her cleaned up and settled. Trixie helped a lot; Molly loves that dog." He cleared his throat. "Sometimes I wonder if old Rocky didn't look down from doggy heaven and send us Trixie, they're so much alike."

"I thought you had a German Shepherd." September let him talk, giving herself time to figure out how to ask him for help.

"Yes, that's when we were first married. The dog of our youth. Lots of dogs between him and Rocky. We adopted Rocky for our thirty-fifth anniversary from a rescue group. He was already seven when we got him. At our age, we didn't want to deal with a puppy, and knew he'd probably be our last dog. Can't imagine why he lost his home, he was as close to perfect as a dog could be. Something special about those old guys. Rocky used to help Molly with the housework, picking up, collecting bits of trash or stray socks from the laundry. Should have seen him Christmas morning, all that stray wrapping paper liked to drive him nuts." The memories transformed his face to a peaceful glow. "Now Trixie does the same thing when she picks up stray socks or towels or stuffed toys at the nursing home, what Alison called thievery. I think Trixie wants things neat, especially herself. That dog loves getting spiffed up, coat groomed, nails done." He laughed. "Molly calls it Trixie's spa day. Never knew a dog to sit still for having her teeth brushed. She's calmer around Trixie, always more willing to talk to the dog than anyone else, even me." He brushed off the hurt, reconciled.

At the word "dog" Shadow raised his head and thumped his tail, and Teddy smiled. "You're a good-dog too." He polished his glasses on the hem of his yellow sweater and put them back on before he turned to September. "What's this about?" He blinked pointedly at the stack of papers she'd set on the coffee table.

She could stand it no longer and jumped up, crossed the room in three long strides and swished the curtains closed over the window before turning back to him. "This morning I had a visit from Sylvester Sanger." She indicated the folder of loose pages on the table. "He'd been working with Humphrey Fish," she returned to the sofa and sat down, "on an investigative report involving sick animals. Pets, wildlife. And maybe people, too."

"Okay." He shrugged. "And this matters to me, why?" He glanced at Shadow, and the pup yawned and panted gently. "Is Shadow sick? Or the cat?" His neck wattle turned rosy with concern.

"No." She shivered, and prayed she wasn't lying. "Well, Macy is at Doc Eugene's."

He eyeballed her. "Isn't he the husband of that tracking woman? Your friend killed last month? He's your vet?"

"Pam, yes. A lot of people got hurt. Pam was Shadow's breeder, so Doc Eugene was the vet of record. I hadn't found anyone else since moving here, so . . ." She shrugged. "Anyway, Macy's sick but it's not related to Sly's investigation. The doctor ran some tests and should know more soon."

"That's too bad." He stared at her, lips tight, and said nothing else for a long moment until she began to fidget. "You going to tell me about the investigation?" He finally stood up. "Or are we going to sit and stare at each other?"

"Yes. I mean no. Crap, Teddy, I'm tripping all over myself, but this could be important." She bit her lip to stop its trembling. "Guess I'm more worried about Macy than I thought." At least that part was true. She took a breath, grabbed the folder, and opened it. "I need your help on a project, something I promised to help Fish out with. There's nobody better at digging out the facts than you."

He blinked. "You're laying it on a little thick, my dear. Be straight with me. What've you got yourself into *this time?*" He underlined the last two words, but smiled, and took the file she handed him. He probably thought nothing could be as bad as the events that first brought them together. She hoped he was right.

"Okay, here's the Cliff's Notes version, but I'm sure there's more detail in the file." She cleared her throat. "Critters are sick. Wildlife first, and now pets. It's like they're aging super-fast, and going senile. But it's not only the old cats and dogs. I mean, that can be a normal part of aging." She hesitated, and then added, "Really old dogs and some cats develop cognitive dysfunction. Similar brain changes, with amyloid deposits, as in people diagnosed with Alzheimer's disease."

Teddy carefully closed the file in his lap, and placed both hands on the cover. "Why me? What does this have to do with me? I don't have pets. Not anymore." The quaver in his voice said he already knew, but wanted her to put it on the table.

"Fish says people are getting sick, too." She had trouble meeting his eyes, and hurried on. "He could be full of it. You know how Fish loves those hand-waving kinds of stories. People who don't have pets also are affected, so there must be something else in common."

He stroked the file but didn't open it. "What sort of symptoms?" He closed his eyes.

"Forgetfulness, losing things. Mood and personality changes. Problems completing familiar tasks. Confusion about what time it is, or where they are."

"Like Molly." He blinked down at the file in his lap. "She's younger than me, you know. The doctors say it's progressing a lot faster than normal. Whatever 'normal' is." He didn't hide his bitterness.

She leaned forward. "Fish says it affects younger folks, too. And Sylvester Sanger disappeared after investigating the story for Fish." She pointed to Fish's file in Teddy's lap. "He started getting calls to his radio show, and kept track. Fish said it's almost night-and-day with some of the people, some way younger than Molly. He thinks the medical community hasn't picked up on it yet because the cases are too scattered, and symptoms too similar to Alzheimer's. So when Sly called him having already done some legwork, he decided to investigate further and sent the reporter to me. Fish thinks it's something different, it happens so fast. "

Like Aaron. The thought shocked her. Aaron had struggled with his memory for several weeks now. Mark laughed it off at first, and later grew

concerned. But he said Aaron was in denial, and refused to see a doctor. She'd
noticed Aaron's vague behavior this morning. Now Aaron had disappeared,
just like Sly. "There's a man named Victor Grant. He's involved somehow
with Sly's disappearance. I'm sure of it. This can't wait. Can you help?"

Teddy stared for a long moment at the folder, but still made no attempt
to open it. Finally he said, "I'll see what I can find out."

"Great, thanks! I've got to go get Macy, but I'll be right back." A pulse
throbbed at his temple, and September worried she'd upset him too much.
"Are you okay?"

"Just peachy." He breathed heavily. "You've implied that my wife's
Alzheimer's could instead be caused by some weird brain-frying zoonosis
spread by wild animals and pets. I'm over the moon with delight." He glared
at her, words so soft she had to strain to hear him. "And on top of that, you
dump this on me," he slapped the files in his lap, "and run off to get your
cat? Because you can't be bothered? Because your life is more important than
an old man who only has his dying wife to care about?" He rose, roaring the
last words and brandishing the file like a club.

"That's not what I meant. I don't know—"

"That's right. You *don't* know. And you don't care to find out."

"Teddy, don't be that way. I'm not dumping this on you. I just have to
get Macy first, and I'll be right back. We'll work together." God, this had
been such a mistake, she should never have involved Teddy. He didn't
understand.

*Victor hid her scars beneath long lacy sleeves and flowing floor-length concert skirts,
and she hungered for each public concert, respite from his oppressive presence. Victor escorted
her onstage—having concocted a story of her neediness—but had to wait for her in the
wings while she performed, only returning to collect her during the applause. She reveled in
sharing an intimate musical conversation he couldn't orchestrate. But his threat to hurt
anyone she told—her parents, the other musicians—kept her bound to him as securely as
the ropes he used to punish imagined infractions. She concocted elaborate escape plans but
never dared do more than dream . . .*

She couldn't go back to that. He'd never let her escape again. "Macy's
sick, I have to get him and make sure he's safe."

"Then you better go get him." Teddy strode to the closet, shrugged on
his coat, and grabbed keys off the wall hook. "Lock up when you leave."

"What? Where are you going?" She jumped off the couch, surprised he'd
not raced to his computer to work his magic.

"Where am I going? Where you should have gone. The police." He
scooped up the file and stomped to the door. "I'm not playing amateur sleuth,
not again. Last time it nearly got you killed, and this time Molly . . ." He
stopped abruptly, cleared his throat and opened the door. "You're a terrible
liar, September. You're not telling me something, and I'm not in the mood
to fly blind, not when it's about Molly." The house shook when he slammed
the door.

Chapter 26

Combs wiped clots of mud off September's phone, crumpled the paper towel, and dropped it into the garbage container hidden under her kitchen sink. In the short time he'd known her, she'd never been without her phone. Or her pets.

He hesitated only a moment before scrolling through recent calls. He could apologize later for intruding. September had always been a twitchy rabbit ready to bolt, the fallout of a stalker experience she refused to talk about. Someone so careful about locks and being responsible wouldn't disappear without any explanation. Maybe her phone would offer a clue as to where she'd gone.

The phone logged his own call early that morning, and the one she'd made to 911 that brought him and Gonzales running later that same day.

September had also phoned All Creatures Veterinary Hospital. "That's it," he breathed, and his shoulders relaxed. Quickly, he hit re-dial and waited for the vet hospital to answer.

"September? Did you forget something? Doc Eugene's getting ready to run Macy's tests right now. He should be ready shortly."

The clinic must have caller ID. He'd used September's phone. He hesitated, not sure what to say to the chirpy young man. "I'm a friend of

September's. Is she on her way home?" Combs wondered what was wrong with Macy. Leaving him couldn't have been easy.

"I guess so. She didn't say. We expect her back anytime now. I left her a message on her home phone, too."

"Tell her…" He smiled. "Tell her dinner's almost ready." Combs disconnected. Getting the meal ready would make up for his snooping and help take her mind off Macy's health issues. He started to shut down the phone, but noted her most recent call to the radio station. "Huh. She's talking to Fish again?"

She'd been adamant about quitting the Pet Peeves show, just when her notoriety would make it take off. That burned Fish's butt, especially since September had dodged his calls for weeks. What made her decide to call him? He set aside the phone. Maybe she'd tell him later, but if he asked, she'd know he'd snooped.

He collected the beer cooler, carried it to her refrigerator—she called it 'Macy's Perch'—and loaded up the door with the beverage. Several covered bowls rested inside, each with plastic or foil covers, most small sizes that held a serving for one. He juggled a few, lifted lids, and moved some around. "Leftover, leftover, leftover, salad." He made a face at the last. It had tomatoes. He hated tomatoes. Combs hoped September wouldn't expect him to eat those red, nasty things.

A large covered dish on the bottom rack looked promising. Combs tipped up the foil. "Jackpot!" He carried the deep-dish lasagna, Anita's specialty, to the oven. After debating temperatures and considering the fancy settings for duration, temperatures, bake/broil/who-knows, he made a guess and set the dish inside to heat. Bake-and-eat frozen pizza was his forte.

The blue flowers would soon wilt. She'd taken the trouble to get the bouquet. The least he could do was put them in a vase. Combs rummaged in one of the overhead cupboards, but didn't see anything resembling a vase. She should have bought a vase when she got the flowers. He rinsed out the Son-of-a-Peach coffee mug that sat in the sink and congratulated himself on choosing a silly gift she'd actually use. He filled it with water, and stuck the handful of blossoms in the container before he carried it into the dining room and centered it on the table.

A phone tweedled. Combs searched his pocket, but it wasn't his cell. He hurried back into the kitchen, and caught up September's ringing phone before it went to voicemail. The caller I.D. said it was Mark. Must be her brother. He answered tentatively. He'd met the family only briefly during April's arraignment, and probably was not their favorite person. "Hello?"

"Hi. Um, who's this?" Mark had a pleasant unremarkable voice. "I think I mis-dialed."

"No, wait. This is September's phone. Are you her brother?"

"Yeah. Who're you?" Suspicion clouded his voice. "Let me speak to her."

"This is Jeff Combs. She's not here right now." He knew the stained glass windows in the room were also courtesy of the man on the phone.

"That cop." Long pause.

His jaw tightened. "Right. I'm that cop." *That cop* who had saved one of Mark's sisters, September, and arrested the other. He waited. Combs crossed to the stained glass table, another Mark creation, to clean up the flower box debris.

Mark broke the silence. "Where is she? Is Aaron there?"

Combs paused. "I'm the only one here."

Then a pause. "Look, sorry for being such a prick. September says you're a good guy, and I trust her judgment. Aaron should have come home hours ago. It's his night to cook—vegetarian goulash. He's not answering his phone."

The prickling at the back of Combs' neck returned. "His truck's here. But he's not." It must have taken a lot for Mark to admit his worry. "Maybe he's with September?"

"Right, and she left her phone at the house? Why'd she do that? She and that phone are joined at the hand—or ear, I guess you could say. Besides, Aaron's acting odd." Mark sounded scared.

He put on his cop voice. "Odd how?"

"I'm coming over. You're at my sister's?" Sudden determination deepened the man's voice. "Maybe he's hurt. He won't listen to me, I tell him and tell him to take it easy." Combs could hear opening and closing doors as though the man retrieved his coat.

"Mark, I've already canvassed the grounds. Neither is here and her car is gone. September lost her phone in the garden, and I bet they're together." Combs gathered up the flower box garbage, crushed it together in one hand while cradling September's cell in the other, and opened the wastebasket cupboard with his booted foot. "No reason for you to run over here, I'm sure Aaron will turn up soon." He stuffed the trash into the basket, and bent to retrieve a card that had fallen out.

"You don't understand." Mark hesitated, and then explained in a rush. "Aaron forgets. He forgets a lot. Not only where he left his keys, or someone's name. He forgets what he's doing, right in the middle of stuff." He plowed on, once started unable to stop the outpouring. "Aaron won't see the doctor. Last week he turned on the burner and left the house, forgot about the oatmeal on the stove. He forgets to put on his pants and leaves the house in his boxers. Jesus, what am I going to do? Aaron's losing his mind. And he's using gas-powered chain saws and God knows what else. He could forget what he's doing and cut off his freakin' leg!"

Combs barely heard the other man. He stared at the crumpled hand-lettered anniversary card in his hand, block red letters screaming as they spelled out *payback*.

Her cello was gone. A bright lamp she loved, and the colorful carpet from the music room. An anniversary commemorated something special, to honor and celebrate a joyful wedding.

September's wedding anniversary had been in June, and the anniversary of her husband's death had passed weeks ago. The card was no celebration, the flowers were a taunt, a bullying threat born of anger and fed by obsession. *Payback.*

He knew what that meant. He didn't know the man's name, but Combs knew exactly who and what this was about. So did September. No need to lock the door when the invader had already breached the walls.

He licked his lips and cleared his throat. "Mark, your sister ever tell you anything about her stalker?"

"What are you talking about?" Incredulous. "You mean that business from when she lived in Chicago?"

"Don't know, Mark, but it's about time we found out." He crossed to the oven and switched it off, and returned the lasagna to the refrigerator. He gazed longingly at the beer, and then closed the door. September was on the run, she wouldn't be home any time soon, and he had no way to find her. But Mark might have a clue. "Can we get together? I'll buy you a steak."

"I'm a vegan, so's Aaron."

"So I'll get you bean burritos. Give me an address. We need to talk."

Chapter 27

Shadow whined and ran after Teddy, but the old man shut the door in his face with a loud bang. What happened? He checked over his shoulder at September, and furrowed his brow. They'd talked loud at each other. Before he left, Teddy's smell changed to an acrid fear-stink that made a good-dog's hackles raise. Shadow didn't like that.

September carried a cloud of fear that clung to her body and didn't wash away even when icy wind blew against her. In the closed-up car, the smell spoiled the fun of a car ride.

He whirled away from the door when a car started outside, and nosed past the fabric fluttering over the windows to see Teddy drive away. Shadow whined again, puffing warm breath against the cold window until his breath-fog froze white and blocked the view.

"Shadow, c'mere baby-dog. I need a kiss." September sounded sad and tired. He bounded to her and pushed his head and shoulders—as much as would fit—into her arms, tail whipping back and forth as she scratched the hard-to-reach itchy spots on his back. He licked her cheek, her mouth, and her eyes. Tasted the salty rain she shed. He nose-poked her, trying to make her laugh. But she hugged him tighter. He didn't struggle; he'd become used to her touch and knew it made her happy.

Finally, she pushed him away, and he sat down without her asking, and tipped his head from side to side, curious what would happen next. She stood up from the sofa, and walked down the long hall to a familiar room. Shadow eagerly padded after her, and hopped up on the bed. He sniffed the comforter, and could still smell his own signature odor, even after the long time since their last visit here. Shadow didn't know exactly how long, but many days and nights, more than he had paws. That was a lot. This time, she didn't ask him to get off the bed, and he sighed, put his head against the cover, and rubbed his face to get rid of the fear-stink her hands had left on his head.

"Maybe Timothy would bring Macy here. What do you think?" She picked up something from Teddy's desk, pushed buttons on the handle, and held it to her ear.

He whapped his tail against the cover when she smiled at him, and fine dust rose in the air. Shadow sneezed. Not a 'let's-play' sneeze, only a tickle sneeze. He heard when someone inside the ear-handle object spoke, and wondered again how people could get inside such tiny objects. A dog wouldn't fit inside.

"I'm September Day, calling about my cat Macy." She listened. "So the test is done? Macy's ready to go home?"

Shadow cocked his head and sat up. He was ready to go home. He yawned. It had been a long day.

She frowned into the mouth-piece. "Can I speak to Timothy? I'll wait." She sat on the bed beside Shadow and gently scratched his chest. He liked that.

"Timothy, it's September. I've had something come up and wondered if there's any way you could bring Macy to me . . ." Her hope-filled voice changed to disappointment. "Oh, I understand. I saw how short-staffed you were. Can Doc Eugene talk now? When I get there? Okay." She made a face. "How long will you be there?" She stood up abruptly. "I didn't realize you closed so soon. I've not had my cell phone with me." She listened again. "No! No, I can't leave Macy overnight. I need to get him now." She ran a hand through her hair, pacing to the desk and back again. "Please, wait for me. Don't close before I get there. I'm maybe twenty minutes away."

She clopped the receiver back on the desk, said, "Shadow, let's go!" and rushed from Teddy's office.

He bounded from the bed, squeezed around her in the hallway and galloped to the door, dancing with eagerness until she could get it open. Shadow raced to the car while September reached inside a metal box beside the window before she fiddled with the doorknob, and then dropped something back in the box with a clank.

"Good-dog. Let's go get Macy." She opened the car and nearly clipped his tail when she slammed the door.

The car moved fast. He liked that and stuck the tip of his nose out the small opening of the rear window. Shadow had to brace himself to keep from being thrown off the seat when September made the car swerve. When they slowed and pulled into the parking lot of the vet clinic, he nose-poked her. She had to take him inside this time. He didn't want to stay alone in the car, not again. They were supposed to stay together.

She slammed open her door, stuffed a folder with papers into her pocket and grabbed Shadow's leash before coming to him. He pressed his ears flat and grinned when she opened his door, and waited impatiently for the long lead to be attached to his harness.

"You be a good-boy, okay? No schmoozing the staff for treats, and no rude nose pokes to the clinic cat, she hates that. Quick trip in and out, pick up Macy, and then we hit the road."

He wagged at the words he knew—*treats* made his tail wag the fastest. September stood back for him to hop out, and scratched under his chin as she closed the car door, and he leaned into the sensation. She hadn't asked him to "seek" anything, so he knew not to surge ahead even though he wore his tracking harness. Shadow walked beside her, not dragging September forward or lagging behind.

He couldn't resist inhaling the orgy of smells surrounding the clinic, though. They were especially plentiful in the bushes right beside the front door. Most of the pee smelled nice, a few spoke to him of nerves. Shadow understood that, a new place could scare dogs that weren't brave like him.

But a few of the smells screamed "different" in a way that itched his fur. Shadow raised his head, sampling the air. Were these different-smelling dogs nearby? The pee smell wasn't fresh, but they might wait to jump at him— jump at his person—on the other side of the door.

Shadow stiffened, watching September's hand reach for and push open the door. He leaped in front of her, barking loudly to warn off any different-scented dogs lurking in the room.

"Shadow! What's wrong with you?" She tightened her grip on his leash. "Sorry, everyone. He's usually a big push-over."

September's disapproving tone stopped his barks, but he remained cautious. She couldn't fool him, she was concerned, too. He scanned the small room from side to side, sniffing the air and staring at the other occupants.

Two women and a man sat on cushions against one wall. One held a cat in a canvas bag. He huffed the air. It smelled scared, but otherwise had the usual weird-cat-smell, nothing the way a good-dog should smell.

At the front desk stood another lady, this one with a bad-smelling curly-furred dog the size of Shadow's head snugged tight in her arms. It made an ear-hurty keening noise and gazed around the room without focus on any one thing. The little dog's hind end, swaddled in soft white fabric, smelled of poop and pee, and she shook and shivered even though the room was toasty-warm.

Shadow wondered what it was like to be held so far above the ground. Was she shivery-scared about being dropped? Maybe that's why she smelled bad? He stretched his neck as far as he could to get a clearer sniff-picture without risking contact.

"Timothy, I'm here for Macy." September touched Shadow's neck, and he followed to the far side of the room, away from the sick-smelly dog and nervous cat. He placed one paw on the cushioned bench, and then took it down when September shook her head. He licked his lips and instead stared out the large floor to ceiling window to watch their car in the lot outside.

"I'll tell Doc Eugene you're here. Go down to room one. Glad you made it before closing. Oh, some guy called looking for you. He said dinner was waiting. Hiya, Shadow." Timothy waved, and then turned to the woman with the dog. "I'll meet you with Butterscotch in room three."

"Crap, I forgot about dinner with Combs." Shadow followed September, and put his ears down and slung his tail back and forth at Timothy. Sometimes he got treats when he did that. This time, though, Timothy turned away and disappeared into a back room as the woman took her keening dog down the hall.

They didn't wait long. Doc Eugene bustled into the room, and stopped with surprise when he saw Shadow. "He's grown, hasn't he? You know, he was one of Pam's favorites."

September didn't say anything, but flinched, and Shadow wondered why. When the tall man in a white coat squatted down and held out his hand, Shadow went to him and happily accepted butt scratches. He turned around, and nailed the man's face with a slurp, and was rewarded with a laugh. Returning to September to lean against her leg, Shadow reacted to her tension and whined.

"But you want to know about Macy. It's what I always fear with Maine Coons. It's his heart." Doc Eugene stood up and placed something on the nearby wall before flicking a switch.

Her breath caught, and Shadow pressed harder against September's leg. He didn't understand the words as the conversation continued, but they kept mentioning Macy and he worried something bad had happened to his cat. That's how he thought of Macy. They were family, so Macy belonged to him like September belonged to him, and he to her. Family belonged to each other.

Finally, Doc Eugene left the room, while September led Shadow out the other door and back to the front desk. Where was Macy, where was his cat? He woofed with concern.

"Shadow, hush. Settle, while I pay the bill and get Macy's medicine. Then we'll go talk to Combs."

The room had emptied. September dropped his leash and turned toward the counter, so Shadow padded across the room and jumped onto the cushions in front of the window. He waited for her to tell him "off," and when she didn't, he smeared nose prints and watched the outside view.

A big truck loomed over their small car outside, like a big dog bullying a puppy. He could hear the engine snarl, the vibration rattled the window and tickled deep inside his ears. Shadow shook his head, and the metal tags on his collar jingled with dog music.

Behind him, the door squealed open, and Shadow whirled and hopped off the seat. Timothy had Macy in the canvas carrier, and the cat meowed and pressed a paw against the front webbing. Shadow panted happily.

"Macy! Kitty, you sure scared me. But you're going to be okay." September smiled, relief in her voice and posture, and held her palm flat against the other side of the webbing. She stuffed the pages from her pocket inside one of the carrier sleeves as Macy rubbed his face against her hand through the fabric.

Timothy held the carrier in nose-sniffing range. Macy didn't even hiss, just made the rumbly sound Shadow could feel as well as hear. "Want me to take him to the car? You've got your hands full."

"That'd be great. I'll unlock it." She fumbled out her keys, pointed them at the window and Shadow saw the car's eye-lights flash. "Shadow, wait with me, I still need to get Macy's meds."

Shadow wagged and huffed, sniffing Macy as best he could through the webbing, while the cat continued to face-rub. Other than the strange hospital smells, Macy smelled like himself, not scary-sick. He was happy his cat would come home with them, and they'd be together again. Family stayed together. Shadow wagged harder, and tried to follow Timothy out the waiting room door but was blocked.

While September stayed at the counter, Shadow returned to the window perch. He tipped his head from side to side, panting softly, following Timothy's progress to their car as Macy's carrier gently swung in one hand.

Someone got out of the bigger truck and walked to meet Timothy. The stranger's face had funny colors. Holes for eyes and nose and mouth. Not like a person at all.

Shadow's mouth closed. His ears came forward. He stood up. The man wore a hat pulled over his face. The two spoke for a minute, and then Timothy shook his head and tried to back away.

Shadow whined. His tail rose, jerky wags, and he whined again deep in his throat. They bubbled into growls and then angry barks when the stranger grabbed Macy's carrier—his cat!

"What? Shadow, settle, what's wrong?"

But he wouldn't stop. There, out the window! Timothy and the stranger played tug-o'-war with Macy's carrier! Shadow paw-pounded the window, barking and snarling so loud that spittle stained the glass.

"Oh my God, no!" September raced to open the door, but Shadow beat her through the opening.

"Stop! What're you doing? Help, someone help!" Timothy yelled and flailed ineffectually at the much bigger man, who shook him off like water from a bath.

Shadow galloped toward the pair. He barked warnings, but his leash tangled in nearby bushes and stopped his rush to protect his cat from the stranger. The man-with-no-face wrested Macy from Timothy and tossed the carrier into the back of the big truck.

Timothy pulled at the man's arm until the strange man snatched up a big digging stick from the truck's open door. He swung. Timothy fell.

Behind him, September screamed and froze in place. But Shadow never paused. He tore free of the leash tangle, and leaped at the man stealing his cat.

The shovel swung.

Chapter 28

Nikki sat in the back seat squeezed between Hank and Willie. Dustin drove like they were in a video game so the tires squealed on sharp turns. He'd promised to drop everyone off after they visited the old barn. Nikki wanted to sit next to Dustin, but Melinda claimed the middle front seat. Zeke sat on her other side.

Melinda was all "Oh, Dustin, you're so great Dustin, sit next to me Dustin" it made Nikki want to gag. She couldn't help giggling when Dustin paid attention to her instead of Melinda, happy he believed her story about the barn. The others probably would have ignored her.

This way, at least they all would share the secret. Nobody would tell on Nikki without getting themselves in trouble.

The barn was spookier at night. Chatter in the car died away when Dustin pulled to a stop and set the brake. Nobody made a move to get out, and Melinda finally giggled, a high-pitched nervous sound that made Nikki jump.

Dustin cleared his throat. "I got a flashlight in the trunk." Nikki was surprised to hear a slight quaver in the older boy's voice, but when he swung out of the car, his swagger remained intact. "Zeke, you and Hank come with me. The rest of you wait in the car."

"No way." Melinda followed the boys out of the car, her jaw shoved forward with determination. "What you gonna do, clobber him with the Eveready?"

Dustin shook his head, and popped the trunk, his voice hushed. "Take care of the little kids. Probably shouldn't have brought them, anyway."

The words were a stomach punch and Nikki blinked back tears. Willie sat quietly in the back seat, and seemed happy to do as he was told. She got halfway out the door before Hank could shut it. "I'm not a little kid!"

"Shh! Quiet, Nikki." Hank narrowed his eyes, and whispered. "This could be dangerous. For you too, Melinda." He threw out his chest and tried to lower his voice but it came off pathetic.

Melinda made a rude noise, and Nikki giggled. "Girl power. Right, Nikki?" The older girl put her hands on her hips. "We're not going to wait around for the pig-sticker to sneak up on the car. We're all in this together, or we all go home, right now."

Nikki held her breath. Maybe Melinda wasn't so bad after all.

Dustin rolled his eyes, but gave in. "Fine. But you're in charge so keep them together. Willie, come stay with your sister." He switched on the flashlight, and it flickered a moment and then burned steady after he thumped it softly against the side of a tire. "Stay close. Hell, we've made enough noise, I'll be amazed if we find anyone lurking around. Lurking in the barn." He said the word again, as if relishing the sound. "Lots of bushes to lurk in."

The group slowly circled the rickety old structure. They startled a hidden animal once, and even Dustin jumped and cried out. "It was nothing." He lowered his voice to a gruff growl, compensating for the loss of he-manliness. Nikki thought it was funny, but was glad he couldn't see her smirk. He'd called her a baby, but she didn't scream and pee her pants. She thought of the sick raccoons and her smile faltered.

The flashlight beam swept back and forth, keeping the path around the barn illuminated as much as possible. A big iron pot rested against the back wall of the structure, blackened wood scattered beneath. Nikki thought it must be a witch's cauldron like in Harry Potter spells, but hadn't been used in forever.

"Don't step in a hole and break an ankle. The armadillos turned the ground into a moonscape." Dustin stayed ahead of the small group, and every few yards stopped and turned back to light the way for those following. It didn't take long before they'd returned to the front of the building. He held the flashlight under his chin to make a scary face. "Nobody here but us chickens."

Nikki giggled. "Don't you want to go inside? Bet the scary man's hiding in there." Her nerves had calmed, but she didn't want the forbidden excitement to end.

"Inside?" Dustin turned to his cousin. "This the hangout you told me about? It's deserted."

Zeke nodded. "It's pretty cool. Cobwebs and creepy crawlies. And cats, like Nikki said."

Hank agreed. "The outside door's padlocked and nobody uses the place anymore, far as we can tell. But we always check before going in. Whoever owns the place would have to unlock the barn door, so we'd know to keep driving by."

"How you get in?" Dustin shined the light over the bleached gray of old boards. Any paint had long since worn off.

Nikki pointed. "There's a loose board." She led the way when Dustin shined the flashlight in that direction. "It sort of swings back and forth on an old nail, wide enough to get through. That's where I ran out today, and Mr. Felch stood right there."

"Nobody's here now." Hank reached the board, pushed it to one side, and eyed Dustin. "Might be a tight fit for you. It's wider at the bottom. You're wearing your good clothes, man. Your mom'll be pissed if you get all grunged up."

"Screw that." Dustin stared at Melinda. "Seriously? You hang out in this dump?"

She crossed her arms and tossed hair over her shoulder. "City boy all scared?" She poked an elbow gently in Nikki's ribs, and Nikki giggled.

His jaw tightened, and he thrust the flashlight at Hank. "You know the place. So go on through, then hold the light for me." He blinked at Melinda. "Unless one of you wants to go first?"

It was a dare. Nikki thought Melinda might go for it, but she laughed instead. "Be my guest," she said.

Hank took the light, pushed the board aside, and turned sideways to sidle through. The light inside the barn made gaps in boards show up in the darkness like a Jack-o-lantern toothy smile. Nikki shivered with delicious chills. She couldn't remember ever having so much fun. Even the stinging of arm scratches faded. The earlier scare was worth it, her admission to being an official member of the cool kids.

Dustin knelt on the damp ground, turned and crawled in sideways with a one-handed posture through the narrow opening. She waited her turn, watching as Zeke followed Hank. She hurried after her brother, and helped hold the board for Willie and then Melinda last.

"Nikki, it's show and tell time. What happened?" Dustin's words were teasing, but not mean. She could live with that.

"There's these cats live here, see? And I feed the mommy cat. I call her Hope. I think they live in that horse stall, because she always come out of there." Nikki pointed and walked toward the area. "I sat right here to feed the kitties. A kitten came out, too. But then these raccoons followed the kitten. Sick ones." She couldn't help shivering. "Maybe sick with rabies. They scared Hope and she clawed me good trying to run, and I got scared and runned. I mean, ran. Out the board. And I saw that man with the gun. Mr. Felch."

"Wait a minute." Dustin held up a hand. "The *cat* scratched your arms?"
She nodded.

"I thought you said this Felch guy hurt you." He glowered.

Nikki licked her lips. They hadn't asked her what had happened. "I only said he had a gun. Maybe even he shot the gun, you know, while I ran away. I heard a boom." Her voice sounded whiny, and she hated that. "He scared me!"

Dustin made a disgusted sound. "Got dragged all the way over here for nothing, for some cat scratches." He took a step closer to her and she reflexively stepped back. "You sure it was cat scratches?"

She bobbed her head again.

"Not raccoon? Not a creepy man?"

She wrinkled her nose. "I'm sorry, but you didn't give me a chance to explain—"

Melinda cut her off. "Never mind, Dustin. Give her a break. You should be glad it's nothing serious." She bent down toward Nikki and whispered, "Girl power," and Nikki didn't feel so bad after all.

"You're right. Sorry Nikki. Friends?" Dustin held out his hand.

Nikki stared at the big, seventeen-year-old boy's hand, and hesitantly put her small girl hand in it and shook. It felt very grown up. Maybe he didn't think she was such a baby after all.

"While we're here, do I get the tour?" Dustin shined the light around the inside of the barn. "Not much to see. Pretty clean, too. I expected it to be trashed."

Hank waved a hand to encompass the entire barn area. "Don't want anyone to know about us, so we always take out any trash we bring."

"How environmentally friendly of you." Dustin laughed. He walked down the center of the barn, shining his light inside each empty stall, three on the left and two on the right.

Nikki gasped. "The door's open." She pointed and ran to the far end of the barn. "Come on, bring the light!"

Next to the stall where Hope and her kittens lived sat a room she'd always imagined must house wonderful secrets, maybe treasures of sparkling jewels, or bags of gold coins. She remembered the bag that Mr. Felch had carried. Maybe this was his stash of treasure. He sort of looked like a pirate, only not as handsome as Johnny Depp.

The wooden plank door to the room had always been closed with a padlock, twin to the one on the outside of the barn but not so rusty. Some sort of grinder with gray-white powder inside sat next to the steps, and now the door swung open, and the lock was gone. If they found money inside, that could change things for her and Hank, and Mom. Especially Mom. It might make that worry spot between her eyes smooth out and go away.

"Hurry up!" She stepped from foot to foot, impatient for the light to come. Tentatively, she stepped up onto the wooden block that served as the single step into the room. Her nose wrinkled. It smelled dusty, powdery.

Dustin reached her and held the light high, illuminating the room. Nikki stepped on something brittle that cracked beneath her feet, and cried out and fell back into his arms, hiding her face.

Bones. The room overflowed with piles of blackened, charred bones.

Chapter 29

The small but tidy workroom held hand crafted items and brilliantly colored stained glass windows and lamps. Combs feared he'd break something, and shifted uneasily, crossing and then uncrossing his legs in the antique cane-back chair.

"Excuse the mess." Mark January sat opposite him. "I'm covered up with holiday orders, so every surface has projects in various degrees of being finished."

"That's okay." Combs shifted again, and then gave up and stood. "I'm worried about your sister."

Mark stood, too. "Mind if I work while we talk? I got a few more pieces to cut for this panel, and like I said, I'm up against a wall. Besides," he wiped his hands on the stained canvas apron, "keeping busy helps keep my mind off Aaron. You're sure I can't file a missing person's report?"

Combs shook his head. "He's an adult. You can file immediately, and missing kids or developmentally disabled adults will get attention right away." He shrugged. "Hate to say it, but depends on the workload how quick the police would get to him. Playing devil's advocate here, they'd argue maybe he took the day off, or his truck wouldn't start and he caught a ride with a friend, or had a tiff with a lover. No offense." He walked to the nearest table, solid, made from rough unfinished pine, and gently touched the jigsaw of cut glass pieces. "Christmas wreath?"

"Yeah, it's a wreath." Mark adjusted safety goggles over his eyes before he scored a large sheet of green glass with a "screeing" sound, lifted it, and broke it cleanly. "He could call me to pick him up. I've left messages, he's not answering his phone." Deft hands turned half the sheet a three-quarter turn, scored it again along a gold-painted line, and split it again.

"Well, I bet he's with September. She left in a hurry. She took a few things. A rose lampshade that was in her office."

"I made that." Mark paused, puzzled. "Why pack a lamp?"

"I didn't see her cello, either. That's what makes me think she ran." Or someone took her. Combs had a bad feeling. "What can you tell me about her stalker?"

Mark shrugged. "Not much." He manipulated a long, thin strip of swirly green glass he'd separated from one end of the larger sheet. "The stalker thing, that was her story, but Mom figured it was an excuse to explain when she messed up." A row of leaves drawn with a gold paint pen marched down the long strip of glass. With quick, sure strokes, Mark scored each in turn, cracked them free, creating a loose pile of rough leaf-shaped pieces. Combs came closer, and got waved back. "Watch your eyes. Shards fly in unexpected directions."

Combs reflexively blinked and took a step away. "She messed up, how? She left school early for some music scholarship. A tour, too, right?"

"Yep. A sixteen-year-old cello prodigy, that's our September. But too young to be on her own." Mark chose one of the small rectangles of green glass and began to shape it, scoring and breaking off bits at a time until the proper inner and outer curves defined each leaf. "My folks had this family friend." He made a face. "Older. Kind of a creep, if you ask me. He was supposed to watch out for September, but apparently he couldn't handle the job. She started spending more time partying than practicing, was a no-show for a couple of concerts, and they kicked her out of the tour."

"A party girl? Drugs?" Combs raised his eyebrows. That didn't sound like the responsible woman he knew today.

"Don't know. Maybe. Probably." Mark added another rough-cut green leaf to the growing pile. "Hell, I did my share of booze and pot growing up here in Heartland, and later in college. A teenager virtually on her own in Chicago? It's likely. Anyway, September finally got scared and called April to rescue her." He peered over the goggles. "You remember April?" The question had extra teeth.

Combs stared back evenly. "September returned the favor, didn't she?" April nearly got herself, her son, and September killed. April remained in the hospital, and probably faced jail time once she was well enough to face a judge.

"Why didn't this family friend help September? Who is he?" Mark had no clue what kind of real trouble September had faced, or how April helped her out, and it wasn't his place to enlighten the man.

Mark stopped, holding the glasscutter in one hand and another strip of glass in the other. "It's been eight years. I haven't a clue where Uncle Vic might be. The family sort of lost touch, and who could blame him? After September's meltdown, she hooked up with Christopher Day, they moved away and eventually got married. What does this have to do with anything?"

"Maybe nothing. Maybe everything. Might have something to do with Aaron. She left her front door unlatched. Not only unlocked, Mark, but unlatched. And I found this." Combs held out the red-lettered card. "On the table, beside a bunch of blue flowers."

"Flowers? Blue ones?" Mark set down the glass cutter, and took off his goggles to examine the note. "Anniversary? What anniversary is that? Today's December eighteenth."

Combs's phone rang. He dug in his pocket, and saw it was Gonzales. "Gotta take this." He walked away from Mark to the front of the room, speaking in a low voice. "Combs here." When Mark held up a hand and then pointed to an adjacent room, he watched the man go. "What's up?"

"You remember Theodore Williams, right? He's here with me and he's got quite a story. Ties in with Sly's visit to September this morning." He chuckled. "Hate to break in on a date with your girlfriend—"

"She's not my girlfriend." The inside joke fell flat. "She stood me up." He hoped that's all it was.

"So she's got better taste than we thought."

Combs cracked his knuckles. "What's Teddy into now?" He'd been instrumental in helping catch his mother's murderer, and become a good friend to September as well. Combs's breath quickened. "Does he know where September is?"

"You're ahead of me already. Yes, as a matter of fact, says he left September at his house."

His shoulders relaxed, and he leaned against one of the tables. She hadn't left town after all. Had he jumped to conclusions on the stalker angle?

"She gave Teddy notes from Humphrey Fish for some story Sly planned to write about animals making people lose their minds." He laughed again, the way kids whistled past a grave. "Crazy, right? Sounds like something Sly would make up. We found nothing in Sly's Gremlin, nothing at his work computer and his laptop is missing. We still haven't found the man. Looking more and more like somebody shut him up. Maybe Fish's notes will tell us why."

Crazy-ass memory loss. Like Aaron? When Mark returned, carrying a picture frame, Combs replied softly, not wanting the other man to hear. "Take Teddy home and I'll meet you there. We can talk to September, too." He pocketed the phone and turned to the other man. "What's that?"

"You said blue flowers." Mark held out the picture, a professional portrait of a somber teenage September with her cello held protectively with one hand, and a bouquet of blue flowers clenched in her other white-knuckled fist. A hatchet-faced balding overweight man with piercing green eyes, bad skin and worse teeth loomed behind September, his hand possessively on her shoulder.

"Who's he?"

"Victor Grant, the man my parents asked to watch out for September when she went on tour. I had to call Mom, and she recognized the date." He tapped the photo. "You said blue flowers, and it reminded me of this picture."

Combs must have looked puzzled.

"Blue flowers. Forget-Me-Nots. Uncle Vic gave her a bouquet of blue flowers after every performance." Mark tapped the picture again. "Eight years ago today September walked out of a concert in Chicago. She hasn't played since."

Chapter 30

September froze, the scream scalding but refusing to leave her throat. She couldn't breathe; terror transformed the action into stuttered slow motion.

Shadow. Ski masked man. Shovel.

Wielded like a club, the wickering sound ripped the air as it swept back and forth at the dancing dog. The stranger's broad shoulders rippled beneath his padded fleece jacket, and his tight jeans revealed muscular thighs as he aimed each swing at Shadow. She braced and flinched, each time anticipating the dull thud against Shadow's furry body and helpless to stop it.

But Shadow managed to dodge until it finally connected a glancing blow off his tail. He yelped, spun away, and launched himself at the man, teeth catching his sleeve. He hung on, snarling and shaking his head, suspended half off the ground with rear paws pin wheeling for purchase. For an endless moment, the attacker juggled the shovel.

The sleeve fabric gave way, and Shadow dropped to the ground, quickly regaining his balance but not fast enough.

Timothy lay crumpled on the ground. He moaned and tried to roll over. The shovel descended and connected with a sodden thump-crunch against his shoulder, prompting a shriek.

Shadow yelped, an echo to the vet tech's cry. He placed himself between the supine figure and the attacker, snarling a warning to back off.

The sound unfroze September's feet as well, and she raced forward. And then stopped, afraid to get too close. "Stop! The police are on the way!" She hoped they were, anyway.

She peered over her shoulder, and saw Doc Eugene through the window with a phone pressed to his ear. She turned back to the masked man. "Why are you doing this?" She heard Macy yowl from inside the truck's bed, and prayed the cat wasn't hurt when the carrier was flung.

Victor was heavy and limped; this man was lean and athletic. "Who are you?!"

He put a gloved finger to his lips and remained silent. Perfect teeth gleamed through the red and blue knit mask for only a moment before he tossed the shovel into the truck bed, climbed inside, slammed the door and peeled out of the lot.

September rushed to Timothy, barely registering the clomping footsteps approaching from the clinic. "Help is on the way. I'm so sorry." She shouldered the dog out of the way. "Shadow, stay back." She had to push the pup away again when he tried to climb into her lap and lick her face.

Doc Eugene grabbed her shoulder and pulled her aside. "I called 911." He knelt beside Timothy, examined him quickly, and then covered him up to his neck with several clean but tattered towels. "He's breathing. Barely. Don't see any bleeding. But I don't want him moved, he got hit in the head." The blunt force trauma left the young man's arms at weird angles when he'd tried to deflect the spade. "Why would anyone do such a thing?"

September sat on the cold pavement, arms around Shadow. "He took my cat." Tears spilled unchecked down her face, freezing in the wind.

Doc Eugene crossed his arms, trying to stay warm. "That makes no sense. Why would he take your cat?" He scowled. "He must know you."

Timothy stirred, blood pooled at his mouth and he blew red bubbles at the corner.

"Be still, Tim, help's on the way." Doc Eugene's voice was unsteady, but his hands held Timothy's head immobile, not allowing movement.

"I didn't recognize him." She wiped her eyes, dodging when Shadow tried to lick her face again. "He had a mask. And gloves. He didn't say anything."

"Yes he did." Timothy's voice, reedy and faint, startled them.

"Don't talk, hang in there." Doc Eugene sounded desperate. "Where the hell is the ambulance?"

One of Timothy's bare hands grabbed September's knee and she flinched before she bent close when he tried to speak again. He mouthed, "Macy?"

She blinked hard, but forced a smile and put her hand over his and gently squeezed. "Don't worry about Macy. You need to take care of yourself."

"I'm sorry." A bloody tear escaped one eye. The other had already begun to swell closed. "He asked if Macy was yours. Couldn't stop him. So sorry . . ."

"Asked about me?" It was Victor's doing. Her heart broke. The monster had targeted Macy, and Timothy had also fallen victim to his payback. She reassured him with lies she didn't believe, and choked on the words. "Macy will be fine. I promise."

"Stop making him talk." Doc Eugene checked Timothy's respiration that grew ever more strained. "September, think. Think! What did he look like? Did you get the license? What color was it? You'll need to give a statement to the police."

The police. That's right, they'd be here any second, and keep her repeating her statement over and over and the son-of-a-bitch would get away. If she followed now she could catch him. How dare he hurt Timothy, and take her cat! Macy's damaged heart could give out at any time.

Timothy's hand flexed under hers, and she leaned close to hear. "Payback," he whispered.

She felt her face blanch. "What?"

"Hurt Macy." Gasp. "Unless." A breath, and he choked. "Meet you." He stopped breathing. His hand fell from her knee, dropping a scribbled note with the same red block lettering as the anniversary card. September grabbed it, stuffing the note in her pocket.

She poised to begin CPR when Doc Eugene shoved her aside and took her place. "No, oh no no no." He took charge, feeling for a pulse before tipping back Timothy's head.

"Let me help." She moved closer.

"Haven't you done enough?" His voice cut her to the quick.

Doc Eugene began rescue breathing as the ambulance arrived. Within seconds, the parking lot swarmed with EMTs.

"You're right. Nothing I can do here will help." September grabbed the end of Shadow's leash. "Let's go for car ride." She whispered the magic phrase and the dog rushed to her car.

Nobody noticed when September slowly drove away from the clinic. She couldn't help Timothy. She'd probably gotten him killed. Besides, Doc Eugene knew as much about the attacker as she.

Payback. Sent by Victor. If she'd doubted before, the note confirmed the author, and she had to do what he demanded. He had Macy.

Chapter 31

Teddy pulled into his driveway and saw Detective Combs climb out of the unmarked car parked at the curb. He unfastened his seatbelt when Detective Gonzales pulled in behind him. What had September gotten him into? Again?

Her car was conspicuously absent, though. She'd dumped this mess in his lap, and run off on an errand to get her cat. He understood her reluctance to get involved in another police investigation. Last time she'd nearly died and still managed to save her nephew, but she hadn't survived unscathed. Hidden injuries hurt worse and took longer to heal, if they ever did.

He got out of the car, and waved at Detective Combs with the folder of notes from September. "Not a reunion I particularly welcome, gentlemen. No offense."

"None taken." Combs stepped to meet Gonzales, and the two waited until Teddy unlocked the door. At least September had seen fit to secure his home. That was the least she could do.

"September's gone." Gonzales stated the obvious. "Slippery little devil." He turned at Combs. "No offense."

"None taken." Combs frowned, forehead wrinkled with worry. "She's hard to keep up with, for sure."

They followed Teddy into the living room, and he waved them to the sofa while he got rid of his coat. "Yep, September's done it again. No offense." He couldn't resist the sarcastic tone.

Gonzales didn't smile this time. "I wanted Combs to hear this, too, since it's related to the call we made out to her house. We never found Sly's notes."

"These are duplicates of Mr. Sanger's notes from Humphrey Fish, out at the radio station. Another familiar name. Deja vu, indeed." He polished his glasses on the hem of his sweater, put them back on, and opened the folder. "She said Mr. Fish enlisted Mr. Sanger to investigate his listener's concerns about wild animals infecting pets. And possibly people."

Gonzales nodded at Combs, who took the lead. "Sick how? That's something the city pound or county extension agent should handle." He frowned at Gonzales. "As for people illness, that's the Health Department's purview."

"Fine." Teddy slapped the cover of the file closed, and offered it to the men. "Take it to them. My wife's not well, and I need to be on call for her, not gallivanting around playing Mr. Marple." He breathed heavily. "September only gave it to me because Molly's got Alzheimer's, and Mr. Fish thinks this is some new variant of the disease."

"Wait. Alzheimer's?" Gonzales held out his hand and took the file. "My wife's aunt has that. Terrible, heartbreaking condition." He spoke sharply to Teddy. "I didn't know animals got Alzheimer's."

Combs leaned forward. "That's not something you catch from your pet, or another person. This is bogus." He stood.

"Don't shoot the messenger." Teddy held up his hands, palms out. "Sorry, bad word choice. The fact is: September dumped that in my lap. I'm being the good citizen and turning it over to the authorities. You want to take it to the health department, I'm all for it."

Gonzales handed the file to Combs, and watched as he quickly scanned the contents, flipping pages. "He's got names. A lot of them. He's been careful to avoid anything litigious, but he's making a case for intentional poisoning."

Combs paced as he quickly read through the notes.

Teddy hesitated, feeling his heart rate increase. "Do you think someone would poison people intentionally?" Molly had been diagnosed only a year ago. Heat flamed his cheeks.

Gonzales stood. "Too soon to tell." He turned to Combs. "Take that to the health department. But first make a copy."

Combs agreed. "With the recent cut in funding and personnel, they can't move too fast, and with the holidays, it could sit for weeks."

"It was the pet owners complained first." Teddy walked them to the door, both relieved and a bit disappointed the puzzle had been handed off. "Bet animal control would have some insight."

"Yeah, or a veterinarian. Someone who treated the pets." Combs's phone buzzed and he searched a pocket for it while he continued to talk.

"September told us Sly had a sick cat she took to the vet. Maybe the kitty has some clues." He added drily, "Just call me the pet detective." He shoved the file at Teddy to hold while he found the phone. "Combs." His eyes widened. "Shit. Okay, on our way." He scowled at Gonzales. "Deja vu strikes again. Or is that redundant?"

Teddy opened the door for them. "What? A big case?"

"Could be." He spoke angrily over Teddy's head to Gonzales. "Assault over at a local vet clinic. September fled the scene."

Chapter 32

September drove quickly, following the single word prompt on the scribbled note the attacker left behind. She gripped the steering wheel so hard her hands began to cramp. After she'd survived last month's horror, she dared to hope God had forgiven her. That she'd atoned for whatever she'd done to deserve Victor's attentions. She'd even attended church a few times, figured she owed Him that much for getting her through the worst. Mom convinced her to play the holiday concert, and actually got her to practice Melody again.

But bad stuff kept coming. She hung on with virtual fingernails to a cliff that threatened to collapse and dump her into a place from which she'd never claw free. Her teeth chattered and her sight shrunk to tunnel vision. "Ten, nine, eight, seven . . ." She tried the counting trick, and bit the inside of her cheek, anything to keep the roller coaster of emotions from jumping the tracks.

"I don't know how to pray," she whispered. "But this is me, trying. Please don't let anyone else get hurt because of me." In the mirror she saw Shadow tipping his head from side to side, and laughed bitterly. "Yeah, like praying's going to help. But can't hurt when we've got nothing else." He barked and she liked to pretend he agreed.

She knew what Victor wanted. He'd professed to love her, his definition of it anyway. He basked in the reflected glory of her audiences' appreciation, and when she left she'd betrayed that love. His humiliation kept him from pursuing her, kept her safe for a time because he expected her to tell, to file charges with the police.

But she couldn't tell, not the whole story anyway. Oh, she told everyone she'd been stalked, including Combs, but never identified him. She'd lied and claimed Victor tried to protect her—otherwise, she knew he'd hurt her family.

She told only enough to get by. To her parents, that she'd been stalked. To the police and her sister April, that she'd been raped. It was the only way to explain giving up her music. The only way to get police protection. And the only way to explain the baby.

Victor didn't know about the baby. His son. Given to April to raise as her own. Combs had figured that out on his own, and she hated the look in his eyes, judging her. Mom would disown her if she found out. She might be damned for not loving Steven, for giving him up, and staying away for eight years. But she'd not destroy April's family or damn that little boy by revealing the secret of his parentage.

She shuddered at what Victor's payback would be if he found out Steven was his son.

Once Victor learned she hadn't identified him, he waited, plotted, and when she'd relaxed her guard, he'd murdered Chris and Dakota. She couldn't prove it was Victor, he'd been too careful. Since she'd never pointed a finger at him before, identifying Victor at this late date would never float.

She knew what he wanted: To humiliate her as she had him. Payback for his hurt. Killing Chris and Dakota was the appetizer, she was the main course, and Victor orchestrated this menu like a virtuoso chef. Now they played a deadly game of hide and seek, this time for keeps.

But this time, she wasn't a frightened child. She had Shadow. And a gun. She'd serve Victor a dessert that would blow him away.

She hated guns. Chris got her one before they married, and made her practice. Here in Texas, she had a carry permit, but in Indiana, she'd felt safer leaving the gun at home and relying on Dakota's Schutzund training. She'd learned the hard way a dog was no match for a bullet.

Last month she'd stashed her gun in the car's glove box, just in case. At the time, her house's security as well as Shadow's presence made the gun less vital. For the first time, September knew she'd use it without hesitation.

September picked up the note in the car seat beside her—*Gazebo*—the one word conjuring memories of happier times. Her first public cello performance took place at the outdoor pavilion, affectionately known as The Gazebo, in the city park next to Heartland Middle School. After that, she'd played at The Gazebo many times. She'd even played for the Middle School graduation. The Gazebo represented the time before the bad; when her future was hopeful and only good lay ahead. Now it, too, was tainted with Victor's special brand of poison.

She turned at the corner. Heartland Middle School sat on the outskirts of town. With school closed for the holidays, and the weather so cold, visitors weren't likely so it made cruel sense to choose the spot.

The man had slung the cat carrier into the back of the pickup like so much trash. With Macy's diagnosis, he might already be dead.

No! She wouldn't think like that. Doc Eugene said the tests showed cardiac changes, but not as severe as they could be. It was the same heart condition that caused young athletes to drop dead on the basketball court. Macy had received his first dose of the medicine before they left. His required exercise restriction would be the biggest challenge—over-exercise could kill him. So could stress.

How much stress did Macy feel right now? Damn Victor!

"You hurt my cat and it's on," she whispered. He could terrorize her, threaten the people she loved, and she'd warn them and sic the cops on him. People could take steps to protect themselves. Well, most people could. Her throat tightened with guilt at her failure to warn and protect Timothy. Like a trusting pet without a clue, Timothy walked right up to the killer. Taking Macy crossed the line.

September sucked in a breath. "You're stupid. Stupid! What were you thinking?" Victor had her so rattled she couldn't think straight. But nobody had to know about Steven. April's secret would stay hidden.

She'd been a terrified kid, beaten down and ashamed to tell her parents. She'd believed Victor's assertions she'd asked for the attention, but she'd been a child. Mom didn't speak to her for years, angry she'd blown off her music career and blamed it on what she called "that stalker fiction." Even April believed the pregnancy to be a result of some bad-boy romance. She didn't need to know Steven was a child of rape.

September's reputation meant nothing, not in the face of murder. She *could* turn in Victor. Press charges. April was an expert at believing what she needed to believe and she'd protect her son with her life.

She didn't care if they never proved Victor murdered Chris and Dakota, or hired Timothy's attack. Pressing charges would shine a spotlight on him, and the public embarrassment alone pulled his fangs. To Victor, that would be worse than anything else. He'd be caught, or disappear for good.

She'd make him pay for all the pain he'd caused. And she'd get her life back.

No need to tell him that, though, not at first. "It's not a sin to lie to the devil, is it, Shadow?" He thumped his tail and she smiled for the first time in hours. That's what she'd do. Two could play at blackmail, because that's how he surely meant to use Macy, as leverage to get her to submit to him.

The school parking lot was deserted. Safety lights illuminated both the school property and the nearby park. As she slowly pulled through the park's high arching entry, she saw a ramshackle truck parked along the back exit beneath a pool of light, like a cat seeking a sunning opportunity.

September took a big, shuddery breath, steeling herself for the confrontation to come. She'd demand he give Macy back, and she'd keep his dirty secret. If he refused, she'd threaten to tell the police about him. *Everything* about him.

And once she had Macy back—and Melody, she wanted her cello, too, dammit!—she'd tell the cops all about his sorry ass.

Finding her own wash of light, September pulled to a stop near The Gazebo. Only the truck across the park showed evidence anyone was here, but there were plenty of dark shadows produced by the buzzing overhead fixtures. The single word on the note mocked her. It had no time for a meeting, no signature, nothing. It would be like Victor to lead her to this deserted place—and never show up.

September opened the glove box, pulled out the gun, made sure it was loaded, and put it in her pocket. She settled in to wait, wishing she had her phone to call Combs. It had been a mistake to shut him out. "Hindsight sucks," she said. "Think with your head next time, not your heart."

But there wouldn't be a next time. Not if she could help it. She was done with drama. Tired of hurting the people who cared about her. Like Teddy. A fresh rush of guilt spilled over her. She'd been incredibly insensitive, and he'd been a good friend to her. Like Combs. It was hard to be her friend, but she'd make it up to him. After this meeting, she'd find Teddy and explain. And apologize. Hope he'd forgive her.

Clack-clack-clack!

She jumped, hit the door lock, and scrambled for the gun in her pocket, heart galloping. Shadow barked and snarled, ears slicked back and spittle flying.

A snaggle-toothed man wearing a blue and red ski mask stood beside the door, tapping her window with the blade of a shovel.

Chapter 33

Teddy wished he'd brought his laptop. The detectives hadn't wanted him to come, but they couldn't legally stop him from following them to the veterinary hospital. He had to park across the street, though.

He'd known as soon as they mentioned the veterinarian that September's cat Macy must be involved, but he couldn't think why. Taking the cat seemed a direct dig at September, a way to keep her attention, or maybe gain leverage over her in some way. Of course the detectives focused on the human victim.

September had been desperate to collect her pet. He could see that now, though she'd tried to hide it from him. He should never have ignored her fear.

Detective Combs said she'd left home so quickly she didn't pack or go back for her phone. To him, that sounded like running away. So who was chasing her? Maybe the same person who took the cat? If he'd stayed and heard her out, he could have persuaded her to go to the police, and maybe none of this would have happened.

Any mention of Molly's illness made him crazy. He lashed out against the helpless feeling, and September had been the handy target. It wasn't her fault Molly's disease couldn't be reversed. He'd gotten riled at the suggestion of finger-pointing blame even though Mr. Fish's notes were anecdotal at best, based on rumor and supposition. Sylvester Sanger's reputation tainted the story with a bad smell. Yet being able to do something in defense of Molly, even as ineffectual as running down a bogus story, gave him purpose. It was good to have a purpose again.

The poor vet tech had been beaten to death, and that trumped anything else. Whatever she'd gotten mixed up in, he knew it wasn't her fault. September had worse luck than Job.

The EMTs had given up trying to resuscitate the technician by the time he'd arrived. Now Teddy sat in the clinic waiting room. A large plate glass window offered a clear view of Detective Gonzales doing whatever detectives do after a murder. Teddy wished they'd cover up the poor boy. Another person arrived, maybe the medical examiner, and conferred with Detective Gonzales before kneeling to examine the body.

Teddy clearly heard Detective Combs interviewing the veterinarian. They hadn't bothered to shut the door to the examining room down a narrow hall where they conferred. Doc Eugene said the staff had departed by the time September arrived to pick up Macy, and only the technician and doctor had stayed to release patients.

"September wanted to get her cat, don't know why the rush. She could have gotten him tomorrow but didn't want to wait." The veterinarian's voice trembled, and then steadied. "We usually close at six p.m. on Thursdays, and office hours are limited over the weekend, but we ran late tonight."

Detective Combs's low voice kept a professional tone. "Did you see the attack?" Pause. "So what did you see?"

Teddy strained to hear.

"Tim offered to take the cat to the car while we finished talking. Timothy—that's my technician. God, he's worked here fifteen years!" The veterinarian needed a moment before he could go on.

"I know this is rough. Take your time." The detective spoke with gentle encouragement, and soon the doctor calmed enough to go on.

"September had Shadow with her," he said. "She'd already paid the bill, but wanted to know about the other cat she brought in. I'd left the chart in the back, and by the time I got it, Shadow started barking. Didn't think much of it at first." He laughed without humor. "This is a vet clinic, after all. But then September yelled, and I could tell the barks were serious."

"Serious? How can you tell?"

"Detective Combs, dogs bark for lots of reasons: boredom, during play, excitement. Shadow's barks meant business, they were alarm barks—something threatened or scared him."

"Okay, so you heard some serious barks. What did you do?"

"Ran back to the front. Both September and the dog were outside, and Timothy was. . . Tim was hurt. On the ground." He paused, and Teddy heard him blow his nose before continuing. "I grabbed some towels, a dog blanket I think, whatever I could find to cover him and keep him warm to counter shock. He tried to talk to September. I made him stop, tried to keep him calm, told him help was on the way. I called 911."

"Did you see anybody else? Any other vehicle?"

"September said somebody in a truck fought Timothy to take Macy. Why would anyone steal a cat?" He blew his nose again. "Tim started to crash, so I gave CPR until the EMTs arrived. That's when I realized September was gone."

Teddy shook his head with dismay. September probably chased whoever took Macy, but leaving the scene made her appear guilty as hell.

Detective Combs said nothing for a moment, and then offered, "I've watched those dog shows on TV. Some dogs—cats too?—must be worth a lot of money."

The veterinarian demurred. "Rare breeds go for a pretty penny, yes, but Maine Coon cats are pretty popular. Macy's gorgeous, very nice example of the breed, but I don't think he's ever been shown."

"Why does that matter? My mom had a cat. The vet told her Simba could produce a hellacious number of kittens if she wasn't fixed. That's a lot of potential cash." Combs floated another speculation when the vet didn't act convinced. "Locals know September won the lottery. Maybe somebody's holding the cat for ransom."

Teddy had thought of that. September would pay anything to keep Macy or Shadow safe.

The doctor agreed. "That makes more sense. Champions can produce some high-dollar litters, but that's the exception with cats, not the norm. Macy's neutered. He shouldn't be bred anyway, not with his HCM—that's a potentially heritable heart ailment."

"Heart problems? Is that why September brought him in?"

"Yes. That, and the other cat. Belonged to…Wait a minute, I left the file out front."

Teddy pretended to read the Humphrey Fish pages when the veterinarian walked behind the front counter. Detective Combs hurried after, saw Teddy in the waiting room, and scowled. "Go home. This is a matter for the police." He paused. "That's my file."

Teddy stood, and pushed his glasses up his nose. "I know, Detective, figured you'd need it. But September's like a daughter to me. I want to help."

"Help by going home. Leave the file with me." He turned to the veterinarian as the doctor riffled through a stack of color-coded paper files.

"Here it is. Sylvester Sanger's cat."

"What?" Teddy hurried to the counter, and set Fish's file on the ledge.

"Damn, she mentioned Sly's cat this morning, I totally forgot." Detective Combs's words ran over Teddy's.

Teddy leaned against the tall counter. His mouth had gone dry and he licked his lips before he could manage to speak. Blood from the dead technician stained Doc Eugene's white coat. "What's wrong with it? The cat, that is, why's it sick?" He imagined the file's information scorched his hands, and dropped it on the counter.

The veterinarian frowned. He saw Teddy stare at the red stains, and shrugged out of the white coat and stuffed it into a garbage can. "You a friend of September, huh? That's good. I think she needs friends, but be careful. Her friends have a way of getting hurt."

Detective Combs flinched, and Teddy wondered how close a friend the detective had become. He knew the veterinarian's murdered wife had been September's friend, too.

"This could be related, Detective." Teddy angrily slapped the folder against the counter. He waited for the doctor to open the file, but Doc Eugene eyeballed the file like it was a snake.

Detective Combs shoved the file closer. "He's right. Sylvester Sanger disappeared this morning. He left his cat with September, said he'd been researching some weird new animal disease. We never found Sly's notes. This supposedly is a recap."

"New critter disease? Don't know if it's new. I've got my own ideas about that." The veterinarian opened the file and began to read. "Uh huh, uh huh. Yep. That's what I've seen, too. But mostly in dogs." He pushed it aside and opened up the clinic's file on Sylvester's pet cat. "This is the first cat case I've seen. It's more obvious with dogs. Cats hide, or they wander off and disappear. People notice when dogs forget house training or tricks they've always known." He rubbed his face. "I understand from a few clients they've seen similar behaviors in wildlife, but that's purely anecdotal. I couldn't confirm or deny that."

Teddy pressed for more details. "September told me cats and dogs can get Alzheimer's, like people. They forget things, get senile."

The veterinarian shook his head. "Not exactly. Yes, they can develop brain changes as they age, and some of the amyloid brain deposits are similar to the human Alzheimer's disease. This is different, though." He sounded puzzled. "Cognitive disorder in pets happens with the really old ones. That would be dogs aged nine or more, and cats older than fourteen or so." He tapped the cat's file. "This new syndrome affects old pets, too, but not exclusively. Mr. Sanger's cat Pinkerton is three or four—now, I wouldn't know for sure if it's the same thing without an examination of the brain changes. But I had a dog come in recently, and the owner authorized the necropsy after euthanasia. I'm still teasing out information on that, sent some slides to pathology, but it has me concerned."

"Is it contagious?" Teddy held his breath.

"Contagious?" The veterinarian looked up sharply. "You mean from pets to people? No."

The front door of the clinic squealed open and Detective Gonzales entered. "You want to see him before they take him away?"

"Be right there." Detective Combs turned back to Teddy. "Like I said, you should let the police handle this. Or turn it over to Parks and Wildlife."

The veterinarian shook his head. "Actually, the county health department should be told. If the pathology comes back as I suspect, the CDC will take over the whole thing."

Detective Gonzales perked up. "Health department?"

"CDC? I thought you said it's not contagious?" Combs shrugged. "It's Sly's pet theories about the sick critters, maybe connected with this mess. Could tie in with the perp taking September's cat."

Sighing, the doctor rubbed at a stain that had bled through to his shirt. "Don't want to speculate too much, or cause a panic. But it's likely some sort of environmental contamination. Probably food. Pet food contamination can affect pet owners, too."

Gonzales nodded. "There was a big scare a few years back with pet food being recalled. Like that?" He paused, opened the door and called, "Hold up, we'll be there in a minute." He shut the door and told Combs, "They want to roll. Why don't you take a gander, and I'll finish up in here."

Combs headed out the door. Teddy saw him hurry to the body.

Gonzales crossed to the counter and leaned on it, standing beside Teddy. The small detective made Teddy feel tall, even with his old man stoop. "So it's not contagious to people, but could cause problems if they're also exposed by handling contaminated food. Like salmonella or E coli. Damn, need to call Mercedes—my wife—and tell her to watch the kids around the dog food."

Teddy wished they'd be quiet. He remembered something, a connection with food and memory, but couldn't quite recall. Wait, had his memory jumped the tracks, too? Would he join Molly in madness?

And there it was. His heart pounded and he put a hand to his chest. He whispered the words. "Mad cow disease?"

Chapter 34

The masked man's happy grin faded when he saw September's gun. He stumbled backwards away from the car, holding his hands and the shovel aloft. "Don't mean no harm. Thought you was here to help." He head-jerked toward the ratty truck parked on the other side of the park.

September steadied the gun, aiming at the man's belly. Chris's lessons came back to her: *Don't point unless you mean to shoot, and always go for the biggest target.* She hoped it wouldn't be necessary, but she was ready. "Drop the shovel. Back away. Farther." She yelled the words to be sure he heard through the closed window. When he'd retreated a safe distance she opened the car door and stepped out. "Take off the mask. Where's my cat?"

"Mask?" He ducked his head, hands still in the air. "Oh." He tugged the ski mask over his head. "I ain't hiding nothing. It's colder than a witch's tits." He frowned. "You lost a cat? I love cats, got me a sweet litter over at the barn." He smiled again, showing teeth in dire need of dental care. "Got me some great hunting dogs, too. Nice one you got there." He didn't sound particularly concerned about her pulling a gun on him. "He won't bite me if you let him out. Dogs know good'uns from bad'uns. They always like me."

Her hand wavered, and slowly she lowered the gun, only then realizing she'd not released the safety. She dared a glance over her shoulder, and saw

Shadow with his nose poked as far as possible through the opening in the window, wagging tail underscoring the stranger's words. This man wasn't a threat. And he hadn't taken Macy. She remembered the toothpaste-bright shine of the attacker's grin, nothing like this man's broken fencepost smile.

"Sorry, mister. Where'd you get the ski mask?" The attacker had worn an identical one.

"Okay for me to pet him?" She nodded but kept distance between them when he approached Shadow. "He wants out. Okay?" The man asked permission—she liked that—and when she agreed, he opened Shadow's door for the dog to hop out.

"Who are you?" She relaxed when Shadow raced to her side, nudging one hand to get a pet. She watched Shadow's reaction closely, hand still tight on the gun hanging at her side, and stepped on the dog's trailing leash to keep him close. The stranger seemed harmless, if a bit odd.

"Call me 'Felch,' everybody does. They gave all of us official gear with the TV colors." He indicated the ski mask, which now bulged from one tattered pocket. "Not supposed to wear 'em out and about till the launch party tomorrow night, but I didn't have nothing else. Mr. Dietz don't want nothing to get in the way of our big-whammy party, so I try to do what's right but on the hush-hush." He held a finger to his lips. "My own fault I got sick. But nobody else ought to pay for my mistake. Couldn't live with myself knowing what I know and not making the effort." He squatted to meet Shadow on his own level, turning his face away when the pup aimed a slurp at his eyes. "Can't sleep no more. My body clock's all bass-ackwards. So got to hurry while I can still think straight. It comes and goes." He stood again, ambled over to the shovel and stopped. "I know what I need to do. But sometimes the why of it gets all foggy." He walked back toward his truck, his figure flickering from into the lamplight to shadow and back again like a stop-action film.

September's eyes took time to adjust when she slowly followed the man. Stepping from bright into dark shuttered her vision as effectively as blinders. "Somebody took my cat. He stole Macy from the vet clinic." Her voice caught. She squinted from the dazzle upon reentering the next spotlight.

Felch hunched his shoulders, but kept walking. "Your cat's sick, too? Sorry. Hurts to lose 'em, and I've lost several. See, it gets the critters sick lots faster than us people. It can take a critter down in a couple months. With people it's maybe a year." He sounded sad. "I got a few more months, I figure. Had other plans, but now they don't matter none. Got to work fast."

"Wait. Mr. Felch, wait. You're saying there's a contagious animal disease making people—making you—sick?" She hurried to keep up with his long stride. "Infected pets make people sick?"

"Naw, the same thing makes people sick gets the critters, too. All get exposed to it, one way or the other, but the animals die quicker. I think that's because they age so much faster, and kitten brains still developing. And the wild ones, they eat direct from the source."

"Eating? Dying?" She stopped at the thought. This was confirmation of Sly and Fish's wild story. September again hurried to catch up. "It's local, though, right?" Please let it be local, and not the beginning of another debacle like the horrific pet food recall of 2007, when nearly 200 brands from a dozen manufactures were intentionally contaminated. This would be worse if it also affected the pet owners.

He hefted the shovel. "The more they eat, the quicker they get sick. I can't clean up that biggest mess by myself. Can't put 'em all out of their misery. But I can collect the bits that I shared, get 'em back, and get rid of 'em. I been working through my list."

They reached his vehicle and he tossed the shovel in the truck bed. His ski mask fell from his pocket and got kicked underneath when he climbed in after the shovel. Felch stood to tug and aimlessly rearrange the contents.

She stood next to the old truck. "If you didn't take my cat, who did? The man wore the same kind of ski mask as you."

He shrugged. "I warned the reporter when he asked, but Mr. Dietz didn't like that, said it could cause a panic. I can't warn 'em all. Mr. Dietz says the show reaches more folks at once, that he'll make it right, lots faster than me with my lonely old shovel. He promised." He motioned to the dusty pile of dirt in the truck bed, sifting over top of bags of fertilizer and stacks of unidentified boxes, some with garden supplies spilling out. There was barely room for him to stand.

"What does any of this have to do with me?" Shadow pressed against her legs, and she followed his gaze. His attention was focused on something in the blackness beyond the pool of light, and she felt more than heard him begin to growl.

Without hesitation or thought, September ran. In the same motion she lifted the gun. But before she'd taken two steps someone grabbed her gun hand and wrenched her arm behind her back.

September screamed, dropped the gun, and was yanked against a muscular form. She twisted to see, but he wore the familiar ski mask. He forced her to bend with him when he scooped up her gun.

"Hey, what y'all doing? Don't hurt her." Felch stepped forward to tower over them from his perch in the truck bed.

Shadow danced around September and her captor, barks mixed with frightened yelps. He feinted bites at the man's legs.

The man took careful aim at the pup, and September screamed again. She couldn't move, kicking accomplished nothing. She turned her head and bit him hard on the jaw through the mask and tasted blood.

He yelled. The shot went awry. His grip never faltered, and instead of releasing her, he head-butted her temple.

The world spun. She would have fallen if not for his support.

Felch whined, confused. "You promised to help."

September screamed at Felch. "Help me! Make him stop!" Her head whipped from side to side, dark hair flagging an SOS as she searched vainly for help. The nearby schoolyard remained deserted. She, Felch and her attacker were alone.

She watched with incredulity when Felch sank to his knees, head cradled in his hands. "I can't remember what I gotta do. You promised!" He reached a hand toward them, and acted surprised at the gunshot. Red blossomed at his neck. He remained motionless an endless moment before he dropped. A cloud of white dust billowed and quickly settled.

September froze for a heartbeat and then redoubled her efforts. Get away, fight, flee. He'd kill her, kill Shadow, she had to get away, stop him, save herself. She kicked, but her rubber soled boots made no dent against his heavy work boots. "Let me go, you son-of-a-bitch, get off, get off!"

Shadow's hysterical barks grew more frantic. His tail flagged in high jerky movements, and snarls shouted fear and indecision. He grabbed and bit the man's pant leg and tugged, nearly pulling him to the ground. September cheered silently, but saved her breath to fight.

He aimed the gun again. More carefully. At Shadow.

"No!" She knocked his arm, and the shot went wild.

"I'll kill your dog. Like before."

His voice. The old familiar terror iced her veins. Victor, his voice, she'd never forget it. The gun followed the dog's movements. "Don't hurt him!"

"Beg." He shook her a little, couldn't do more with only one arm snugged her vise-tight, but it was enough. "Just like old times. Let me hear you beg."

"Please don't hurt my dog." She couldn't stop the sobs that choked her and could barely speak past the grief. "Whatever you want, but don't hurt him."

"You're so predictable." He laughed, delighted. "Call him off or I'll shoot him."

She swallowed hard. "Wait. Shadow, it's okay. Settle, baby-dog. Wait." Her voice cracked, but turned to steel to issue the commands to save her boy's life. He had to obey. Had to, or he'd die.

"Put this on. Backwards." Victor grabbed her by the hair, and she bit her lip not to scream. He held the gun trained on her, and turned loose her hair long enough to pull another ski mask from his pocket and toss it to her. "Do it." He aimed the gun again at Shadow.

She could run, and he'd kill Shadow and still come after her. "Shadow, hush. Sit. Wait, good-dog." Her voice trembled when he planted his tail. He yawned and whined his distress, licked his lips to signal "no threat" in the hope the scary situation would go away. When it didn't, he watched her with a furrowed brow, clearly conflicted whether to obey or not. "Please be a good-dog, wait. That's it. Wait."

Victor turned the gun toward her face. September took a breath and pulled on the ski mask, eyehole and mouth openings turned to the back. She could see the floodlights filter through, but no details. "Wait, Shadow, good-dog!" She kept calling, the command more a plea and a prayer as she let herself be dragged to the truck. Victor shoved her into the cab and started to climb in after.

With a furious roar, Shadow broke the stay. She heard him thunder close, could imagine him savaging Victor's legs.

God, no! He only wanted to help but he'd be killed. She saw Victor's silhouette, arm raised, pointing. She didn't hesitate.

"Shadow, *show-me GUN!*"

Victor cursed. The gun popped. Shadow screamed.

Chapter 35

Combs watched the EMTs load the vet tech's body into the ambulance, and slowly roll out of the parking lot. No lights. No hurry. He cracked his knuckles and flexed his neck, releasing tension that had settled into place like a vagrant no matter how often he tried to evict the unwelcome intruder.

He turned to the ME who waited nearby, leaning against his car, foot bouncing with impatience. "Sorry for the wait. COD pretty obvious? Blunt force trauma?"

The doctor agreed. "One massive tear caused all the bleeding. Something like a hatchet, some weight behind it but the blade was rather dull. Not so much a stab or cut as a tear. Caught him on the side of his neck and laterally down his chest. Another blow took out one knee and took him down. His right ulna, bone in the forearm, is fractured. Maybe more, but that much I could tell from this prelim."

"Defensive wounds." Combs demonstrated, holding up his right arm in a protective gesture. "The object came down and his arms came up, protecting his head."

"Probably." The ME nodded shortly. "Don't know the order yet, but at least one blow got through his defenses and cracked him a good one beneath the hairline. Likely a concussion, subdural hematoma—a brain bleed—could be what killed him. I'll know more when I get him on the table." He sighed. "There goes my nice, quiet holiday plans. Tell me this won't be a repeat of last Thanksgiving."

"Sure hope not." Back at the brightly lit clinic Combs could see Doc Eugene, Teddy and Gonzales still chewing the fat. Must be the veterinarian's worst nightmare to have this happen. Not only bad for business, but a horrible reminder of his wife's tragic end.

Once again, September was at the center of it all.

His phone rang. He frowned when he recognized the caller. "Hey Melinda. Daddy's working, can I call you back?" She knew better than to call during his shift. Well, to be fair, his regular shift should be over by now. Overtime would be the name of the game for the foreseeable future.

"You gotta come home. I mean, come over to our house. It's important. I'm scared."

He'd been ready to brush her off until the last two words. Combs straightened. "What is it, baby? Scared of what?"

"Somebody stole Mom's garden stuff. We had it stacked up in the garage, and came home and somebody broke in and—"

Combs ran a gloved hand over his head, tipped his face to the sky and mouthed, "Why me?" But he counted to five before answering. "You had a break in. Did you leave the garage door open again?"

"Maybe. I don't know."

"Anything else taken? Or only the fertilizer?"

"Daa-aaad. I don't know! But Mom's gonna freak. You know how she is about her roses. This is supposed to be some fancy exclusive stuff makes them grow like crazy, and you can't get it any more 'cuz the guy who makes it won't share the recipe, and Mom's already pissed I took off with my friends instead of going Christmas shopping with her and—"

"That's between you and your mother, Lindy."

Dead silence. "You don't know, Daddy. It's hard. Mom's acting weird lately. She can't remember anything, and blames me and William. Even Uncle Rick notices. And...and I miss you." Her voice cracked on the last.

Combs's hand tightened on the phone. 'Uncle Rick,' Cassie's new husband. At least Lindy didn't call the man "dad." That would kill him. After the tiff they'd had, he wanted nothing more than to leave Gonzales to the investigation, race to his kids and hug them close. "I know it's hard, baby. Hard for me, too. Hard for your Mom. And you gotta admit, that's not the first time Mom acted weird."

She laughed. As he'd hoped.

"I got to go. But I'll check in later, promise."

"What about the watch party? Mom said I could invite anybody I wanted. There'll be celebrities and swag giveaways, free food." Her voice got small. "Could you come?"

He arched his neck, and blew out his breath. He wanted to say yes. But didn't want to let her down. That happened too often. Better to say no than to disappoint. "Text me the details. I got a new case, but you know I'll be there if I can."

"New case?" Her voice was resigned. She'd grown up with him being a cop. The job trumping family stuff was nothing new. "You'll be careful, right?" She waited for the expected response.

"Careful as a three-legged dog with a fire hydrant. Bye, Lindy." He hung up the phone as Gonzales came out of the clinic. They walked together to the car.

"Everything okay?" Gonzales pulled out the car keys.

"Yeah, fine. Kids stuff. Ex-wife stuff. The usual." Combs pulled open the passenger door and climbed in. "Anything new from the vet? Teddy still playing detective?"

"Yep." Gonzales started the car. He adjusted the blower to keep windows clear. "He's convinced the pet angle is connected. I'm not so sure. Probably wishful thinking because of his wife. Wants something to blame." He changed gear and the subject. "Whatdya know about the stalker situation? You know September better than anyone. Why else would someone swipe her cat?"

Combs agreed. "I'm thinking it's personal. The cat's leverage over September. For ransom? Or something else." He pulled her cell phone out of his pocket. "Maybe we'll get lucky and the call to ransom her cat will come through September's phone."

She'd only told him bits and pieces about her stalker, but more than what Mark seemed to know. Her brother's assessment didn't jive with September's PTSD. "I think the stalker's here. Or someone pretending to be him scared her off. I got a name. And a picture. Victor Grant. Her brother said he was a family friend supposed to watch out for her, but I think instead he took advantage. For my money, Victor Grant is her stalker."

"Makes as much sense as anything. She built that fortress for a reason." The car increased speed. They were headed back to headquarters to write up the report, and later would swing over to the ME's office for further details once the vet tech's body had been processed. "Hard for September to stay under the radar after everything blew up last month."

"True that." Combs stared out the window.

"At least she has the dog with her."

Combs shook his head. "Shadow's a service dog; she never trained him for protection. He scopes out the house and warns of intruders, but I think he's more for emotional support than anything else."

"Whatever. I still wouldn't want to go up against his teeth."

"For the stalker to know about her cat, he must have been around for a while. This wasn't spontaneous, it was planned." He wished September would let them help. There was no way to reach her. Knowing September, she'd gone after the guy to get Macy back. "We need to find Victor Grant. If he's in the clear, then it's something other than the stalker."

Gonzales gnawed his mustache. "We don't know for sure this Grant is her stalker, if she never named him. But whoever it is, probably somebody new to town at least since Thanksgiving. Look at hotels for long-term stays, and apartments for recent rentals. Damn, that's a lot of people. Man, it is the holidays."

"September claimed the stalker killed her husband, but the local PD didn't buy it. I'm betting they at least took a look, even if they didn't clue her in." He paused. "Call Chicago PD, too. Uncle Stan knows people there, and her husband worked SVU there before they got married." Uncle Stan, retired after forty years on the force, still had plenty of connections.

Combs didn't need September to quote chapter and verse. It didn't take an Einstein to scope out what happened. Her sister April had never given birth, which begged the question about Steven's birth parents. Put it all together and it wasn't a huge leap what had happened.

September's stalker found out he had a kid, got pissed, and came after her.

Gonzales's phone rang, and he plucked it from a front pocket and thumbed it on. "Yeah, Gonzales." He listened, and his posture subtly straightened. "Yes, sir. Right away, sir, we're on our way."

Combs braced against the door when Gonzales slowed at the next intersection and pulled a fast U-turn. "What?"

"The Captain." He pushed the gas, hard. "Pecan gleaners in the south of the county, over the other side of Cottontail Mountain, found a pile of bones. A big pile. Deer mostly, probably a hunters' dump."

"Yeah, it's still deer season."

"There's not much left besides bones. Coyotes and other critters picked them clean. Hell of a place to harvest nuts." He pressed the accelerator hard.

"Pickings kind of slim by this time of year." Wild pecans commanded a decent price by the pound, and for some had become supplemental income. Commercial growers used motorized engines to shake down the nuts, but the gleaners banged branches with long poles and scrounged the ground to gather the pecans before squirrels beat them to the punch. Hard work, back breaking to gather up the bounty for not much reward, but that'd put the gleaners nose-to-nose with God-knew-what might be found in the scrub country. "Captain wants a pecan pie?"

Gonzales snorted.

"So what'd they find? Or should I say, glean?"

"A body. Face gone, so are the hands, probably cut off and tossed somewhere else to stymie ID. Wallet gone, too. But Captain says the fellow has a press badge the killer didn't find. Sylvester Sanger."

"Son-of-a-bitch. September was right. Somebody nailed that sorry bastard, and then moved the body."

Gonzales smoothed his mustache. "Somebody tried to kill Sly's investigation when they disappeared him. Another few days among the critters, and there would've been nothing left."

Chapter 36

Shadow banged his nose into the side of the truck when the stranger slammed the door. He jumped high against the side of the truck, barking-barking-barking as loud as he could. He clawed the metal as the truck started to move.

He heard September inside, crying. Shadow tried even harder to reach her.

A good-dog protected his person. She was his family. He'd tried even though the bad man pointed the gun at him. Shadow knew guns could reach out and bite, his ear stung with the memory. He didn't want September to get bit, either. So when she shouted *'show-me'* he nose-punched so hard the gun flew from the man's hand.

But September didn't climb out after the gun fell in the dusty road. Why didn't she come back to him?

Instead, she stayed with the bad man in the truck. It moved faster and faster, down the road and past September's parked car. Shadow barked for the truck to stop, and when it didn't, he chased after, trying to grab the tires with his teeth. He had to stop it from taking his person away.

But once it spun out of the lighted park onto the dark, hard car path, it raced faster and faster, so fast he couldn't keep up. Shadow ran after the truck anyway, chasing the truck into the night and crying for September to stop, to wait for him. But she'd left him behind.

Panting became more important than barking. He needed every breath to chase after them. No matter how hard he ran, the truck sped faster and soon its eye lights faded into the distance. He was left alone in the dark.

Shadow settled into a distance-eating rhythm, head held high to taste the air for the signature odor of the truck that had stolen his person. He loped along, focused only on the thread of scent, one paw padding after another, panting breath and pounding feet a hypnotic rhythm syncopated with his heart. On and on he ran; the odor fresh and blood hot in his nostrils. He didn't need light to see, his ears and his paws kept the path true, straight down the middle of the deserted car path. Without need to think, the scent told him where to turn, and although it grew fainter with time, it pointed the way as bright and sure as sunlight on a good-dog's back.

Trucks and cars followed car paths. Their four wheels spun faster than four dog-paws could gallop, but they always stopped. He'd catch up to the truck and his person as long as he didn't stop. One paw after another. No matter how long it takes. Follow the scent. Turn at the corner, run up the hill. Keep running. On and on. Don't stop. A good-dog finds his person.

Light haloed him from behind and made a dog-shadow leap out before him, but he ignored the shine. When the TOOOOT! sounded, he jumped, but quickly turned back and kept running. The scent pointed. He followed.

TOOOOT! The horn sounded again, and Shadow moved to the side of the road so the car with its shining eye lights could pass by.

"Hey boy. Hey dog?" The car pulled alongside and slowed to keep pace while the stranger talked to him out the window.

But Shadow kept running. Panting harder now. Running slower. But still moving. He couldn't stop. September was waiting for him. When the truck stopped and he caught up they'd be together again. They were family, and family belonged together.

"Dog with a mission, right? C'mon, boy, you're gonna collapse. Why doncha take a break."

Shadow's ears flicked. He didn't need to pee and poop. He didn't know why the stranger suggested take-a-break. He ignored the man's words. Only the scent mattered. The scent ruled. There. On ahead.

He stumbled. Caught himself, and pushed ahead. What was that whistle? His breath. It made whispery whistle sounds. Shadow came to another crossroads, ignoring the car that followed beside him, and paused. He knew which way to go, but paused. Another step. His head hung to the ground and he whined. Step. Pause. Step, step. Breathe.

The stranger's car stopped beside him. "Man, you're gonna kill yourself, dog. Doncha want a car ride?"

His ears flicked again, but he didn't raise his head. For a moment, catch his breath. There, over there, the scent-path continued. He took another step, licked his lips and whined. Panted. Jagged breaths pumping in and out.

"That's it, that's enough." The man got out of the car and walked slowly toward him, and Shadow watched warily. "Car ride?"

He raised his head, and barked at the man. His voice sounded funny. He barked again. *Car ride.* It wasn't September's car. But cars traveled fast, faster than dog paws, maybe faster than strange trucks that stole away a dog's special person.

"You want a car ride, dog? Sounds like a deal." The man opened the passenger door, and stood back.

Shadow whined, looked from the road's scent path to the open door. Finally, he limped to the car and climbed in. It took two tries to jump into the seat, and he leaked a bit of urine on the way in.

"Good-dog, that's a boy." The man carefully closed the car door, trotted around to the driver's side, and climbed in. He and Shadow stared at each other, until Shadow whined and reached out to gently sniff the man's offered hand. "Good boy, you're a beauty, aren't you?" He scratched Shadow's neck, and played with the jingle-sounding dog music on his collar. "So your name's Shadow?"

He cocked his head and barked once, but softly. It didn't occur to Shadow to wonder how the stranger knew his name. People knew things that dogs didn't. That's the way things were. Shadow watched out the window, sniffed the closed glass, and woofed again. He wanted the car to go. To go THAT way, where September had gone.

"Okay, Shadow, chill and rest. And we'll get you back where you belong."

The car started, and Shadow wagged with excitement. His tail thumped. But then he yelped, and pawed at the glass when the car turned around.

They were going the wrong way! He barked and pawed the glass again.

But the strange man only made soothing sounds. And drove Shadow away from any chance of finding September.

Chapter 37

Teddy took off his glasses, plucked a tissue from the box on the front counter and polished them, more a habit than anything. They weren't dirty. But it gave him time to think. He wished the whole situation would go away, but he owed it to September—and maybe Molly—to dig deeper into the story. He hoped it truly was only a "Fish" story.

"It's been a long, hellacious day. I want to lock up and go home." Doc Eugene rubbed his own eyes. "The patients have already been walked and fed, Timothy took care of that before he…" He turned away, busied himself gathering and stacking file folders.

"I'm sorry for your loss." Teddy carefully placed his glasses back on.

"Tim's family needs to be notified. Do I do that? Or the police?" The veterinarian slumped into a chair. "When my wife died, I got a call from the cops. I was out of town at a conference in Houston. It was our thirtieth wedding anniversary, did you know that?"

Teddy didn't know what to say.

"The blizzard grounded planes, and I couldn't get home for three days." The hurt remained raw, his words bitter. "She'd be alive today if it wasn't for September."

"September thinks so, too. And you're both wrong." Teddy held up a hand to stop angry words. "A lot of people were hurt. I lost a dear friend, and I'm terribly sorry for your loss. September will punish herself forever. Yet the only thing she's guilty of was trying to save the lives of her sister and nephew. And your wife helped her do that."

Doc Eugene started to say something, and then shrugged. "Pam never needed to be asked twice, that's true, she loved SAR work, hands on with the dogs to save people's lives." He smiled. "Seeing Shadow today was a treat. He's from one of the last litters Pam bred. I've placed his littermates with people who will help the pups reach their full potential. I don't have time to run a practice and train the dogs, too. And frankly, the dogs that are left— Heike, Uschi and Bruno—just remind me of my loss." He picked up a picture from the desk, of Pam surrounded by her dogs. "Bruno didn't eat for a week, thought I'd lose him, too. God, they were a sight together, especially on the trail. Don't know who enjoyed it more, Pam or the dogs." He turned the picture around for Teddy to admire.

"Good times, too. Right?" Teddy reached out a hand and squeezed his shoulder. "My wife Molly looks the same. But she's only really present now and then." When the veterinarian tipped his head, questioning, he said, "Alzheimer's."

"Aha. Sorry." Doc Eugene stood again and shuffled through the files he'd stacked, pulling one free and opening it. "That's why you're so interested in this."

"Mad cow disease. Here in Heartland." Teddy shivered.

"I didn't say it was spongiform encephalopathy. Far as I'm aware, prion disease has never been reported to affect dogs, but there is a feline spongiform encephalopathy thought to relate to the bovine form. Then there's scrapie, which affects goats and sheep. I don't know what this is, but the signs are similar." The veterinarian met his eyes. "There are other prion diseases that affect wildlife, rarely. Mink get it, and chronic wasting disease affects deer and elk. Again, that shouldn't impact the pet population, or humans. If it did, the CDC would already be here with sirens wailing."

Teddy shook his head. "There was a scare some years ago about infected cows and contamination of the food supply. I thought they cleared all that up."

"Right. There was a major outbreak in the UK back in the 80s and 90s. They test for it now so it can't get into the food supply." The veterinarian shrugged. "Mutations in a gene can cause spontaneous prion disease, no contamination necessary. But in people it's damn rare, maybe one in a million every year, with an incubation of months to decades, so nearly impossible to track even if it gets diagnosed. Creutzfeldt-Jakob disease is the human form, and it's thought the variant of that arose from the bovine disease. The only way to diagnose is to examine brain tissue. Tiny pinprick holes develop in the cortex and turn the brain into a sponge." He tapped the stack of folders. "That's why I sent off samples of that dog's brain, it appeared suspicious. I don't know what this is, maybe something entirely innocuous. Coincidence does happen, you know. Like September associated with another murder." Despite the wry tone, the joke fell flat. "Sorry, I know she's a friend."

Teddy didn't acknowledge the comment. He shared the man's bitterness over life's random attrition. He couldn't shake the notion—hope was too strong a word—that something other than Alzheimer's might be the cause of Molly's illness. Maybe something treatable, if it could only be identified.

Teddy didn't know what mad cow looked like, only that it affected the brain. "They banned beef imports for a while, right? From Canada and the UK. I forget all the details. Me and Molly still had our dogs then, and I remember she wouldn't buy beef for us and switched to a lamb and rice food for the pets." He smiled sadly. "At the time, all the experts said it wouldn't affect cats and dogs, but that didn't matter to Molly. Price of beef plummeted, but nobody bought it for a while. Not if a rare steak could drive you mad."

The doctor shook his head. "A cooked steak is as infectious. Cooking doesn't kill prions."

Teddy leaned on the counter. "If it's mad cow disease making the pets sick, it could affect people, too." He paused, and then asked the money question. "Can it be treated?"

Doc Eugene pushed the file to one side. "I know what you're asking. Alzheimer's disease is heartbreaking, but there are medications that help slow the progression. There's nothing for prion disease."

"Something's making people sick. Not only folks Molly's age, but youngsters, too. I know of at least two people in their thirties recently diagnosed with what the doctors *say* is Alzheimer's disease." He emphasized the word to show his doubt. He poked a finger at the file belonging to the infected dog. "Of course, they'd have to eat the same infected food as the animals, I suppose. How many people feed their cats and dogs steak? How often does wildlife get to chow down on prime rib?"

The veterinarian shrugged. "Coyotes and raccoons eat anything. They're scavengers, raid garbage cans like it's a smorgasbord, so theoretically the same food source could be accessed." He opened the file in front of him. "Then there's the raw feeders and home cookers. Mr. Benson's been feeding his dogs a raw ration for years."

"Raw?" Teddy made a face. "I like my rare beef as much as the next Texan, but that sounds like it's asking for trouble.

Doc Eugene laughed. "The veterinary community's shared your concern for years. Nevertheless, lots of my clients' pets get fed raw or homemade diets. That massive food recall that poisoned so many pets also created a whole new cottage industry. People lost faith in commercial foods and started mixing up their own recipes." He shrugged. "It can be done. Takes more time and there are some downsides. You gotta do it right. Sometimes I recommend home prepared foods, but consider them more of a therapeutic option for special cases. Some of my alternative medicine colleagues beg to differ." He laughed. "There's a reason they call it the *practice* of medicine.

Often it's more art than science."

"But you say this Mr. Benson's dog got sick and he feeds raw food? Any of his other dogs sick? Do the other sick pets also eat raw food?"

"He's a hunter. You probably know him from that new reality show."

Teddy made another face. "Not a fan of reality programming."

"Well, it's pretty popular. Mr. Benson's become a local celebrity. He only brought in the one animal, but I'm sure he feeds all his hunting dogs the same. The other animals, don't know if it's the same illness or similar signs. Good idea to research common food sources. I investigated at Mr. Benson's behest. But it could affect commercial pet rations as easily. I think Mr. Benson uses a commercial supplement."

"What's that? The supplement?"

"Usually a vitamin and mineral pre-mix that makes sure the homemade recipe is balanced. Lots of them out there, the internet lists millions of self-proclaimed expert recommendations." He flipped through pages in the file. "It's documented here somewhere. I don't carry such things anymore, not worth the trouble when so much is available cheaper. The internet again." He closed the file. "It'll be a couple of days at least before the pathology on the brain tissue comes back. Until then, we're guessing."

"None of this helps us find September, either." Or helps Molly, he thought. If she'd caught this "new" disease, it'd be trading one horror for another. "If September had her phone, I could've used GPS to find her." At Doc Eugene's surprised expression, Teddy offered a sheepish expression. "You could say I have certain skills that allow me to bypass official channels. Only for good."

"Right. The geriatric Lone Ranger."

Teddy barked a laugh. "I like that."

Doc Eugene suddenly straightened and drew in a deep breath. "I wonder . . ." He held up one hand, and flipped once again through the stack of file folders. "GPS. We've got a new product we're trying out. Tracking device for pets, mostly used to keep hunting dogs from wandering too far. Timothy thinks it'd be—I mean, he *thought* the product would make a great holiday promotion." Awkwardly, the veterinarian corrected his tense. Teddy knew it would take a while before the young man's death felt real.

The doctor pulled out Macy's file, flipped it open, read, and paused. "Well how about that?" He turned the chart around so Teddy could see. "September bought a collar tracking system for her cat. If Timothy's killer still has Macy, we can find him with the cat's GPS."

Teddy's pulse quickened. He pulled the file closer, but frowned. "Wouldn't the unit have to be charged?" The veterinarian handed him a duplicate of the product and he quickly scanned the information, and pointed. "See here? It runs on a rechargeable battery."

"Timothy made a note. He charged the unit and put it on Macy's collar before the cat was released." Doc Eugene smiled again, and reached for the phone. He had one of the detective's cards in his hand.

"Wait." Teddy stopped him. "The unit has to be configured. September didn't have time to do that. Or would she give Timothy access to her phone or computer codes?" The veterinarian shook his head, disappointed. "You define acceptable territory, and then tell the GPS feed to send alerts to a designated account." He paused, thinking.

The veterinarian's face fell. "Oh. Right. Guess that's no help."

"Not necessarily." He polished his glasses. "Did I mention I have skills?"

Chapter 38

September slowly regained consciousness when the ancient truck's jounced movement stopped. Her head throbbed. The driver's side door squealed open, and the shot springs jiggled when someone climbed out. He left the door open—she assumed it was Victor—and icy air laced with a hot, gag-making smell poured in.

She couldn't see. Panic. Had the head blow left her blind? The knit mask itched her face, and memory assuaged the panic but only a little. The blindfold snugged tighter over her eyes and around her head than before so no light leaked through. Her temple throbbed. How long had she been out?

Shadow! He'd shot her dog! Then she remembered hearing muffled barking before she passed out, and could breathe again. Knowing he was still alive, that one small victory made the pain worthwhile.

Careful to remain still, September blinked, testing the limits of her vision. Eyelashes scrubbed against the fuzzy knit mask. She heard steps shuffle outside the truck. Victor probably could see her through the windows. Best to play possum as long as possible. Maybe she could learn something useful, leave a message for would-be rescuers, or even figure out how to escape. She'd escaped before.

After a smitten fan sent her flowers—Forget-Me-Not blossoms—Victor became enraged and threatened to smash Melody, her only connection to normalcy, to life before, to the real September. Once he destroyed the music, she'd be next. September knew her daydream of escape must become a reality.

The chance came three months later, December eighteenth, after Victor escorted her onstage. She seated herself, situated Melody between her knees and took the bow. She didn't look at Victor when he brushed a kiss on her forehead, fearing he'd read her intent. He hesitated, and September forced a smile, prayed he couldn't hear her thrumming heart.

Vic exited stage right and stared as she prepared to play.

September nodded at the conductor, the orchestra played, she placed her bow and fingered the strings, took a deep breath—and stood. She ran into the wings, cradling her cello like a beloved child. Gathering her long skirt in her bow-hand, September raced down the stage stairs into the audience, thundered up the aisle and out through the rear double doors. Audience members began to murmur and rustle but she didn't hesitate, and dashed down the first set of red-carpeted stairs, turned the corner, and continued to the ground level.

She terrified the coat-check girl when she suffered her first panic attack, certain Victor would convince everyone her "mental breakdown" required his personal intervention. But the girl let her in and September burrowed between hanging coats to hide, holding Melody like a shield, like the life preserver she truly was.

A half hour later, Detective Christopher Day and the police team appeared. Victor Grant disappeared.

And now he was back.

The truck jostled with accompanying thumps and grunts of effort. He must be in the truck's bed, moving Felch's body. Felch must have helped steal Macy, even if he hadn't understood the implications.

And what *was* that smell? September breathed through her mouth, but the odor coated her nostrils and clawed at the back of her throat. She could almost taste the acrid, cloying smell. They must be at the county dump. She turned to the window and leaned her shrouded brow against the glass, welcoming the cold but afraid she'd vomit into the knit cover and choke to death. That'd serve Victor right. But she wouldn't get much satisfaction, either.

September heard him drag a large object from the back of the truck. Gravel or sand beneath the weight screed against the metal bed. Her seat jounced again when Victor jumped off the back of the pickup, grunted a few times to drag the object off, and a sodden thump hit what sounded like wet leaves. Sound faded as he dragged the object some distance away from the truck.

Before he could return, September quickly explored her face with her hands. Her wrists were bound by tape. More tape wound around her head and across her eyes over top of the knit covering. That explained her loss of sight.

His face and voice haunted her nightmares. She didn't need to see Victor to know it was him, but the blindfold kept her helpless, and literally in the dark about where they were going. Or what he was doing here at the dump.

There must be something, some way to leave a message. The police would talk to Doc Eugene, and he'd tell them she'd been there. Victor could have taken her at the house, but he didn't. Instead, he left the flowers so she'd run. He wanted her to run, and when she didn't, he took her.

Combs might think otherwise. She'd discouraged his attentions for so long, he might decide he'd had enough. How long could you push someone away before they gave up trying? A brief, clutching grief nearly crippled her before she pushed it away as well.

Her car. They'd find it eventually. She'd left the keys behind. Surely they'd know that wasn't right. Maybe Victor had finally screwed up. She had to do something, leave a signal. She had to trust they would look.

September patted her coat pockets. The noxious rotting odor faded into the background as she struggled to wriggle one hand inside the zippered front. A hard object, long and pointed. And a round cylinder, a pill bottle, no help at all. A pencil might work to scribble a note, or if sharp enough, pierce the tape on her wrists, or stab as a weapon.

She traced the outline and recognized the blunt-nosed Sharpie Marker with disappointment. There was no way she could get it out of her pocket, un-cap and write a message before Victor returned to the car.

This had to be more than payback from the mercenary son-of-a-bitch. It had something to do with Sly; the terrible day had started with him. Then there was Felch's confusion, clumsy gait and insistence on "fixing" some wrong. He said the ski mask was some official merchandise. A TV show, that's it. If she could figure out where Victor fit in, she might still get out of this alive.

She heard Victor returning to the truck. *No time, no time, leave something behind in the truck, something that could come only from her.* He'd notice if she kicked off a boot. She'd cut her nails short to practice cello, and they couldn't leave noticeable marks. No buttons to tear, and the ski mask had contained her tears or blood, if any. She wore no jewelry, so had no watch to drop onto the floorboards, nothing that identified her.

The pill bottle. Macy's prescription. She hiccupped, and grappled to pull it out, and the cap pulled off. Normally the child-proof bottles were a bitch to open. Never mind, it wasn't the pills—it was the label on the bottle that mattered.

She managed to milk the bottle up out of her pocket until it dropped. Most of the small, white tablets scattered down her front. September kicked the bottle out of sight beneath the seat and shifted, brushing off pills caught in the fabric folds of her coat.

Knowing Victor, he'd probably dumped Macy somewhere. Her eyes filled. One more innocent victim because of her. If she didn't survive, Macy's pill bottle found under the seat would convict Victor. That was a damn fine legacy for her beloved cat.

The truck bounced as he climbed back into the cab and slammed shut the door. "So my sleeping beauty awakes."

She refused to answer. But in the back of the truck, another voice replied. "Meowring?"

Macy was alive.

Chapter 39

Combs put a hand up to his mouth, trying to stifle the smell. "That's disgusting." One of the uniforms looked green. "You gonna toss your cookies, do it over by the road. I don't want you contaminating the crime scene."

It had taken more than half an hour to find the place. After traveling down main highways and turning onto twisty farm-to-market roads, they'd come to a graveled path that took them deeper into the scrub. Gnarly bois d'arc trees and a few honey locusts fought for supremacy among the native cedar elm, mountain ash and burr oak. He hadn't a clue how the gleaners found the cluster of pecan trees. Maybe they passed the information down the family line the way granny's pecan pie recipe became an heirloom.

As if reading his mind, Gonzales said, "Won't be thinking about pecan pie the same way ever again." He spoke through a paisley bandanna.

"Love the new style. Like you're ready to bushwhack a stagecoach." Combs coughed, his eyes watered. "Yee-haw. Don't suppose you've got an extra?"

Gonzales shook his head, and the bandanna covering his mouth and nose rippled when he spoke. "But I got some Vicks."

"Gimme." Combs accepted the small bottle and liberally smeared his upper lip. It didn't help. "Don't know how the ME handles it." He acknowledged the little man crouched over the remains.

"Nose transplant. You think?" Gonzales led the way over to the small group of onlookers, the pecan-gathering group who stumbled across the body. Literally. "Which one of you called?"

The older woman raised her hand. "I did." She had a young girl of perhaps twelve clutched tight under one arm, and a lanky pimple-faced teenage boy stood nearby trying to pretend he was bored and failing. All three shared the same dark uni-eyebrows, upturned freckled noses and tiny gray eyes. "Daddy found it." She pointed at an even older man standing with his back braced against the tree. "I got the only phone, for emergencies. This qualified."

"I'll say." The teenage boy wiped his runny nose on his coat sleeve.

Combs noticed none of the family acted bothered by the smell. Maybe long-term exposure deadened smell sense the way overuse of perfume made some women overdo the cologne.

"What's your name?" Gonzales took the lead. The wind had picked up, which made audio recording iffy, so he took notes on the small pad.

"Feeny. Glory Feeny. This here's Gina. That's George Junior, and over there's Daddy. My dad, that is, George Feeny, Senior." The little girl shivered, and Glory gave her shoulders a squeeze.

"You called right away?" Gonzales scribbled the names.

"Yep. Soon as Daddy uncovered the boot. First off, thought some hunter done tossed out an old pair, and Daddy needs new ones so he tried the size. 'Cepting the feller was still wearing them."

"Touch anything else?" Combs took in the family's worn clothes, and the loose fabric bags at their feet. Or maybe other pickings. "Mind if I take a peek?"

"Help yourself." She nudged one of the bags with her foot. Dirty, worn tennis shoes peeked from the cuffs of baggy sweatpants. "All you'll find is nuts." She didn't sound angry, only resigned.

"The pigs got him."

Combs glanced up. The old man stood with eyes closed, loose lips mumbling maybe in prayer. "What'd you say?"

He opened his eyes and repeated. "Just what I told Glory. Them feral pigs got him." The old man's words gave Combs the creeps. "Then when they was finished, the coyotes took a turn. Maybe some coons got in on it. And finally the black birds flocked over top, they're gleaners like us, take the leavings. This here's like a trough for the critters, they kin all belly up to the bar."

"Daddy, that's enough." Glory gave him a look. Combs wasn't sure what it meant.

"You've known about this place for a while?" Gonzales asked the question before he could. "Other people come out here on a regular basis, do they? I'll need the names."

Glory shrugged, but stared daggers again at her father. "Hunters know the spot. Don't know no names. They keep to themselves, and we do likewise." She nodded at the trees. "Don't need no competition for the pecans, and sure don't have no interest fighting the pigs for that garbage. We's poor, maybe, but I feed my kids healthy." Her chin jutted out.

"No disrespect, Ms. Feeny. Just trying to figure out who might have dumped this man out here." Gonzales pulled down the bandanna so she could see him smile. "We appreciate you being good citizens and calling us. You didn't recognize him?"

She shook her head. "Like Daddy said, the pigs got him. Nothing to recognize." She took a breath. "Can I go? Want to get my kids and Daddy back home. We been out here for too long."

"Just a couple more questions, ma'am." Combs thought Gonzales was a better man than him, going without the bandanna filter. He licked his teeth, to be sure the smell hadn't made them melt. "You got out here what time?"

"Don't have no watch. Early afternoon, though. We ate lunch before we came."

"And when was the last time you came here for the pecans? I mean, before this."

"Last week." Glory turned to her son, and he shrugged. "First day out of school for the kids, so we come up here and scouted around. Not too many pecans that day."

"Did you pick around this same area? So the body wasn't here last week. What day was that?" He stared back at the three pairs of tiny gray eyes. The old man wouldn't meet his eyes. Huh. Something there.

"Monday last. Nobody here that day but us." She crossed her arms. "Can we go?"

"Thanks for your time. Yes, you can go. We may have more questions later, so don't leave town." Gonzales paused. "I need your address."

"Where would we go?" She huffed, but readily gave Gonzales the address of the low rent apartment complex where they lived. "Just so ya know, the phone's disposable and almost done. We ain't got a line at the house so you'll have to catch us when you can." She stooped and scooped up the pecan bag, and the teenager grabbed the other two before they all made their way to a distant rust-bucket sedan.

Gonzales tugged the bandanna back into place. "Doesn't help a damn. But I look so cool." He cocked his head at Combs. "You look like a snot-nosed kid."

"It's a choice. Not a good one, but what can you do." Combs breathed through his mouth for a minute, and the wind in his face also helped. "What do you think?"

"The old guy knew more. Glory knows Daddy could get in trouble and wants him to shut his pie-hole." Gonzales closed his eyes. "Damn, and I used to love pecan pie."

Combs shrugged. "So we'll follow up with Daddy when Glory isn't around." They waited for the ME to approach. "Sly disappeared from September's place on Thursday morning and hasn't been seen since, after she claimed to see his dead body. So somebody flew in and scooped him up after she saw him—"

"—or he walked out under his own power and got transported later." Gonzales shuddered. "Hope to God the man was dead before they dumped him. Feral pigs, nasty beasts. Sure do fast work."

The ME ambled up to the detectives, wheezing from the climb out of the trough. "Sometimes I hate my job."

"Only sometimes?" Combs sounded like he had a cold, and tried again. "What's the word?"

"Dead before he got here."

Gonzales let out his breath. "Sly was a low-brow gossip monger, but even he didn't deserve this."

The ME went on. "Several blows to the torso, and the COD appears to be a baseball bat to the head. A Louisville Slugger, to be exact."

"Got your crystal ball mojo going, do you?" Combs forgot and breathed through his nose, and nearly gagged.

"Nope, nothing so woo-woo. Found the baseball bat. Under the body." He motioned over his shoulder to where the CSIs continued to process the scene. "It's pretty distinctive, has the words *King Thwacker* wood-burned into it. Yep, it's an old fashioned wood bat, not a new-fangled modern aluminum or whatever the hell the Rangers use these days. A lot of good that does 'em," he said.

Combs didn't let his surprise show. He grunted. "September's bat. Must have come from her place. She said they had words."

Gonzales picked up the thread. "More than words. Somebody heard or saw the argument, and took the next step. Doesn't look good for her." He held up a palm to stop Combs's reply. "Just saying. Whoever whaled on Sly meant it to incriminate her." His phone rang, and he frowned as he listened.

The ME continued. "We'll have to confirm ID once we get him back to the morgue."

"I thought the responding officer found his wallet?" Combs raised his eyebrows. "No?"

"Wallet's gone, whoever killed him probably disposed of that. Even cut off his hands and bashed in his teeth, obviously trying to hide who he was. And the critters took care of the rest." The ME shrugged. "They missed his press badge, on a lanyard under his shirt. Sometimes we get lucky, when others get stupid."

Gonzales hung up the phone and crossed back to them. "Found September's car."

"Where? She okay?" Combs breathed through his nose again, but this time he was prepared. Damn, he must be getting used it. He wondered if his sense of smell would be permanently damaged.

"At a park next to Heartland Middle School. She's not there. But get this: they found her gun, and it had been discharged."

"Shit." Combs started running toward their car. "Anything else, tell me while I drive."

Gonzales jogged after him, and swung into the car in the same synchronized motion as Combs. "They found a stocking cap on the ground, weird colors. Somebody recognized it. The characters from that reality hog hunting show wear them."

"Hog hunting?" Combs jammed the keys into the ignition and shoved the car into gear. He didn't watch reality TV and had enough of guns during his day-job. "Hogs, like feral pigs?" The car bucked over the uneven gravel road, but began to make better progress once back on the paved FM highway. "There's a whole film crew in town, I think the actors are local but betcha there's some out-of-towners. Wonder if any of them joined the party since Thanksgiving?"

"Haven't had time to canvass motels. But I got a list of possibles, right age bracket and name match to Victor Grant or close derivatives." Gonzales swerved around a squirrel and nearly went off the road. "Damn tree rats," he muttered, and then louder. "Any word from the Chicago PD or from South Bend?"

Combs shook his head. "Not yet. Like you said, it's the holiday. Case moving too fast." His phone rang and he grabbed it and tried to answer, but nobody was there. It tweedled again, and his eyes widened. It wasn't his phone. "That's September's phone." He dug it out of his pocket, and handed the phone to Gonzales to answer. "Put it on speaker."

"It's an unknown local number." Gonzales punched it on. "Hello? Who's this?"

A man's baritone spoke, cheerful and excited, while in the background a dog barked and yelped. "Hey man, I got great news for you. I found your dog Shadow."

Chapter 40

She stumbled, and Victor's bruising grip kept her from falling. September bit her lip to keep from crying out, wouldn't give him the satisfaction. She knew from experience any complaint fueled an increase in the abuse.

They'd driven for quite a spell away from the dump. The smell faded quickly, and she silently thanked the winter wind, but worried about Macy left in the back of the truck. At least Macy was alive. Thank goodness for Maine Coon fur.

She'd managed to surreptitiously collect half a dozen of the Atenolol tablets. Maybe Victor hadn't noticed, but she couldn't be sure. He might simply wait until later to surprise her with his retaliation. Or he might believe himself so in control of the situation, nothing she could do mattered.

September tried to keep track of turns, even counting the number of seconds between them. That always worked in the movies. But she suspected Victor purposely drove in aimless circles for a time to thwart that possibility. Even if her guesses proved accurate, she had no way to know.

Once they slowed and parked, Macy meowed when Victor collected the cat's carrier and helped September out of the truck. The uneven ground sported large tufts of vegetation, maybe grass or winter rye. Icy wind made her hands stiffen and prickle, the Reynaud's syndrome making an expected appearance.

She listened. It sounded like the middle of nowhere. No traffic or train sounds, no street light buzz or any of the subliminal ambiance that saturated every urban setting. Only the crunching of their feet on frozen ground broke the silence. Her fingertips stung, and she could imagine the nails turning blue in response to the drop in temperature. September curled her bound hands protectively into her chest. She'd need as much function as possible if she were to do anything in her defense.

A soft thump prompted another meowed protest. He'd banged the cat's soft sided carrier against something solid. Still blindfolded, she remained helpless to do anything to protect herself or her cat.

They'd entered some sort of a shelter. She could tell by the change in air pressure and smooth feel of hard-packed dirt beneath her boots. September heard the thump of the duffel drop to the ground, and Macy's guttural reply.

"This is temporary." They stopped. He released her arm. She didn't try to run—run where, blindfolded and bound? Instead she shivered elaborately and whimpered for Victor's benefit. Let him think she was totally cowed. He did have control, but overconfidence might create mistakes. Right now, that was her only hope.

Metal on metal rasped followed by the scream of rusty hinges. "Go on, inside, step up." He pushed her, and she reached out with both clenched hands, found the wooden doorframe and felt with a foot for the step before she cautiously climbed inside.

A room. Small, confined. Smelled dusty and musty, like old lawn clippings. Hay?

"Here's your cat."

He shoved Macy's carrier against her shin, and she crouched to touch the webbing, smiling with relief when the cat's cold, wet nose pushed against her hand through the mesh.

"There's a bucket straight ahead of you on the far wall for the obvious bodily functions. A sleeping bag beside it, in case you get chilly or want to sleep. Not much left of the night anyway, it's nearly dawn." He moved around, and she could hear his boots clop on the wood floor. "Got Felch to clean out all the bones. Didn't seem to bother him, but he was an animal himself. Hell, his own shack up the hill isn't much better. And there's a table to your right with a thermos. Coffee, for the caffeine addict." He laughed. "See, I remember, something we have in common. Neither of us could ever get enough coffee." He paused, and she heard him move around the room again. "Collected all your favorite things here. Just for you." He turned serious, and it was all she could do to stand her ground when she heard him draw near. "It's not how I planned. But you'll never leave me again. You need me, September." His arms came around her. Hot breath burned her neck, and she stiffened.

A phone burbled. Victor's arms tightened for a moment before he stepped away. "Rain check."

She said nothing. Didn't move, although her instinct screamed to put as much distance between them as possible. September reminded herself he'd graduated to murder, and he had her gun. He could aim the gun and shoot her and she'd have no warning.

He answered the phone. "Yes, what?" He listened. Aggravation colored his reply. "I've got everything covered, except I need a ride. Felch's truck slid into the dry gulch at the dump site, can't get it out. Yeah, that's why I'm not back yet." He listened. "I took care of Felch. Hey, we agreed, it had to be done. They shoot horses, don't they?" He laughed. "Great movie. Besides, he couldn't be trusted after what he did to that reporter, and too much of a loose cannon. Hell, he'd show up for the party and start wagging his jaw, and we'd be done." Another pause. "Nobody will tie anything to us, after a couple of days there won't be anything to find. You plan what you'll say when he's a no-show at the party tonight. I still need a ride. No, not one of the new guys, they'd have too many questions. Send BeeBo, he can give me a lift to my car. There's still a few loose ends to tie up before the party tonight." Another pause. "Yeah, grabbing the cat smoked her out but there was a minor complication. Felch will take the heat on that, too. I know what I'm doing. Don't worry," he finished, "I can guarantee she won't be a problem."

September sucked in a silent breath. This *was* bigger than Victor's personal obsession with her. If Felch had something to do with Sly's disappearance, then her kidnapping involved Sly's investigation, and his partnership with Fish.

"You'll manage. You don't need me there. Sunny and the other stars will make the appearance; nobody will notice one less goober. Local yokels will believe anything you tell them," he said drily. He lowered his voice, but she could still hear. "No, I need to move tonight, before then. It's personal." He made a frustrated sound. "Oh, all right. But if you want me there, I want my bonus as soon as we wrap. I'll send wire instructions for the rest, but I need traveling money tonight." He listened. "You don't want to test me. I know where all the bodies are buried. Literally." He hung up. Footsteps thumped the floor. The squeal of the door announced his departure.

"Stop! Please, Victor!" She couldn't help the pleading tone in her voice. That wasn't faked.

The footsteps paused, but he remained silent, waiting for what she'd say.

"How long will you be? Can you at least take off the blindfold? I already know your face, and haven't a clue where we are. Besides, there's nobody to tell." She motioned with her taped hands. "I can't do anything taped up and blind."

Nobody knew she was here. What if something happened to him? She could be stuck here for days before someone found her, if they ever did.

"Plans changed." He wasn't happy. "I'll be back tonight, and we can finish our reunion. That sleeping bag isn't the Ritz but it'll do in a pinch. Soon, very soon, I'll be my own man answerable only to myself, but tonight I've got a command performance I can't escape." He paused. "There's no way out. No windows, no lights, new padlock on the door, and nobody to hear you scream, but go ahead and knock yourself out."

His hand touched her face, spider-light against the ski mask, and she jerked away. "Just remember there are consequences to everything you do. That cat you love so much? Treat me nice or I'll wring its neck." The hinges squealed and door slammed.

September gathered Macy's carrier close, shaking as a padlock snicked closed. Soft footsteps faded, and she craned to hear, remaining motionless until the distant truck's engine roared to life. Once it drove away, she wasted no time.

"Macy, I'm gonna get us out of here. I won't let him hurt you. Or me." The cat mewed back and head-butted the mesh. "I know, I know you want out. Me too." First, though, she needed to see. She'd have to risk Victor's consequences. The alternative didn't bear consideration.

She still grasped half a dozen of Macy's pills in one hand, and awkwardly dropped them into one of her pockets so she could use both hands to work off the mask. Depending on how long they were stuck here, she might need to medicate Macy. Or maybe poison Victor? She wondered what effect Atenolol might have on a person.

She wasn't a scared, gullible teenager any longer. Nothing he could threaten would keep her from fighting him. The chameleon lied as a matter of course. For all she knew, this place was a luxury get-away and the bucket a sick joke designed to torment her.

September quickly rolled the breath-wet soggy knit cap upward, uncovering her lips and nostrils. Cold, fresh air invigorated her efforts.

It took longer to work the taped portion off, the pressure against her closed eyelids creating dark sparkles that slowly faded when she tossed the ski mask free. For a long moment she was afraid to open her eyes, afraid it wouldn't make a difference and that Victor's assertion of no windows would continue to block further effort to see.

Macy yowled, and September blinked. Opening her eyes wider, she turned her head. He hadn't lied for once. No windows. But chinks in old planks allowed dim light to filter through. September levered herself upright, and walked carefully across the floor to the wall, placing her eye to a knothole. Moon glow bathed a rough field with light. The horizon had begun to brighten.

Still dark, but near dawn on this icy December morning, so it must be Friday about 7:30 a.m. Victor's meeting was tonight, what time he hadn't said. But she couldn't count on him keeping to a schedule. She needed to make plans quickly and set them immediately in motion.

Her eyes grew accustomed to the dim light, and before anything else, she tried the door. She grasped and shook the handle to no avail.

The hinges were attached on the other side, so even if she'd had the tools, there was no way to access them. Anyway, she'd need her hands free to do anything.

September bit at the tape, and tried to get a purchase on the material. Gaffer's tape, but she couldn't get the right angle to tear it, and Victor had used nearly a whole roll. The multiple layers made it impossible to remove without a cutting edge.

The bucket squatted against the wall, sure enough, with a roll of toilet paper. The small table held a thermos as well as the missing rose lamp stolen from her office. Was it plugged in?

She hurried to the table, and when the sound of her shoes across the plank floor changed, she realized Victor had placed a carpet over the floor. It was hard to tell in the near darkness, but she suspected it had also been taken from her house. He'd chosen things she would have never left behind when running away. These were items meant to furnish a future life together. She shuddered. "Over my dead body." It might come to that.

She found the cord to the lamp, coiled and neatly tied, and dropped to her knees to search for outlets. No outlets, but Melody was there.

She pulled out the cello, and saw the strings were gone. Crap. The A-string might have cut the tape on her wrists. Any of the strings could have worked as a garrote or trip-wire to surprise Victor upon his return. Hmm. Maybe the cord from the lamp could work to trip him?

Because she would NOT go quietly.

Within minutes she'd explored the tiny confines of the room. Old wooden planks made up the floor, four walls, and low ceiling. Multiple empty nail and screw holes peppered the walls where hooks, shelves or other accessories no longer rested. Nothing remained, no sharps able to injure or threaten a captor, and nothing useful to signal a rescue. Originally used as a tack room or for tool storage, someone had transformed it into a bare box, a prison to keep September contained until Victor could spirit them both away.

Macy yowled, the sound a bit desperate. "Okay, I know I promised. We'll figure something out, right?" She hurried to the cat carrier, sat on the floor and zippered open the top.

He eeled out of the container, stretching first one fore paw followed by the diagonal rear leg and then stroked his full length against September's thigh. Macy climbed into her lap, pushing his cheeks in turn hard against her face. "I know, it's been forever, I missed you, too." His purr vibrated beneath her stroking hands. Somehow that made everything better. Fear and panic slowly began to subside, replaced by angry resolve.

The sticky tape between her wrists caught the cat's fur and he flinched and pulled away. Macy sniffed the tape, and tasted it, and then stretched out on his tummy against the familiar carpet and honed his claws.

"Not even your claws will do the trick on this tape," she said. Macy circled the small room, sniffing the floor for whatever animal scents remained and stopped to cheek-rub the few items: the bucket, the table leg, nose-touched the rubber tip of Melody's endpin.

The endpin! September stumbled in her hurry to reach the cello, and released the holding screw to pull out the long metal rod. Light-weight titanium and about two feet wide, the rubber stop fit over a sharp point. With effort, she got the rubber end off, braced the rod between her knees and used the dagger point to sever the tape binding her wrists.

"Yes!" She pulled off the rest of the tape and grasped the endpin, swinging it through the air as though testing a bat or fencing an invisible adversary. Though sharp, the light-weight rod designed to enhance tone of the instrument had never been meant as a weapon. "Use what you got, September."

She returned to the cat carrier. After taking Fish's notes to the vet clinic, she'd had no time to discuss them with Doc Eugene or Timothy, after the vet tech was attacked. At least she'd stuffed them inside the carrier. She set the file aside and searched another pocket, pulling out a small spray vial of synthetic cat pheromone used to reduce feline stress. She put it in her pocket, and added the small penlight used for Macy's chase-the-light game.

Feeling the half dozen loose pills in her pocket, she debated giving the cat a pill. Doc Eugene had explained about titrating the dose—starting small and slowly increasing as needed—and had given Macy his first dose before she'd picked him up. She couldn't risk giving him too much and overdosing him.

That made her wonder again what an overdose might do to a person. Atenolol was a beta-blocker. She glanced at the coffee thermos, and for the first time began to feel hope.

Macy pawed one edge of the carpet in a corner of the small room. He sniffed, and then sneezed.

"What'd you find?" He meowed back at her, and she joined him. "Going to help me get the bad guy? Like you nailed them the last time?" She didn't know how soon Victor would be back and there wasn't time to train new behaviors. "Use what you have," she whispered again, her new mantra.

Claws caught on the edge of the carpet, and Macy lifted the covering enough for her to see in the dim light: a cat-size black hole in the floor on the inner wall.

Chapter 41

Teddy had fooled with Macy's GPS setup for nearly an hour. His eyes itched and didn't want to focus. Cleaning his glasses didn't help. Besides, Doc Eugene's tiny office, outdated desktop and slow internet connection made him want to bite nails and throw the computer against the wall.

"Had to create an account. Email is required to send alerts via email or text, so I plugged in my own info. But that's as far as I got." Teddy's frustration made him even more tired. "I don't have a clue what to set the local portal parameters to, without a general idea of Macy's location."

Doc Eugene rubbed his own eyes. "Usually the local boundary is the pet's home. I've got September's address, if that'll help." He yawned. "Sorry, so tired. I've not slept well lately anyway."

Teddy yawned, too. "Doubt either of us will sleep much tonight, either. I mean today. It's nearly dawn." Teddy refolded the brochure with the setup information. "Nifty device, works something like the Amber Alert tracking options for kids, but without all the bells and whistles. The kid version has multiple zones you can define, and as long as the child wears the device, you can get updates every minute or so and track movements 24/7. You can even set it up for when you go on vacation or for the Little League practice park. And it all tracks on your computer or smart phone."

"Nice. Didn't know they had that for kids." Doc Eugene half smiled. "Bet that would drive teenagers nuts, though."

Teddy agreed. "But for the little ones, and the wanderers—like autistic children—it could be a lifesaver. They use a combo of GPS and cell phone towers to track." He tapped the pet tracking brochure. "This system, though, tracks pets with a separate handheld device. You set up the boundaries on your computer, but the handheld detects signals only within about a two-mile range. It alerts when the pet crosses the designated boundary." He made a face. "That's actually to our benefit, most of these pet trackers only work up to about six hundred feet or so. I still need to set up the boundary, make a best guess to get the location within that two-mile limit. We need straight line-of-sight for best case results. And then pray the batteries on the cat's collar last long enough for us to zero in on Macy. Even the kid version of this technology says batteries need a re-charge every forty-eight hours."

"That's a lot of ifs." Doc Eugene picked up the brochure, flipped it over, and read for a moment. "Wait, here it says they have a GPS option."

Teddy nodded. "Yes, but we're dealing with the basic package. The bonus options would get us eyeballs on the cat from a computer map using satellite technology, but there's an extra fee and a forty-eight-hour set up delay." He paused.

"I could pay the fee, that's not a problem." Doc Eugene leaned forward. "I know September didn't intend for Pam to die, or for Timothy to get hurt. Macy is my patient, and he got taken from my clinic, so there's that. I want him found. Besides," he tipped his head, "I hear you've got skills. Maybe the ability to speed up that forty-eight-hour lag time?" He smiled. "I've got my laptop in the car. It's old, but you're welcome to use it if that'll help."

Teddy smiled back. "Funny you should mention that." He flexed his shoulders and rolled the chair away from the desk. "Does your laptop have a mobile Wi-Fi, you know, one of those plug-and-play hotspots?" The veterinarian shook his head. "Then I'll have to run home and get mine." He stood, collected the materials he'd need, and headed to the front waiting area. "Thanks for letting me stay."

Doc Eugene followed with the keys to the front door, but stopped when the clinic phone rang. He sighed. "What the hell, I'm still here. And I need to record a message we'll be closed today, and cancel the appointments. After Timothy's death, I won't ask the staff to come in, not until Monday." He unlocked the door for Teddy, and then trotted back to the counter and leaned over to reach the phone. "All Creatures Veterinary Hospital."

Teddy lifted a hand to wave, and started out the door. It'd be a twenty-minute drive to retrieve his laptop. Figuring out how to track Macy was busywork, though, and there were no guarantees the thief still had the cat or that September was anywhere nearby. But he owed it to September to try. That was all they had.

"Wait! Hey, Teddy, hold up."

He turned, caught the door before it closed and re-entered the waiting area when Doc Eugene yelled. The veterinarian held the phone receiver in one hand. "It's one of the detectives from before. Somebody found Shadow, they want to drop him off here."

"What?" Teddy hurried back into the clinic, and held out his hand for the receiver. "This is Theodore Williams, what's this about the dog? Was September with him?"

"Teddy, it's Combs." He sounded as exhausted as Teddy felt. "Some guy called. He picked up Shadow way the hell out on FM 1417, said he was a dog with a purpose and running down the road at a pretty good clip."

"What was he doing out there? Where's September?"

A pause. "We haven't found her, but her car was identified over at The Gazebo. That's a park next to the middle school. We think someone took her, maybe the same one took the cat. Could a dog follow the truck, maybe track where it went?"

Teddy relayed Comb's question to the veterinarian. "Maybe." Doc Eugene sounded excited. "Shadow sure has the bloodlines for it."

Teddy spoke into the receiver. "If the dog's pickup was, say, within two miles of the cat's current location, and September's with the cat, I can find them. Macy has a GPS on his collar. Tell me the location."

He hung up the phone, eyes shining. "Combs will meet us out on FM 1417 with Shadow. I need to get my laptop along the way. You drive. I don't do night driving. And pray there's enough time for me to finagle the GPS."

Chapter 42

The hole in the floor measured eighteen inches by five inches where one old plank had split and fallen through. Animal fur fuzzed the splintered edges of the opening, clearly used as a critter path into the barn's tack room.

September guessed this was a barn, probably abandoned since wildlife claimed the building. More likely feral cats set up housekeeping, if her nose wasn't mistaken. Cat urine had its own special ambiance. Macy certainly thought the place an aromatic delight.

She crouched to shine the penlight into the hole. "No, stay back." September gently restrained Macy. "We'll play later."

But they wouldn't play, maybe never again. She pushed aside the crippling thought, and stopped him again when he would have followed the light into the hole, the chase-the-light game so ingrained he had only to see the shine to follow its path. He loved cubbyholes, and probably could squeeze his twenty-three-pound body through. But what then? How would she ever get him back?

Or should she try?

September remembered the step up to get into the place. There must be a crawl space under the floor, and the fur snagged on the hole pointed to another exit into the interior of the barn. Maybe an escape not only for Macy, but also for her. No way could she squeeze through. Not yet, anyway.

But if she could pry up another board or two, she could wiggle through. If the crawl space was deep enough. And if it led anywhere besides dead space under the floor. And if Victor was gone long enough. What time was his meeting tonight? Tonight—that meant after dark. So at least several hours, anyway.

Too many ifs. But no other options presented themselves.

Dropping her hand through the hole, September shined the penlight around inside, illuminating the dirt-floored crawl space. A well-worn path led toward the hidden stair step, back into the barn's interior. That must be the way out.

She stretched out on the floor and pushed her arm as far inside the hole as she could reach to determine the depth of the crawl space. Cold ground stopped her hand about two feet down, and she flexed her icy fingers to keep circulation going. Two feet would be a tight squeeze.

She'd make it work. No other choice. She grappled left and then right, blindly, with one bare hand. Fluffy, soft material crinkled with something that sounded like paper and sticky cobwebs. Probably fur, desiccated vegetation, dust bunnies. Nesting material. At least it was too cold for spiders. She hoped nothing inside the burrow would mistake her fingers for hors d'oeuvres.

Reaching far forward, she brushed more wood, possibly the continuation of the wall, and followed its surface until she found another narrow opening. Her arm wasn't long enough, nor could she see around the corner. But if the cats used it to gain access to the crawl space, it must be at least as large as the one into this room. Macy could get out.

"He could die." She said the words aloud, and then wished she could take them back. Sending Macy into the crawl space put him at risk from coyotes, or the sick wildlife. He was a house pet, and had never had to hunt for a living beyond "killing" his toys.

His heart could give out.

As much as she yearned to hold him safe in her arms, she couldn't protect Macy once Victor returned. Staying with her, Macy would die. Sending him away gave him a chance.

She couldn't explain to the cat. If she showed him the hole, would he run, or instead try to come back to her? Would she have to scare him to make him leave? If she survived this—no, WHEN she survived this, would he hate her? Would he forgive her? How would she find him again?

Eight years ago after she'd escaped, she'd put the cello away because Victor might track her through the music. Turning her back on Melody nearly killed her, and she adopted Macy to ease the empty ache in her arms. Macy taught her to laugh again. Pets were safer than people; they didn't pretend or wear a mask.

Shadow could track Macy. He'd survived the gunshot. She'd heard him follow the truck at least for a while. Would he follow this far, track her to the barn? He'd never been taught to track people, and wouldn't know what to do on his own.

September wiped away tears, and with them the fantasy of a Lassie-inspired rescue. Once on the scent trail, Shadow ignored everything. On the road and oblivious to danger, he could be hit by a car. Or he could be bleeding from Victor's gunshot. Shadow might be lost, alone and dying. That was the reality. "Baby-dog, please forgive me."

And Macy was damned if he stayed and damned if he ran. He had a chance to survive only if he ran.

She knew what she'd tell clients. Some lost cats traveled miraculous distances to find their way home. The reality was grimmer.

God, she didn't want to make this choice! This was Macy: the furry wonder who had healed her heart with his silly antics, his demands for attention and affection, his never-give-up pestering attitude and brilliant understanding of her moods. Macy gave her the courage to love again, to say yes to Chris and find some peace. For a while.

The big cat burbled and trilled, climbed into her lap and turned three times before settling into the makeshift nest of her crossed legs. He turned upside down, presenting his white chin and chest for scratches, half closing his eyes and increasing the volume on his Mac-truck purr.

He had something on his collar. She frowned, turning Macy around to better examine the object. "Hold still, buddy." She shined the penlight. "Oh wow, I forgot about the GPS!"

A small plastic object had been attached to his collar. Timothy promised to charge the device, so all she'd have to do was finish the setup at home. That is, if she ever got home.

She would! By damn, she would get home again.

"Thank you, Timothy." She stroked Macy, and his purr rumbled the small room. "Once I get out of here, that GPS will bring you home to me. Keep yourself safe until then, buddy, until I can set up the tracking. I promise."

That eased her heart a little. It was still iffy, but she had to take the risk and turn the cat loose. Victor could return anytime now. "Maybe somebody will find you. Wish you could talk. You'd tell them how to find me, wouldn't you?" The cat cheek-rubbed September's face, smearing the tears she couldn't control.

Pull yourself together. What do I do when a lost pet shows up? Even before finding someone to scan for a microchip, what do I do? "Check for a tag."

September quickly rummaged in her pocket and retrieved the Sharpie marker she'd found earlier. "Hold still, Macy." His rabies tag had her name and contact information, just as Shadow's did. But that wouldn't help anyone find *her*.

She turned the cat around, and wrote on the GPS tag. And then for good measure, she wrote in block letters on Macy's white fur apron.

That finished, she reached for Fish's file. Victor's mention of the reporter indicated a connection that might be the key to getting out of this mess.

The thick file contained pages of scribbled notes nearly impossible to read in the dim glare of the penlight. It also included several internet printouts, some dated from several years earlier.

Scrapie. Wasting disease. Prions.

"It's a brain disease." That's what made the animals sick? "Okay, Sly, tell me how they get it. And are people at risk?" That was the issue.

The government cracked down on foreign imports and tightened processing requirements. Today, even pet food manufacturers had layers of inspection to avoid a repeat of the crippling recall. But Felch said the pets and people got sick from the same cause. She skimmed the documents, and found the answer stapled to the back of the file. A slick flier, folded in three, included a red font that shouted the headline.

HOG HEAVEN HOSTS Hog Hell

Hog Hell. Pig hunts. She knew feral pigs made wallows out of plowed fields, uprooted crops, got into garbage and frequented dumps. They'd made a mess of her garden, too, and aggravated the crap out of Aaron.

She wrinkled her forehead, putting it together. Chronic wasting disease affected deer, but hunters harvested deer and took only the prime venison cuts, leaving behind the spine, legs, and head if it wasn't trophy-worthy. People wouldn't eat the deer parts that could infect them—the brain, especially.

But pigs would.

Feral hogs left nothing; they were nature's garbage disposals. They ate acorns, dug up pastures and trashed seeded fields. They'd eat scraps hunters left behind. Like infectious deer parts? And if hogs ate something contaminated by sick deer, and people harvested the hogs…

"Oh, my God. It's the hogs!"

Macy meowed at the exclamation and leaped off September's lap.

That had to be it. Felch and BeeBo starred in the *Hog Hell* show. BeeBo's dog was sick. Felch claimed to be sick, and had a run-in with the reporter, maybe to quash the story's connection to the TV show. Lots of money was involved in making a show a success, not to mention rich endorsement deals for the stars. They had lots of incentive to make the story go away. She read the flier again, and realized what it meant. "Oh dear God, they're feeding everyone at the party!"

Barbecued feral hog would be served at the Hog Heaven restaurant. Tonight. That must be the important meeting Victor must attend. And Piggy Panache gift boxes of what they called "piggy treats" distributed for the holiday gift giving season.

Horrified, she read that the TV show would offer ordering information to viewers. No wonder they wanted to keep any rumors quiet, at least until after the premier. If the meals and the samples were contaminated, a widespread infection could affect thousands or even millions of innocent victims. How long would it take for the disease to cripple the fans?

It sounded bizarre, like one of Sly's wild, made up stories. But a farfetched rumor would kill the show as effectively as the real thing. They must be desperate to keep things quiet.

She didn't know how Victor became involved. Was he one of the actors, too? She'd never seen the show, but that would explain his willingness to protect his job.

Victor knew Sly had talked to her, so he had even more reason to keep her under wraps, and then whisk her out of town. He would have killed her already, if he didn't have other plans for her.

It wasn't about outwitting a stalker anymore. September had to get out before Victor came back. She had to stop the poison from being served.

She nuzzled the cat. "You're not going alone, Macy. Time to get that hole bigger." September retrieved the cello endpin and set to work.

Chapter 43

Dietz took in the packed restaurant with satisfaction. The kitchen behind him bustled, metal clatter of utensils a percussionist's dream. Roast pork, barbecue sauce, grilled corn and coleslaw teased the air in a medley of complementary aromas that ebbed and flowed like a musical cannon.

Picnic tables boasted *Hog Hell* red and blue checkerboard oilcloth. Tall plastic glasses of sweet tea (unsweetened for the unenlightened) sat at each place setting. But most guests of legal age were enjoying the complimentary beer.

Posters plastered rough barn-door walls and featured BeeBo, Felch, Sunny (in suitably revealing attire) and several of their dogs. He'd wanted a couple of the hounds present—some fans acted more passionate about the dogs than the people—but the health department killed that idea.

At the moment, Sunny "The Babe" Babcock flirted outrageously with Humphrey Fish. He'd arranged to have Fish sit at the head table with the cast, ostensibly for interview ease, but actually to keep an eye on the fellow. Sunny had very specific instructions, and so far, she'd followed the script to the letter and stroked Fish's ego while deflecting any mention of problems. Sunny knew who wrote the checks.

Butterflies, not hunger, quivered his insides. He didn't trust Grady. But he had no choice. At least Grady had the balls to get rid of the reporter's body, and stop Felch from doing any more damage. "God bless the hungry little piggies," he muttered, and then smiled and raised his hand when BeeBo entered the restaurant to loud cheers from the patrons.

Fish hopped from his chair and pumped BeeBo's hand when he joined the head table. Dietz raised his eyebrows at Sunny, and she gave him a thumbs-up from across the room. She'd keep BeeBo from spouting off on the forbidden tangents.

They'd been lucky Grady saw the behaviorist talking with the reporter. Containing fallout from that bigmouth's rumor had become a nightmare. His stomach rolled, and Dietz popped three antacid tablets. He didn't want to know how Grady planned to keep the woman out of sight. They were in too deep now to be squeamish, and soon they'd be over the hump, as long as Grady showed up to finish the job.

Dietz had his own plans for some down time with the tasty babe-o-licious Sunny. Tonight set in motion all his future success. Dietz glanced at his watch. Another fifteen minutes until show time. Two big screen TVs gave everyone in the place a great view.

Dietz always was surprised at the cross-section of fans. Hunters should be the go-to demographic, but teenage boys—and even a few girls in the audience reflected the most recent polls. Here and there, well-dressed couples sipped their beverages of choice—mostly Lone Star—with a few overdressed people thinking "premier = evening attire" appearing mildly uncomfortable and out of place.

For the locals, this was the event of the season, though, and anyone able to snag a ticket to the limited seating made sure to attend. Dietz smiled. At least some plans worked.

By the time Felch went south, it was too late to cancel the watch party, even if he'd wanted. Besides, if the worst happened, Dietz had deniability. *He* hadn't killed anyone, or stashed any bodies. *He* didn't know any details. *He* was a producer/director/host of a reality show. The missing Felch was the bad guy here, and with any luck, he'd never be found. And if he were found, Dietz'd be properly shocked and appalled, and lay blame squarely where it belonged: on Grady's shoulders.

Dietz had been a damn fine actor, after all. But so had Grady, and that made him wonder how much of the man's story was true. He popped another antacid.

Grady entered the restaurant, and relief washed over Dietz as he waved him over. "You clean up good." He wore the official show ski mask rolled up to perch atop his head. Grady wore the show uniform of camouflage hunter's garb, with the blood-red hog silhouette outlined in DayGlow on the back of his jacket. Grady saw one sleeve of the new coat was torn and roughly stitched up. "Wait, is that makeup?" He peered closer at the man's face. "What happened? Wait, I don't want to know."

Grady fingered the spot. "Best I could do on short notice. Got bit, but nothing serious."

"She bit you? What the hell? You said everything's under control! Did she see your face?" That was key. He didn't want any more blood on his hands, but if September could identify Grady—and hence, the connection to him—all bets were off.

"Wore the mask like you said. Relax, nobody's the wiser."

"Counting on that." He breathed in, out, in, out, waiting for his heartbeat to calm. "Okay, I'll introduce you. Be the character. Remember, you love hunting and your hunting dogs are your life. The regular spiel. We good?"

Grady nodded, and a goober-grin lit up his face. "Juss fine and dandy." He wiped his nose with the back of his hand, and Dietz grimaced.

"Drawl is fine, but lose the drool. You're not one of BeeBo's hounds." Dietz jerked his head toward the front of the screen. "Let's get the others."

Dietz made his way to where BeeBo held forth at the head table, entertaining the rest of the crew. He tapped the big man on his massive bare shoulder. BeeBo wore his signature camouflage pants and matching vest with a torn, stained—but clean—tee shirt, and he'd knocked the dirt clods off his boots. He also wore the official show hat, as did most of the crew members at the table. Sunny hadn't put hers on yet, probably didn't want to muss her hair. She'd cut the fingertips out of the blue gloves to show off her new manicure. Whatever.

"Hats on, everybody." Dietz pulled one out of his pocket and pulled it onto his head. "We got two hundred of them, one for everybody in the restaurant." The buzzing crowd started to quiet, sensing the evening entertainment was ready to begin. "Hope we have enough. Pass them out, BeeBo. You too, Sunny and Grady. And I'll get this road on the show." He embraced the rush that came with the virtual curtain rising, grabbed the mic at the front of the room and switched it on.

"Everyone having a great time?" The tentative response prompted a repeat of the question. "I said, having a GREAT TIME?" He flashed his practiced host smile when the room yelled back affirmative, and laughed out loud when a table of youngsters made pig-snorting sounds. Soon the whole room took up the noise. He held up a hand to quiet them. "Sounds like *Hog Hell*—music to my ears." Cheers erupted and again he waited for the noise to fade. "I'm delighted you joined us tonight for a special evening, a watch party celebrating the renewal of Heartland's very own reality show, *Hog Hell*. And your stars are here. BeeBo Benson." He pointed, and the room cheered, while the big man's moonlike face beamed with an 'aw-shucks' expression, clutching the trademark unlit cigar between his lips. "Sunny Babcock." More cheers, mixed with wolf whistles as she struck a pose. "And a new cast member you'll see more of soon, Vince Grady." Grady doffed his cap and bowed, to polite applause. "Unfortunately, Randy Felch couldn't be with us tonight." Disappointed sounds and a few boos came from the youngsters' table, and one of the adults shushed them with a stern expression. "Sorry. I'm disappointed, too. Called out of town indefinitely. You ask me," he dropped his voice and stage whispered into the mic, "he got a call to Hollywood for his own show. But don't tell, it's a secret." The room laughed, and Dietz knew he had them. Nothing better than when the crowd bit on every nugget, it fed their energy back to the performer. Magic.

"I hope you enjoy your own official *Hog Hell* gear. The cap and ski mask combo'll keep your head warm and face toasty on those bitter cold days during a hunt. I can't guarantee they'll protect you from the flu, but it can't hurt. Oh, and it'll advertise the show, too." He leaned forward. "I'm all about keeping locals working. Well, and me paid, too." He laughed again at the happy response.

Most of the kids in the crowd immediately donned the ski masks, and a few of the adult men did as well. The ladies set the caps aside, but that was okay. He wanted as many men as possible out and about wearing the gear in the weeks ahead, to deflect any potential connection to the show if by chance Grady or Felch had been seen during their clean-up efforts.

"The fine people here at Hog Heaven have cooked up a great meal. Hmm, some lip-smacking food'll be served any minute now. And I wanted everyone to know about our new project, a cooking show featuring more ways to roast up those tasty hogs, while getting rid of a problem that damages local economy. That's right, *High On The Hog* cooking show airs right after the New Year, and our first featured restaurant is none other than your local homegrown talent here at Hog Heaven! C'mon out here, Louisa and Jim Sams, take a bow. The owners of Hog Heaven and hosts for tonight's watch party!"

The middle-aged couple hurried out of the kitchen, smiling with embarrassed excitement at the applause and attention. Jim carried a cardboard carton, and Louisa held aloft a holiday themed cellophane-wrapped box like a candy sampler.

Dietz wished he'd thought to have them wear the official cooking show gear, instead of the stained bib-style aprons. The barbecue sauce dripped like blood. But there was nothing to do about it now.

"To help promote *High On the Hog*, we're giving you a sneak preview taste of holiday gift sets we call Piggy Panache, gourmet samplers available for order right now—but you heard it first. It'll be announced on the show tonight." Jim began moving down the aisles, holding the carton for Louisa to distribute the meat samplers, one to each family. "Could I have a volunteer to help? The show's about to start and I know our hosts want to get back into the kitchen to monitor the meal."

A couple of the teenagers from the rowdy table jumped up to take the carton from Jim. "Thanks, fellows." Dietz watched the distribution with interest.

As they received the Piggy Panache treat samplers, men in the crowd immediately tore open their packages to taste the various bacon, jerky, and sausage offerings. The ladies for the most part set aside the samplers with the hat. Dietz guessed many of the gift boxes would end up getting mailed to hard-to-shop-for relatives. "Before you leave tonight, be sure to have Mr. Grady get your name on the mailing list for future special deals. We want to give our Heartland family the first chance at trying out all the great new features."

Dietz hoped they appreciated the samples. The website ordering information listed each package at $29.95 plus shipping and handling, a tidy profit for product that cost him less than $4, and that mostly for the processing and packaging.

He'd keep harping on the "homegrown" angle as long as it paid, but wanted to cash out sooner rather than later. Two potential buyers had already expressed interest, but would probably move the filming to Louisiana where there were better financial incentives for the industry. They had the funds to take *Hog Hell* to the next level, and he'd still get the income from the new cooking show, a helluva safer way to do TV. No more wading through pig shit, or waiting for someone to discover Grady's clean-up attempts.

He switched on the big screen TVs. "And now, without further ado, enjoy the premier episode of this year's *Hog Hell!*" Dietz cranked up the volume, set down the microphone, and took his place at the head table as Grady and BeeBo joined him. He patted Sunny's luscious backside, and felt better than he had in a week.

The waiters moved between the tables with teaming plates of pork, sides of thick onion slices, potato salad, coleslaw, and grilled corn on the cob. Dietz held up his glass of beer in a silent toast to the TV screen as the opening credits rolled, and the rest of the table followed suit. His stomach rumbled, and he laughed. Butterflies gone, it was time to eat.

Dietz had the first fork of tender barbecue pork halfway to his mouth when the police burst through the door.

Chapter 44

"No, go on, get out of my way." Combs pushed the big pup. Shadow again tried to climb into his lap, making it impossible to drive. "Back! Shadow, get in the back."

The dog wouldn't stop crying. "I thought shepherds were supposed to be fierce, buddy. Can you give me a break?"

Combs opened one of the back windows partway. He remembered September always did that. Finally, Shadow pretzeled himself in the front passenger seat enough to turn around and squeeze through the narrow opening between the front seats into the back. He stuck half his head out the opening. And whined some more.

The dog shivered and panted, his sides a bellows until Combs feared he would pass out. The cold temperature made Shadow's breath fog the glass, which then froze in fairy patterns, and Combs couldn't tell if the pup was exhausted or excited. "Maybe both. Huh, boy?"

He didn't know much about dogs. How September communicated with the pup was magical to him, and he hoped that would translate into the dog pointing to where she'd disappeared.

He'd planned to leave Shadow with the vet. But Doc Eugene had given Teddy a ride in his Jeep, so the dog had to stay with Combs. Finding the cat with GPS seemed a long shot at best, but he didn't want to discourage Teddy. The old man had good intentions, and at this point Combs wouldn't turn down any help.

Shadow's tracking ability was their best shot. Amazing that the dog traveled so far from September's abandoned car at the school, more than twelve miles before the Good Samaritan picked him up. Combs figured they'd start at the pickup point, turn the dog loose, and follow Shadow to wherever September was being held.

Combs's phone rang, and the dog woofed. "Hold your horses, I'll get it. Do you answer September's phone for her, too?" Shadow barked again, and stuck his head back out the window. His tail waved. That meant he was happy, right?

He answered briskly. "Combs."

"It's me." Gonzales spoke over crowd noises. "It's a zoo here. More than two hundred people at the restaurant, it'll take the rest of the night to process them. And you're not going to believe this. Everybody here has one of those hats."

Combs groaned. "What about the production personnel? Anyone missing?"

"We got the whole crew in custody. They made it easy, everyone sitting at the head table. Actually, three head tables but one with the stars and host—and Humphrey Fish. He's eating this up, got his audio recorder going, and keeps lamenting the radio station didn't set up a live feed." He made a disgusted sound. "I had no idea it took so many people to point a camera. Some are missing, were outside smoking or whatever, and ducked out the back when we came in. Don't know how many but we'll get names and track them down. A guy named Felch, one of the stars, was a no show. The head honcho says he got an offer and took off for Hollywood."

"You buying that?"

"Shit, no. Dietz—that's the host producer guy—he's squirmy as a cornered rat."

"Nobody named Victor Grant in the group?" Of the dozen or so possibles Gonzales had found, only a few had previous run-ins with the law, and none were recent. "Got that picture of him with September?"

"Yeah, that and a bunch of other possibles." The crowd noise waxed and waned. "Haven't had a chance to show any pictures. If Grant's our guy he probably changed his name. And maybe his face. Don't actors do that a lot? You know, facelift and Botox and stuff."

"What about Felch? He's missing; September's missing. Felch could be our guy. Might not be her stalker, could be somebody wanted to keep a lid on the contaminated pigs rumor. TV folks have the most to lose when word gets out about that." He hesitated. "Listen, people hadn't started eating that mess, had they?"

Gonzales sighed. "Some had, but got it shut down quick. Oh, and I sent your wife and kids on home, figured we could talk to them later."

"My wife?" His foot jerked in reaction, and the car surged. Shadow barked and nose-poked him as if to chide his carelessness. "Cassie? She was there, with the kids?"

"Sorry, I mean *ex*-wife. Yeah, she was here with your two and a table full of teenage yahoos. Good kids I think, but causing a ruckus."

Combs white-knuckled the steering wheel. Melinda had mentioned plans to attend the premier, even invited him. Why hadn't he picked up on that? "They didn't eat any of the, uh, the food, did they?" He licked his lips and cleared his throat.

Gonzales paused, and answered carefully. "Don't know. Hey, they'll be fine. Like I said, we got here as they started serving. I gotta go, but will keep you posted. You do the same."

The phone went dead, but almost immediately rang again. Maybe it was Cassie? Or one of the kids? "This is Combs."

"Detective, it's me, Teddy. Where are you?"

Sighing, Combs relaxed his grip on the phone. "I'm on my way. *We're* on our way, I mean. I got September's dog." At the last word, Shadow nose-poked him again as if to hurry them along. "ETA ten minutes."

"Good. We're at the intersection. And I got good news. The GPS works."

Chapter 45

Nikki crossed her arms and pouted. It wasn't fair. She wanted to stay and see what other exciting stuff might happen next. But Mrs. Harrison, Willie and Melinda's mom, made them all leave the restaurant. Now she sat squeezed in the back seat, in the middle as always, with Hank on one side and Willie on the other.

"Why couldn't we talk to the cops? Everybody else got to stay." Hank leaned forward to speak to Mrs. Harrison. "I could've got a ride back with Dustin and Zeke."

"I'm not responsible for Dustin and Zeke. But I am responsible for you. Your mother trusts me to take care of you. She can decide if you need to talk to the police."

The restaurant was fun, especially when the boys made funny pig noises and got everyone snorting. Nikki giggled at the thought. She loved the Hog Hell cap, and cradled her gift box of treats. Hank already ate his, but she saved hers for Hope-Kitty. "Why'd the police stop the show, anyway?" She stared out the window. The TV people said Mr. Felch wasn't on the show anymore and went to Hollywood. Had he taken Hope with him?

"I don't know." Mrs. Harrison didn't elaborate. She hunched in the driver's seat, neck stuck forward to peer out the windshield, and slowed at nearly every intersection to read the street signs.

"Will Daddy come talk to us?" Willie kicked his foot against the back of the passenger seat until Melinda turned around and glared.

"Your father will talk to you, if that's necessary. But I think the police have more than enough people to talk to at the restaurant." The car nearly stopped, and then sped up again.

Nikki braced herself against the front seat and her seatbelt cramped across her lap. Willie didn't notice, but Hank put his finger to his lips and shook his head when Nikki would have complained about the jerky driving.

She knew Melinda and Willie's dad was a cop. He didn't live with them anymore because they all got divorced. It was sort of like her and Hank not having Daddy home, even though he and Mom were still married. It sure would be nice when Daddy finally came back from the war.

Mrs. Harrison rubbed her eyes like they hurt, and the car sped up. "What a fiasco."

"What's a fiasco? Is that like a Spanish party?" Willie poked Nikki. "Fiasco, fiesta, get it?"

Melinda groaned, but Nikki giggled despite herself, and poked him back. "Good one." Daddy liked puns, too.

"Mom, you missed the turn." Melinda spoke softly.

Mrs. Harrison bit her lip. "My eyes won't focus. We'll go around the block." She peered at Hank in the mirror. "Your mom told me she wouldn't be home for another hour. I left her a voicemail you'd both be with me. She can pick you up from our house." She paused, and then muttered, "If I can find the damn turn. There it is!" She put on the signal, and the car banked sharply.

Hank shook his head. "That's okay, Mrs. Harrison. You can drop us at home. Right, Nikki?" He elbowed her.

"That's right." She took the prompt. "Mom has Hank watch me every day after school. Even though I'm not a baby." She smiled when Melinda met her eyes. "Girl power, right?"

"Totes." Melinda again turned to her mom. "The road is back there. Mo-om!"

"Let me drive! I know the way home, for heaven's sake."

But Nikki thought she acted confused, maybe even a little scared?

She continued to complain. "What an embarrassment. An embarrassment to the city, to the Chamber, and to me personally. And where's the effin' house?"

"Mom." Melinda turned in her seat. "Are you okay?"

"Just dandy." Mrs. Harrison patted her hair. "Need to get a cut, maybe time for a new style. What do you think, Lindy?" The car stopped at the corner with a jerk, and she cupped her face in both hands.

"Um, Mrs. Harrison? Please, you can drop us at home, that'd be fine. It's two blocks over that way." Hank leaned forward and started to pat the woman on her shoulder, and then thought better of it. "Just turn right. And then at the next block turn left."

Mrs. Harrison straightened up. "That whole restaurant situation blows my mind, you know? Got me totally rattled. A fiasco." She cranked the wheel and gunned the engine, and the car slid around the corner. "Hang tight." She laughed, and then stopped at the next corner. "Which way? You, boy, what's-yer-name, you have to tell me how to get there. I've never been to your house."

"She picked us up two hours ago," Nikki whispered to Hank. "What's wrong with her?"

"Turn left here." Hank's hand squeezed Nikki's knee, and she made a silent "ouch" shape with her lips but took the hint and shut up.

The car made the turn and zoomed four blocks before the driver slowed to a stop, well past their house. Melinda mouthed, "Sorry," as Nikki and Hank climbed out of the car. Willie acted ready to cry.

"Thanks for the ride, Mrs. Harrison." Hank opened the car door, and held it until Nikki slid out. "Lindy, maybe you should call your dad?"

Melinda nodded. Mrs. Harrison barely waited for the car door to slam before zooming away.

"Wow, that was epic." Nikki hugged herself.

"Yeah, an epic fail." Hank shrugged, and grabbed her sleeve. "I didn't see Mrs. Harrison drink anything but sweet tea. Weird." He pulled the *Hog Hell* cap down over his face and stared out of the ski mask holes. "It's cold. Let's go home."

She hesitated, and then cocked her head and smiled. "Race you! On your mark, get set, GO!"

She watched him pelt down the sidewalk, ducking through a neighbor's yard and vaulting a low fence. He never looked back.

Nikki turned around, and jogged in the other direction. With a bit of luck, she'd be home before she was missed. If he told Mom about the barn, tonight might be her last chance to see Hope.

Chapter 46

She'd worked for hours, and the hole still wasn't large enough to squeeze through. Although exhausted, September couldn't let herself rest. The sleeping bag shrugged around her shoulders fended off the worst of the cold, and sunlight filtering through chinks in the boards offered work light for a while.

But now the sun had set, and she feverishly worked by feel, trying to conserve the batteries in the penlight. She feared Victor had drugged the thermos, but thirst and a threatening migraine forced her to risk one cup of strong coffee. It tasted fine, and the caffeine held her headache at bay. Not knowing how long she'd be trapped, though, she saved the rest for later. That also reduced the need for bucket use, a vulnerable experience she didn't want to repeat.

Victor had said he'd be back tonight. She had no time to waste.

September leaned on the endpin, and the third board gave way with a satisfying crack. She moved it aside and shooed Macy out of the way. He wanted to push his face into the hole.

"Yes, I know, smells lovely." She wrinkled her nose at the pungent aroma, but Macy purred with delight. "Big enough for you to get through, anyway. Gotta hope the exit out the other end will let your fluffiness out, too."

She couldn't stop revisiting the what-ifs that brought her to this place. If she hadn't insisted on leaving home at sixteen. If she'd blown the whistle on Victor right away. If Chris hadn't thought he could save her. And if she hadn't bought the stupid lottery ticket.

To Chris, the windfall meant they could start a family, no more excuses. The thought of a baby terrified her, and nearly prompted a panic attack. After a horrible fight, Chris stormed out with Dakota while she wept into Macy's fur. An hour passed. Then another hour. She called his cell and the police answered. And she knew, even before they told her about the blue flowers scattered over Chris and Dakota's bodies. No chance to apologize. No way to explain. She never got to say goodbye.

She dropped the cello endpin to fist the tears from her eyes. Wishing the past away wouldn't change the present. But by damn, she'd decide her own future.

September pushed one arm and shoulder through the opening, gingerly followed by her head. While by no means overweight, the opening barely accommodated her shoulders. It'd take at least one more board width to allow her hips to pass. She shined the penlight and the beam lasered the crawl space, stopped by wooden planks on all sides.

"Oh, no. There must be a way out." What she'd thought to be the exit instead was the hollow of a stair step.

Macy head-butted her thigh, and September raked the light one more time around the perimeter of the enclosure, this time at the juncture of dirt floor and planking.

"There! Thank God." A small cone of excavated dirt marked entry to a tunnel originating beneath the stair. The wood was solid but the nails rusty and loose, and the critters had burrowed underneath. Macy would easily fit through. And if she could get one more board pried loose and squirm the rest of the way into the crawl space, September could kick out the rickety step and also escape.

She heard somebody.

"Kitty, here kitty kitty kitty." The nest under the floor muffled the high-pitched voice.

September froze, and then scrambled to pull herself out of the hole. Sounded like a kid. But what was a child doing here?

"Hope, I got treats for you. Are you here?"

What to do? Could the child get her out?

Macy chirruped and then gave a long, drawn out meeerow in response to the "treat" word. Crap!

"Hope!" Footsteps pattered closer.

Decision made for her, September stood, flipping the carpet back over the hole to keep Macy from diving through too soon. "Hello! I'm in here." She crossed the door and pulled, rattled and then banged on it. "I'm trapped, can you let me out?" Macy yowled again, and the footsteps paused.

"What are you doing in there?" The child came to the other side of the door. "There's a lock. It's a new one, wasn't here before. Sort of like the ones on my school locker, but without the combo dial."

"A padlock." Damn, no way to get past that without bolt cutters. "Before? You come here a lot? Do your parents know?" September's heart raced. "Here's what I need you to do. What's your name?"

"Nikki." The little girl hesitated. "I come to feed the cats. Is Hope-Kitty with you? The TV guy said Mr. Felch went away, so there'd be nobody to take care of her. She's a big cat, and I think some of her kittens are still here, too."

"My name is September."

Nikki laughed. "Like the month?"

"Yes, exactly like the month. Listen to me carefully, Nikki. I need you to find an adult and tell them about me."

There was a long silence. "I'm not supposed to be here. I sneaked off from my brother, and Mom'll get mad if she finds out. I'll get in trouble." She sounded miserable. "Mom's allergic to cats."

"Please! You have to get help before . . ." She hesitated. Telling the girl about Victor might scare her so much she wouldn't tell anyone. Macy cried again. "That's Macy. He's sick. I know you love cats, so you'd be helping him, too."

"How'd you get stuck in there, anyway?" It sounded like Nikki pulled on the padlock.

"Never mind, that's not important. Isn't there anyone you could tell? Maybe your brother?"

Nikki didn't say anything, and Macy meowed again and pawed the door. "I'm sorry your kitty is sick," she said, her voice small. "I guess I could tell Hank. He's my brother."

September switched off the penlight to conserve the batteries. The room plunged back into darkness. "Nikki? Do you have a light out there? How'd you see the padlock?"

"My cell phone." Nikki held it up to a crack in the door. "But it goes out and I gotta keep pushing the refresh."

"Nikki! Call 911, call the police. You know how to do that? Tell them September is locked in the barn. You don't even have to give your name, so you won't get in trouble or anything. Call them—"

"Hey, somebody's coming. A car pulled up." Nikki stepped away from the door, and the light from her phone shut off. "It's a man." She sounded relieved. "Betcha he can get that lock off."

"Nikki, no! Run, please run!"

Oh, God. Why hadn't she sent the girl away immediately? That had to be Victor.

Nikki screamed.

Chapter 47

"Let go of me! Let go! I'll tell." Nikki struggled and kicked, but the man was too big and she couldn't get away.

He didn't say anything, and that was scarier even than his ski mask. It matched the *Hog Hell* souvenir cap she wore. "You were at the restaurant, too."

He gripped her arm tighter, right on top of the scratches Hope had left. He marched her back into the barn. Was he mad about Hope? Her lip began to tremble. "Are you Mr. Felch?"

The man paused, and stared at her a long moment, considering. Then he nodded.

"Why'd you lock that lady up?" She wouldn't cry. Her brother Hank wouldn't cry if he'd gotten caught, and neither would Melinda, so she wouldn't either. Despite the silent assertion, a tear dripped off her cheek. "What're you gonna do? Please, Mr. Felch, let me go. I won't tell. Cross my heart."

It was wrong to lie. Mom said so all the time. But Nikki didn't care, she'd tell the biggest lie she could if he'd let her go. And then tell on him anyway! She was pretty sure it was against the law to scare kids. And for sure, it wasn't legal to lock up ladies in barns.

He held a big heavy flashlight like a club and she shivered. She could see lots better than from the light her phone made, before he stomped it and broke it to pieces. Another fat tear slid down her nose. Daddy gave her that phone. Now she couldn't text him or anything.

They reached the padlocked door, he found a key, and unlocked it. Her teeth chattered. He'd lock her inside, too. She remembered the school lesson on stranger danger, and what to do. Run. But she couldn't run. Scream. That she could do.

The door swung open, and Mr. Felch pointed his flashlight into the woman's terrified face. September yelled, "Macy, *KILL IT!*"

Nikki saw a pinprick of light focused on the man's ski mask. Nikki screamed.

Mr. Felch yelled, too, when a furry projectile hit him claws first in the ski mask.

Chapter 48

September dropped the penlight, ferocious in her joy that Macy had escaped. Now it was her turn. She'd dodge past Victor, and run like hell.

She held one of the broken boards like a batter warming up on the mound. September cocked her arm, but before she could swing, Victor thrust Nikki forward into her arms and the weapon fell with a clatter.

He stepped into the room, booted the improvised bat across the room, and slammed the door. Macy had ripped the ski mask from his face, loosened the moorings of a hairpiece, and left his clawed cheeks slimed with bloody war paint.

Not Victor at all. He was a stranger.

Nikki shuddered in September's arms. "You're not Mr. Felch. You're Grady." She turned, and buried her face in September's chest. "I want my mommy!"

Grady? Not Victor. "Sorry, so sorry. I thought you were someone else. We need to get out of here before he comes back." September's arms hugged the weeping child.

"Should have killed that cat when I had the chance."

She gasped. The voice was Victor's even if the face wasn't. She could see a swelling bruise, hidden by smeared makeup, on one side of his jaw where she'd bitten him through the ski mask. Her skin crawled.

He breathed heavily. "Took years to save up for my new face. Just for you. To please you, September." He aimed the flashlight at his face like a spotlight and his smile gleamed toothpaste bright in the glow. He preened in a model's pose. "That damn cat better not have ruined my face. Lost a hundred pounds, too. All for you."

Victor. The shape of his face, the droopy ears, his piggy eyes, his height, but most of all the voice—and those hands, oh God, his hands!—conjured memories. She moved Nikki behind her to shield the child. "It was never about your looks, Victor."

"Then why did you leave me?" He roared, and September scrambled backwards, pushing Nikki with her. Her instinct was to cower; the old buried impulses reborn in an instant.

The nightmare man. The demon haunting her nights and stalking her days. Thief of her childhood. She'd blanked out the worst, but the body's sense memory couldn't forget.

Every touch. Every cut. Every burn, every beating. Every caress. She gagged, and thought she might throw up. She'd survived only because she learned to freeze, become invisible, go to another place in her mind and convince herself the pain and terror were happening to someone else. A different September.

Terrified animals react in one of three hardwired behaviors: freeze, flight or fight. She was an animal. Freeze, so the predator won't see you. Flight, to outrun the hunter, find a bolt hole to hide. . .

"Took a while to find you, and then you were all over the news. The perfect job opened up right in your back yard. Everything came together, the timing was perfect. We're meant to be together, and this time, you'll never leave me." Boasting. Proud of himself. Wanting her admiration.

Freezing made her a target. Running triggered the predator's chase. She took in Nikki, another innocent victim. Only one option left. It was time to fight.

"Let Nikki go. It's me you want. I'll go with you, do whatever you say, only let her go." She hugged the child as a cover to whisper to her. "Hole in floor under the rug. Go!" She pushed the girl behind her. Nikki was the right size; she'd be safe in the crawlspace. Keep him distracted and focused on her until the child was safe.

He waved his hand dismissively, and the flashlight stayed on his figure like a theater follow spot he clearly relished. "You nailed the lid on the kid's coffin when your cat unveiled me." He tsk-tsked. "What a shame. She saw my face."

September's mouth turned to dust. He was right. If only she'd stayed quiet and not asked Nikki for help. If she'd sent the girl away immediately to call the police. If she'd delayed Macy's command. Any of these choices would have kept Nikki safe. If Nikki were hurt, it'd be her fault. So many wrong choices, all wrong. How could she trust herself to get them out?

She had no choice. Survival was up to her.

He waxed poetic, a thespian writing his own script for a captive audience. "I say *jump*, and Dietz asks *how high*." His shoulders shook as he chuckled. "Had Dietz so worried about that reporter's fairy tale he nearly wet himself with relief when I cleaned up the mess. Even got a bonus lined up. A bonus for us, for our life together, a gift that keeps on giving."

She couldn't stop her lip curl reaction. Victor still didn't get it.

He pointed at her and she flinched. "I remade myself, for you, for us! And you spit on me—again—like you're so much better than me." He took another step toward her, anticipating her scared rabbit response of the past.

No more running. Her heart quickened. Nowhere to hide, even if she'd wanted to. Time to end this, once and for all. Her shoulders straightened, she breathed in-out-in and a weight melted from her heart with the exhalations. She'd been lost for a lot of years, but tonight she'd found herself. September was reborn.

Out of the corner of her eye, she saw Nikki kneel on the floor and finger the carpet. September nodded encouragement but kept her focus on Victor. She'd goad him, distract him until Nikki wiggled through the hole. She'd lure him further into the room, get him tripped up on the sleeping bag, make a dash for the door, and lock him inside. She took a breath, planted her feet, and smiled. "Fixing your outside doesn't change who you are. A bully and a sadist."

He lunged at her, and she dodged but miscalculated. God, he was quick! His fist caught her jaw, and she went down, hard, landing on top of the pet carrier. If Macy had been inside, the cat would have been crushed. *Please God let Macy avoid coyotes—and don't let his heart give out.*

Victor came after September, and she crabbed backwards, feeling the carpet give way to rough wood. "Nikki, hurry! Go, go, go!" Something jangled, and her hand closed around cool metal, recognized it, and raised the cello endpin like a sword above her. It gleamed in the limited light.

Nikki squealed as Victor remained focused on September, following her and standing over her. "A bully? A sadist?" He panted. "You ungrateful bitch. I loved you!" He kicked her, and September cried out. "I took care of you." He kicked again, and she scrambled sideways.

Nikki sat wide-eyed but frozen against the wall, the uncovered hole forgotten before her.

"Go! Nikki, get out, now! Run!"

She jumped, a terrified bunny-scamper aimed not into the crawl space as directed, but toward the closed door from which Victor had stepped away.

Victor easily countered, caught the little girl's arm and shook her. He crashed Nikki into the closed door. She crumbled, fell to the floor.

"No!" September scrambled to her feet.

"That was your fault." Victor snarled. He transformed into a deranged clown figure, the skewed wig flapped and bloody cheeks distorted his features. Grabbing Nikki's coat collar, he dragged her away from the door and dumped her at the center of the room. "I gave up my own career, my own art to make you a star!"

She whipped the endpin through the air like a fencer's foil and the silver gleamed in an arc that kept him at bay. "You never loved me. You wanted to own me, that's all."

He feinted, dancing in and away. His new athletic physique gave him an advantage, and she hoped her tingling cold fingers could keep fast their grip. She caught him on the wrist and the metal rod made a satisfying meaty sound.

He hissed and retreated, flexing that hand—oh God his hands! Fingers that pinched, fists that punched—her nostrils flared with satisfaction.

"You ungrateful bitch, flaunting yourself, making men want you. I did what any man would do to protect what's his, and teach you right from wrong."

She padded in a semi-circle to get closer to Nikki. The little girl curled into a protective ball, knees hugged to her chest and eyes squeezed closed, frozen in fear.

"Bastard! Picking on little girls make you feel like a big man?" She softened her voice. "Nikki, honey, I know it's scary. I'm getting you out of here. Nod if you understand." The child nodded and her eyes squeezed even tighter shut. "I want you to go under that table over there, okay?" Nikki squinted, located the spot, and scrambled beneath the table and hid behind the cello.

September didn't take her eyes off of Victor. She positioned herself between him and the girl's minimal shelter.

He stood between them and freedom, blocking the door as he mocked her. "You've changed. Sound like a mother." He stepped back closer to the opening to guard the door. But she had no intention of escaping. She'd finish this tonight, once and for all. "How are you going to save her? You couldn't even save yourself. Don't make promises you can't keep."

"Hypocrite!" Like a lanced abscess, the vitriol poured forth, using the words to enrage him and lure him in. "Love doesn't lock you away. Love doesn't teach lessons with whips. Love doesn't punish with lit cigarettes on your neck." Her long hair covered the scars, but the emotional hurt might never heal. Fighting back salved the wounds better than any miracle cure. *Closer, just a little more.* She hefted the endpin, balanced her feet well apart, and readied herself for the swing to take him out.

He took another step closer but then backed away, shaking with anger. "You ruined my life, made me a laughingstock. I couldn't show my face, nobody believed I could deliver, not in the concert hall and never again on stage. I had to reinvent myself."

"Good! You deserve every bad thing that happened." She shook with anger, and it felt good, God it felt so much better than fear. "A normal person doesn't rape someone and call it love. A normal person doesn't murder someone's husband. You killed my dog!" Her voice broke.

Be strong. Do this is for Chris. Do it for Dakota. And for Timothy, for the lost Macy and Shadow-pup. And do this for Nikki, who should never have been here in the first place. "I'm not the same scared kid you tortured into believing she had no value without you. I know what you are. No amount of surgery changes that. You're a freak."

He roared, and came at her at last, the flashlight an improvised sledge.

She dodged to the side, stepped in, and with all her strength whipped the endpin. Its shimmer whickered through the air.

He whirled, countered. Banged into the table.

Nikki screamed. Scrambled. The cello fell over.

September reset, followed him, swung again.

He backed away. Face surprised. Then concerned. Finally angry, he retaliated with the flashlight blinding her eyes.

She ducked. Blocked his blow with the endpin. Metal hit metal so hard her finger and arms stung, but she hung on to her weapon.

He pressed the advantage, scooped up the cello—*no, not Melody!*—and swung the instrument toward her.

Shoulder hunched, she spun away to absorb the blow, and fell to one knee with the impact. He held the cello like an ax, and chopped her exposed knee. She saw Melody fall in slow motion, heard a distinct POP before the pain flooded her knee.

September shrieked, fell to the ground, and rolled. The joint screamed, it was never meant to turn that way. Victor tossed Melody aside and swung the massive flashlight toward her face.

She held the endpin overhead between both hands to block the blow. The pin flew out of her hands, and clanged against the wooden wall, rolled and disappeared down the hole into the crawlspace.

Victor leaned down, loose wig flopping, and took his time as he cocked his arm for the killing blow.

Nikki smashed the used metal bucket over Victor's head, and immediately scurried away, gasping with fear.

Her knee. Unbearable pain. *You've felt worse.* September dug in her pocket. She couldn't move, couldn't get away. Could only wait. Her fingers found what they sought.

Victor wrenched off the bucket, face and hairpiece wet from its contents, and flung it across the room at Nikki in disgust. The girl squealed at the impact, and dodged away.

He turned back to September, ripped the bedraggled wig off, mopped the blood from his cheeks, and threw it into her face.

She brought up the bottle of synthetic cat pheromone, and sprayed directly into his eyes.

He screamed, anguished, the alcohol in the suspension burning his ravaged skin and eyes. Victor knuckled his eyelids, dropping the flashlight as he backed away and reached blindly for the door. "I'll kill you for this! You'll die, do you hear me?"

Nikki raced to September's side.

"Now, get out, now's your chance Nikki, go go go!" September waved toward the door Victor had managed to open and stagger out.

Before the little girl could reach the handle, the door slammed shut. The padlock snicked, locking them both inside.

Chapter 49

"You got the GPS working?" Combs couldn't help grinning. What do you know, the old man came through. Maybe something finally would go right. "Man, you're a freakin' wizard."

"Not so much." Teddy's frustration made his voice crack. "Thing is, the cat's moving, and going fast. Gonna to be out of range soon, if I sit here and wait for you."

"What? Why?" He pressed harder on the accelerator. "The cat's moving? There's a range?"

"I'll explain later. Had to jerry-rig the system, and it's like hitting the lottery to even get a reading. Macy goes into a tunnel or behind a hill, and we're screwed. What you want me to do? Wait for you or go after the cat?"

Combs considered the options. "Go after the cat. Odds are Macy's with September. They're making a run for it. Try to get eyes on the vehicle." Whoever the guy was, he hadn't wasted any time racing from the restaurant to collect his victim.

"Won't work, Detective. The GPS isn't following the road, not the way a car or a person would travel. The signal's heading cross-country. I think Macy got away or was dumped. Something must have scared him to death, he's really moving." He sounded anguished. "Have to track him on foot. Don't know if I can catch him. My joints don't listen to me these days."

He didn't have to think. "Do it. Whatever it takes. Get that cat. Maybe September got a message on him." That'd be like her. And if the cat started running, that meant September might be close by and running, too.

Behind him, Shadow pawed his arm and yawned. "We can find the initial location of the signal, and from there do a ground to ground search. I'll call it in. The guy must have some out of the way place to hold September."

"That could take hours! I don't think we have much time. And besides," Teddy added, "There's no way to know if the first GPS location came from where she's being held. Macy could have been on the run for a while. That's the first spot we registered once I got it going."

"Go after the cat, Teddy. You handle that, and when I get there with the dog we'll see if he can't point us in the right direction."

Shadow woofed, as if he understood every word. Combs hoped he did.

Chapter 50

Shadow stood in the back seat of the car, and stuck his head through the window. He liked the man driving the car because September liked him. His name was Combs, and he acted like an awkward pup around September, but that was okay. If she didn't mind, neither did Shadow.

He'd enjoyed the car ride with Combs, too, because he got to stick his whole face into the wind. Usually the window only opened a crack for the tip of his nose. He leaned further out, most of his neck also feeling the cold wind, and tasted the scents riding the night sky.

He wasn't sure where they drove. But the man mentioned September several times, so Shadow hoped that meant they'd go find her. He wondered why she'd left him behind. It was a good-dog's job to stay with his person, and it puzzled him why she didn't understand. His paws hurt from running after the truck she'd been in. He hadn't caught the truck, but he'd finally caught his breath.

The car slowed, and Shadow nervously licked his lips. Now what? It was dark, but another car's eye lights stabbed the night.

"Stay in the car, Shadow." Combs got out. "Be right back." He closed the car door, and walked over to talk to a smaller stooped man who got out.

Shadow wagged harder when he recognized Teddy. The old man fed him bacon and scratched Shadow's ears.

"My old legs couldn't manage off road. So Doc Eugene's tracking Macy."

Macy? The familiar name made Shadow come to attention, and he pointed his ears forward. Why did Teddy talk about Shadow's cat? He tipped his head and searched the dark roadside with nose, ears and eyes. Macy only went outside at September's house when he wore a harness and leash—a flimsy thing dogs could chew off, not like Shadow's proper *hide-and-seek* harness. When Macy wore that, September followed behind gripping the line.

His heart quickened at the thought, and he arched his neck. Was September out in the dark, walking Macy? Why else would Shadow's cat be here? That must be why Combs and Teddy brought him here, so they could be together. Did they want him to *seek* Macy, like before?

He felt funny when they weren't together. He took care of September, and she took care of him, and they both took care of Macy. That's what family did for each other.

He liked Macy all right, even if he smelled funny, not like a dog at all. But Shadow only felt like himself when he was with September. Sometimes it was hard to breathe when she touched his neck, stroked his ears, and called him "good-dog." A spot inside his chest grew warm and swelled so big he thought he'd burst with the happy feeling.

Right now, icy dread filled his body, different than the cold air, but he didn't know why. September would know what to do to make him feel better. His brow furrowed and he whined, and then lifted his nose into the breeze. Was she here? With his cat? He sifted scents, seeking…seeking…

The two men stood close together talking, and Shadow listened while he continued to test the air. His ears twitched when he heard his name. He woofed, a polite understated sound the way a good-dog should.

Combs turned to him. Shadow wanted out. How to tell the man to open the car door? He needed a closer sniff, to press his nose into the ground where scent clung to grass and pooled in the lees of ditches. Shadow barked louder. Why wouldn't Combs listen?

Then the breeze shifted, and he froze—Macy scent!—and he couldn't stop barking, pawing the door, lunging to get out the half opened window.

Combs raced back to the car. "Hey boy, settle down. Stop, you'll hurt yourself." His voice barked back with disapproval.

Couldn't he understand? Combs acted like he couldn't smell Macy, and Shadow's frustration grew when people ignored important scents. That's why they should listen to good-dogs. The wind shifted again, and Macy scent disappeared.

Shadow howled! He pushed his head and chest through the window opening, and got one foreleg out, too. Out, he needed out. Follow the cat smell, find September.

Teddy hurried to join Combs. "Let the dog out, for God's sake. He knows something. I watched how he tracked Molly." He reached out with an upturned palm. "Want to play *hide-and-seek?*"

Yes! Shadow yelped, and licked Teddy's hand. Teddy understood. He knew the right words. He let the old man's gentle touch push his paw and head back into the car, and waited impatiently for the door to open.

"He's got a long lead still attached to his harness." Teddy put his hand on the outside of the car. "Don't know if he'll pay attention to me, he's pretty riled up. So get ready to grab that line when I open the door." He spoke directly to Shadow. "Wait. You know what that means, right? Shadow, *wait.*"

Teddy made strong eye contact. Shadow yawned, and turned his head aside in polite deference to the older man. He whined, panting with excitement, and backed away from the door. It opened, and he trembled, barely able to contain the urge to leap out.

"Okay." Teddy gave the release word, and Shadow hopped out and immediately dropped his nose to the pavement. "Shadow, *seek.*"

Someone grabbed the leash, he could tell by the tension that tugged his back, but Shadow remained focused on smells. Shadow tracked left, breathing in with quick snuffles and out with short huffs, clearing his nostrils every so often to better read the scents.

Pulling hard, he swerved off the car path, burying his face for a moment in the dry crinkled vegetation mounding the roadside. Mice. Coyote. Bird poop. Old glove. No Macy.

"Don't we have to give him something to smell?" Combs let himself be tugged after the dog.

"I suppose so. But we don't have anything." Teddy spoke softly but with authority. "Shadow, where's September? Find September, big guy. *Seek.*"

Shadow paused, and stared at Teddy, puzzled. He'd never tracked a person. In the *hide-and-seek* game it was a good-dog's job to find other dogs and cats. And September always gave him a sniff-sample to tell him what to *seek.*

Was this a new game? With new rules? He wished September was here. But he didn't hear or smell her at all. That fleeting Macy-scent teased the sensitive smell place deep in his muzzle almost to his eyes. Finding Macy was the next best thing.

Never mind what Teddy said. Dogs knew better sometimes. Smells and sounds never spoke to people like they did to good-dogs.

Shadow put down his head and tracked to the right this time, still searching for any hint of Macy. He snuffled past the mid-line point of the highway, stopped and came back.

There! That smell: that was Shadow pee-smell, there in the road. He'd been here before.

The wind ruffled his fur, and Shadow lifted his face to the stream, tasting and drinking deep of the myriad smells. There. Macy smell.

He leaped ahead, crossed the car path and dove down the embankment into a stubbled field. And hit the end of the line. Shadow tugged and pulled, yelped with frustrated effort, but Combs planted his heels and tugged back.

"What's he doing? Teddy, he's not following the road. I think he found a squirrel or something."

"Listen to the dog. Follow Shadow." Teddy limped after them in a hopscotch gait, and slowed to stumble down the incline off the road.

Shadow whined, lowered his head to the ground and snorted. He paced back and forth in a half circle, the long line taut where it unraveled from Combs's grip. Too slow! He pulled, threw his weight against the harness, and the tension disappeared like fog battered by sun. There, again the Macy smell beckoned, and Shadow leaped ahead, ignoring Comb's exclamation of pain.

Free of the man's grip, Shadow coursed first one way and then the other in a steady, space-eating jog through the field. His nose barely skimmed the grass. The teasing breeze with its intermittent scent shouted louder than any people words and beckoned his paws to hurry, faster, and faster still. To the left. Now to the right. Ahead for a spell and back left again. And—

There! He stopped. Nosed the spot, inhaling deeply, tail wagging with growing excitement. He told himself *good-dog*, but it wasn't the same. He'd found Macy smell at last. Fresh. His cat had rested here a moment.

Fear stink from the cat's paws made Shadow's hackles bristle. He sniffed again, tracked right and then left and centered on the paw pad trail. Macy's path wound through tufts of grass taller than Shadow, and his signature odor marked the frozen ground and everything his fur brushed.

Shadow increased his pace. The cat spore grew ever more fresh. Maybe September would be with his cat, and they could all be together. His leash-line dragged behind, snaking after him through the rubble. It hung on something, and impatiently Shadow jerked it free, and continued to run forward. Up a small incline. Down the other side. There, beneath that tree. The smell so fresh it glowed clear as star-fire in the night sky.

A hiss. Eerie eye glow, a blink and another hiss. Macy, but terrified, not recognizing Shadow. And September nowhere around.

Shadow stopped. His tail drooped with disappointment, and he whined. Macy spit, and Shadow dropped to the ground. That was how he told September he'd found the lost when they played *hide-and-seek*. It also told other scared dogs and cats not to worry, that he was no threat.

He looked away from the cat's eye-shine and yawned to show he meant no harm. And he woofed, but very softly. He didn't want to scare his cat any further.

Macy growled, but then he mewed—a cautious cat question that sounded puzzled. Shadow didn't dare move or stare directly at the cat. In a moment, Macy delicately sniffed the air, stood, and paced carefully toward him.

Shadow couldn't contain himself any longer and stood, tail flagged high and nose-touched his cat. He sniffed Macy from head to toe as the cat rubbed his length against Shadow's front legs.

The cat stopped and lay down, panting. Macy must be tired from running.

September smell covered the cat. Fresh scent, too. Shadow knew she couldn't be far away. But there was no trail on the ground to find her.

"Here kitty kitty kitty. Macy, I know you're there."

Both Shadow and his cat froze, both furry faces swung toward the familiar voice. Macy tensed, ready to spring away until Shadow nose-touched his cheek again and wagged. Footsteps crunched over frozen grass. Macy pressed against Shadow's side.

"There you are!" A light spilled onto the ground from the man's outstretched hand, and he crouched without moving forward any further. "Well, well, and Shadow, too. How'd you get here? Good-dog, you found Macy."

Shadow plastered his ears and wagged harder, but stayed in place when Macy meowed and trotted over to Doc Eugene.

"How about that, the GPS worked." Doc Eugene gathered Macy into his arms, and grunted as he stood. "Shadow, let's go." He patted his leg. "Come, boy. Back to the car."

He barked, and backed away. It wasn't time for a car ride. Dogs got locked inside cars. September wasn't here, but she wasn't in the car, either. Shadow barked again.

"You know better than that. Hell, you knew how to sit and down and come before you left our house as a pup. Pam teaches all her pups before they're re-homed. So COME!" He took a step toward Shadow, impatience in his voice. He juggled Macy, and the cat settled into Doc Eugene's arms, mouth open and still panting.

September wasn't here. But he could smell her touch on Macy's fur even from where his cat now rested. Macy had been with September so recently, her scent spilled off the cat's body in waves. Macy's fur-contact painted Shadow's leg with the faint aroma of her signature odor. Everything the cat had touched, each tree trunk and grass hummock, carried that telltale clue.

He could find September by playing the game backwards. *Seek* in reverse. Shadow would track not where Macy was, but where the cat had been. *Good-dog!*

Shadow whirled, ignoring Doc Eugene's concerned voice, and found the trail. The man's voice faded in the distance as Shadow ran, his nose barely skimming the trail, picking up the bread crumb smell clues along the way.

By the time he'd passed through the wooded area and padded up the hill, he panted heavily and his paws hurt again. The scent was less strong—older—but still distinct when he burst into a clearing and saw the old building. It smelled of dusty wood and sick animals. Raccoons? Stale cat pee from several other cats.

Macy's trail, tainted with fear-scent that burned his nostrils, led inside.

Shadow didn't slow his pace when a car sitting in front of the old building roared to life. The vehicle's eye-lights speared him in the hard-pack soil of the car-path, its tires spun clots of dirt. The car ran at him.

He gathered tired muscles to dodge away. But then Shadow froze in shock when September yelled.

Chapter 51

"Tell me you got something, Gonzales. I got nothing here, and worse."
Combs blew on his rope-burned palm, and shook it, wishing he'd worn
gloves.

"What happened?" Background noise from before had disappeared.
Gonzales must have left the restaurant.

"Met up with Teddy. He rigged a way to track September's missing cat.
Seems to've found the signal and that's still in play, but no results yet." He
stood outside the car, leaning against the door while Doc Eugene tramped
somewhere out in the darkness supposedly hot on the trail—or tail, of the
missing cat.

"Don't you have the dog with you? Get it to track."

"Gee, why didn't I think of that?" The heavy sarcasm targeted his own
inept handling of the situation. "The dog must have Greyhound in him, he
took off so fast. Couldn't keep up or see him in the dark. How do those SAR
teams do it?" He'd never had a dog, other than a tiny mop of a pooch
belonging to Cassie when they were first married. Muffy could have doubled
for house slippers.

"So we got both September's cat and dog in the wind, and they were our
best chance to find her." Gonzales sounded disgusted, but then brightened.

"Leaned on Dietz and he's in denial about any contaminated meat, says it's a smear campaign born of jealousy." He laughed. "I kid you not, that's a direct quote—born of jealousy. He's one of those woo-woo artsy types, a smug bastard acts like his shit don't stink."

"Any leads? No-shows at the restaurant?" It still made Combs's skin crawl to think Cassie had taken the kids to the event. What was she thinking? Couldn't have predicted a bust, granted, but it didn't sound like his social-climbing former wife.

"Couple names, yeah. The AD—that's the assistant to the director—says one of the cast, a goofy-ass character, goes by Felch, can't be found. They announced at the dinner he's been replaced. Everyone we interviewed so far confirmed that." He blew out a breath, obviously as tired as Combs. They'd both been running nonstop for nearly twenty-four hours. "Still going through the witnesses and taking statements, only about half done. I had to take a break."

"Felch likely?"

"Involved for sure. Got pictures galore, he's on all the posters and other promo material. Felch is a local, but kind of a recluse, one of those back-to-the-land self-sufficient guys. Lives out in the area you're searching, actually, so might want to run by his place if you got nothing else encouraging."

Combs scribbled down the address. Better than doing nothing while waiting on cat schematics. "Good. Who's the other? You said a couple possibles."

"Guy named Vincent Grady, new to the team. AD says they brought him on less than six weeks ago as the set PA, in charge of wrangling the talent and other chores. Best I can tell, a glorified gopher. He's also replacing Felch in the cast lineup."

Combs cracked his knuckles. "Six weeks. Timing's right. About the time the Blizzard Murders hit national wires."

Gonzales agreed. "Grady got a raise and new title. Pissed off the AD something fierce."

"You can stop with the alphabet soup, Gonzales. I left my scrabble board at home."

"Can you spell AWOL?" He paused. "Grady attended the launch party but disappeared in the roundup. Nobody's seen him since."

"You need to lean on this Dietz character. He's the head honcho—director or producer or something, whatever initials they call them. He's got to know something. Tell him he's responsible. Hell, he probably is."

"Great minds." Now Gonzales sounded sarcastic, and Combs cracked his knuckles. "Rattled him like a box of Good 'N Plenties. Told him we found Sly, and I thought he'd shit a brick. You ask me, Dietz already knew about Sly. Got his composure back pretty quick, like those actor guys do, but I could tell he was surprised we found the body. Took Dietz all of ten seconds to point fingers at both Felch and Grady."

"How convenient they're both missing." Combs saw Teddy motioning to him, and pushed off from the car. "I got something. Maybe. Hold on." He crossed over to the old man, and saw Teddy staring off the road, into the dark.

"Something moving over there." Teddy pointed. "I think it's Doc Eugene."

A flashlight wavered, and then steadied as it floated disembodied over the ground. The figure drew closer until they could make out the veterinarian.

Doc Eugene cradled Macy in his arms. "He was running loose. Shadow found him, too, but I couldn't catch the dog." The vet carefully climbed the embankment, struggling with the added weight. "Cat's stressed, too. Got to get him calmed down." He crossed to his vehicle, opened the back and climbed in with the cat. Teddy followed, shoulders stooped, defeated. He started to climb in the passenger side.

"God dammit to hell, can't catch a break!" Combs put the phone back to his ear. "Just found the cat. It was loose." What a waste of time. "I'll go visit this Felch character's place since we got nothing here." He disconnected.

Before Combs reached his own car, Teddy yelled. "Detective, you must see this, we've got something." He adjusted his glasses as Combs jogged over to the car.

"What?" He peered into the car's interior.

"Couldn't see it out in the dark," said the veterinarian. "But Macy brought us a message. Mean anything?" He'd removed the GPS tag, and handed it to Combs.

Someone had written on the tag with black marker. "V. Gra." He met the men's expectant expressions. "We think that's the name of September's stalker. Victor Grant." He shook his head, frustrated. *Or it could be Vincent Grady. Hmm.* "Doesn't help find him. Or September."

"Victor Grant. September mentioned him. She said he had something to do with Sly's disappearance when she gave me Fish's file." Teddy grimaced, apologetic. "I should have mentioned that sooner."

Combs grunted. "That's confirmation, anyway, but it doesn't help find him, either."

"Maybe this will help." The veterinarian held Macy up, smoothing the cat's fur.

Purrs rumbled as the man stroked Macy's white throat and chest, what September referred to as his bib. She'd used the marker to write on his fur. "Do that one more time, smooth a little to the side. Yes, right there." When the fur laid the right way, it was easy to read. "*Barn.* She tried to write his name on the tag, and the location on the fur." Combs pulled out his phone and hit speed dial to reach Gonzales.

Teddy already had his laptop out, balanced on the hood of the car, the mobile hot-spot providing internet access. The screen filled with an overhead view of the area. His fingers flew, and the image grew brighter, and larger.

Gonzales answered. "What you got?"

"Barn. Give me a list, any structure that could be described as a barn in," he looked around, "maybe a three mile radius of this location."

"On it."

Teddy's fingers clacked on the keyboard, and he gasped. "Oh, no." He glanced up at Combs. "I think I found it."

Gonzales came back on the line. "Hey, man, go figure, Felch's address I already gave you has a barn. I'm on my way."

"Meet you there." He turned to Teddy. The man should be happy or relieved, not stricken. "What?"

Teddy's eyes didn't move from the computer, and pointed to a bright spot on the screen. "I hope that's not the right barn. It's on fire."

Chapter 52

Hot pain radiated from her knee outward, encompassed her thigh and throbbed in rhythm with September's pulse. She reached for the flashlight Victor had left behind, and yelled with frustration and agony when her fingers fell short. Any movement made invisible knives stab deeper into the wound, and left her panting.

"He locked the door. Why'd he do that? Why'd he hurt us?" Nikki's eyes reflected twin pools of shock, and a purpling goose-egg marred her forehead. She hugged herself.

September gritted her teeth. Forced herself to slow her breathing. Deep breath in, blow the pain out, breathe in, blow out. *Focus, focus.* "Nikki, can you see anything? There's a crack in the door." *The reason didn't matter. How could she explain Victor, when she didn't understand him herself? Only getting help mattered.*

The little girl peered through the chink. "It's too dark. Wait." She turned her head for a better angle. "I see something. A light. It's a match, I think." She fell silent, and then backed away from the door, stuttering with fear. "Fire, it's a fire. He set a fire!" She pounded on the door. "Let us out! Let us out!" When it wouldn't give, Nikki turned her tear-streaked face. "He's going to burn us." Her voice was anguished.

"No, he's not. Nikki, listen. Look at me. Nikki!" She put command and conviction into her voice, the same tone she'd learned to use with Dakota. And with Shadow. *Would she ever see the pup again? Or Macy? Not if she didn't get them out of here.* "You won't burn. I'll get you out. I promise. Do you believe me?"

Nikki sniffled, but kept tossing worried glances at the door. "Smoke. Do you smell it?"

The acrid aroma tickled her nose, but soon would choke out the limited air in the tiny space. "We have to work fast. I can't move very well, so you'll have to do what I tell you. Trust me, okay?"

"Okay." She sniffled again.

"Bring me the flashlight." September stretched her hand to take it, wincing at even that minimal movement. She covered the expression with a laugh, to reduce Nikki's fear. The girl's deer-in-the-headlights emotions wouldn't take much more.

Using the light as she had with Macy, September pointed the light at specific objects as she talked. "There on the table, see the thermos? Bring that. And over there, the ski mask. Take off your hat, too."

Nikki brought everything to September, kneeling beside her. "Sorry about your leg."

"Me too. You're pretty handy with the bucket."

She wrinkled her nose. "It smelled bad. He's a stupid-head and deserved it."

Laughing, September agreed. "You saved my life, you know. That was brave. Can you be brave a little while longer?"

"I guess so." She looked at the door and pointed. "Smoke. It's getting worse."

The chinks in the old boards leaked foggy tendrils that floated upward to hang in the upper third of the small room. Tinder-dry wood and animal bedding would burn quickly. There wasn't much time.

September opened the canister of coffee, thankful she'd left most of it in the thermos, and poured brown liquid over the two ski masks. "You're too young to drink coffee, Nikki, so I don't want you trying to get a caffeine fix." She winked at the girl to show it was a joke, and got a tentative smile back for her efforts. "It'll feel nasty but you need to wear the mask with the wet parts against your nose and mouth. Breathing through the wet helps filter out the smoke. And see how the smoke stays up high?" Nikki looked up. "That's why we need to stay down low, the lower the better. Okay?"

"But there's no way out. And there's not enough coffee to put out the fire."

Shining the light again, September pointed it to the far corner where the carpet rucked over the hole she'd enlarged. "That's the way out."

Nikki slowly shook her head. "I don't like little places like that." Her lower lip trembled. "Hard to breathe in little places. And besides, it smells."

The girl was claustrophobic? That sucked. "Yep, it smells bad. I think some cats hang out there."

"Hope-Kitty?" Her pitch turned up a notch. "She could burn up, too!" Nikki crawled over to the opening and pulled back the rug, and stared down into the black hole, doubt and fear chasing one another across her face.

"I can't get through that little opening. But you can. Nikki, I need you to go get help." She thought Nikki would refuse, and couldn't quell her own rising panic. At the least, Nikki had to get out and save herself. A crackle and whoosh beyond the locked door created another puff of heavier smoke. "There's not much time, Nikki. You already saved my life once. You're the only one who can do this. I'm counting on you."

Her narrow shoulders hunched forward. "Okay," she whispered.

"Quickly then." September dumped more coffee on one of the ski masks, and held it out to the girl. "Put it on." She watched as Nikki pulled the soggy mess over her head and covered her face, and then donned the second soaked mask herself, and poured the rest of the lukewarm liquid over the carpet. If she couldn't get into the crawl space, her only chance was to roll up in the wet carpet and pray Nikki got help here in time.

First, get the girl safe. "I'll hold the light for you." September took a breath, braced for the pain, and then rolled onto the side with her good leg, and pulled herself closer to the hole, dragging the wet carpet up over her exposed legs. "Hurry, Nikki. The fire's spreading." The flashlight speared through the hole. A pair of eyes reflected the light back before the animal scampered away.

"It's Hope! Hope is really here!" It gave her the needed incentive, and Nikki sat on the edge of the hole, feet dangling through, and butt-scooted forward. She closed her eyes, took a breath and held it, and dropped into the crawl space as though jumping into a swimming pool.

"Never mind the cat for now. Nikki, find the hole, over there." September pointed with her light as the crackling fire sound grew louder. "Hope will come with you. I promise!" The girl had to go now, before the barn collapsed on top of them.

September dropped her head and shoulders through the narrow opening, ignoring the pain in her knee that had swollen to twice its normal size. She pointed with the light. "Go, Nikki, go!"

The girl quickly crawled to the narrow opening, but stopped to check back over her shoulder. The ski mask turned her into a freakish figure. "What about you?"

"I'll be fine." September smiled, but it was hidden by her own wet mask. She steadied her voice to make the lie more believable. "I'm coming right after you, okay? Don't want to slow you down with my bum knee, so you run and get help. Just go, go now!"

Nikki turned to the small opening excavated by animals, perhaps by her beloved Hope-kitty, and dove through. She wiggled until only the bottom of her shoes could be seen. And then they too were gone.

September wanted to cry with relief. Nikki would tell the authorities about Victor, so he'd be punished. She'd won. After eight years of terror, it was over. For a moment she relaxed and closed her eyes. She'd done all that she could.

Heat blasted her legs. She jerked, and her knee punished her for the reflex.

The wet carpet offered little protection. Her butt and legs splayed out on the floor above might as well be bare. Her upper body dangled from the waist through the hole, so she'd survive longer even while her lower extremities trapped above cooked like a roasted pig.

She dropped the flashlight into the crawl space. Her arms reached for the underside of the floor, seeking purchase. She needed leverage.

September strained, and managed to pull more of her body into the hole. Her hips became a cork that plugged the opening. She screamed, and screamed again. Twisted. Squirmed. Clothing tore. Skin ripped.

Her body dropped, knocking her breathless and pressing her coffee-wet mask into clotted fur and dusty spider webs. Craning her neck, she saw her injured leg still caught in the hole above, and September reached up and managed to tug it down. The thumped landing prompted another scream, but why be brave? Nobody would hear her die. Through the hole, light and shadow danced as flames gnawed the old wood above and around her.

September reached for the flashlight, and it clinked against metal. The cello endpin—all that was left of Melody—gave her an adrenalin boost of hope. Her injured leg made the wood-kicking plan impossible, even if she could have turned her body around. But the metal could help her dig her way out.

She squirmed toward the dugout next to the wooden steps. The agony in her leg belonged to someone else. She *willed it so.* Just as she'd gone to that other place during the Victor years, where the torment visited on that *other* September couldn't touch her, she divorced herself from the pain.

The endpin gouged the frozen earth as she sought to enlarge the frozen dirt tunnel. But within two or three strikes, September realized the barn sat on a cement pad with decades of hard-packed dirt over top. The tunnel couldn't go deeper, she couldn't breach the concrete, and the eight-inch height of the opening didn't come close to allowing her through.

Coughing turned to sobs, and she let her face fall into her arms. At least the smoke would kill her before the flames. She imagined she heard barking, and her tears intensified. *Hope somebody finds you, baby-dog. You deserve a good home. Someone to love you.*

"September? Are you there?"

She roused. "Nikki, what are you doing?" She saw the girl's masked face peering through the tunnel. "Get out, get out!"

Shadow barked.

"Shadow? Oh my God, is that my Shadow?" September coughed again. Smoke had begun to seep into the crawl space.

The dog cried and pushed Nikki aside, scrambling to get his head into the hole. "No, get back, Shadow, it's too small." His powerful shoulders made the old two by six boards flex.

"The bad man was in his car waiting. I couldn't leave." Nikki chattered like the youngster she was, no longer cowed but excited by the adventure. "He almost hit the dog when he drove away. Shadow—is that his name?—heard you scream. We couldn't leave you here."

Her mind raced. "Nikki, I appreciate that, I truly do. You can do one thing for me, but then you have to run. Not walk, you *run* out of here for help." The drill sergeant demand brooked no argument, and she didn't wait for the girl to respond. "Does Shadow still have his leash?"

At the sound of his name, the dog yelped. "Hold still, dog. Um…yeah, it's a long line." Nikki paused. "What should I do?"

All she needed was one board-width. "Hand me the end of the line." She gathered it up through the hole when Nikki poked it through. "Now get the hell out of here, Nikki! Run, run!"

The girl scrambled to her feet, footsteps pounding. A pause. And then a scream of pure delight. "Daddy! Daddy, you're here!"

September couldn't wonder about who might be outside. She couldn't wait for a rescue. Rescue was here. Rescue was a midnight-black baby-dog.

"Good-dog, Shadow, you're such a good boy. You found me, didn't you?" She had to work fast, or she'd kill them both.

Shadow barked. Joy colored his voice, and not a little fear and worry.

September pulled a third of the length of Shadow's tracking line through the excavated hole, pulled it up and over to poke the end out a chink in the first board until it dropped to the ground. She clawed up that end again, and tied it off, leaving plenty of play in the leash for the dog to maneuver. "We're gonna play tug. Want to play, Shadow? Good-dog, this is a new game and I know you can do it." *Please God let him do it!*

He barked again, ready for anything, and backed away from the tethered board.

September found the cello rod again, and attacked the exposed end of the board. Yes! The sharp end of rusty nails still poked through toward her. She pried at the board, loosening them a bit, and then traded the endpin for the metal flashlight. Using it like a hammer, she pounded them to back the nails out of the wood. Some proved so old, they simply broke off, and she quit when the flashlight bent others and made the situation worse.

It was up to Shadow. If he failed, he'd be burned alive with her, unable to break the tether to escape the barn. And if he died by her hand, she wouldn't want to live anyway.

"Shadow, let's play tug." She coughed, cleared her throat, and put a teasing lilt in the game-words. "I've got it, it's mine and you can't have it. Ready, set, TUG!"

He barked, and grabbed the end of the leash in his jaws and pulled. It slid through his teeth. He couldn't get purchase, but the board shifted.

"Again, baby-dog. Ready, set, TUG!"

She timed it, and shoved from her side when he pulled. Once more, the board shifted. But not enough.

It wouldn't work. Not in time to save them, anyway. Think, think! He wasn't trained the way sledding dogs or weight-pull dogs competed. Shadow was trained NOT to pull when on leash.

Except when tracking.

"Shadow! Good-dog, what a good boy! Wait, it's okay, chill." He panted, and then coughed, and pawed the opening in the dirt. "Shadow, let's play *hide-and-seek*. Where's Macy?"

He cocked his head. The fire lit the area enough that she could see the movement through the narrow opening in the board.

She knew Macy was long gone, perhaps never to be found again. She couldn't think about that painful reality now. The cat could save them, though, even if he lived only in memory. Shadow knew the cat's scent, had been drilled to find Macy, and the trail was fresh from this doorway out of the barn. She needed him to run out of the barn, and pull the damn board off the wall, tug it to hell and gone out of the barn. If she couldn't get out in time, at least he might survive.

"Shadow, where's Macy? *SEEK!*"

He didn't pause. He didn't test for scent. Shadow whirled, put his head down, and bulldozed away. He was caught short by the end of the tether, but the board creaked and moved.

"Good-dog, God, you're such a good boy!" She couldn't see through the smoke and tears. "*SEEK, Shadow, SEEK!*"

He did. The board squealed. And it flew free.

Hope raced past September out the opening and streaked from the barn to rejoin Nikki. September followed more slowly, gasping as she found her way by feel. She crawled on hands and one knee, dragging her injured leg, amazed that safety beckoned less than six feet away. It might be too far.

Her eyes wouldn't focus. Were those cars out there? They circled the burning barn, and as she watched a fire truck with flashing lights pulled up.

Shadow barked and howled, and struggled to get back to her. Thank God, somebody held him back. It looked like Teddy, what was Teddy doing here?

She dragged herself another two feet, and paused to strip the wet mask from her face. Better to see than to breathe, she'd hold her breath the last short distance.

September saw Nikki huddled against a man—her father?—wearing military attire. When a puff of wind momentarily cleared smoke he saw September's struggles, and pushed Nikki gently aside to take three hurried long steps toward her.

But another figure outran him, dodging flames to reach her. He startled a massive flock of tree-roosting birds, flushing them into a feathery explosion that blackened the fire-lit sky before the cloud spun, turned in concert, and finally evaporated into the night.

Combs scooped September into his arms, and carried her the last several feet into the fresh air. For the first time in eight years, September felt safe.

Chapter 53

September hobbled into the kitchen, Shadow never far from her side, and smiled at the array of food still to be eaten. Anita bustled from the refrigerator to the stained glass table, replacing spent dishes with refills.

Shadow licked his lips and stared hopefully at his empty dish. Anita took the cue, grabbed a square of cheese and lobbed it expertly toward the bowl. He leaped forward and snapped it out of the air before it landed.

"He'll get fat." But September didn't mind, not tonight. He deserved as many treats as he wanted. Tonight they celebrated the cusp of a new year, and for her, a new life. Shadow made that possible. So had Macy.

"Get out of here. Go entertain your guests." Anita made shooing motions with her green and red lacquered nails, and flipped dark hair over her shoulder that tonight boasted a matching green streak.

"Got to give Macy his pill." The cat lounged atop the refrigerator, supervising the activity. September stroked Macy's white throat, and rumbled purrs spilled forth. Dark stains from the Sharpie-drawn message had yet to fade, but she considered it a badge of honor. She wouldn't inflict the indignity of a bath on the feline hero.

"Pill time, Macy." She shook out one of his prescriptions. He stood and stretched, and then sat and waited for the medicine. "Open." As soon as his mouth stretched wide, she made a tongue-click noise to signal he'd chosen the right behavior, and quickly popped in the pill immediately followed by a sliver of cheese. "Good boy, Macy!" The cat chewed, swallowed, and pawed her hand. She obliged with another treat and followed up with a cheek scratch.

"Will that cure him? Never knew a cat to open wide like that for a pill." Anita smiled with admiration. "Mine'll take my head off if I think about pills."

September laughed. "Most cats hate pills, true. Macy isn't a fan, but the treat trumps the pill. He knows he only gets treats afterwards. I like to think he knows they make him feel better, too." She shrugged. "There's no cure for cardiomyopathy. Doc Eugene says Macy's is the milder form, and the medicine helps." Thank goodness Doc Eugene was a board certified veterinary internist with a specialty in cardiology. Macy would get an annual echocardiogram from now on, to monitor any heart changes.

Macy's DNA test showed he carried only one copy of the gene so he had a more encouraging prognosis. Maine Coon cats with two copies of the A31 mutation were eighteen times more likely to develop problems and often died by age four.

Anita joined September at the refrigerator to scratch Macy's other cheek, and the cat closed his eyes with pleasure. "At least my mutt cats are immune." At September's frown, she stopped scratching, and Macy head-butted her hand until she continued. "No?"

"All cats can get it. Experts suspect the disease happens as the result of a heritable heart gene mutation—that's been proven in a couple of cat breeds, but not all—so responsible breeders screen for HCM to avoid spreading the problem. Persians have an incidence of up to forty percent, Maine Coons like Macy, Ragdolls, American Shorthair, Sphynx—several breeds are known to be affected. But it's in other breeds, and even mix breed cats and ferals aren't immune. They may get sick and die without being diagnosed, so I suppose we can't know the true incidence in pet cats." She stroked Macy's thick fur. "God bless Winn Feline Foundation. They're funding research to find ways to identify and eliminate the disease from breeding programs, and that can help the general cat population—including your kitties."

The phone rang and Anita started across the room to get it. "Who'd call this late on New Year's Eve?"

"That's the business line. Let the machine get it." Tonight she didn't want anything to put a damper on the festivities.

"Forgot to tell you." Anita bit her lip and plucked a Post-It from the wall phone and handed it to September. "Message from some O'Dell woman, there's the number. She sounded pretty upset you'd not returned her calls." She made a face. "About that time the cookies started to burn, and I got so busy with the food, it totally slipped my mind. Sorry."

"That's okay. With pet lovers, everything needs immediate attention even if the problem's gone on for months. I'll call her later." September stuck the

Post-It on the face of the refrigerator, and dropped Macy's pills back into a drawer. She leaned against the granite counter top. "Thanks for all this. I couldn't do it without your help. Still have quite a hitch in my git-along."

"Love doing it." Anita wore a silver sequin-encrusted cocktail dress with matching spike heels and glittered like a tarnished tree ornament. "My postage stamp apartment won't fit more'n four people, and I love parties. Only chance I get to wear my sparkles." She eyed September critically. "At least your crutches got retired. Hard to host a party when you walk like Lurch from *The Addams Family*."

Stifling a giggle, September poured wine into a glass, and sipped. "I don't do sparkles." Hell, she rarely did skirts, either, and preferred sweats or jeans. She'd surprised Combs by wearing a calf-length emerald velvet gown, the long sleeves, high neck and long skirt not only festive but practical. The dress hid both past and recent scars, including the knee brace stabilizing the ACL tear. Doctors predicted a full recovery with strict adherence to rehab.

"Go on. Get back to your party. I've got this covered." Anita sipped her cocktail. "I'll join you in a minute. It's a half hour to the new year, so go stop Fish from being a conversation hog." She made a face. "Maybe not a good choice of words."

September shuddered. It would be a long time before she'd risk eating pork again. Fish, though, had somehow managed to turn the *Hog Hell* debacle into an opportunity. Rather than shutting down the TV show, controversy vaulted it to even greater ratings, and he'd been tapped to replace Tommy Dietz as the host.

Anita was over the moon when Fish brought her on board as his assistant. Tonight was the closest Anita and Fish had come to having a real date. September hid a smile. Fish didn't stand a chance of squirming out of Anita's shiny net.

When she limped from the kitchen into the dining area, September saw several groups scattered throughout the room. As Anita predicted, Fish held forth in one corner, entertaining Detective Gonzales and his wife Mercedes along with Doc Eugene.

She'd hesitated to invite the veterinarian, knowing how he felt about her, but breathed easier when he'd accepted. He raised his glass when she entered, and September smiled back, grateful they'd been able begin the process of reconciliation. She'd promised to spend time with the dogs Pam had loved so much, and perhaps get them back into tracking form. Shadow would enjoy the canine company.

Shadow stayed glued to her side. He'd not left her sight since the fire, not even when she'd gone to the hospital for evaluation. Combs insisted she and her service dog couldn't be separated, and the medics took one look at his badge and her face, and didn't argue.

Combs smiled from across the room and left Teddy to meet her. "You're gorgeous."

Heat warmed her cheeks.

"So are you, Shadow. Handsome, I mean." Combs held out his hand for the dog to sniff, and the pup politely nose-touched. He pressed closer to September, and stayed between her and the man.

Combs leaned in to whisper to September. "I think he's jealous. And we still haven't had our first date."

She bit her lip, flustered. "Don't be ridiculous." Her hand fell to Shadow's ruff, and the butterflies settled.

Teddy joined them. "What a lovely couple."

What was this, a conspiracy? September sipped her wine and kept her eyes lowered.

Teddy added, "And you're pretty dapper tonight yourself, Detective Combs."

September sputtered. "Good one."

He scratched Shadow's chin. The pup wagged happily. Teddy turned somber when he turned to September. "How's Aaron?"

She took another sip of the wine, and leaned against a chair, more to give herself time than for any need of support. They'd found Aaron wandering, alive but suffering from frostbite, blood loss and hypothermia. And what they all suspected to be a new prion disease, courtesy of *Hog Hell*.

"Not good. They saved his arm." He'd hurt himself, bled all over the garden, and got turned around when he tried to go for help. Aaron exited out the back of the fence and walked more than a mile before he sat down on the shoulder of a road and was found by a passing driver. "He's lucky he didn't die of shock, lucky the weather wasn't worse. They're still running tests." She raised her eyebrows at Combs, asking permission, and at his slight nod, she continued. "Cassie Harrison has it, too."

Teddy was surprised. "That's your ex-wife, right?" Combs nodded. "I understand how Mr. Felch got sick, and the dogs from the show. But Aaron and your ex-wife, what's their connection? The restaurant says they never served harvested feral pig before the launch party."

When Shadow whined and nudged her, September smoothed his brow. He read her emotions as easily as she read music. "Aaron's a vegetarian. He'd never eat barbecue."

Teddy sounded properly shocked. "Hey, Mr. Fish? Can you explain something for us?" From across the room Fish jutted his chin whiskers in acknowledgment and strutted over, the others in his group following. Teddy continued. "You're on the inside track now. So how'd the barbecue get contaminated?"

Fish hemmed and hawed, and September enjoyed watching the little man squirm. "See, I had to sign a nondisclosure agreement. That's part of my new contract." He preened. "Going to bring some Fish style to the show. I'm the new host, you know. Moving the show to Louisiana, though."

Anita guffawed from the kitchen doorway before joining the party.

"Everyone knows you ditched radio and got kicked upstairs. Couldn't sign that contract fast enough." She carried a fresh bottle in one hand, and her own cocktail glass in the other. "Anyone? Refills? More cold beer in the fridge. September, say the word when you want the champagne opened. It's twenty minutes till midnight."

September answered when Fish wouldn't. "The CDC has to sort it all out. Felch is dead, and he was already so sick he probably couldn't tell us anything anyway." She sipped her wine. "BeeBo's got to explain what he knows. I don't think any nondisclosure will protect him. Besides, he'll do it for his dogs. The man's a true dog lover. I don't think he had any idea or intention to cause problems. Dietz is the criminal." Dietz and Victor used each other, and in her mind, were equally to blame.

"Dietz claims he knows nothing." Gonzales waggled his empty beer bottle, and smoothed his mustache. "Time for a refill." He hurried to the kitchen.

Combs set his beer on the table and cracked his knuckles. "I don't buy Dietz's denial." He leaned closer to September, and her first instinct was to back away, but she took a breath and tried to relax. "Your theory works for me," he said. "Tell them."

All eyes focused on her, and she licked her lips. The unfamiliar taste of lipstick jarred her for a moment. Shadow pushed against her knee, the good one, and she steadied at his touch.

"I've done some research, and Doc Eugene put me in touch with some experts." She smiled thanks at the veterinarian. "White tail deer can develop spontaneous prion disease. It's called chronic wasting disease." She took a breath. "When hunters take a deer, they don't harvest the whole thing and the waste gets dumped. That's typically the feet, the offal, and if it's not trophy-worthy, the head. Sometimes they take the haunches, and dump the rest of the carcass."

Doc Eugene rattled the ice in his glass, needing a refill but reluctant to leave the conversation. "They're supposed to dispose of the waste properly. Not dump it in a ravine."

"A ravine where other animals scavenge. Enter the feral hogs." September drained her wine glass. "Pigs eat anything. The most common way to become infected with a prion disease is to eat contaminated tissue, most typically the brain or spine."

Teddy sat on the arm of the chair. "Sorry, my arthritis leaves me achy." He cleared his throat. "If I understand so far, infected deer get eaten by pigs, and people eat contaminated pigs. But that still doesn't explain Aaron, if he doesn't eat meat. Or Cassie Henderson, unless that single launch party meal exposure was enough to make her sick."

"I don't think any of them got sick from eating the pigs. Well, maybe the hunter's dogs, and Felch's barn cats." September ran her thumb over the rim of the wine glass so it sang. "Nikki said several of the kittens became sick and died."

Doc Eugene straightened and smiled broadly. "Did I tell you Nikki's parents gave her permission to keep the mother cat?"

"She got to keep Hope? That's fantastic." September would never have forgiven herself if Nikki had been hurt. After the child's terrifying experience, she deserved some happy news. "Between getting a cat for Christmas and having her dad come home, she must be walking on air. From what I understand, Nikki and her brother attended the TV launch while their mother picked up the dad at the airport, for a surprise." She smiled at Doc Eugene. "So did you put in a word to her mom about dealing with cat allergies?"

"You bet I did. Nikki's a sweet kid, totally cat crazy. She's going to help Saturday mornings cleaning kennels and whatnot, in exchange for some basic cat care. I'm a bit short staffed at the moment with Timothy gone." Doc Eugene's voice turned gruff for a moment and then steadied. "I gave my test results to the CDC officials. BeeBo's dog and Mr. Sanger's cat Pinkerton were both positive for prion disease. Maybe a new variant."

Gonzales returned to the group with fresh beer, and handed a bottle to Combs. Mercedes linked an arm through her husband's and sipped her own wine.

Teddy took off his glasses and pointed them at September. "You say only the pets got it from eating the tainted meat?"

"Raw fed." Doc Eugene shrugged. "Probably contaminated with neuro matter."

"But not the people." She sighed, twirled the wine glass again, and then carefully set it down before she accidentally broke it. "It's complicated, but follow me here. Nikki said when the kids visited Felch's barn earlier, they found a pile of bones."

"Bones?" Mercedes hugged her husband's arm and shivered. "He collected bones?"

September cocked her head. "Collected from the hunters' ravine drop, yes. Felch processed them, and sold the result." It explained everything, how the prions were distributed and people were exposed with no contact with the meat. "Felch boiled and charred them and then crushed up the bones into a fine powder, and sold it in bags to gardeners as bone meal fertilizer."

Teddy's stricken expression spoke volumes. "Molly bought a dozen bags of fertilizer a couple years ago from a local man. Bet it was Mr. Felch. I shared them with the local Master Gardener club when she had no more use for it, and even took a couple bags over to Sunnydale Nursing Home." He rubbed his eyes, and put glasses back on with trembling hands. "That day you brought Shadow, we found Molly out in the garden area with one of the bags. Maybe she knew what had made her sick. She tried to tell me."

September hugged him. "It's not your fault. It's not anyone's fault. Felch tried to make a buck recycling natural materials. Lots of people do that, and never have a problem. Besides, this is only a theory. But it would explain why

Aaron and Cassie contracted the illness, too, if that's what they've got." The fault lay in Dietz trying to cover it up.

Doc Eugene drained the watery dregs of his drink. "There have been documented cases of prion disease contracted by inhaling contaminated material, like bone dust."

"We've rounded up all the bags we can find." Gonzales smiled at his wife. "Felch tried to be a good guy. He was on a mission to retrieve all the bags. That's what he meant by damage control."

Combs agreed. "Dietz wants us to believe that Felch killed Sly, but there's no evidence of that." He took a long pull on the beer. "I think Grady killed him to shut him up and didn't expect September to find the body, or call the police. Then he told Dietz he'd clean up the mess in exchange for a cut of the show proceeds. We found a newly signed agreement in Dietz's office." He bent toward September. "He left Felch's truck at one of the dump sites, with Macy's prescription pill bottle under the seat, like you said, so that ties his vehicle to your kidnapping. No prints from Grady, though, so it's circumstantial, not a slam-dunk."

September resisted the urge to ask about leads on Victor, aka Grady. He'd disappeared, left Dietz holding the bag, and she feared the chameleon had again escaped justice.

At her urging, the CSIs collected claw trimmings from Macy, so they had Victor/Grady DNA. He wasn't in any criminal database, though. To prove him guilty they had to catch him first.

It'd been two weeks. He'd disappeared before for years. The thought of him at large, at any moment able to again victimize her or someone else, made her want to scream. She shook herself and forced a smile. She wouldn't let anything spoil this night.

"This is a party. Enough of the gloom and doom, let's concentrate on the positives." September picked up her empty wine glass. "Anita, time to break out something stronger."

"After the champagne, sure." Anita took her glass. "But we've got some toasts first, and only bubbly will do the trick."

Her brow furrowed, but September waited as Anita and Fish bustled to the kitchen and returned with champagne for everyone.

Fish took the floor. "I've got the first toast. To a new career." He winked. "Sometimes you can turn a sow's ear into a silk purse."

Everyone laughed, toasted, and sipped.

"Me next." Gonzales held up his cell phone and winked at his wife. "Not even Combs knows this. Got the word a few minutes ago when getting my beer. The Captain has impeccable timing." Combs groaned. More laughs. "Victor, aka Grady, is in custody"

Mercedes and Anita gasped and then gently clinked glasses.

The room rocked. September grabbed for anything to stay upright. "They caught him? Really?" Combs's arm tightened around her shoulders. "They caught him."

He beamed. "Best news I've heard all day. Here, here!"

She couldn't stop smiling as she lifted her glass, and nearly choked when she tried to swallow the beverage. "He'll try to wiggle out of it."

"That cat's DNA evidence combined with eye witness accounts—yours and Nikki's—nail his balls to the wall." Gonzales flinched when Mercedes punched him for the language, but everyone laughed. A giddy atmosphere overtook the room.

"Me next. First, sit down here." Teddy pulled forward one of the dining room chairs for September and hurried to the office/music room next door.

Puzzled, but too happy and excited to object, September seated herself in the chosen chair. She smoothed the soft fabric of her dress, and leaned forward to rub Shadow's ears when he settled beside her. The rest of the guests watched her face with smiles of anticipation.

"Close your eyes." Combs touched her shoulder.

"What's happening? Not sure I like where this is going." But she did as he asked. "Everyone's in on this, I suppose?"

Teddy's limping footsteps approached, muffled on the deep carpet. "Hold out your hands."

She did. And encountered a cool hard surface, silk smooth, familiar. Her eyes flew open.

"A cello?" She saw each excited face, all claiming the group gift, and her heart expanded, too full to contain all her emotion. "You got me a cello." She took the bow Teddy presented with a flourish.

"That pole thing that sticks in the end? It's there." Combs pointed at the metal endpin that had helped her escape, and she bent down to release it, biting her lip to stop the trembling. "We recovered that from the barn. Part of your first cello, right?" Combs's hand on her shoulder squeezed, and she put hers atop it and squeezed back. September didn't bother wiping her eyes.

"I don't know what to say. Except thank you." She sniffled, and held up her glass. "To my friends."

"To friends," they echoed.

The clock began to strike midnight as Macy strolled into the room and curled up beside Shadow on the floor next to her. September stroked a hand from the cat's domed head to the dog's arched neck. "And to chosen family."

Shadow barked at her words, licked her hand and banged his tail. September had no doubt they thought with the same mind, and loved with the same heart.

Everyone echoed the toast. "To chosen family."

"And to new beginnings." Combs stared into her eyes, and this time she met them without flinching away.

"Yes, to new beginnings." She smiled.

He touched the gorgeous scroll of the instrument. "Play something?"

September quickly tested the strings, adjusted the tuning, and settled the cello between her knees. Where Melody had been as dark as her own sable hair, the face of this instrument shone as bright as the unfamiliar but welcome hope now filling her heart. She set her bow on the strings. "I'll call you Harmony," she whispered, and began to play a new joyous song.

The room fell still, listening, as the clock chimed midnight, announcing the beginning of the New Year.

Macy's "ack-ack-ack-ack" lion cough answered the cello's sweet voice, and Shadow tipped up his head and added his howl, a raucous trio the most beautiful sound of all.

"Everyone's a critic." September laughed, but didn't stop. She'd never stop playing again.

EPILOGUE

Claire O'Dell clutched the phone, willing it to ring. She'd lost count of the times she'd called since last November, begging for help. But never a reply. How unfair, how wicked to help one child, but sentence hundreds of others to this purgatory of uncertainty.

She and Mike gambled on a miracle for Tracy, and got it. For a while, they basked in the glow of their little girl's transformation, and marveled at the six-year-old's unlocked abilities. But as Tracy's medicine cost drained savings, tempers flared. Worry filled every waking moment as the remaining doses in Tracy's bottle shrank.

No parent should suffer such anguish. The joyous dream became a nightmare. What had they done? Tracy would suffer horrendous side effects caused by a sudden withdrawal. They tried to hide their worry from Tracy. But somehow, she knew.

This morning, Claire's worry transformed to horror. Last night sometime, while Mike worked double-shifts, Tracy vanished along with her last bottle of precious pills. Before Claire could unfreeze her brain to react, to call Mike, to do anything, her best friend called, equally terrified for her autistic son. Lenny had also disappeared, taking Tracy with him.

With the clock ticking, Claire made frantic plans. She'd call Mike from the road, so he couldn't stop her. She knew where they'd gone: Heartland, Texas, where their miracle derailed. All because of that meddling woman.

She'd make September Day fix this, somehow, some way. Tracy's life depended on it.

FACT, FICTION & ACKNOWLEDGEMENTS

Publishing a debut novel is nearly impossible. That's a fact. A second novel is even more difficult to accomplish. That's also a fact. For me it's taken more than twenty years for fiction to become a reality. In dog years I should be dead.

I come from the nonfiction world and love intertwining fiction story elements with fact. But what's real, and what's fantasy? My publisher Bob Mayer writes "factual fiction" so I'm borrowing from him to offer nuggets related to this story. As September might say, here's the Cliff's Notes version with some additional resources for those curious for "just the facts" in HIDE AND SEEK.

As with LOST AND FOUND that launched this dog viewpoint series, much of this book is based on science, especially dog and cat behavior and learning theory, and the benefits of service dogs. A vast number of veterinarians, behaviorists, consultants, trainers and pet-centric writers and rescue organizations offer their incredible resources and support to help make the pet-centric storyline as accurate as possible. Find further information at IAABC.org, APDT.com, DWAA.org and CatWriters.com.

FACT: The *show-me* game is real, created by trainer Kayce Cover as a vocabulary game used with a variety of animals, which my own dog loves to play. See http://synalia.com/

FACT: The German Shepherd Dog on the cover is a real nine-month-old titled tracking dog that achieved her TD at age six months. Yes, that's a girl on the cover! (Don't tell Shadow…) Gillian Salling, a tracking dog expert and owner of Fernheim German Shepherds, graciously allowed her gorgeous and talented Uschi Von Fernheim, TD to serve as Shadow's cover dog model.

FICTION: Shadow's viewpoint chapters are pure speculation, although I'd love to be able to read doggy minds. However, every attempt has been made to base both Macy and Shadow's motivations and actions on what is known about canine and feline body language, scent discrimination and the science behind the human-animal bond.

FACT: Some of the pet characters in HIDE AND SEEK are based on real-life pets. Fifty terrific names were suggested with over 4100 votes during the "Name That Dog" and "Name That Cat" contest. Marci DeLisle suggested **Pinkerton** in honor of a favorite longhaired feral tabby cat with a bright pink nose surrounded by white fur. Pinkerton considered himself the resident security guard for the feral cat colony. Patricia suggested **Hope,** which seemed incredibly appropriate and actually helped focus the theme of the book. Patricia is a double winner, also suggesting the dog name **Rocky** for Teddy and Molly's much beloved heart-dog of the past. I made Rocky a twin to the current therapy dog at the nursing home, named Trixie. **Trixie** received an astounding 805 votes and was suggested by Kristi Brashier who lives with the real-life Trixie described as a very dark red Golden Retriever diva dog, whose goal in life is to have everyone pet her and tell her she's pretty. Trixie is also known as the neighborhood thief because she retrieves things from the neighbors. The winners received advance copies of the book, their pets' namesakes serving heroic roles in the book, and my eternal gratitude. Watch for future "Name That Dog/Cat" contests for future stories.

FACT: Therapy dogs can work wonders when partnered with Alzheimer's patients. Emotional support dogs also partner with a variety of people, from children to adults, including those suffering from post-traumatic stress disorder (PTSD). Not only dogs, but cats, parrots and other critters may be suited to become one of these incredible helpers. Learn more about pet-people partnerships at http://petpartners.org (formerly Delta Society).

FACT: All cats are at risk for hypertrophic cardiomyopathy (HCM), even that random-bred rescue beauty sleeping on your lap. Gene tests for the disease are available for a few select cat breeds including Maine Coon cats. Research funds are needed to make tests more widely available and ferret out the cause(s) of HCM and other cat-specific illnesses that take our cat friends from us far too early. As an added bonus, research into pet diseases often has applications and benefits to human health. The Winn Feline Foundation http://www.winnfelinehealth.org) is worthy of your support in this endeavor. Give generously—it could save your cat's life.

FACT: Canine cognitive disorder has been widely recognized in dogs. The brain changes appear to resemble some aspects of human Alzheimer's disease and drugs beneficial for humans appear to help dogs. The illness is found less commonly in cats. Studies indicate a combination of drug intervention, special antioxidant diets and behavior modification and training games (use it or lose it, to prevent "brain rust") can actually reverse some of these old-pet behaviors. The AKC Canine Health Foundation http://www.akcchf.org/ and Morris Animal Health Foundation http://morrisanimalfoundation.com/ fund research into these and other vital animal health challenges.

FACT: Feral pigs are such a huge environmental problem in Texas that experts agree there's no way to hunt, trap or barbecue our way out of the mess. You can learn more about feral hogs here: http://www.invasivespeciesinfo.gov/animals/wildboar.shtml

FACT: Prion diseases can arise spontaneously in nature and affects a small percentage of people each year. And yes, during the 'mad cow' scare, a few documented cases of cat infections were reported. A good place to start research is http://www.cdc.gov/ncidod/dvrd/prions/

FACT: Human cases of prion disease have been associated with inhalation of infective bone dust. Hey, some things you just can't make up!

FICTION: There is no evidence to support the notion that feral pigs contract prion disease by eating infective deer remains, or that barbecued feral hog poses risk to humans. The shivery notion arose from my decidedly twisted imagination.

FACT: This book would not have happened without my PAW-some tribe of friends, family and accomplished colleagues. Cool Gus Publishing, Bob Mayer and Jennifer Talty created an author-friendly professional venue for "outliers" with unique vision to succeed and support each other's success. My Cuchara gang continues to inspire and support my crazy notions and helped birth this book and many others during our times on the Mountain. Special thanks to my first readers Kristi Brashier, Dr. Lorie Huston and Frank Steele for your eagle eyes, spot-on comments and unflagging encouragement and support.

I am incredibly indebted to International Thriller Writers and the Debut Authors Program. The people who make up this organization are some of the most generous and supportive folks I have ever met, and my fictioning journey would never have become a reality or continued without this organization. Steve Berry's inspiring address to the 2013 Debut Class was the kick in the furry britches this writer needed to git-er-done and write the next book. And the next. And the next after that. I'm wearing my bunny slippers with teeth and loving it!

Finally, I'm grateful to all the cats and dogs I've met over the years who have shared my heart and sometimes my pillow. These days, Magical-Dawg and Seren-Kitty are my furry inspiration for all-things-pets. And of course, deepest thanks to my husband Mahmoud, who continues to support my writing passion even when he doesn't completely understand it.

I love hearing from you. Please drop me a line at my Bling, Bitches & Blood blog at AmyShojai.com or find more pet-centric books at http://www.shojai.com where you can watch for the latest dog-viewpoint THRILLERS WITH BITE!

SEPTEMBER'S STORY CONTINUES in SHOW AND TELL...

An animal behaviorist and her service dog race a deadly storm to expose a treacherous secret others will kill to protect.

A BLACKMAILER returns to sell a deadly cure.
A MOTHER'S DENIAL dooms millions of children.
AND A DOG shows true loyalty...when he runs away.

*"**SHOW AND TELL** is one of those rare thrillers that hits you in the heart as well as the head. Amy Shojai hits the ground running and never slows down. Damaged souls of both the two and four-legged variety join forces to rescue others along with themselves. Riveting, wholly satisfying ...makes us care."* --**Jon Land, *USA Today* bestselling author**

KEEP READING for a sample of **SHOW AND TELL!**

SHOW AND TELL: Chapter 1

Eighty pounds of German Shepherd vaulted onto her bed and startled September from a sound sleep. She froze, mouse-quiet in the dark. Her heart trip-hammered in concert with the dog's low, bubbled growl that shook the bed, the vibration more felt than heard.

The downstairs clock struck five times. Clouds moved aside for moonlight to spill through the wooden blinds, painting the room silver with black shadows. The dog leaned closer. White-bright fangs glistened from his sooty muzzle, and September didn't need to see Shadow's expression to understand the dog's warning.

Shadow had good reasons for everything he did. He'd saved her life more than once.

The big black dog licked her face, and she pushed against his muscled chest, urging him off the bed so she could rise. His hackles continued to bristle despite her soothing touch, a warning she couldn't ignore. He was concerned, but not in full protection mode. Probably a furry trespasser. Better to see what had him on alert. She hadn't said a word, and didn't need to. The two partners were so in sync with each other, they might as well have read each other's mind. Shadow's tail flagged with excitement, anticipating her command to *check-it-out,* his signal to investigate and ensure no danger loomed.

Before she could move, a coffee-dark streak of fur leaped into her arms. The cat's bottlebrush tail echoed Shadow's concern, and September's mouth turned dry with fear. She briefly hugged Macy and brushed aside her long disheveled locks that matched the Maine Coon's fur. Even the stark lock of white hair at September's temple matched Macy's snowy bib. The cat's tilted green eyes, twin to September's, glowed a stoplight warning. Macy shivered. Even the cat reacted to Shadow's concern.

The dog's concern heightened the foreboding that had lived inside September as long as she could remember, despite knowing the ghosts from the past couldn't hurt her. It had taken a year since moving home to Texas for her to begin to heal. Shadow's solid presence and the purring warmth of Macy anchored September in the here-and-now. *They* were real. *They* were chosen family. The crawly sensation on the back of her neck mocked her newfound confidence.

September jumped out of bed, berating herself and silencing the what-ifs. Shadow's alert had been silent, not the full-on bark-warning given for a household intruder. Besides, the house alarms hadn't triggered. She took a calming breath with that realization. Clear the house, and then check the grounds outside.

With a plan in place, September hugged Macy again, and plopped the cat back onto the bed. Best to lock the cat in her bedroom and keep him out of harm's way. Macy didn't need more stress on his heart.

She showed the cat her closed fist. He obediently sat and began self-grooming, a way to calm himself down. September wished she had the ability to self-medicate with purrs.

September cautiously opened the bedroom door, stepped outside with the dog, then closed and latched the door. Shadow pressed against her, and she knelt and gave him a quick hug before signaling with the silent hand-wave command to *check-it-out*.

He bounded ahead, a silent black wraith invisible in the dark. She could track his progress from his thumping paw-jumps down the stairs, claw scrabbling on the wooden entry, and huffing breath as he tasted the air from room to room.

Finally, after clearing the house, Shadow raced back up the stairs, sat before her, and barked once. Her shoulders relaxed, and her grin nearly split her face.

"Baby-dog, what a good dog!" Not such a baby-dog anymore, with his first birthday nearly here, just a week after Valentine's Day. Her first shepherd Dakota taught her to love again, but Shadow became her heart.

She followed him down the stairs, encouraged when her knee gave barely a twinge. After surgery repaired the injury, physical therapy—what she called specialized torture—had her nearly back to normal even though she hated water therapy. After weeks of therapy, she could tread water for twenty minutes without breaking a sweat.

September paused in the office/music room. Playing her cello honored the memory of her old instrument. The gift from Combs and her new circle of friends meant perhaps a new life was possible, too.

September debated calling Combs to come check out the house. But no, she had to take charge of her life. Calling for help meant her stalker still controlled her from his jail cell. Courage meant moving forward despite the fear, and she wanted to be independent.

She still couldn't believe someone like Detective Jeff Combs—handsome, smart, accomplished—wanted to be with her. He'd promised no pressure, yet he wouldn't take no for an answer. So after several "not-a-date" casual lunches or dinners with friends, a couple of coffee meetings, and countless phone calls and texts, September surprised herself by saying yes to a for-real formal date.

Butterflies threw a party in her midsection. It felt good.

The kitchen's stained glass windows usually splashed the slate floor with peacock colors but sunrise wouldn't arrive for another two hours. Several phone messages beckoned on the landline reserved for her pet tracking and behavior consulting business, and September resisted the urge to review them. They could wait.

Shadow insisted something outside needed attention. It was his job to *check-it-out* whenever they returned home, or visited somewhere new. Anything different—a sound, a smell—could set off his alert, and she'd rather Shadow err on the side of caution. Even if they found nothing she didn't want to discourage the dog by ignoring his concern. Training never stopped, after all. She'd learned the hard way to trust her gut, and her dog. Shadow yawned and stretched, but his tail continued to signal his agitation.

Six months ago, she'd have locked the bedroom door and called the police. No more, not after what she'd survived in the last few weeks. She'd take her dog for a walk, and check out the property, like any other normal person. *Let it be a squirrel or raccoon.*

Shadow spun and twirled, nearly running into the wall in his excitement when she slipped on her coat, and stuffed bare feet into mud-caked garden shoes. She grabbed his leash on the way to the door.

"*Sit. Wait.*" She bent to hook the leash to Shadow's collar, and unlocked the kitchen door to the back patio, keyed in the security, and switched on the outside lights. If someone intended harm, the lights would either flush them out or send them scurrying on their way. With luck, any interlopers would be kids taking a dare to trespass on the notorious property. Nobody had any legitimate business being out here so early at five-frickin' o'clock. She slammed the door shut. It had a nasty habit of unlatching and swinging open in the wind.

No stars broke through the overcast sky, and the setting moon's glow tarnished heavy clouds. She should have pulled on a pair of sweats. The down-filled coat, a remnant from her years in Chicago, made her look like the Michelin Man, but covered only her upper thighs. Despite the muggy atmosphere, her bare legs chilled in the sixty-degree temperature.

She couldn't walk too fast in the sloppy garden shoes, and the dog adjusted his gait but remained insistent. Every time he paused to sniff, she found herself dodging one of the dozens of wind chimes she'd hung from every available spot. They served as a low-tech security system. The tinkle of bells, clatter of shells, and rattle of pottery shards played a counterpoint to the clop-shuffle-clop of her awkward shoes on the brick pathway.

She stepped off bricks and into grass when they rounded the house, and the soil squished. The rain finally stopped last night, at least for a while, but the countywide flash flood warnings continued. February more often unleashed ice storms that coated trees, broke branches and downed phone and power lines, so nobody complained about the extra rain. Except maybe her garden, if the plants hadn't drowned. Maybe they'd all die, and she'd have a good excuse to get rid of the roses that had become thorny memories of past pain.

Shadow led her to the wooden ladder next to the carriage house/garage. She'd created the set up as part of his training. You never knew what a search might require of a tracking dog, even climbing a ladder. She'd never met a dog so hungry to learn new things. He sniffed the area thoroughly before moving on.

September scanned the end of the driveway. A pair of carriage lamps on each side spilled light through the bars of the closed green gate, throwing jailhouse shadows in her path. No traffic lit the county road. She started to relax. Maybe the intruder had left. Shadow hadn't alerted to anything yet. *Trust the dog.*

He slowly made his way down the drive, and stuck his nose through the gate, tasting the air. He huffed, and pulled harder, and she noticed an old car parked some distance away, half hidden beneath a live oak. Her throat tightened as Shadow delicately sniffed one side of the gate. His nose hit the ground.

Okay then. She squared her shoulders. "*Seek,* Shadow. *Seek!*"

He towed her quickly up the other half-circle of the drive. September could barely keep up and cursed her decision to wear the sloppy shoes. Shadow dragged her up the front steps, exploring the front door's brick landing. Her heart thumped faster.

The dog continued to track his prey. He pulled September off the side of the front steps, across the lawn and padded quickly around to the other side of the house. They'd made a full circle. The dog moved faster and faster, signaling the target was near. His head came up.

Shadow's tension traveled up the leash and she trembled in response. His bristled fur made him look half again as large when he stalked stiff legged toward the kitchen door that now stood ajar. No wind had tugged it open; she'd latched the door securely.

His deep-throated roar shattered the quiet. September grabbed the leash with both hands to contain Shadow's sudden lunge. He wasn't a Schutzhundtrained protection dog, but after what they'd gone through together, Shadow had every right to be defensive when a stranger invaded their home.

September put a hand on his ruff, and he quieted into a down position, but continued to shake and huff with tension. She had to steady her own voice, outrage as much as fear fueling her emotions.

"Who's there? I'll send in the dog." At her words Shadow lept to his feet. This time, September didn't correct him, but watched when Shadow whined and cocked his head, listening. She wished she'd collected her gun from the SUV's glove box while they'd been near the garage, or brought along her cell phone to call Combs for backup. Screw being self-sufficient, she'd welcome some help. But they were on their own. She'd have to trust Shadow to do his job.

September leaned down, stroked both sides of Shadow's face, and he wagged at her touch. She unhooked the leash but held his collar a moment longer, and whispered. "Good-dog, Shadow. You know what to do." She spoke the command full-voice. "*Check-it-out*," and released his collar.

Shadow sprang forward, claws scrabbling on the slate floor of the kitchen. He paused, then dropped his nose and traced the scent of the stranger's tread. September edged inside, and stood in the doorway to watch him work. His tail wagged with excitement. Shadow loved hide and seek games.

He tested the edge of the table where someone must have touched before he raced from the kitchen to the adjoining dining/living room. September hurried to keep up, but he easily outran her.

She didn't bother to switch on lights. Scent lit up rooms for a dog brighter than any lamp. Shadow raced into the dark living room, sniffed past the big table and across the carpet until his claws tap-danced on the wooden entry, with September in his wake.

September nearly ran into Shadow when he stopped to nose the handle on the front door. The deadbolt and other locks remained engaged, though. His head whipped around, attention drawn to the music/office room. A split second later, September heard the soft sobbing breath, too, and tore after the sound.

Shadow blocked the doorway, lay down, and barked once, his signal of a successful find.

The soft snuffling came from the kneehole of the desk. Someone as small as a kid. They'd have to be small to have wiggled through the bars on the green gate.

"Come out. I know you're in there." September took a cautious step into the room, and finally turned on the stained glass lamp. "Good-dog, Shadow. *Wait.*"

A girl called back. A tremor in her voice. "I only want to talk. Please don't send the dog after me."

Shadow wagged and stuck his head forward, but didn't break the *wait* command. He'd gotten better about that. His attitude, more excitement than defense, bolstered September's confidence. If the dog showed no fear, she'd trust his judgment.

"Come out from under there. Shadow won't hurt you. Unless you do something stupid." She stood with elbows wide, chest out, and tried to quiet her noisy breathing. Nobody showed up at five in the morning and walked into a stranger's house.

Shadow tipped his head, looking quizzical as the stranger finally pushed the chair away from the desk, and cautiously crawled out of the hiding spot.

"Where'd you come from? Who are you?" She softened her words for Shadow's sake when his ears went down and he yawned and turned away. Despite his scary size, shepherds were sensitive and he didn't like loud voices.

"Came from Chicago. Claire O'Dell." She answered quickly, but moved with slow caution to put the chair between herself and Shadow. "I parked outside your gate, I rang the bell, and when nobody came, I walked around the house. I've called you before, but you never answered, never returned my calls." Her tone became strident. "So I had to come. Beg you to help."

Not a girl, but a petite woman stood trembling, gaze locked on Shadow. Claire's head barely came level with September's shoulders. The whites of her eyes shined in the dim light, and she held up her hands in surrender. "Is he going to bite me?" Her voice traveled up an octave.

"No, he won't bite. Sit down already." September's exasperation made Shadow slick back his ears. "But stop staring at him, no dog likes that." She waited until Claire perched on the edge of the desk chair. "I'm calling the police."

"Oh no, you can't." She wrung her hands. "If you call the police, my little girl will die." Claire sobbed.

Shadow broke his *wait* command. With an apologetic glance at September for disobeying, he trotted over to the stranger, and licked clean her tears.

(end of sample)

To find out what happens next, get **SHOW AND TELL** now!

Have you read the first books in the September Day series? Ask your favorite booksellers for your copies today! Stay tuned for the next installment and find out what happens next to September, Shadow and all their friends.

Stay up to date by subscribing to PETS PEEVES newsletter

www.SHOJAI.com

ABOUT THE AUTHOR

Amy Shojai is a certified animal behavior consultant, and the award-winning author of more than 30 bestselling pet books that cover furry babies to old fogies, first aid to natural healing, and behavior/training to Chicken Soupicity. She has been featured as an expert in hundreds of print venues including The New York times, Reader's Digest, and Family Circle, as well as television networks such as CNN, and Animal Planet's DOGS 101 and CATS 101. Amy brings her unique pet-centric viewpoint to public appearances. She is also a playwright and co-author of STRAYS, THE MUSICAL and the author of the critically acclaimed September Day pet-centric thriller series. Stay up to date with new books and appearances by subscribing to Amy's Pets Peeves newsletter at www.SHOJAI.com.

Made in United States
North Haven, CT
07 August 2024

55794709R00148